THE
VANISHED
CHILD

———

THE
VANISHED
CHILD

Sarah Smith

BALLANTINE BOOKS
New York

Library of Congress Cataloging-in-Publication Data
Smith, Sarah, 1947–
The vanished child / Sarah Smith.
p.   cm.
ISBN 0-345-37350-2
I. Title
PS3569.M5379758V3   1992
813'.54—dc20   91-55573
CIP

TEXT DESIGN BY DEBBY JAY

Manufactured in the United States of America

First Edition: April 1992

10 9 8 7 6 5 4 3 2 1

To
S.M.B.
M.B.C.P.
J.R.O.P.
with my love
omnia mei dona Dei

[The disappearances of children] are stories of bereavements sharper than death. The sorrow of a fixed and finished calamity abates with time; the sorrow of suspense grows intenser the longer it endures. . . . The loss of a child by the hand of man involves treachery and cruelty, the despair of the family, the misery of the child, its rearing in crime and shame for ruin, or—less wretched fate—its early death . . . [Yet the child] is not forgotten in the heart of infinite love; not unwatched by the veil that never sleeps. The hand that has spread the veil will lift it.

> —C. P. Krauth, introduction to
> *Charley Ross the Kidnapped Child*
> (1876)

O God, who for the Three Children didst assuage the flames of fire: mercifully grant that the flames of sin may not consume us Thy servants.

> —Baltimore Catechism

THE
VANISHED
CHILD

———

CHAPTER 1

THE BARON ALEXANDER VON REISDEN went mad after his young wife died, and in five years he had not got himself sane. His friends were concerned about him. He had tried suicide once, early on, and had not succeeded; this was encouraging in a man who was usually both well-prepared and lucky; but even mad, Reisden might reasonably have assumed that he could shoot himself through the heart without missing, and, knowing himself, at the first moment he could, he would have learned how to do it better. He still had the gun, in a box in his top drawer behind his collar studs, and he still suffered from what had led him to the act, his singular and inexplicable and apparently incurable madness.

"Do you still think you killed her?" Louis asked.

Reisden looked up from making notes in his lab book. "I did kill her. That isn't the question."

It was Christmas Eve, 1905, in the cold lab of the chemistry labs at the University of Lausanne. Reisden's notes on neuromuscular connections were spread out on his lab bench beside a refrigerated box, glass-topped and

3

glass-sided, into which the string galvanometer and Reisden's other testing apparatus fit; but because one could not have visibility and insulation too, the whole lab was not much warmer than the box. The refrigeration coils and an electric motor took up most of the back wall; Louis had to shout above its rattle. Reisden, cold in his coat, held his hands over the Bunsen burner. In a tin pan nearby lay three frogs half stretched out, stunned by the cold. One of them stirred, disturbed by the shadow of his hands.

"But you know it was an accident," Louis persisted.

"Of course." Reisden picked up a pithing needle and opened the glass box. How much, he wondered, will the experiment be disturbed because the experimenter is warm-blooded? He measured the frog's temperature and brushed his hand across the frog's back, making it hop, panicked, across the lab bench until it stopped, paralyzed by the cold and the toxins building up in its muscles. Bending the frog's neck forward, Reisden felt along the smooth skin and slid the needle into the base of the skull, upward into the brain. He moved the needle back and forth. The frog gave one slow shudder and relaxed in his hands. The procedure was supposed to be painless, which Reisden had always considered irrelevant, as if painless death were more excusable. Tasy had died instantly and probably without pain.

I know it was an accident, Reisden thought. I never had any trouble knowing that.

The frog flopped limply in his hand. Frog a moment ago, preparation now. He cut quickly through the skin of the leg, dissecting out the nerve and muscle.

Louis Dalloz peered over his shoulder, snuffling like one of the pigs he studied, puffing vapory breaths like a wrathful French Santa Claus. From the sleeves of his old overcoat rose a rich odor of large animals and barns. His muffler, which his wife had knit for him, bulged the neck of his coat. He looked like an accident with a hat, and even in his own university he had been taken for the janitor. Only his hands, short-fingered and delicate and stained with acid like Reisden's, looked like a chemist's. "How can you stand this cold?"

"How do you stand pigs? The cold slows down the recovery reaction."

"Yours too. This isn't an experiment, it's a hair shirt." Louis sniffed. He squinted at the string galvanometer. "What happened to your lab assistant?"

"Gone to Zurich for Christmas."

"And you stay here doing work that any lab assistant could do. If you were in Paris . . . Berthet doesn't let a twenty-seven-year-old man act like a monk. Not in Paris."

Reisden reached over and turned off the refrigerator. For a moment the silence deafened them both.

"I'm not going to Paris."

Louis snorted and glared up at him.

"You will hear me, Louis." Reisden kept his voice neutral. "I like Berthet's people. Yes, I'd probably be good there. Yes, I would like living in Paris. We've been through that. I am not going."

"You don't think you're good enough."

"It won't work, Louis. I've seen all your bait before."

"You like Switzerland. You want to stay here and make money." Louis fiddled with Reisden's big microscope, spinning it up, then twiddling it into focus again. "Whose slide?"

"Ramón y Cajal's."

"Pretty."

"New stain. I'm not out of touch here," Reisden said.

Louis looked up at him. "No," said Louis, "only with yourself. You've locked yourself away so long that you don't remember how to come into a room with people in it, eh? Or tell a joke that doesn't have an edge to it. You're like a wild animal in the corner of a pen, going *grrrr*"—Louis bared his teeth and growled convincingly—"because he doesn't know what else to do. And he thinks even to himself, *Je suis la bête sauvage,* I'm mad. But isn't he only afraid of what's going to happen next? Don't look down your nose at me, Sacha, like the Baron von Reisden. I knew you when you were nineteen."

Reisden sighed and put the frog down. "Make yourself useful, would you? Write while I measure."

Louis sighed loudly and took the pen. Onto the string galvanometer Reisden fit a translucent string of frog preparation, once frog. The current barely made the muscle twitch. Reisden moved the dial in tiny increments, reading out numbers.

"Just for a few days, come with me to Genoa," Louis said. "It's Christmas. It's not good for you to stay here alone. Jeanne will fuss over you. We'll have a nice roast pig. Everyone from the lab will be there. You can look down your nose at our research methods."

"No, I shall spend Christmas day cutting apart innocent little frogs."

Louis opened his mouth and closed it.

Now, thought Reisden, we will get into deep waters. Louis would ask, did Reisden know that most suicides happened at holidays? Louis, he thought, look here, Louis, one doesn't shoot oneself because it's Christmas.

"You were my best student," Louis said forcefully, holding up his hand as if he were about to swear to something. "Now you are——" He waggled his fingers, looking for words. "Now you can choose between working for Berthet or Sherrington. But you're wasting it, you're not doing chemistry, you're just being sorry for yourself and calling it guilt. I'm here out of interest for you, that's all, freezing my ass in this refrigerator you call a lab on the day before Christmas, to tell you that you are being stupid. You didn't mean to kill her. You had a nervous breakdown and thought you did. And that was five years ago."

Ah, was it? "And in another country, and besides, the wench is dead. And it will never happen again. But I'm not going to Paris."

Louis glared up at him, his face reddening. "Sometimes I want to throw a bomb at you. Take the job, and don't play Saint Alexander in the Icebox. It's not good for you."

Reisden let that go. He watched the hand move instead. That was Louis' gesture, what one would take of him first if one were to act him: holding the hand up, wiggling the fingers. This is my hand. Why does it move? At nineteen Reisden had taken Louis' undergraduate chemistry course because the passion of his life had been acting and he had wanted those French-peasant gestures. He had found instead a question that he had been unable to answer.

And that had kept them allies ever since: that and Louis' persistence. Sometimes Reisden was grateful for Louis. Not by any means always.

"Look," Reisden said, "when is the next train to Genoa?"

"Two hours," Louis said instantly and added, "Will you come?"

"I'll take you to the train. You don't want to be away from Jeanne at Christmas, do you? We'll stop at your hotel and get your luggage."

"We can't get a cab at four in the morning. I'll have to stay."

Reisden looked out into the dark streets; his breath fogged the ice crystals that grew up the window. "I'll drive you," he offered.

"In the *auto*!" Louis said under his breath, rounding his eyes sarcastically. "In Saint Alexander Reisden's holy cursed automobile! *Vierge Marie!*"

I do give rides, Reisden thought, suddenly very tired. I don't kill everybody. He checked the still-living frogs and picked up one. The frog stirred a bit in the warmth of his hand. "Live," he said to the frog, and let it drop back among the rest.

IN EARLY MORNING, the station was a smudge of black and grey. Under the electric lights outside, Reisden's automobile had drawn two or three station porters into the street. Its racing colors were bronze and a coppery green, the only trace of color in the cold. Louis went off to the left-property office and reappeared wheeling an enormous packing case. *"Merde alors,"* Reisden murmured; *"merde absolue."* The case squealed desperately and Louis knelt by the breathing holes at one end, murmuring into unseen large hairy ears. "Pig, piggy darling, *mon petit chou,* just one horrible little train ride, then you will be on a lovely large farm near Genoa where pigs of your beauty are appreciated." Where in Lausanne in December had Louis found a pig?

Underneath the peasant look Louis was real peasant. As a boy he had tramped barefoot around France, learning the feeding and the raising and the genealogy of pigs. He had been a near-illiterate farmhand plodding through a chemistry course in Paris when the Revolution of 1870 had broken out. When the Paris Commune failed, Louis' friends had got him to Germany, to the only man they could think of who was asking the same sorts of questions about farm animals. What Rudolf Maty had taught Louis, from remote professorial heights, was that how the pig grew was only a part of it, that everything was a whole of parts, molecules and atoms, linked together into gut and muscles and fat and bone; that molecules broke and linked, transformed from food to what ate the food, that everything ate and lived in a great ring, corn and pig and farmer. "The chemistry of life," Louis had called his lectures. As an aristocrat, of course, Reisden had been expected to be at best amused by them. One is supposed to know that men such as Louis have nothing to say.

Reisden's family had been ennobled by Charlemagne. Reisdens had lived in Rezény castle from the thirteenth century until the last bits of roof had fallen, fifteen years ago, sending Reisden's two decrepit aunts scuttling to furnished rooms in Salzburg. As an aristocrat Reisden was deplorably modern: He had a profession and he made money. It was vulgar to concern oneself with a profession or with the earning of money, Reisden's guardian had told him; he would marry well because of his name. Instead Reisden had found the stock market, just about the time he had got interested in research biochemistry; and vulgarly, ever since, he had learned how to make the stock market pay for the lab.

"He needs a distraction," Louis said to the pig. "He should do what you do, eh, little boy?"

Have experiments run on him, be sacrificed for science, or screw pigs? "Don't bother, Louis," Reisden murmured. He moved off down the station platform, lighting a cigaret against the faint odor of boar. Louis thought Reisden should marry again. Jeanne picked out good women and sat them next to him at dinner when he went to Genoa. But, Reisden knew, no one hallucinates for a long time without a good reason. Biochemical or genetic? Graf Leo and the aunts were dead long ago and he had no one to ask about bad genes. In any case he had no intense interest in reproducing himself; there would be no more Reisdens.

The electric lights were hazed; it had begun to snow again, sharp half-transparent spicules. As if coincidentally, Louis followed him down the platform.

"Get on the train, you could be in Paris in a few hours. See how it feels."

Reisden shrugged. "I like working alone."

"No," Louis said. Reisden looked at him startled. "Don't tell yourself lies. Sacha, you live here like a dead man. You maybe say a word to your lab assistant? And maybe your barber, and the waiter at whatever restaurant you eat at? Sacha, do you always eat alone? You write to me, beautiful lab reports and one sentence at the bottom of them, 'All well here, it continues to snow.' You're usually at your lab at night because no one else is there to mind the cold. Except tomorrow, being Christmas, no one will be there at any hour, so you'll work in the daytime too. Do you think you're happy? Do you think something will change without your changing it? Don't get comfortable. I taught in Germany twelve years, and every morning I prayed on my knees, 'Don't let me forget I want to get out.' "

The porter came by. "Monsieur, your train is loading."

The two walked out onto the platform. It was grey dawn. The wind had risen and the snow stung their faces. Beyond the city rose snowclouds, coming in fast, and the black shadows of the high Alps, tunneling the wind and cutting off the light of day. They were taller than anything should be. They filled half the sky, massive and fragmented, like vicious dreams.

I would like to live in a low country, Reisden thought.

The wind bit at their faces. Soon the passes would close for the winter. The Simplon Tunnel would not be finished this year; it would be hard to get to Paris, or Genoa, or anywhere.

"My love to Jeanne," Reisden said.

"Hers to you, Reisden." Louis put his foot on the train step, turned around. "Merry Christmas."

"Merry Christmas, Louis." Louis would worry over him, and there was nothing to be done about it.

Louis' coat passed in a blur behind the windows of the railroad car; then Louis' face peered out at him. Being insane is like losing one sense, whatever it is that keeps other people sane. One cannot explain its loss. One can only feel unbalanced and wrong. Reisden sighed, out of an inaccuracy of feelings that was not quite amusement and was not quite despair.

Of course one could go to Paris. One was not a chemist if one didn't. And, for all practical purposes, he was quite sane.

Louis rattled the window down. "You could come to visit at New Year's—"

"I'll send you the results from the end of this series at New Year's. The pass will be closed."

"Not quite yet; we could talk—" Louis suddenly leaned forward, half through the window, and squinted through the snow.

"Sacha, who's that?"

On the platform across the tracks from theirs, a man was looking at them. An old man, about sixty—a short, shabby-looking man, wearing a badly cut suit and a comic small hat perched foreign-style on the back of his head. There was nothing unusual about him, nothing to draw the eye, but Reisden felt caught in that stare, the intensity of his look, as if the old man were seeing death, or a ghost, or God: something familiar, lovely, and terrible. It was a look like the moment before death, something to be avoided.

"He knows you," Louis said.

"No." But the stranger raised his hand tentatively, half hailing Reisden and half not, as a man does when he is not sure whether he is approaching the right person. Reisden flinched, appalled. The man began to stumble forward, not looking where he was going, and Reisden wanted to be somewhere else, not seeing whatever was going to happen.

The platforms were a meter or so higher than the tracks, the two sets of which were set in a well between them. A woman caught the old man's elbow at the edge of the platform. He said something to her and kneeled arthritically to sit on the brink, carefully let himself down into the well, and began picking his way across the iron tracks and the ties.

Down the track, like melodrama, a train was gliding into the station. The wheels gave a thin mournful shriek, the banshee sound of wheels on snow; the locomotive glided forward, crying warning, seeming not to slow at all. Somebody on the other platform screamed.

Reisden could have jumped down into the track well and pulled the old man out of the way. There was time, but he did not move, he stood completely still, not so much as breathing, while two railway guards ran past him, took the old foreigner by the elbows, and pushed him up onto the near platform. And, staggering to his feet, the old man kept coming toward him.

"Richard, do you know me?"

I would have let him fall under the train, Reisden thought.

"I am Alexander Reisden," he said violently. "I have never seen you in my life." The worst was that so far as he knew it was true.

"*Sacha, qu'est-ce qu'il dit?*" Louis called from the train.

"He says I am someone called Richard." Reisden's voice was abruptly shaking; he steadied it.

"Then Jay really killed him," the old man said, and suddenly he paled until his lips blued and his eyes rolled up. His legs sagged and he slumped suddenly between the two guards. They laid him down on the platform, in the falling snow and the slush.

Louis butted his way through the people who were beginning to gather.

"You'll miss your train." Reisden leaned against one of the pillars of the platform, feeling odd and cold, and stared at the old man.

"Who is Richard?" Louis asked. Reisden shook his head. The guards were putting a blanket over the old man, but not over the face. "Not dead," Louis said. The comic hat had fallen off; Reisden picked it up and read the stamping inside the crown. "Dr. Charles Adair. Boston."

The name meant nothing. Reisden knelt in the snow and put his hand on the man's throat, feeling for a pulse. It jumped weakly against his fingers. He stood up quickly, brushing his hand against his coat.

"Richard?" he said. "I don't know. I don't know at all."

CHAPTER 2

"Dr. CHARLES ADAIR," said Victor Wills, leaning forward fascinated over the café table. "Charlie Adair, in this wonderful year of 1906. Think of your seeing the name in his hat. He must be getting old— Heavens, it's eighteen years since the Knights were killed. August 1887. He didn't die, I hope," Victor said.

"No." Reisden lit a cigaret and blew out smoke. "But he wasn't well; I think he went back to his country. Victor, Dr. Charles Adair lives in Boston, Massachusetts, and Louis has got me scheduled to go to a Harvard conference near Boston this spring to deliver a paper. I'm wondering whether I should cancel. I wouldn't like doing to anyone else whatever I did to him."

"He thought you were Jay French?"

"No, someone named Richard."

"A boy," Victor said absently. "Yes, I know about Jay and Richard and the Knight murder case, and I suppose, dear boy, that you had better know too."

Victor Wills and Alexander Reisden were sitting in one of the little cafés by the Piazza San Marco. The glass shutters were up; outside the New Year's rain stormed across the plaza, and the pigeons and the tourists had taken shelter. The rain would be snow on the Simplon, Reisden thought, wondering why he had taken the chance of traveling to the Italian side. Inside, heat and heavy gilt held back the winter weather. White-haired Victor held his cup of caffe latte in two hands and stared happily about him.

Victor was a friend from almost as far back as Reisden could remember, a British Museum gossip-monger now retired to Italy. When Reisden had been at English prep school, the London literary man Victor, who was newly converted to Catholicism, had seen him act in a school play and invited him to his flat to discuss the Trinity. Victor had spoken rather oddly about Catholicism and, with some authority, about Havelock Ellis, Frank Harris, and Wilde. Reisden had been innocent enough then not to see immediately that Victor intended to seduce him; but when he had caught on, a little before Victor's intentions would have become unmistakable, he had somehow distracted Victor from his initial purpose and got him talking about Wilde, Victor's own life as a professional writer, and finally about the poems of Mallarmé and the future of the British Liberal Party, about which they could agree. Victor had remained a friend, amusing Reisden inwardly with a succession of episodes involving Italian waiters, lost manuscripts, and the local government board on which Victor titularly had worked. He had retired to Italy in the aftermath of the Wilde affair. The love of Victor's writing life was poetry—privately published, tinted ink on tinted paper, Beardsleyesque illustrations—but since his retirement, he had become a hack writer "to keep the wolf, dear boy, if not from the door, at least not wholly upstairs with one and sharing the covers." His bread and butter was True Crime.

Victor wrote as Detective Sergeant Thomas Butcher (Retired), whose thrilling exploits of famous crimes appeared in the *Pink 'Un* every week. He was the author of three volumes of *Great American Crimes, by a New York Detective,* and about thirty other books, including *Blood and Diamonds, by A Female Spy.* ("Such *fun,* my dear boy.") Such as his profession was, Victor was at the top of it.

"The infamous Knight case. I warn you, dear Alexander, you may not like it. Jay French was a murderer, dear boy—a multiple murderer, quite as good as dear Lizzie Borden. Jay French the Child Killer. I kept the Knights out of *American Crimes,* you know. My editor wanted to include the material, and I had photographs. But I wouldn't do it."

"Oh?"

"I told him it would inconvenience a dear friend. I shall give you quite the worst first. It's curious," Victor said delicately, "that Adair thought you were *Richard.*" Victor pushed a photograph over the table. "John Jay French," he said. "He and Richard were cousins."

The image was small, about the size of a visiting card. Reisden recognized individual features: brow, nose, a jaw like the one Reisden shaved every morning. Suddenly the features were a face and the face was his. Reisden shuddered violently and handed it back.

"Are you sure you like this, my dear boy?"

"Curiosity merely startles the cat. Go on."

"Quite sure? After ten years writing blood, what shocks me would make a pudding crawl. Well, then, I shall be my usual caustic self and let the chips fall where they may. Here is what happened to the Knights."

FIRST, said Victor, you must realize that the crimes of the rich have essentially to do with money. And particularly so in America, where they've no morals, no tradition, nothing but lucre. William Knight was made by money. Eventually the man who couldn't be his heir killed him.

William Knight was the son of a poor Irish immigrant, born on the ship that brought him to America. He ran away to sea at ten and owned his first sailing ship at twenty. Much of his trade was in cotton goods. He was rich by the beginning of the American Civil War.

Then he dealt with the Confederacy.

He was already over sixty, but William Knight traveled to England and to the Confederacy itself, keeping up the cotton trade. He was completely ostracized. Trading with the South was simply not done, and three of his own sons were fighting for the North.

But he became very rich indeed.

He's quite mad-looking in the photos: an evil ancient Lincoln, with the nastiest twisted mouth and great dark eyes like a cave full of spiders. He let his hair grow long because the Bible told him to. He built churches, held public prayer meetings in his offices, and sued his neighbors over trifles. He owned parts of thirty-six companies, but he always ate the same thing, meat loaf and toast and gravy at the nearest cheap restaurant. He married three women—*they* all expired, you can imagine—

and sired enormous numbers of children, seven of whom grew to adulthood.

And, quite young, they began to die off.

Of the seven, William Knight, Jr., John, and Alphonsus died in the Civil War and left no known children. Isabella died of some female disease, unmarried, no children. Clement Knight committed suicide, unmarried, leaving no children. William's fifth son, Gilbert Howard Knight, refused either to marry or to go into the business. He was disinherited and forgotten, and when William Knight died, Gilbert was an itinerant used-book seller, of all things.

Late in life William sired a sixth son, Thomas Robert Knight. Dear Alexander, from all accounts you would have liked Thomas Robert. And Thomas Robert died with his wife Sophie, in a boating accident in 1883, leaving one son, Richard Knight.

The Richard, dear boy, that Charles Adair took you for.

I do like Richard Knight and by all accounts he didn't have a pleasant life with William. I've seen pictures; he was a handsome boy, dark-haired as you, vivid, proud, with the most marvelous eyes. One senses a great curiosity in him: the sort of boy who would have known where all the birds' nests were, but might have watched them rather than smash the eggs. From the day Richard arrived William started training him to be a millionaire. Tutors in mathematics and finance and deportment. William wanted Richard to succeed, you see, to wipe the stain from William's money by the force of Richard's charm.

Richard, one feels, would have somehow done it—if that was what he wanted to do.

Then came Jay French.

Jay French came from the South. No date of birth, no birthplace, no next of kin. He must have been born right after the war, or during it, to have been in his twenties in 1887. So he might have been a child of one of the Knight sons who died in the war, or for that matter, a son of William Knight himself. He looked like a Knight, dark-haired, good bones. Like you.

He appears first in the Knight Company ledgers in 1884 as a clerk-secretary, but by the beginning of 1885 he was William Knight's private assistant. He was short and thin, as though he had grown up starved, and was something of a dandy in a quiet way. A little, thin young man, cool and competent and always there. From all one hears, he was a very good man of business and almost the only man who got on well with William Knight.

Alexander, can you imagine them together? William needed an adult, responsible heir. Richard was only a boy. But Jay was illegitimate, and bastards cannot inherit under American law.

After Jay arrived, Richard seems to have spent more time away from Boston, at the family's house in New Hampshire. It was a house by a lake. Often Jay went with him. Richard seems to have quite suddenly become a sickly little boy, because in 1886 William hired for him a personal doctor. You met him on the station platform. His name was Charles Adair.

Now, my dear, things get interesting.

Here is Jay the illegitimate and Richard the legitimate. And here is a lake convenient for drowning. Oh, wouldn't *you* have, if you were the villain of the piece? It would have been so easy. A little push, the tiniest accident with a boat, the poor child would have been among the angels. And there, inevitably, at William's dark and bony side, would have been the mourning, the so-deserving Jay. One could have worked out the inheritance somehow, if there were no other heir.

But of course Jay murdered William first.

On the night of August sixth, 1887, William Knight and Jay French were staying at the house by Lake Matatonic. They ate dinner with Dr. Charles Adair in attendance. He says there was no disagreement between William Knight and Jay. Richard was not in the company; he had been sent to bed as being unwell. After the meal Jay French went upstairs to his office, at the head of the stairs opposite Richard's bedroom, to examine accounts. William Knight spoke with Adair and then began to clean a collection of some pistols and revolvers that he kept mounted on a board in the parlor. He was sitting in a large rocking chair, the guns on a table beside him and the windows open.

Dr. Adair had left the house and was on the road toward the village. The road led by the lake. By looking back over his shoulder, he could see the lights of the Knight house over the water. He heard a sharp bang, he says, like the sound of a dictionary being dropped. A man called out. He began running back toward the house. Whenever the trees were thin, he looked through them toward the house. He saw gaslight shadows on the windowpanes. Then Jay banged open the front door and ran away from the house with a staggering motion. "I'll get you for this!" Jay French shouted; really, you would think people would have some imagination. He fired at the house, a window broke. Jay ran off toward the woods beyond the barn. Silence, silence, silence. The doctor ran down the path, reached the house. Servants were coming downstairs, screaming and crying. William Knight was dead, shot dead, in the front room. A blood-bath, a shambles. Jay was gone. Richard Knight was downstairs, by his grandfather's body, deep in shock. (Prepare to be astounded, my dear.) The doctor asks the child, "Richard, did you see anything?" And what does Richard say?

"I won't tell," says Richard. "I'll never tell."

THE SLEETY RAIN rattled the glass. Victor leaned back, watching Reisden.

"And he never did. Three days later, under almost impossible conditions, Richard Knight was kidnapped. He was with his doctor and his uncle Gilbert in seclusion at the town's hotel. Guards in the corridor, guards downstairs. At one in the afternoon, Dr. Adair and Gilbert Knight left the room together. The boy was alone. Not five minutes later the guard checked the room.

"Richard was gone.

"And they never have found him."

The espresso machine hissed behind the bar. Reisden said nothing; his face was immobile. Victor's eyes drifted over Reisden's shoulder to another diner, a very young blond boy who had frankly been listening to the end of the story. Victor smiled dazzlingly. The boy blushed and looked away. Victor looked back at Reisden, who was still quiet and white.

"My dear boy," said Victor penitently, "I shouldn't have told you."

"It has nothing to do with me."

Victor had debated whether to show him the picture of Jay French. Better that Alexander see it from a friend.

But with Alexander and murder one was on so dreadfully shaky ground. One did have to make one's living
by turning murder into entertainment? One couldn't
simply prostitute oneself on the street, old as one was?

Reisden lit another cigaret; his hands seemed quite
steady but the match flame jittered. Victor waited.

"Why did the boy say what he did?" Reisden asked.

"Oh, my dear, if that were all. Why did Jay murder
William, when they apparently got on so well? Why did
Jay kidnap Richard? How did he get the boy out of the
hotel, past the guards? Did Jay kill him? Why didn't he
simply kill the boy there? The Knight case is so beautifully without explanations."

"The boy said 'I won't tell,' not 'I don't know.'"

"Could he have possibly been Jay's confederate, or
seen something that explained why Jay did it? I've wondered." Victor pursed his lips and held a forefinger to
them. "Let me see: Jay is lavender. He turns the dear
little boy Richard to his wicked devices. William discov-
ers them. Jay kills William to avoid being exposed.
Richard won't tell on his friend. Jay rescues him from
the hotel. They are now living in connubial pleasure in
Canada, troubled by only the slightest of bad dreams."
Victor shook his head. "I could write it but I couldn't
sell it, so I hope it isn't true."

Reisden smiled. "Who is Adair?"

"A curious man. A very simple man. Quite religious—in the Third Order Secular of St. Francis, I
believe. He runs a charitable hospital for children, and
doesn't simply run it, he lives there with the children.
You saw, of course, how much of the case depends on
his story. But he wouldn't have harmed Richard."

"For no one hurts the thing he loves." Reisden's

voice was quite flat. Victor reached out and took his hand in a gesture that he tried to make not flirtatious at all. *For each man kills the thing he loves.* Poor dear Oscar had been right about so many things.

"Dear boy, don't torment yourself forever. She really wouldn't want it."

"Yes. Don't worry." Reisden clasped his hand and let it go. "What happened after Richard disappeared?"

"Eventually Gilbert Knight got the money," Victor went on. "Did I mention that his father had completely disinherited him? Now he has it all. Millions and millions and millions of dollars."

"Does that make him the chief villain?"

"So *dull.* He was absolutely the first person one would have suspected. I want Jay French to have done it. He didn't have any reason, it was impossible for him to have got Richard out of the hotel. He must have done it."

"One can do things without motive," Reisden demurred carefully.

Victor nodded. They were on shaky ground again. "But generally, you know, murders have some reason. Jay French should have had some grudge against William, or have been dismissed by him. And there wasn't anything of the sort. Jay simply went upstairs, came downstairs, shot William, and kidnapped Richard."

"No explanation."

"None, dear boy."

"Would anyone at the Harvard conference, or in Boston, think I looked like one of the Knights? Anyone other than Adair, I mean."

"Oh, no, no, no, dear boy. You must go if you want to. Even darling Lizzie Borden isn't recognized on the

street. And you are the Baron von Reisden, not Richard
at all."

"Then I will go," Reisden said.

Victor looked at him shrewdly. Reisden raised both
eyebrows.

"Don't go, dear boy. You don't have to."

"I'm giving a paper at the Harvard conference."
Reisden smiled. "And going to New York afterward.
Opening doors, as Louis says."

"He could read it."

"He could." Reisden mimed a push on an invisible,
rather heavy door, then ducked as it swung back and hit
him. It was cleverly done, Victor thought, done like an
actor. Uneasiness mimed so well that it hardly seemed to
belong to Alexander. "I don't have to go to Harvard, or
to Paris. Except that Louis's right. It's go or give up."

"Then, dear boy, find out what happened to Richard.
I'll give you forty percent of the book royalties and you
won't have to write a line. No, I'll go half, *and* dinner
at Bauer-Grünwald. For once I could afford to take
you."

Reisden laughed and shook his head.

"Oh, do," Victor purred. "I would get three hundred
pounds on the advance alone."

CHAPTER 3

IT WAS NOT A HOUSE without music, but never before this evening had the staid Boston neighborhood heard the kind of music that was blaring and bouncing down Commonwealth Avenue. Harry Boulding had wanted a real dance band, and the best one in Boston had been crammed onto the second-floor landing, playing Boston-starch-collared versions of ragtime. The caterers' wagons had rolled up the avenue all afternoon, and the buffet had been laid on the heavy, old-fashioned dining-room table, on the thick, dated linen that the old butler had brought out from the least accessible closets. The florists had hidden the dark carved paneling with its gargoyles under seasonal flowers: poinsettias, holiday greens, rosettes of red ribbon. Harry had grumbled, "They got rid of all their leftover Christmas muck on us," but now that the party had started no one seemed to mind. What could go wrong, what could be less than perfect, for the coming-of-age party of Gilbert Knight's adopted heir?

The carriages stretched all up and down Commonwealth Avenue, the horses stamping in the snow. Some men from the Iroquois Club had come in a sleigh and were giving some girls from Wellesley rides up and down the avenue and around the Public Garden. As the sleigh swooped drunkenly in the snow, the Iroquois boys hallooed at windows and threw snowballs, and passersby ducked to get out of the way. The first floor was packed with guests. Big burly teammates of Harry's clustered around the dining-room buffet, tearing at chickens with their fingers. They talked seriously about Yale games, spring training, good plays. In the little parlor, Harry was opening joke birthday presents; there was a shocked universal shriek from the girls. "Oh, you! What do you want to show a girl a thing like that for!"

"Harry, what's your old man getting you for your birthday?" someone yelled. "Boston Harbor to sail in?"

"He'll have an announcement," Harry said carefully, enunciating around a few beers and perhaps just a little too much gin. He was not drunk, just incredibly happy. All his friends were here, it was his birthday, and for once the dull old house was lively. He held up the offending present in two fingers. "This, my friends, is shhhh——" He shook his head, dropped the present sadly, and held his finger to his mouth. "Shush. *Be* quiet. This, my lovely friends, is what the horses do on the street. My friend Joseph here has sent a wicked and an offensive thing to me. So what do we do?"

"What do we do?" the whole room yelled.

Harry grinned maniacally. "Let's dance!"

Not that the big parlor wasn't already crowded. All the furniture had been put against the walls and the rugs taken up for the evening, but no Boston house was really meant for serious dancing. People were dancing cheek to cheek, elbow to elbow, dancing in a mass, tuxedos crushed, corsages a flat mess against bosoms that were much closer to their partners' starched shirt fronts than etiquette and dancing school required. Harry, tall and burly, roiled into the center like a halfback into a scrimmage. "Pet! Pet! Perdita! I want to dance! Where's my girl?"

"OH, UNCLE GILBERT, what a party!"

Perdita Halley had escaped five minutes earlier, up the stairs and behind the dance band into the library on the second floor.

Behind the thick doors, in the dark quiet of his library, Gilbert Knight was sitting in anxious retreat from the party. He had one role to play that night, and no more than fifteen words to say. He had been resisting saying them for ten years. She slipped into the room and listened for him. In the dark she was completely blind; she heard the murmur of the fire and Gilbert stirring in his usual chair. She sat down in her chair beside him, reaching silently for his hand.

"My dear, is it actually going *well*?" Gilbert Knight shook his head. "Have we actually raised him to adulthood at last?"

"We have eaten a cow and two turkeys. Lothrop Ames had a fight with his cousin in the back yard and they're both in the kitchen drying off. The under-housemaid got kicked in the ankle by one of the football players and *she*'s in the kitchen with her ankle on ice. Miss Lucy Blackstone sent her footman over from next door to complain; I had Mr. Phillips send her over some of the refreshments, and we'll save her a piece of the birthday cake. Miss Emma Blackstone is here. The police came to the door to ask if they should arrest the Iroquois boys with the sleigh. I told them if they did, please take the girls too or we would be short on dance partners." She combed her hair back absently with the fingers of her free hand. In the damp and the heat it had frizzed out into a cloud; it always did. "Cousin Efnie says that every girl here is the smartest-looking in Boston. Phillips says they're all like a crowd of Gibson girls. I am frightfully jealous."

She was only seventeen. Boston society might let its young men run wild down Commonwealth Avenue, but for girls there were rules. No matter that the shopgirls at Filene's piled their hair high at sixteen and wore slim, long Gibson skirts that let show only a peek of a glamorous high-heeled slipper. No girl of good family could put her hair up or wear floor-length skirts until she was eighteen. For the long limbo of Boston seventeen, Perdita wore plain dresses with wide skirts, flat slippers, and lisle stockings. Her hair streamed down her back, and between her skirts and the floor was a shameful expanse of stockinged ankle. Tonight, at Harry's party, with all the fashionable older girls there, she spared a moment's regret for being eight months too young. Blind as a bat she might be, and Providence have reasons; but why couldn't she be old enough to dress like a grownup at her own boyfriend's party? Never mind. Despairs and rebellions were good only for laughter. Uncle Gilbert needed her tonight.

"Well," said Gilbert. "Only one more thing to do, my dear, and then I suppose we will have done everything we can."

"When will you do it?" She felt like an executioner.

"My dear, might we put it forward half an hour? If I were to wait until midnight, I don't know that I could do it at all."

She nodded. "That will suit Harry better too. He's still afraid that you won't do it, you know."

"I have made up my mind." Gilbert sounded doubtful, as if his mere decision to do something did not count for very much. He shifted restlessly in his chair. "My dear, I think I'll take a small glass of sherry."

"Of course, Uncle Gilbert, I'll get it for you." Uncle Gilbert had perhaps four glasses of sherry in a year. She moved over toward the drinks cabinet and felt among the bottles, moving her fingers over the raised letters on the little silver tabs on each, until she touched the label SHERRY. She poured carefully, judging by weight and sound how full the glass was.

"Thank you, my dear."

She sat down beside him on one of his old, brittle chairs.

"My dear——" he said after a time, and cleared his throat. "I suppose you know that declaring Richard dead is not entirely my desire."

"I know," she said steadily. Bucky Pelham, her real uncle if not her favorite, was Gilbert Knight's chief lawyer. Uncle B. had told her at length how important it was to declare Richard dead, and so had Harry in their boyfriend-and-girlfriend talks together.

"I must make Harry the heir to everything," Gilbert said, and his old voice shook a little. "I have never fully inherited from Richard. I don't own the money free and clear until Richard is declared——not alive."

"Uncle Gilbert, if Richard could, he would have come back." She pressed her lips a little together; those were Uncle Bucky's words. She sympathized with Uncle Gilbert, whether or not she should.

His voice went down an octave suddenly, quavered, and rang for a moment as if there were metal in it. "If he were dead I think that I would *know*, you see. He was my brother's only child." He stood up, a blur against the fire, whispering, half voiceless under the little crackle of the flames. "I have never felt that he was wholly gone. My dear, God grant I don't do wrong tonight."

He said nothing for a while, and then came back and sat down by her, taking her by the hand. "At any rate, my dear, when we have had the one announcement, and Harry is the heir to the Knight Company, perhaps we shall have another? And perhaps we will have more parties in this house? A wedding party, and someday a christening? You are my true child, you know, and I do long for you and Harry to be married."

"Oh, Uncle Gilbert!" She shook her head. "Harry hasn't asked me yet. And who knows whether I shall have him when he does?"

The door opened and a blast of sound from the party erupted in at them.

"Not marry Harry?" Gilbert said. "Oh, Charlie! Charlie, we didn't expect you for weeks yet. Dear friend! Come in!"

"Uncle Charlie!" Perdita exclaimed in delight.

"I couldn't stay away." His voice sounded tired, she thought. Why was he back from Europe so soon?

"Isn't our party vasty and grand, Charlie? Do you think Harry will be an adult after this?"

"After tonight," Charlie agreed, "we'll have finished looking after the boy, and high time too. Perdita, my darling, you're prettier than ever and dressed to death. Let the old boys talk for a few minutes, will you?"

"Of course. I should look at the party."

"CHARLIE, am I doing the right thing?"

Charlie Adair stretched his aching legs toward the

fire. It warmed them and took the travel-tiredness out of them, but it didn't take the ache from his heart. That's the worst of being old, he thought, you don't know whether your heart's broken or you need a good night's sleep. No, the worst is, whichever it is, the good night's sleep will take care of it. The doctor doesn't prescribe eternal sorrows for old men. He wanted to go to Mass and recapture his grief, or have a good glass of whiskey and forget it.

"This is the only right thing," he said almost automatically. "Harry's your own boy."

"Not the same way. I wish he were. Charlie, there are so many abandoned children who need my love, and I have one of the best of them and I've adopted him. But I can't love him as if he were Richard, not as much as you love any child in your clinic, any child off the street. I wish I had your heart, Charlie."

"Ah, no you don't, not my old ticker." Charlie liked the young: the children from the clinic, his niece and her boyfriend, everything green and growing. Bert Knight's grief, for all it paralyzed Bert, kept him green. Since the railway station in Lausanne, Charlie Adair felt as old as dead leaves. Seeing that man had taken something out of him. He could not think of Richard anymore, only of how Richard could stir up things better left to die.

Charlie Adair dug into his bulging pockets, pulling out string, lollipops for the babies, and his Franciscan crown, which he rolled in his fingers as if he could take pagan comfort from the rosary beads. So much of the Rosary was about children: the Annunciation, the Visitation, the Nativity. Mary meeting her Son for the first time since His death and Resurrection. Resurrection was her greatest joy, in which Charlie could not share. For him, every Hail Mary would be *thank God the man at the train was not Richard.*

Bless me, Father, for I have sinned. I want my comfort. I want my morning chat with You, the next best thing to being asleep in bed, and my little bit of bread that says You died for my sins so that I don't have to. I want my peace that passeth understanding, I want, I want. I don't want things to change. "Ah, Bert, I'm too old for the grand opera. I'd be glad if your nephew was the Knight Company heir and my niece was married to him."

"That is how it will be," Gilbert Knight said sadly.

"And why should we be sad about it?"

Above the mantelpiece, softly illuminated, hung a portrait. It looked a little unreal, like most portraits taken from a single photograph. A little boy sat in a tangle of grass in front of a rosebush. The boy's hand was on the head of a black-and-white mongrel dog, and the dog's chin lay contentedly on the boy's knee. Roses out of season stood in a vase underneath the portrait; in the fire's heat they were giving up their perfume, so that Charlie Adair smelled roses just as he had when he had taken the little boy's photograph eighteen years ago. For all his words Charlie closed his eyes, stabbed with irreparable loss. God bless you, Richard, forever and ever.

"Do you remember how many people thought they saw him, the first year or two?" Charlie asked. "They were all wrong."

"People would write to me, come to me," Gilbert said. "They'd have pictures that looked like him. They'd bring children."

"Do you remember the old woman from New Jersey?

Bert, she brought the boy she'd adopted all the way up from Montclair to us on the train. She'd dressed him up like he was going to church, all new clothes, and her sitting there with her apron all mends and tatters. Not hugging him, not touching him. She was sure he was ours, you see, because she wanted him as much as the world.''

"But he wasn't."

Charlie kept looking up at the picture. His fingers closed round his beads. "Ah, it was as if he was, but she had got him and not us. I don't know if you remember what you did the rest of that day. The old lady stopped me trackless. I was going back to the hospital, but I never got there. Halfway there, I remember, I went up the nearest church stairs—not even a Catholic church, God forgive me—and spent the whole afternoon putting calluses on my knees, saying St. Francis' prayer over and over. 'Lord, make me an instrument of Thy peace . . . help me to love.' I was shamed by that old girl, she was so full of love. Help me to love, I prayed. Teach me what to do. Help me love so much that nothing else matters." Charlie smiled. "That night I was down at Boston City, the emergency room, a little girl comes in, kicked by a horse and deaf. Four years old, the poor kid. And three days later, I'm on your doorstep with my hat in my hand asking for a hundred dollars for the family. Four kids there were, three of them deaf. God had children for me when I knew to ask Him."

Thank God the young man in Switzerland was not Richard. Thank You, Lord God, that You gave me these children. And Bert has Harry, and what would Harry do if Richard were alive? "Bert, you took Harry into your house almost ten years ago. You've adopted him. You can't hold out any longer. You're not being fair to the boy. Give him your heart."

Gilbert put down the sherry glass on a spindle-legged old table and bent his shoulders and clasped his hands in a hunching approximation of prayer. He looked as if he were about to be whipped. Suddenly he unclasped his hands and put them flat down on his knees.

"I would lie to God, Charlie, if I prayed that Richard is dead."

But not I, thought Charlie Adair, saddened. Not I.

DOWNSTAIRS the noise hit Perdita like a tidal wave. For guidance she usually depended on her ears and on the known location of furniture and lights. Tonight everything was smothered in greenery, cleared away or moved around; she stood blind in a chaos of colors. She was whirled off the last step of the stairs and into the crowd. Elbows poked at her, somebody jabbed her in the side. "Look out! Can't you see where you're going?" No, you— She mentally stuffed the words unsaid back into her box of rebellions.

"Why, if it isn't little Perdita!"

"Good evening, Miss Blackstone," Perdita sighed.

A huge, warm, powder-smelling shape flashed a lorgnette at her. "Are you going to play the piano for us? I did so enjoy your little recital at Mrs. Beach's. She says you are quite promising—such praise from a woman of her eminence!"

To get anyone's attention with a piano tonight, Perdita would have had to hit them with it.

"Miss Emma, have you seen Harry?"

"Why, child, he is all over." Miss Blackstone lowered her voice. "I understand he is about to become a young man with very great expectations——?"

"Oh, Miss Emma, I know nothing about that."
Sometimes it paid to be seventeen.

"Oh, of course not, my dear. A girl should never
think of such things. But what is wrong with your
uncle? Your uncle Charlie, my dear, came rushing in as
if he were bringing a bucket to a fire. I hope he is
considering his health; he is just back from Europe, and
you know one can get such terrible diseases abroad. I do
so look forward to hearing everything that he learned on
his Tour—will he host a little *collazione* at the Children's Clinic, perhaps a photographic slide lecture?"

"The buffet is in the dining room," Perdita said a
little acidly, but Miss Emma Blackstone just cooed and
sailed off toward the rear of the house. Perdita hoped
everyone who wanted eclairs had already got one. Miss
Blackstone hunted eclairs as Teddy Roosevelt shot buf-
falo, by the hundreds and thousands.

There was a huge roar over the heads of the crowd:
Harry's voice. "Where's my girl?"

"Oh, Harry!"

He caught her up in a big bear hug. "Pet," he said,
"Pet, this is the happiest night of my life. The thing is
I love you. I want to dance. Dance with me."

She sheltered herself in his arms, molding her movements to his shuffle. Harry laughed. "I dance like a
football player, don't I, Pet?" He did; but it was endear-
ing, like everything about big, blond, athletic Harry.
They swayed among the crowded dancers.

"From tonight I am king of England, tsar of all the
Russias, sultan of Turkey," he murmured in her ear.
"Rich as Jay Gould, almost, and I deserve it. Just be-
tween you and me, Pet, I'm going to head up the Knight

companies better than anyone else in the world."

She hugged him. Up in the library Uncle Charlie and Uncle Gilbert were mourning the boy they really wanted. She kept her arms around him. Harry, how can I protect you? Only by telling you you are loved.

Suddenly, around them people had stopped dancing; shivers rippled through the crowd, stirrings, all in one direction. Under her palms, Harry's hard muscled back tensed like an animal's in a storm. The band stopped playing, not all at once but dying away in a fray of instruments. Someone pushed a champagne glass into her hand.

"It is nearly midnight," Uncle Gilbert's ready voice fluted above the noise. He sounded so shaky, so sad. "And I would like to propose a toast to Harry—Harry Boulding—who is twenty-one at midnight. And it is my expectation, my hope—" He paused for a very long time and Perdita held her breath. Uncle Charlie said something in an undertone from the same place on the steps. Gilbert finished, like a little child rattling off the end of something only half memorized, "That the company my father founded will, in the fullness of time, be in good hands under Harry."

That was all there was to the speech. For a moment no one said or did anything, as if they were still trying to work out exactly what Gilbert had said. Then one by one, among Harry's friends, there was a ragged beginning of cheers for him. Finally everybody started cheering, as if they felt it was the thing to do. "Get up, Harry! Take a bow!" yelled Harry's friend Joe, who could always be counted on to make a racket. "Hip, hip, hooray! Drink up, everybody!" Perdita touched her lips to the chill, sour wine.

Harry touched her arm. "Do you love me?" Harry asked under his breath.

"Oh, Harry, of course."

"Nobody cares about me but you. *He* doesn't care. You know that."

He pushed away from her and elbowed his way up the stairs. "Thank you, Uncle Gilbert. That was short but sweet. Now, you guys, quiet down a moment. Joseph, don't drink it all yet, you pig. I have an announcement that is going to outrun and outhit everything. Pet, come up here." Someone pushed her forward. She felt the railing of the stairs underneath her hand. "Stand here. I want everybody here to see you. See what a girl I've got." He put his fingers to his lips and blew a loud whistle. "Ladies and gentlemen! Cut it out for a minute! You, too, Efnie. I've got something to say."

The crowd noise quieted to a low buzzing. Perdita, standing on the stairs, could feel their eyes on her.

"You all know that I came here ten years ago. The first person I saw here was this lovely little girl. Well, now I'm older, and this lovely little girl is older— though you wouldn't think it to look at her."

"Baby-stealer, Harry!" someone shouted.

"You said it, Turk, I'd better steal her before someone else does. So I'm saying tonight, right here and now, to my lovely girl Perdita: Pet, will you marry me?"

There was a chorus of real cheering, or it was only her blood singing in her ears. You are my true child. She sat right down on the stairs in surprise and put her hands to her mouth. Oh, Harry. Harry her husband, she his wife, and their children; and Uncle Gilbert would truly care for Harry at last.

"Oh Harry," she said laughing, "thank you!"

Some of the people below burst out laughing, and she supposed it was funny; but she knew they were laughing with her. "What a kid!" Harry breathed into her ear as he kissed her. She felt a little link slip over her finger as Harry held her hand up: engagement ring, she thought, astonished because she was going to be married. It was as if the whole world had changed. She was *engaged* and she was going to be *married* to Harry, and he would be her *husband*. She said the words silently, the round heavy words of married love, and they rolled in her mouth as unfamiliar as rocks or rings.

"You love me," Harry said. "You love me best of all."

CHAPTER 4

CHEMISTRY IS HYPOTHESIS, followed by seeing and touching and measurement. The work of observation is inspiring; if one is good at picking a subject, one will see things that no human being has seen before. But at its worst it is drudgery, and for Reisden it was drudgery for all the winter and spring of 1906.

Reisden's own work was in muscle contraction, one of the most exciting and most frustrating areas of the field. For a hundred years the motion of muscles had been "understood"—nerves move muscles by stimulating them with small electrical charges. By using Eint-hoven's string galvanometer, one could actually observe an electrical charge passing through the nerves and causing contractions in the muscle. But it had only become clear within the past few years that the electrical charge was actually some extremely complex form of electro-chemical reaction.

What was its nature? Neural messages did not act like electricity in wires. They were probably a series of discrete chemical reactions, moving much more slowly than electricity in wires or water—electricity in the nervous system of a frog was slower than a racing car. Moreover, at least in frogs, the neuromuscular system was affected by changes in temperature to a degree far greater than could be easily explained by known electro-chemical reactions. A frog outside on a frosty day was so inefficient that a few hops would exhaust it for an hour.

Did the cold change the frogs' usual reactions, or merely slow them down? Reisden hypothesized it only slowed them down. Were they slow enough to make observation of the recovery reaction easier? If so, by mincing the nerves at different stages of the recovery from stimulation, one would get a stop-motion view of the chemical changes that took place during the recovery process. In the winter and spring of 1906, that was what Reisden was doing, studying the formation and break-down of several cofactor compounds in the nerves of dissected frogs, their temperatures lowered to precise measurements.

He was not an enthusiastic vivisectionist, though he had known researchers who were; it hurt him to kill frogs. When he was well, he accepted doing it; when he found himself getting unbalanced, he usually found himself hating it. That spring, almost constantly, he hated it.

He didn't know whether it was the difficulty of keeping the temperatures right, or having turned down the Paris job, which he did just after New Year's. The weather was bad that season. The snow settled in hard over Lausanne, building up in the streets and turning the slushy grey colors of soot and horse dung. Reisden's series of refrigeration experiments finally finished in March, and, though he had more than enough material to talk about, it seemed to him as though he were missing some essential point.

He avoided seeing Louis at all. Louis was going to spend the whole summer over in America, mostly at the Connecticut Agricultural Station but partly with a man in New York, and Reisden had promised to help him with translating the lectures he would deliver there.

Looking for a method, a new angle, means letting one's imagination loose. Reisden roamed restlessly, spending two uncomfortable days in Paris with Berthet and talking with colleagues and old friends, long lost track of, at a conference in Giessen. But to travel, to visit, had unfortunate meaning of its own: Berthet, Reisden realized, was sounding him again about coming to Paris. He felt like Lazarus risen from the grave, not having meant to do it and finding it frightening. He felt pointless and dangerous to everyone.

Being with so many people turned his nerve ends raw. The conversation had holes in which, very politely of course, no one asked him about either his past or his future. They talked chemistry. It seemed a temporizing, and he felt he had nothing intelligent to say.

And sometimes, over the weeks and months, he thought of the Knights; and then, unusual for such a curious man, he realized he was trying not to think of them.

HARVARD'S CAMBRIDGE was a small, comfortable, stodgy town, all red brick and May green: redbrick buildings, verdigrised copper cupolas and young ivy, all very pleasant to look at in the height of the American spring. In Maytime in Cambridge, bearded men were sniffing the lilacs, discussing baseball, and packing for summer trips; students were trying to catch up on the semester, or taking long lunches and going for walks on the marshy banks of the Charles; browsers were buying books; friends about to graduate stayed up all night to talk. It was a strange beginning-and-ending time, Maytime in Cambridge. And on it, in May 1906, the biochemists descended for an international conference, filling deserted lecture halls, talking about zymase and Harden-Young esters, ultramicroscopes, the elegant affirmation of entropy through Einstein's theory of relativity, and whether there existed a good American beer. Reisden, at odds with himself, was among his colleagues.

Cambridge was a city of lodging houses, not hotels, and with some of the other chemists, Reisden and Louis were quartered in Boston. In an ambitious mood, they walked the distance every morning, through a sea-smelling salt-marsh river basin. The seagulls screamed and wheeled in the pale American sky, and the wide, winding, tide-ribbed river bobbed with wild ducks diving for breakfast. Downriver was the low brown city; ahead, the spires of the college; in the middle, springtime in a foreign country, unexpected and unknown.

Reisden gave his own talk the second day of the conference. The room was surprisingly full. Reisden knew many of the audience by name and work; too many personally. The next three days of the conference were his, to speak to as many of these people as he could, to trade information with them and get whatever ideas might help his project.

He learned little. Harden and Young's confirmation of catalysis among enzymes was exciting, of course, but Reisden already knew Harden well. Researchers at Columbia and Harvard were working on isolating further organic phosphates. Thompson of MIT believed that the problem of muscle motion was essentially mechanical and that one could work it out by developing a microscope powerful enough to see it. Reisden and Peter Miller of Johns Hopkins had a generally futile argument with him about the size of what he wanted to see, relative to the wavelength of visible light. They met Louis' contact from New York, a Maurice O'Brien, who was developing some interesting ideas on how electrical impulse and catalysis interacted. O'Brien, Miller, and Reisden talked most of Tuesday evening and part of Wednesday. *Why* does cold stop muscle reaction? The muscle was building up toxins, lactic acid principally; but a frog dissected after *resting* still showed— Louis descended on them and waved his hands about heats of formation of amines and basal metabolic rates. "You mean we should do it all on paper," Peter Miller snorted.

On Wednesday night Reisden went to the college library to check a question in organic chemistry. The library was housed in a small and antiquated granite building, Gore Hall. The weather had turned warm suddenly, and Gore Hall's crowded reading room smelled of undergraduate sweat, tobacco, and books; someone had spilled a bottle of ink and Reisden smelled that too, a mix of charcoal and solvent and iron. At the reading tables, a thread of cooler air came in through the windows. He filled out the slips for the materials he wanted and sat at a reading desk waiting for them, facing up to what else he could do in a Massachusetts library. There was no reason for him to be so much as interested in the Knights. Still, he scribbled the call slips for three more books: the bound volumes for three local newspapers for August 1887. And there, in the hubbub and flat echoes of the Gore Hall reading room, feeling odd and clandestine, he read about the Knight murder case.

The case had splashed blood over the front pages of the Boston newspapers. Most still followed the old custom of carrying advertisements on the front page, so the news of the murder was mixed with advertisements for patent clocks, Well-Man's Electric Tonic, and the summer sales at Jordan Marsh. "The body of Mr. Knight was slumped terribly mutilated on the floor." (Amplified rustle of pages down the Gore Hall reading room; a cough.) "The desperate murderer had vanished without trace from the scene." (Reverberation of a heavy book thumping onto a desk.) The newspaper artists of the *Illustrated Weekly* had produced unlikely woodcuts of the murder scene, with a hard-faced dwarf pointing a pistol at a benevolent white-haired man, while a child cowered behind the door.

He turned forward to the news of Richard's disappearance.

For that, a law firm, Winthrop, Pelham, and Doane, had taken out reward advertisements, banishing Electric Tonic and summer-weight suits from the front pages.

All three papers flared out in pictures. "A CHILD-KILLER!" shrieked the headlines over the picture of Jay French that Reisden had seen before. He looked at the other one.

"HAVE YOU SEEN THIS CHILD?"

He had little experience in looking at children and he didn't know what he wanted to see. The recognition was all he knew. He felt the picture through a skin of memories, his own almost forgotten childhood, the sound of voices down the long empty corridors at Graf Leo's country *Schloss*, the scratch of school-uniform braid against his neck. He had no pictures of himself that young. He remembered the face, like something seen dimly in a winter window, more dim, the memory of something long forgotten.

He stared at the picture, daring it to stay something he knew, until the face dissolved to shading and lines. Then he banged the big volume closed, so loud that readers looked up.

The Knights had nothing to do with him, and he would do no more about them.

THAT NIGHT, for the first time in perhaps a year, he dreamed about the murder he had done.

November. Very early morning. He and Tasy are outside London in the New Forest, in a racing car on a good straight road. Grey English sunrise, the light barely through the trees. "Can I come with you?" she calls. It's only a trial run. "Come on, dear love!" She climbs into the seat next to him and turns her face to his. For a moment, kissing her casually, he has a certainty of happiness.

The steering wheel is under his hands. He has bound it with black electrical tape, inelegant, but most wheels are slippery and his is not. The roar of the motor increases to a whine as he guns the car up to fifty English miles an hour, sixty, down the long, straight, empty road. The trees passing have their own sound: *whump, whump,* pounding like hearts.

Something's wrong with the steering. The wheel swings free in his hands, then locks. Something jars and rips in the undercarriage, there's another sound—metal?—a scream. Her voice, cut off in the middle. All sounds stop at once. There are broken-off branches in the car. He calls her name, turns to look at her, and sees great smears of red across the windshield glass.

She is lying outside the car, on a mat of leaves under the tree they hit. Her right arm is outstretched, she is lying on her side. Blood has come out of her mouth and nostrils, her eyes are open. She is dead.

And he is purely, joyously thankful, he is glad. He meant to do this. He liked it.

No— It is all dark and he does not want to be here.

He fought his way out of sleep with Louis pounding on the door. "Yes, of course, I'm all right." He stared up at the dark ceiling of the hotel room, listening to the slow clop of a delivery wagon from the street outside, then turned on the lights. It was three o'clock in the morning, but he wouldn't sleep.

Usually when he was wakeful at night he looked after his stocks, but he didn't know the American exchanges and he wasn't going to learn them tonight. He had packed light for the trip and had already read what he had; he was temporarily bookless.

The hotel room had a copy of the City Directory.

Reisden looked at the dark-blue-bound book for an inordinately long time before he opened it and turned to the Ks.

KNIGHT, Gilbert H......263 Commonwealth Avenue
  —H. P. Boulding.

The address was an easy walk from his hotel.

Sometime before dawn he took the walk. The house was a double frontage of granite blocks and gargoyles, outsized for the street of narrow brownstones. The Knights had apparently possessed a talent for the conspicuous. The blinds were drawn; perhaps no one was home, perhaps they were all asleep. What would happen if he rang the doorbell? "Tell me why I think I recognized Richard Knight." He did not stay long in front of the house; he took a long walk. Like a tourist, he saw the Public Garden with its amusing King Ludwig swan boats and then bought himself coffee at a shop with a counter, open early. He and the counter girl were the only persons in the shop.

He asked her, "Have you ever believed anything you're certain isn't true?"

"Sure," she said. "I keep believing my brother'll get a job."

"Have you ever thought you might be someone else?"

She looked at him sideways and moved down the counter, laughing. "That'd be crazy."

"Of course," he said. "Everything has a simple explanation."

THAT DAY, which was Thursday, Louis went down to Connecticut to start looking at pigs, and at the conference, Reisden played a game. He had played it once before, in London when Tasy was still alive. "Tell me your earliest memory," he said to everyone he talked with. "And tell me how old you were."

Back in London, the game had been started by someone who "needed to recover my childhood, darlings" in order to play a role in a pantomime. She needed earliest recollections. "An elephant," Reisden had said. An elephant standing in the river. It was Africa; he had recognized the mud-yellow color of the water. The elephant trumpeted, then blew water onto itself. In the wonderful omnipresent sunlight the water was full of rainbows. The elephant spread its ears; it seemed that there could be nothing outside such magnificence. It faded slowly, back into an Africa he could barely remember. There were words with it, only his own younger voice saying his name, *I am Alexander von Reisden.*

A researcher from Chicago remembered the rocking horse he had had at two years old. Peter Miller remembered eating cornbread batter with a spoon. "Anytime. Four, maybe. But I still eat it." William James the philosopher remembered his brother as a baby "and he is a year younger than I." The New York researcher, Maurice O'Brien, remembered drawing with a bright red crayon: two years old. The curve peaked somewhere around four, but there were outliers in both directions. The most extreme, a biologist from the Lawrence Scientific School, had almost no memories before fifteen.

Reisden himself, he thought, had been ten.

He had never really felt anything was wrong. It was not an uncommon thing to repress very large portions of one's memories. In the ordinary course of life, most people remembered only the smallest portion of what happened to them, and few people who knew them, even close and loving companions, remembered the same things. Parents or brothers or sisters filled in some blanks, but often their memories were surprisingly different. It was particularly so with childhood; and for many persons, some part of childhood was gone completely.

For Reisden it was almost everything that had happened to him before Graf Leo had brought him to Graz from his birthplace in Africa.

Reisden had asked other people the question, off and on, specifically to graph the connection between mental stability and lack of childhood memories. There was none as far as he could tell. It was really no more than intriguing that some people remembered more of their childhood than he did of his.

Is it odd, though, not to remember one's birthday? Reisden didn't remember the date of his, though he had been told it often enough; it fell repeatedly out of his head, and finally, out of exasperation at himself, he had simply added a year to his age every New Year's. Tasia had chosen him a birthdate just before they were married; that date he remembered, but he had never been able to remember his own.

So: a small thing, but odd.

In odd moments Reisden had read up on the literature of loss of memory. It came in two kinds, specific and general. Either kind could come from physical damage, such as a blow, or from a psychic shock. Specific amnesia usually came from a sudden shock; it killed little bits of memory before and after the shock and was almost always permanent. William James, who was just back from California and full of earthquake stories, had several anecdotes about San Franciscans who had received some sort of shock or injury and, to their annoyance, had forgot the earthquake.

In general amnesia, the kind so loved by Victorian melodrama, one forgot one's identity completely. The Victorians liked to show general amnesia being cured years later. "Phyllis! It comes back to me! You—our little home—our babies," et cetera. All wrong. General amnesia repaired itself within weeks or not at all.

There were a handful of exceptions. Not many.

General memory loss was uncommon in healthy adults, but, to some degree, almost universal in children. Children got fevers and thumps on the head. More interestingly, children became adult, or at least self-aware. The Lawrence School biologist had got his research approach at fifteen, and everything before that, he said, became irrelevant.

Reisden had come to Europe from Africa when he was ten, according to that birthdate he could never remember. As far as he or anyone could tell, his parents had died when he was about five, in one of the nameless skirmishes and barn-burnings that preceded the war. How they had died, and how he hadn't, he didn't remember at all. Of the time between, he had some fragments: at the edge of a city, stunted trees standing on a plain; a monkey on the arm of a Moslem trader in a market; the taste of burnt peanuts in a stew. By concentrating he could bring more of it back. He had slept under a bridge sometimes, sometimes under the raised floors of houses; he still remembered the smell of the earth and the not unpleasant beetles, and had once woken to find a snake sleeping next him. For a while he had worked for a junkseller, but the man had died.

Before that, or after, he had stolen food.

He remembered the elephant.

Graf Leo had been at a table behind him, turning over papers. ". . . the son of my friend Franz von Reisden. That is who you are. You understand that. See, here is the paper that tells who your parents were." *I am Alexander von Reisden,* he had said to himself, a delighted child. And in the river the elephant had raised his big trunk, trumpeted, and spread his ears. It had been that very moment when Reisden had understood that he was unique, himself, because someone else had said so. At that moment he had known exactly who he was, and his sense of himself had been as close to him as the pulse in his neck.

I am Alexander von Reisden, born in Africa, son of Franz Eugen and Charlotte-Elisabeth von Reisden. He did not doubt it for an instant.

But Graf Leo was as dead now as Franz Eugen and Charlotte-Elisabeth; and out of Reisden's own memories he could not prove who he was.

THE LAST DAY of the conference dragged, dedicated to the banalities of a formal lunch and speeches. An anticlimax on top of an anticlimax; for Reisden, nothing had come clearly out of the conference, no research angle, no persuasive news. He was leaving that night for New York, to visit Louis and O'Brien and then go back to Europe. He wanted to be gone already, but someone he didn't know had left a message asking for an appointment at three o'clock, at the Harvard science museum. A Mr. Roy Daugherty: not a professor, not involved in the field, wouldn't give his business. A mystery.

The lunch was an official one, long and with speeches,

the serious ones about the future of international coop-
eration among scientists and the funny ones, which were
mercifully shorter. He sat at an English-speaking table
with several men he had met during the conference. One
of Berthet's researchers, of all people, had shown up
from Paris and was sitting some distance away, at a table
where they were speaking French. The Paris man
looked over to him and beckoned to him, and he shook
his head, smiling. He didn't see any end to it; Louis
trying to get him to work on that team; Reisden knowing that his best research would come from working
there; Reisden nevertheless trying to stay away from
Paris. Why had he thought it neutral to come to America? His life appalled him. Suddenly he could not meet
anyone, talk with anyone; he needed to be alone. He got
out with the first wave of those who left.

After that, having left so early, there was nothing he
could do to justify the passage of time. He was enervated
and physically exhausted, having learned too much pe-
ripheral to him. He walked up and down in a courtyard,
nervous as though there were something dreaded and
essential he had not done; but it was simply that he did
not know what to do. For all of his working life he had
been a chemist, and he had been lucky enough to find his
research approach early. It had kept him going, for a
while, after Tasy died.

Now it didn't. Now, all at once, in a little closed
courtyard within four walls, on a Friday in a foreign
country, chemistry left him. *This is my hand. Why does
it move?* Because the striated muscle moves; and what
pulls it? Chemicals and electricity, but what makes them,
where do they come from, why do they move? The
questions were dim and faraway, and the only one he

cared about was why, a long time ago on a November morning, he had known he had wanted to kill Tasy.

Because I am mad.

Stop it, he told himself.

He took a walk. He was to meet Daugherty by the steps of the Museum of Ethnology. He walked to the museum, since there must be something there to take him out of his mood. He went first to the Blaschka glass flowers, which did not hold him long: a large, dull botanical exhibition, imperceptibly made of glass. The museum went on from room to room. It was early afternoon of a May day and the big display rooms were deserted of everything but what could not get outside, the exhibits. Glass cases reflecting each other, inside them stiff animals, dusty fur, glass eyes. Whole walls cobwebbed with the skeletons of birds. Around a corner, suddenly, filling a huge hall, the dead-tree bones of a dinosaur, the ribs of a skeleton whale encircling a walkway. He walked through. He concentrated carefully on the American touches: the stuffed elephant, donated by subscription, shapeless where its straw was leaking away; the pheasants that had been sent to George Washington. He saw mothballs in the corner of their painted case. There were too many stuffed animals. They were too silent, too very much unlike animals. Preparing them for exhibition had made them much more like each other than any were like the living species they mocked. Louis would say, he thought, Only Reisden is such a fool as to notice everything in a museum is dead.

The dust hung in the air; the glass cases reflected one another, the bones hung in figured patterns on the dusty velvet inside. He heard a scratching sound. A mouse had come out to investigate and peered around bewildered, then sped back to its hole. It left the room as quiet as the inside of a stopped heart. Reisden was left alone.

He wanted to get outside, to talk with someone, with Louis, it didn't matter who; he looked for the exit; and then he got lost, it seemed for hours, in the endless corridors of the museum. He went back through all the still rooms, by the stuffed birds with their frozen uplifted wings, under the ribs of the baleen whale reaching down from the ceiling. He stood on the walkway that passed through the ribs of the whale; he looked down at the floor below and at his hands on the railing of the walkway, clenched into fists, veins and bones like an anatomy. Finally he found a stairway. At the bottom, outside the door, he sat on the steps and leaned his head against a railing. The side of the building was warm. It was still light outside, a May afternoon.

"Dr. Reisden? Dr. von Reisden?"

The man at the bottom of the steps looked like a wrestler. He had the knurled ears and the scarred hands; his hair was cut so short it looked like a disfigurement. He wore thick glasses.

"Are you Roy Daugherty?" Reisden asked, bringing the name to mind. He was astonished that he'd come anywhere close to keeping the appointment.

"You're the Baron Alexander von Reisden?" the man repeated. "Lives in Lausanne, Switzerland?"

He was holding a copy of the *Almanach de Gotha,* the European register of nobility; the binding was unmistakable. Reisden shrugged. "Yes, I'm in that book."

Daugherty pulled out a notebook, old, worn-edged leather, the book of a man who spent a great deal of time noting down information. "You are——?" Reisden asked.

"I'm a detective, Baron. A lawyer some, but mostly a detective."

"Oh?"

"Have you ever heard of Richard Knight, sir?"

Reisden's tiredness drained away from him, leaving him cold to the bones.

"More than I care for. Who are you?" he said sharply.

"I got a proposition for you such as you never heard before in your life. Now, you probably ain't going to say yes. No reason why you should; you ain't connected with the Knights and you don't know me from a dead rat. But if you've got a few minutes to spare, I'd like to tell you a story. If you don't mind?"

Reisden looked down the steps at him, quite sure he minded.

"OK if I sit down?" Daugherty asked.

Reisden nodded. Yes, sit down. Daugherty sat down with a *whoof* on the curbing of the steps. "Hot day, ain't it?"

"Mr. Daugherty, I am familiar with the technique of getting the subject relaxed with small talk. Shall we go on?"

Daugherty stared up at him. "Well, they said you wasn't dim."

"I am not dim. I am also surprised that you consider it your business to ask about me. Do you, by the way, think that I am either Richard Knight or Jay French, or any other Knight? You, Mr. Daugherty, may answer yes or no."

"Whoa, now, we know you can't be Jay nor Richard neither. You were right in that nobility book with the Kaiser and the King of England. I'm sorry Charlie Adair caused you trouble, but he didn't know what he was doing. It's just because you ain't Richard that I want to talk with you."

"Does this have anything to do with the Knight murders?"

"No."

"Good. Talk. Please do make it short."

Roy Daugherty hesitated and took a deep breath. "I work for the Knights' lawyers. They got a real bad legal problem. This ain't common knowledge, mind." Reisden nodded. "Do you know anything about inheritance?"

"Not a great deal."

"With the Knights, there's a real complex situation. William Knight left his money to Richard. Richard disappeared. If Richard's dead, next heir is Gilbert Knight and everything's fine." Daugherty licked his lips. "But Richard ain't never been declared dead."

The two men looked warily at each other. Daugherty went on.

"I know you got most of your time spent on chemistry already, and the folks around here say you're a coming man. So what I'm going to ask is something real peculiar for a man like you. Won't take more than a couple of days. But it's peculiar." Roy Daugherty took a deep breath. "We got to have someone pretend to be Richard Knight."

Oh, G-d. This was a hallucination. Roy Daugherty shifted from ham to ham. He wore square-toed heavy boots, a little out of date, and the crown of his head was going bald. Reisden closed his eyes. What was the hallucination, what was frightening, was that he wanted to know about this.

"You want to listen to the whole story?" Daugherty asked.

CHAPTER 5

THE OFFICES of the Knights' lawyers were on Beacon Street overlooking Boston Common, the city's central public park. In the late Friday afternoon they were almost deserted. A secretary had brought coffee. The two men sat near the windows, in the sun. The coffee was good, Reisden supposed. It smelled good but he couldn't drink it. He held the cup two-handed for warmth.

Five years ago, after Reisden had got out of the hospital, he had been taken for recuperation to an asylum. Very gentlemanly, very proper, but an asylum nevertheless. He felt now the way he had when he had first seen the asylum gates: Whatever happens next, one cannot possibly prepare for.

"What it's about is money," the lawyer, Roy Daugherty, said. In Reisden's head, Victor whispered, *The crimes of the rich have essentially to do with money.* "Who gets the money after Gilbert Knight dies."

Daugherty drew on a piece of paper: William Knight at the top of a page. Below him a genealogy of sons and daughters, all slashed off without children. Then Daugherty drew in two other sons of William Knight. One son line he marked "Gilbert Knight," still living but with no wife or children. Finally, at the right, he drew in another son line, and the son of that son, Richard Knight.

"William Knight founded the Knight Company. When he made his will he had one son living and one grandson. No other relatives whatsoever. We even went back to England and Ireland to find some, but there ain't none.

"That's what I've spent most of my c'reer doing," Daugherty put in parenthetically. "I know more about genealogy than any six Mormons."

Daugherty surrounded Richard Knight's name with dollar signs and exclamation points.

"William's will made his grandson, Richard Knight, his only heir. Richard got the Knight Company, all t'other little bits and pieces William owned, all the houses, everything. Down to William's old socks and neckties. Richard got everything."

Daugherty drew a picket fence between William Knight's name and his son Gilbert's.

"William'd had a fight with Gilbert back around the time of the Civil War. So William laid back and said in his will that Gilbert Knight would never inherit a penny from him. I'd be a rubber-tired reindeer before I wrote a will like that for anyone, the trouble it's caused. Gilbert didn't get anything from William, and on his own account he never would'a. Knight Company had to hire him to give him livin' money, after William passed on."

"William was murdered," Reisden prompted.

"So he was. And Richard inherited everything."

Daugherty crossed out William Knight's name, and penciled in the line between William and Richard so that it became a thick conduit for the flow of money.

"Richard Knight got kidnapped just after his grandfather died. Richard had a trusteeship, on account of having about two million dollars from his father, and so he had a will and Gilbert Knight was his heir. Gilbert Knight couldn't inherit from William Knight. But he could from Richard.

"*If* Richard was dead."

Daugherty drew a loop from Richard back up to Gilbert. But this line was dotted with question marks. Daugherty scribbled against it, *Only if Richard's dead.*

"Well, we were the trustees. We didn't find Richard alive and we didn't find him dead, and the firm administered the estate for Richard if he showed up and for Gilbert if Richard was dead. And seven years went by.

"There's a law in this country, don't know if you've got it over in Europe. If a person's been missing for seven years, you can go in front of a judge and have that person declared dead. It sort of cuts the complications." Daugherty added to his annotations on the line of question marks, *This takes seven years.*

"And the senior partner here, Bucky Pelham, was Richard's executor and conservator. That means he's got an obligation in law, you see, that he's got to distribute the estate—give the money out where it belongs.

"By the end of that seven years we had got real tired of wondering who we was working for. So Bucky Pelham went to see Gilbert Knight. 'Mr. Knight,' he says, 'time to have Richard declared dead.'

"Gilbert Knight says no."

"Why?" Reisden interrupted.

" 'Cause he don't think Richard is dead."

"Nonsense," said a fine bass voice at the door of the

office. "Roy, it's because he's utterly neurotic about the money."

The man matched the voice: a tall, smooth, grey-maned man in a perfectly fitted grey suit. He looked at Daugherty and Reisden as if at two insignificant but dirty secrets, and did not so much as acknowledge Reisden's presence. "Roy, I won't disturb you." The man smoothly bowed himself out and closed the door.

"Your senior partner?" Reisden asked.

"Yup, that's Bucky. This is his office; mine's out back. He went to Harvard." Roy Daugherty examined his knuckles critically. Reisden looked around the office. A view of the Boston public park out the window; well-matched and immaculate law books; a desk with an equally immaculate blotter. It looked like a good gentlemen's club.

"How much of your firm's business comes from the Knights?" Reisden asked.

"Mostly all of Bucky's. Others of us, we got other clients."

"Bucky is the Knights' private lawyer," Reisden prompted.

"He's good; I'm saying no different. And he pulls a lot of money in. Anyway," Daugherty said, "Gilbert not declarin' Richard dead. Gilbert had a point, at least then he did. It wasn't like Richard just completely disappeared and no trace of him was found; it never is that way with a kidnapping. Folks were always thinkin' they saw him, Wisconsin and Indian Territory and I don't know where all. Even seven years later we were still getting two or three sightin's a year.

"Well, time went on, Bucky kept askin', Gilbert kept

saying no. Three, four years. It gets to be Richard's been dead eleven years, Bucky's getting nervous. Bucky's got an obligation to distribute the estate in a timely manner, you see. He should petition the court that Richard's legally dead. Firm's paying itself to administer the estate. Firm's beginning to look bad. Bar Association is goin' to go after us.''

Daugherty drew a little tap from the great conduit of money going from William to Richard. The tap was leaky, and Daugherty drew a little man underneath with his mouth open and a blissful smile on his face. The little man's mustache and suit had a distinct resemblance to Bucky Pelham's.

"Bucky sees Gilbert. 'Look, I don't have a choice—I got a canon of professional ethics. I got to declare Richard dead, I got to distribute the estate. If I don't do it, I'm going to get disbarred. Somebody else will be appointed trustee, and *they'll* declare Richard dead.' Gilbert says, 'But Richard ain't dead.' That's all Gilbert's got to say.

"Bucky starts thinking about how to get Gilbert to declare Richard dead. Bucky gets together with Charlie Adair, you know Charlie, and the two of 'em find Gilbert an orphan. Orphan's name is Harry Boulding. Harry comes to live with Gilbert. Gilbert says, 'Harry is my heir.'

"Fine enough. Bucky's happy, for about five minutes.

"Except what Gilbert means, and what he says, is that Harry's *his* heir, not Richard Knight's. When Gilbert dies, Harry gets Gilbert's old suits and all his old books. But he don't get the Knight companies. 'Cause Gilbert hasn't inherited 'em, 'cause Richard ain't dead.''

Daugherty scribbled more on his genealogy chart:

Harry Boulding huddled by himself, down in a corner; a dotted line meandering from Gilbert to Harry, the very smallest and most tentative of dotted lines, representing old suits and secondhand books. The money line still went from William to Richard, still dripping into Bucky's mouth, and stopped there. The line of question marks went from Richard to Gilbert, with the notation by it: *Only if Richard's dead.*

"Well, now, we got to get Gilbert to will the money to Harry. And that don't stick unless Gilbert has the money, which he don't unless Richard's dead. We could go to court and try to make Gilbert declare Richard dead, if we were darn fools. Bar Association's been after us to do just that thing. If Bucky didn't go to the right clubs, he'd a been in the papers before now.

"But if we petition the court and get an adjudication, then Gilbert's going to change lawyers, and we don't need that neither."

Daugherty's genealogy was now a maze of dead people, tentative inheritance lines, dripping faucets, and question marks. Reisden remembered Victor's murmuring about the curse on the Knight money and the obsessive William Knight training his heir. What had started in tragedy was ending in an odd, black kind of farce. Suitable comedy for the entertainment of madmen: He could hardly have thought of anything better himself.

"So when Gilbert Knight dies there will be no heir at all," Reisden prompted.

"Well," Daugherty said, "genealogy's a wonderful thing. There ain't no better way to use up time than genealogy. Bucky ain't been precisely sittin' on a wooden egg all these years. He's been figurin' out who Richard's heirs are if they ain't Gilbert. You see, the law has a concept called phantom issue. Since Richard didn't have no kids, Richard's heirs could be the heirs of his parents—or of his grandparents—or of his great-grandparents, and so on all the way back to Adam. It's real important to find out who all those phantom heirs are, Bucky keeps telling the courts. Can't possibly distribute the estate until he knows who to distribute it to." Daugherty shook his head admiringly. "You never saw a man could move sideways as slow as Bucky."

"And did he find heirs?" Reisden said.

"On the Knight side there ain't no heirs at all, till you count Jay French. We been looking; we got old ladies looking up parish records in places you can't spell nor find in the atlas. Richard's mother got some family, not here in America, but France and Holland. Third cousins twice removed of somebody's grandmother. Commonwealth of Massachusetts won't get the money, that's one consolation. Bucky would fry in a hot place with the Bar Association if they did. But Bucky don't want to deal with no Dutchies. He wants Harry and no other."

Daugherty paused for dramatic effect and drew a line from Bucky Pelham to Harry.

"And Bucky wants that mostly because, the day Harry Boulding turned twenty-one, he got himself engaged to Bucky's niece."

Reisden took a deep breath, almost laughing, but holding it in. "Let me tell you what I hear you saying. Your law firm has administered the Knight estate for over eighteen years. The Knight Company needs an owner. For good reasons, you support this man Harry Boulding, who will inherit from Gilbert. Now your senior partner has a small conflict of interest, since his niece will be married to Harry."

"We *had* Gilbert." Daugherty punched his open hand with his fist. "Gilbert was finally going to have Richard declared dead. Bucky told him what a position it was putting Harry in, not knowing whether he was rich or poor or what he was going to do with his life. Gilbert said he'd *do* it."

"What happened to change his mind?"

Roy Daugherty didn't say anything for a few seconds. He reached up and took off his glasses and cleaned them with a big cotton handkerchief from his back pants pocket. It was a spotted bandanna handkerchief, an old-fashioned color, yellow and brown, such as a carpenter or a metal worker would have carried to put around his neck. Daugherty peered at the glasses as he cleaned them, then fitted them slowly on again; his small eyes suddenly jumped into prominence, looking very hard straight at Reisden.

"You did," he said.

Reisden's coffee was cold. He put it down slowly. "I'm not Richard Knight," he said in exactly the right tone.

"When Charlie saw you, there was somebody from Boston with him who sat down and wrote us, which, if you ask me, he needn't a done. So we had a sighting. Gilbert was as close to signing as his pen on the paper. Wouldn't sign. Made us go back and find you." Daugherty snorted. "All I knew was someone had called you a baron, and that was *all* I knew. Took me two weeks to think of that nobility book, and another two weeks to get to the Rs. Anyway, while we was tracing, we got to thinking."

It took Reisden a moment to understand.

"You don't need Richard Knight, of course, any

more than you need the distant cousins. Harry's the known quantity; even Richard wouldn't be."

Daugherty nodded reluctantly.

"Yup. Bucky just longs in his heart to have everything settled."

"If Gilbert Knight agrees to have Richard declared dead, everything is settled. Gilbert inherits from Richard, and eventually Harry from Gilbert."

"And Bucky don't get disbarred nor lose the Knight account, and Bucky's niece gets married to Harry. And the Bar Association gets off of our doorstep."

This is madder than I am, Reisden thought.

"Then tell me," he said. "What do you want me to do?"

FRIDAY, five-thirty in the afternoon, and he was still in Daugherty's hot, deserted offices. Daugherty had gone out and come back with cigarets, a cheap American kind. From the way he held his cigaret Reisden had the idea he didn't smoke very often. Reisden lit one and blew smoke into the gilded light. For the rest of his life madness would taste like this, rough Virginian tobacco. Whatever happens next one cannot prepare for.

"You essentially want me to scare Gilbert Knight," Reisden said.

"That's Bucky's idea."

"Not a good one."

"It ain't *so* awful," Daugherty said. "Here's Bert been safe all these years, because he never found anybody who was Richard. And Bucky lying awake at night thinkin' of someone like the Tichborne Claimant."

"My heartfelt sympathy. Buy yourself a body and pass it off."

"Bucky thought of that."

"Really."

"All we're asking is you should do a little pretending. *Supposing* you thought it might be possible you were Richard. Say you were adopted."

"Reisdens don't adopt. The point of the *Almanach* nonsense is that we're descended from someone. It's not done."

"Say your whole family was dead and they needed somebody to inherit, like the Knights. That's *done.*" Daugherty's tone put heavy quotation marks around the word. Right, thought Reisden, I'm acting the baron again. Daugherty took a bite of sandwich and spoke around it. "Bucky used to get together examples of important people adopting heirs, to show Gilbert. Didn't cut no ice with Gilbert, though."

"Your idea is that I should say to Bucky, 'Look here, I think I'm Richard Knight.'"

"Yup. Then Bucky has to find out whether you're Richard or not. You don't have to do nothing. Like I said, Bucky's good at being slow. And Gilbert has to sit around and think whether he really wants to lose all that money. He can think how bad he's done by Harry."

"Then, when he has shivered sufficiently, we can tell him, 'Oh, sorry, we scared you.' What if Gilbert believes I'm Richard?"

"He ain't going to. You don't know nothing about Richard."

"And why should I say so? Why should *I* believe I'm Richard?"

Daugherty blinked.

"I am Alexander von Reisden. I know who I am. To think anything else would be stupid, greedy, malicious, or insane. No, I do not want to say to anyone that I am Richard Knight."

One knows what one wants by refusing it. Daugherty nodded, and Reisden closed his eyes in a depression like a terrible tiredness. He would go back to Lausanne and everything would be as it had been.

"There is a way," Reisden said.

He got up and moved over to the window. From the second floor, all the trees in the Common were strange shapes out of proportion. The air was hot, hot enough, Reisden thought, to let reactions happen very fast. Reisden rattled up the window and breathed the smells of the city, asphalt, horse smell, foreign smell. Outside, a floor below the long windows, Beacon Street and the artificial, pretty gardens dozed in the afternoon sun. Beyond trees, in a corner of the Frog Pond, a swan boat was just gliding through its lazy turn, dazzling white and strange, something on stage. What we want from memory is what we want from our own city, a sense of being at home, or at least known, a sense of ourselves.

"I won't remember anything." He breathed cigaret smoke out into the hot air. It dissolved as he was dissolving. "It must be Bucky Pelham or yourself, not I, who thinks I am Richard. Because I will have nothing to do with the whole thing; I won't care. I won't so much as remember who Gilbert Knight is." It was as if the ideas were written on the hot air; he had only to speak them. "Let him insist, if he wants to, that I am wrong and I am Richard. But let him do it alone. Let him be mad and think it, or let him be sane and let Richard go."

CHAPTER 6

GILBERT KNIGHT'S EMINENT LAWYER drummed his fingers on the immaculate surface of his desk as he read Roy's notes. "I am to tell Gilbert that we think this man may be Richard. But due to insufficiency of evidence, we cannot be sure. Gilbert will see him; Gilbert will deny it. But since Gilbert is incompetent to recognize Richard—as, may I add, to do anything else—I will continue to investigate this man, who may be Richard Knight. The man will deny it. What, pray tell, does the man do in the meantime? Do we put him up in a hotel, or does he go back where he came from?"

"Back. Unless Gilbert recognizes him."

A faint smile disturbed Bucky Pelham's mustache. "Gilbert Knight would not swear to his own identity," he said. "I take it there will be no trouble amassing evidence to prove he is not Richard."

"I got copies of Reisden's birth certificate, Bucky."

Bucky pursed his somewhat full lips. "I didn't ask you what you *have*, Roy, I asked you what you will be able to have. Please remember the distinction."

"Sure, Bucky. No trouble."

"Let me see your notes on the man." Bucky read. "H'm. Doctorate in biological chemistry, University of London, 1905; has published articles in his field; races automobiles—does he win, Roy?—makes money on the stock market. Amateur actor in college and graduate school, to universal applause. That will come in handy, I suppose. Catholic—excommunicated! For what?"

"Being corresponding secretary of a"—Roy Daugherty peered at his notes upside-down—" 'Neo-Malthusian Society, and openly advocating the separation of sex from the act of procreation.' He was sixteen."

"H'm. And, five years ago, he had a nervous breakdown after the death of his wife. Intellectual, immoral, and unstable. I don't like him, Roy."

"Don't say nothing about him then, Bucky."

Buckingham Pelham fixed Daugherty with a very cold eye.

"The essential is that he cannot possibly be Richard. I want to get rid of him when I want to."

"He says he's going back to Europe and he don't care if he never sees any of us again."

"See that he does as he says." Bucky folded Roy's notes in half and handed them back with the air of not quite having seen them. "Have you explained to him that Richard was actually murdered, and that we cannot absolutely guarantee this man's safety against Jay?"

"Yup. He weren't a lot concerned, Bucky."

"I want you to be concerned for him, Roy. I have had really enough trouble with one dead Richard. Two of them would be far too much."

CHAPTER 7

SCOLLAY SQUARE was not Harry's Boston. Even in the spring night, the worst of Boston collected here in an urban and fetid mass, a far cry from the Knight house on Commonwealth Avenue or Harry's club at Harvard. When he came into his money, Harry thought, he'd help to clean this place out. Sooty Southern Negroes jostled greasy Jewish storekeepers and greasier Italians from the North End. Outside the garishly lit Old Howard, a streetwalker bulging out of a tight checked dress yelled at Harry. "College boy, want to take a course from me?" On the street corners the Irish micks looked him up and down, eyes glinting under their flat caps. I'll take any six of you now, Harry thought. And when I take my place, I'll send you all back where you belong.

You and the d--ned Baron von Reisden.

Daugherty had said they'd meet at Corbin's pistol range. The place was in the basement of a decrepit alley building that had been falling apart in Paul Revere's time, down stairs that stank of urine. There were scratches in the dirty counter and the range was not quite big enough, so that the targets looked too close. Six little gasfires flickered down the wall, spitting smoky light. A gaslight at the front threw Daugherty's fat-boxer shadow at the wall.

"I suppose the guy picked this place, Daugherty. But

you didn't have to go along with him." Harry thought of taking off his seersucker suit coat, because the place was hot, but he wasn't going to lay it across that filthy counter.

"Neither one of us, I think, wanted to meet at the Harvard Club," said a third voice.

All Harry saw at first was a shadow. The man who had spoken had to duck as he came down the stairs, so he was an inch or two taller than Harry. His voice was deeper than Harry's. Then he came into the light, and Harry tensed all his muscles and gauged the man's size and strength as if he'd have to fight him.

On the stairs of the house on Commonwealth Avenue hung portraits of all of William's sons: William, Alphonsus, John, Clement, Thomas Robert. Up and down the stairs every day, Harry passed a long row of Knight men, dark-haired, long-nosed, with the same build of eyebrow and eyelid and the same half-colorless grey eyes. Looking at the Baron von Reisden, Harry was overcome with indignation, as if the man's very look was a trick, a falsity; he looked as if he should have been painted.

"You're Harry." The Austrian baron was thin, dressed in a dark suit and coat, not in fashion for the summer; but he had the look, absurdly, of a man who was used to being in charge.

Not in charge here, Harry thought. He could play cool too. "Daugherty here says you're a gentleman. A gentleman wouldn't do what you're doing."

"Anecdotal evidence suggests there are exceptions. Would you like to play games or shall we talk?"

"What?" Harry smiled. The man even spoke like a portrait.

"I don't like this. I assume you don't either. Let's not waste time proving it." The man went to the counter of the shooting gallery and casually took a gun out of his pocket. Harry blinked. "Am I really supposed to show you I can use this?" Reisden asked Daugherty.

"Bucky's nervous. He keeps thinking about Jay French."

"Jay French, at least, knows I'm not Richard Knight." The Austrian took out a box from his other coat pocket, opened it, and began fitting bullets into the gun with quick, economical movements. "Daugherty, could you find fresh targets?" Daugherty lumbered up the stairs. Harry was left alone with Reisden.

"I'm Alexander Reisden," the man said, turning around with the gun still in his hands. "I'm twenty-seven years old. I'm a chemist. I am going to briefly and unsuccessfully impersonate your cousin. I thought you should meet me first."

"I'm Harry Boulding," Harry said, but nothing more.

"You are Gilbert Knight's adopted son?"

"So he says. I can't say he does much about it." Harry felt he was complaining. Not to this man.

"Yes, he's being foolish."

"I didn't say that." Harry moved away from him. The Austrian opened his mouth, then closed it again without saying anything. Shut up, you paint on canvas.

Daugherty came clattering downstairs with fresh targets. "Thank you," Reisden said, and Daugherty reeled in the targets on their wires without being asked.

"Gilbert Knight and Richard didn't know each other very well," Reisden said after a moment. "Gilbert is unlikely to be certain of anything, except, I hope, that he doesn't want Richard."

"He won't think you're Richard."

Daugherty came back behind the counter. "You ready, Reisden?"

Reisden casually stood behind the counter, bracing his gun hand with the other, and fired off six shots, steadily as a clock ticks. Daugherty looked at the target solemnly, counted the holes near the center, unclipped it, and folded and pocketed it. "So's to tell Bucky he don't need to worry," he explained.

"Where'd you learn to shoot like that?" Harry asked in spite of himself.

Reisden looked at him, uninterested. "Targets don't hurt. That makes them easy."

Bastard.

When the two other men had gone, Harry went upstairs.

"Give me a gun," he said.

The targets were farther away than they looked, but Harry blazed away at them, round after round, trying to shoot a hole in something he didn't want to give a name to.

CHAPTER 8

RICHARD, RICHARD . . .

All morning Gilbert Knight's anonymous old carriage drove around and around the Common; and there were two inside, Gilbert Knight and his fear. Fear drew the blinds for him and he trembled in the darkness.

The last time he had been so frightened was long ago, that August, before Bucky Pelham's telegram had come. He had known that something was about to happen and had taken his broken-springed book wagon out into the country, selling books among the farms, to escape knowing too soon. He remembered one afternoon he had stopped at a farm. Apple trees in an orchard, apples falling one by one, thudding like a fist swatting flies, and the sweet sweet smell of apples. He had sold a copy of *Moby Dick* to the orchardman's wife, secondhand, but a good copy, because she said she wanted to read the book he had been reading; he looked so scared, she said, it must be a first-rate haunt. And then he had come back from the apples to time and the telegram waiting for him, and the news that was so much worse than anything he had imagined.

Oh, Richard.

Gilbert sat inside, not thinking, just hearing sounds inside his head, *clop clop* and the squeal of the springs, the hum and creak of the rubber tires. The heat came through the ceiling of the old carriage and let out smells, leather and dust and mildew, because he never used the carriage although it was supposed to be always prepared; and with the shades down it grew hotter and hotter, until there was nothing in his head but rattle and heat.

Richard, what will you think of me?

After Roy Daugherty had told him, Gilbert had tried to find Richard's photograph. The painted picture hadn't been good enough; he wanted to find his own familiar record of the light that had shone on Richard's real face, to see if he might find some forgiveness there. But the picture in its silver frame had gone. He had wanted to see the little boy in the garden at Matatonic, with the dog and the scraped knees, the little boy smiling. For once Richard had been happy. See, Gilbert could have said, you were happy. But the picture was gone.

What could he say to redeem himself? Do you remember I sent you a Barlow knife at Christmas when you were six? Gilbert had been allowed to give only a handful of presents, mostly books from his stock. I was your uncle. I loved you. Love hadn't been enough. Gilbert knew what Richard would say to him. When you should have helped me, you were afraid.

"Now, if this ain't Richard—" Roy Daugherty had said.

Gilbert was shocked at his feeling of relief when he thought this man might not be Richard. Then it would still be all right. No one would confront him. Then, Gilbert thought, perhaps he could believe Richard was dead. He would give Harry all he deserved. He would declare Richard dead right away, and then no one would know what Richard had known.

Gilbert Knight had known he was a coward since the summer he was seventeen. It was the first year of the war; his much older half-brother, who had just got his commission, was showing off his new uniforms for the family. When all the rest of them went downstairs, Gilbert stayed behind, turning over in his hands his brother's new service revolver. He sighted down it; he hefted the weight of it in his hands; and unwillingly, with the gun between his loose fingers, he began to understand what the war was. Camaraderie and uniforms he did not understand; he was a rather shy boy, he wore glasses, he would have been one of those soldiers whose swords drag on the ground. All of war was

in those long-bodied bullets he loaded into his brother's
gun. "May I shoot your revolver?" he asked, and took
it out into the waste ground behind the house and fired
it at a half-ripe pumpkin, which exploded. He brought
the gun back silently and laid it down. When his class-
mates went off to war in cockades and bright ribbons, he
enrolled himself silently in the Ambulance Corps. His
brothers died valiantly. Gilbert went through the war
uncelebrated, unharmed, and afraid. His father never
spoke to him again.

For his whole life Gilbert would grope among better
and more decisive men; with women and in business he
held back, playing follow-the-leader through life like a
shy boy on the edge of a playground. When he was
thirty-four Gilbert spent a summer in Boston. Tom, his
tall, young half-brother, was nineteen. Once in a dark
conservatory at a dance, Gilbert saw Tom with beautiful
Sophie Hilary from New York. Desperate whispers and
rustles of clothing, hands and kisses where no book had
told Gilbert hands and kisses might be. The mystery of
love was verified for Gilbert in an instant, and he blinked
and turned away from their privacy, but felt blessed.
Tom and Sophie's wedding had to be hurried. On the
day of her bridal Sophie was pale, awkward, triumphant,
rounding at bosom and waist. Gilbert sat among the row
of disapproving faces in the family pew, sick maidenly
Isabella and the servants, and the family friends, old dry
voices snickering and whispering. But, Gilbert thought,
Tom and Sophie are happy. Through Sophie's veil,
under the white virgin's silk, Gilbert saw Sophie's lush
breasts; he was suddenly young with desire, as if he had
sown and reaped too. How young they were at the
wedding party afterward; girls of eighteen and seven-

teen, talking in high voices, laughing and crying; beardless boys, barely shaving, mouths mustached with a few brave hairs; careful of bright dresses, new shoes, flowers. Oh, I have missed this, Gilbert thought; but he wandered through the party as though he too had a new suit to wear, a hand to hold.

Father had cursed Sophie and her baby to come, and stayed away; and when Tom and Sophie had died, Father had taken the child.

Richard, how could I leave you?

But shall I wish you dead, so no one will know I wronged you?

The bells of the Arlington Street Church tolled the three-quarter-hour after one, and his carriage turned and crawled up Tremont Street and then by Boylston toward Park again, and the gilded hands of the Park Street Church clock said one-fifty-four, so soon, so soon, all around the tall square tower. He knocked with his cane against the carriage roof. The carriage turned up toward Beacon Hill, past the State House high and serene, and down again, to Bucky Pelham's office on Beacon Street.

The stairs were steep and dim, the door at the top was closed. He took the doorknob in his hand and stood without going in.

It was time to give up all his hope of Richard. He would not leave this office today without signing the papers.

Goodbye, Richard. Goodbye, brother Tom.

He turned the doorknob and let the door open.

Chairs, sun, a quiet place. No lawyers, no reporters. No one but a thin, dark-haired man he did not recognize, standing by the window looking out. Gilbert closed the door with a little click, and when he turned back the young man was facing him.

It was then, only then, he saw.

The young man's grey eyes widened and he moved back and stood with his back to the window, head high, palms pressed against the windowsill. His eyes looked through Gilbert, the whites were blazing, in anger or disdain or simply denial.

Richard should have been a happy little boy with scraped knees, holding his puppy, smiling. In a good world there would have been still a little boy to love. What does one want but someone to love, someone to do for, to accept what one has to give? Easy with a painted picture, easy with a child. The man stood unmoving, so that there was an inflexible distance between them; and what to call that distance Gilbert didn't know, but he knew where it had come from.

The young man raised his head, looked at Gilbert straight. "No. *No,*" he said. It was insistence; it was a warning.

There would be no little boy smiling. Why would Richard want to come back, or to remember, or least of all to be happy? That was the recognition, and Gilbert met the look in those cold wide eyes. So little had happened to Gilbert. But when it did, he knew. At last Gilbert had been given something to do, and he did it.

"Yes," Gilbert said.

CHAPTER 9

"Well, Miss, if Mr. Gilbert hasn't even told *you*—"
Lucy the housemaid sniffed disconsolately.

That afternoon Perdita Halley was alone in the music room at the Knights' house, practicing. It was unusual for her to be quite so alone. The music room was just across the hall from Uncle Gilbert's library. He did bookbinding, and usually, while she did scales, she could smell leather and neat's-foot oil and three different kinds of glue. Not today. "He went out this morning, Miss, all mysterious," Lucy continued. "*And* he was upset, but no telling why."

Any change in routine was upsetting to the young housemaids and the middle-aged housekeeper and butler. They liked things as quiet as a woods-pond. Even battle-ax Mrs. Martin, the housekeeper, was already beginning to work up a panic for the wedding, which wouldn't be until Christmas. "Don't worry, Lucy, we shall find out about it soon."

"I hope so, Miss. He wore the wrong tie with his suit today, and that isn't like him at all."

Perdita was working today on a new piece of music. One hand held the magnifying glass over two inches of notes, the other hand learned the fingering. She worked her way through the music two inches at a time, trying not to think too hard of how she would make rhythm and sense of them until she had the notes down. Slow measure in the right hand, a springy beat like a jump rope on the top of the octave line. Left hand, waltz until measure 5. Right hand changing articulations in measures 9–10 and in 11–12. The right-hand part was all thumb and fifth-finger substitutions, enough to give you palm cramps just thinking about it. Perdita practiced slowly, relaxing her hands as she learned, building up toward the right tempo. She peeked forward to the second section, looked at the first measures, a formidable black blur on the page, and sighed. She had to learn that fingering today too. And all this morning she had had fittings for her wedding clothes, which cut dreadfully into practice time.

"Miss? Miss, something awful!"

Lucy burst open the door without knocking. "Oh, Miss! Miss Emma Blackstone's maid has just come from next door and says Miss Emma heard they've found the little boy. Master Richard. And he's alive!"

"Lucy, what?" Miss Emma went everywhere and heard everything, but only half of it was true. "I think we would hear first."

"Master Harry wants to see you downstairs."

She jumped up off the piano bench and found her way past Lucy's black-and-white bulk into the hall. In the dark she was immediately blind as a bat; she felt her way down the familiar stairs.

"Miss Emma says he was locked up in a madhouse," Lucy whispered behind her, "and when they found him all he could say was 'Blood and horror! Blood and horror!' His hair's completely white and he doesn't remember so much as his own name."

"Oh, Lucy, hush. That is nonsense. What is that

sound?" There was a confused shouting from outside the door.

"People outside, Miss—" Downstairs the door burst open, spilling light in a white cloud into the hall. Lucy screamed as if she had been bit by snakes, but with an undertone of triumph. "Oh, Miss, reporters!" Lucy rushed forward and Perdita held her back.

"You can't come in!" Mr. Phillips, the old butler, was actually yelling. Mrs. Martin was screaming behind him, "We will call the police!" The light wavered, wide then narrow, as if Mr. Phillips were trying to close the door against resistance.

"Miss Perdita, you stay away from them," Mrs. Martin said. A camera flash went off in her face; she squeezed her eyes tight. At least she had talked to reporters once or twice after recitals.

"Mr. Phillips, don't you let any of them get inside." She squared her shoulders and eased open the door.

"Miss Halley! What is Harry Boulding going to do?"

"Is the wedding off?"

She raised her voice as high as she could make it. "We don't know anything, this is a surprise to us, and your cameras are hurting my eyes. You must wait outside. Lucy will serve you tea. As soon as we know something, we will tell you at once." She hoped the food would distract them. "But you must wait outside or we must call the police."

Mr. Phillips put his shoulder to the door and the hall went completely black, suddenly quiet.

"Journalists!" Mr. Phillips said under his breath. "Disgraceful."

"Tea, Miss?" quavered Lucy.

"Yes, and sandwiches and whatever else we have. Tell Mrs. Stelling, and take Mr. Phillips with you."

"And if you talk, girl, you'll have no reference from me," Mrs. Martin said.

"Where is Harry?"

She found him in the dining room. The blinds were closed; she closed the door too. He must have heard the reporters in the hall and for a moment she wondered that he hadn't come to throw them out. By that she knew how hurt he was.

"You didn't have to give them food!" he whispered at her angrily, then stopped himself. "Pet, I don't mean it. You know I'm not angry at you."

"Oh, Harry!" She sat down beside him and put her arms around him.

"I'm going out of this house and I'll never come here again."

"Shhh, Harry."

"This man isn't Richard. I've met him, Pet. He doesn't even pretend to be Richard. My ex-uncle doesn't know anything about him—not *anything*—" He walked up and down the room, then sat down again beside her. "I'm not going to suffer like this."

She held his hand and he snatched it away. He pounded the table with his fist as if he wanted to splinter the heavy mahogany.

"Come with me, Pet. We'll get married at City Hall today, then we'll move to another city. Come on." He stood up and tugged at her.

"Harry, it's a mistake, it will all come out right. You'll see."

He fell down to his knees and buried his face in her

lap. "It won't come out right. Nothing in my life has ever been fair. Love me, Pet. Love me forever the way I love you."

Outside in the hall there were loud voices again, then a slam. "I won't stay here," Harry said.

"Yes, go over to Joe's house, stay with him."

"I wonder if Joe's still my friend when something like this happens. The only person I don't wonder about is you. I'm getting married to you if it's the last thing I do in my life. I'm going over to Bucky's," said Harry grimly. "I've got a few things to say to him. You stay here," Harry said. "If Gilbert comes back, tell him he's never seeing me again."

When he was gone, she made her way up the stairs. Upstairs in the music room she brushed the music aside.

What if this person were Richard Knight? Gilbert would be glad and Harry would hate him. How could she choose between Gilbert's happiness and Harry's?

"No," she said aloud. Harry was still Gilbert's adopted son. It would be terrible for all of them. Harry would hurt too much, and Gilbert and herself and even the unknown Richard Knight.

She automatically put the music back in its folder and the magnifying glass away in its drawer. Then she began playing from memory, the finale from Hayden's Sonata in C Minor, with its anxious, passionate theme. She reached and held the skein of the music, half in each hand and the whole in her body until she and the music melded and there was no piano, no thoughts, no body, only passionate fear and hope, only the prayer that those she loved best would win through. And when it was done she sat back, feeling as if she had cried for an hour, with her resolution taken.

If this was Richard Knight, the whole family must learn to live with him. And she must learn to love him as much as she loved Gilbert and Harry.

CHAPTER 10

"YOU CANNOT POSSIBLY BELIEVE I am Richard," Reisden said. Gilbert Knight grimaced at him, smiling through fear. Gilbert Knight, terrified, turned to Roy Daugherty and Bucky Pelham and insisted it was so.

Bucky shouted at him. Roy said it wasn't likely to be so. Reisden moved back and simply watched. Gilbert Knight had his face. Seeing one's own face in a photograph was bad. Seeing it on a living man had made Reisden close to physically ill. "I want to leave here," he said in an undertone to Daugherty.

"He thinks you're Richard."

"What the h--l am I supposed to do about that?"

This was Richard, Gilbert repeated.

"We'll be glad to put the man up in a hotel," Bucky said smoothly, "while—"

"But you don't understand, Mr. Pelham, he is *home.*"

In the end there was nothing they could do. "We got reporters outside, which is something we ain't counted on. You're better in the house for now than in a hotel where they'll get to you. Go with him," Daugherty muttered to Reisden. "Keep telling him you ain't Richard."

And so, finally, the Knights' carriage was brought

around to the side entrance and Gilbert Knight and Reisden were closed in it together, like relatives.

It was by then the hour in the afternoon when everyone in Boston went home. Around the Common, Beacon Street was a snarl of traffic: closed cabs and horse-drawn buses and jitneys, bicycles darting by the legs of the horses, and everywhere people on foot. The Knight carriage blinds were pulled down, closing out light and air.

Reisden said nothing, not knowing what to say. They were both tall men and could not sit in the carriage without being crowded together; their legs got in the way of each other. Reisden moved his to the side. The black carriage jerked forward slowly. The heat was tremendous, and the carriage smelled of mildew and mold and of the old man. Reisden looked out at the traffic through the edge of the blind but saw only incoherent slivers, the red side of a delivery van or a horse's rolling eye.

He glanced at Gilbert Knight. Line of jaw, set of eyes: He recognized the fragments of the Knight face from Victor's newspaper clippings of Jay French and the child Richard. What Gilbert had of his own was fear. Gilbert Knight's face blanched as Reisden looked at him, Reisden's look pinned him against the carriage wall, and Reisden turned away in a cold sweat, ill, as if he had seen himself afraid of himself.

He was Alexander von Reisden. He held hard to what he knew but at the moment it did no good at all.

"Richard, I think we're here."

For a moment, of course, he did not know Gilbert Knight was talking to him. "I am not your Richard," he spat back with a vehemence that surprised even him.

"Are there . . . people outside?" Gilbert Knight twitched the shade up on the other side of the carriage.

"There's a reporter." He looked again. "More than one."

Gilbert Knight looked at him blankly; Reisden swallowed bile and said, "You must deal with them yourself. I will not."

Gilbert slowly nodded, as if he had expected this too. I cannot look at him for one more moment, Reisden thought. "Have your driver take me to the back entrance."

Through the slit at the edge of the blind he caught sight of Gilbert Knight, being mobbed by reporters, running toward the door of the Knight house. He remembered the big grey front of the house from walking past it in the dawn. He put his head down, really afraid he was going to be ill.

In the alley behind the avenue, the Knights' back entrance was easy to find; the same granite blocks walled it off from the street and a heavy iron door was set into the wall. The door creaked closed behind Reisden. He shot the bolt and leaned against the door.

For a moment he was alone.

He closed his eyes and waited for the taste of the carriage to clear from his mouth. The air was cool against his skin, and fresh, and smelled of flowers. The back of the house faced west, so that late sunshine warmed its stones; there were no gargoyles, only ivy turning the stones to leaf, and on a trellis espaliered rosebushes climbed, still in bud. By the flagstones near the house, a few late daffodils still bloomed among striped tulips. Bleeding hearts arched by the wall among lilies of the valley, and snowball bushes bloomed below magnificent purple and white lilacs. The whole garden smelled of the fragrance of lilacs. In the center of the grass rose an apple tree, and its falling petals spilled white across the grass.

By the apple tree a girl was standing.

The spring light touched her white dress and the dark cloud of her hair. For the moment the girl was only a feeling, a sensation, indivisible, like a drawn breath, like being taken out of himself.

"I waited for you," she said.

She was very young. Older than a child, perhaps sixteen, and growing into beauty; the lines and shadows of her delicate face would have made a woman beautiful; but she was not a woman yet, she had never thought of being one. He looked at her for as long as he might have breathed twice.

"Who are you?" he asked.

"I'm Perdita," she said.

She did not really see him. The wind blew across the garden and the blossoms fell around her like bride's-petals. Harry's fiancée was almost blind, Daugherty had told Reisden. What Reisden had not expected, not at all, was that Harry's fiancée and Bucky Pelham's niece would be as absolutely innocent as spring.

No. She was just a pretty girl, standing in a garden; a very young girl, a child.

"Are you Richard?" she said.

"No. Gilbert Knight thinks I am. That's all."

She came across to him and took his hand shyly. He let her lead him over to a bench. She sat by him. There were petals on her hair, and she brushed one hand through it. He saw the glint of her engagement ring on her finger. The other hand she kept loosely in his. He kept his eyes on her: her beauty was a kind of sanity. She appeared to watch him too, but not precisely, as if she saw him through a dazzle, or while thinking intently about something. It was an odd sensation, being watched by someone who could not really see him: It made him feel alone, and alone with her.

She didn't say anything. He didn't know how much Harry had told her, or how much of Harry's situation she would appreciate for herself.

"Look," he said, groping for words. "I am sorry to intrude on you, for however short a time. Gilbert Knight has made a mistake. I could not possibly be Richard. I'm someone else, I am here by misapprehension, and he's—I don't know why he thinks so. It is not true."

She simply waited.

"Do tell Harry this is all a mistake."

She nodded, a little color rising in her cheeks. They were still holding hands. She moved as if to take hers away, then didn't.

"When Harry came here," she said after a while, "he and I walked here, in this garden. He was eleven and I was eight. I told him that Uncle Gilbert loved him, and he knew it wasn't true and so did I. Uncle Gilbert is very loving. But he wants Richard. Don't mind Harry and me. If you are Richard you shouldn't deny it or go away."

She stood up quickly in a whirl of skirts. "I'm going now." And she ran toward the house, leaving him staring after her.

CHAPTER 11

AT THE HOUSE, Gilbert took himself in hand. He sent the servants downstairs. Yes, Mr. Richard was here. No, they were not to talk to reporters. Mrs. Stelling must prepare her most elaborate meal and the big bedroom at the head of the stairs must be got ready.

It was late, Gilbert realized suddenly. When Father had been alive they had eaten after the sun had set. Even when Gilbert was a little boy, they had been "genteel" enough, in his father's eyes, to sit like gentlemen and ladies, eating in the dark. His sister had eaten the fruit out of the ornamental fruit bowl on the sideboard. That was what he remembered out of his childhood, being hungry while it got dark.

Gilbert invited Richard inside, into the library. Gilbert moved around the library, lighting lamps to push away the dusk, forgetting for the moment that the servants were supposed to do it. He wondered if Richard would think it was an imposition, lighting without asking him. Without thinking, he also turned on the electric lights by the two paintings.

"That is William Knight and that is Richard," Richard said.

Over the north mantel stood Father, larger than life size. Richard would remember him like this, an immense frowning presence, the Almighty in formal dress, dark against darkness. Over the south mantel, a little boy smiling with a dog in the sunlight of the rose garden. Gilbert thought, How I have lied to myself, to live with myself all these years. The child should never have been painted as if he had been happy.

"Why did you say I am Richard?" Richard was standing by one of the two big leather chairs, his hand on the back, on the other side of it from Gilbert, keeping it between them.

"Richard, sit down. You are at home."

"I'm not Richard. Do please answer." At least Richard sat down. That was something, Gilbert thought.

How could he say it? If you were not Richard you would say that you were glad I was your uncle. I would say that I was glad you were here.

"You are like your father," Gilbert said vaguely. "Like Tom." It was the tiniest part of the truth.

"That's not enough."

"How much do you remember of Father, Richard?" he asked, hesitating between the words. "Of your grandfather?"

"I don't remember anything," Richard said brusquely. "Look: Unless by any chance you have some reason to think positively I am Richard Knight, you cannot say that I am. If you have a reason, give it."

"Oh," Gilbert said, trying to pull out of the horrible wholeness something that could be talked about by itself. "Oh, yes, I suppose, I have reasons."

"What?"

It was as if he were still at the train station, when they had told him, so long ago, that Father had been murdered. The telegram was in one hand. The reporters asked him about Father's death. He tried to look shocked, even be shocked. Why should he be shocked? Reasons. He could go and get Richard, Gilbert had thought then. They would not stay in Father's house. He would take Richard back with him to the wagon. They would be peddlers together, or perhaps open up a real bookshop so that the boy could go to school in the winter. The boy would sit in the shop in the afternoons and read. On the top shelves of the bookshop, Gilbert would set apples to dry—wooden shelves are good for drying apples—and the bookshop would smell of apple-leather and of old paper, and Richard would read there in the winter afternoons, under the lamplight, and Richard would have been happy. That was the way it should have been. "Richard," he said, "why did you come back?"

"You are the only one who believes I am Richard."

"But here you are," Gilbert said, puzzled.

Richard leaned his head back on the chair and looked questioningly at Gilbert. Gilbert remembered just such a gesture of Tom's: Oh, yes, he thought, having something to answer Richard with, but just too late.

"As far as I'm concerned I am only someone who looks vaguely like you," Richard said. He leaned forward and spoke with vehemence. "*I do not remember anything about Richard.* I don't know you. *You* haven't seen your nephew since he was four. What gives you the presumption to break into my life and call me him?"

Presumption, Gilbert thought; well, he deserved worse. And then he really listened to what Richard was saying.

"Do you mean," Gilbert said, "when Mr. Pelham said you didn't remember anything— Richard, you actually don't remember? You don't remember Father?"

"William Knight? I don't remember anything because *I am not Richard.*"

Gilbert turned back to the painting for a moment. Father, he has forgot you. There was Father in the painting as Gilbert remembered him, with his wide wrinkled lips tightly closed, his hand around a stick, his eyes blazing. But Richard didn't know him. Richard didn't know anything. And there was Richard himself in the other painting. That was how he might think of himself: a little boy with a dog, smiling.

Thank the kind God, Who had given Richard back to Gilbert. And more mercifully, had given him back without his memory.

For the first time since the lawyers' offices, Gilbert met Richard's eyes. Richard had not come back happily or easily; he did not want to be here; he wanted to be told to go away. But he had come, and Gilbert was willing to do anything that was needed to keep him. "What would it be," Gilbert said hesitatingly, "if we never talked about the past?"

I will lie to you, Gilbert resolved, and get Charlie to lie to you. You will be happy.

"I don't mean that we *must never* talk about it, but it might be more pleasant for us"—*pleasant!* Gilbert thought—"to put off discussing the past. Not forever, you know. But a while. As long as you want. A few months. A few years. We could—you know—think about the future."

To his own ears, Gilbert's words sounded strange. How often had he said anything, to anyone, about the future?

CHAPTER 12

"You did something so he'd think you were Richard," Harry said.

Reisden leaned back in his chair. "I told him he was wrong."

Daugherty, Reisden, and Harry Boulding were conferring in Daugherty's office. It was a measure of Bucky's disgust with them that even Harry had been relegated here. The room was crowded with Knight family records and with its own furnishings, a desk of imposing bulk, cast down from a more imposing office, a fan because Daugherty's office was hot, a lamp because it was dark. Daugherty's one window looked out over a rear court.

For three days Reisden had played the role of Reisden unwillingly being Richard Knight. He had watched himself being polite to Gilbert Knight, to Harry, to Perdita Halley, the fiancée. Roles and acting, in the long-ago time when he had done such things, usually had released him and given him his emotions. But not now. He was numb as if he were dead.

"You twisted him," Harry said. "You did something!"

Reisden looked him up and down. "I told him I was not Richard," he said levelly. "I told him I have not a single memory of being Richard. He said, 'Good.' I want to know what I did as much as you do."

Harry turned and strode over to the other side of the room, his shoulders tight like a caged lion's. Somewhere under that rage was the howl of a boy who was really not much loved. Harry had wanted Gilbert Knight to drop the idea of Richard; he had counted on it as much as Reisden himself had. Now Harry raged to keep his pride. Reisden understood, but he didn't care much for Harry's style.

"He said you recognized him," Harry said.

"I didn't bloody well recognize him, he looks like me and I wasn't prepared for it. Take it as read that we didn't want this to happen and we're all terribly, terribly embarrassed. How shall we get out of it? Daugherty, what does Bucky say?"

"Bucky don't know whether to spit nails or cry."

"Show him your birth certificate," Harry said. "Prove you're not Richard."

Reisden looked at Daugherty. "That won't prove that Richard is dead."

Daugherty nodded. "We got ourselves a Richard that wa'n't no Richard, and Gilbert took him like a fish takes a hook, 'scuse me Reisden. Now Bucky wants enough proof to shake even Gilbert. He wants Richard dead on Gilbert's doormat and tomorrow morning wouldn't be too soon. What do you think, Reisden? What do you want to do?"

"I want to leave. But since we have the situation, we might do something useful with it."

"What?" Harry asked.

Reisden lit a cigaret. Since I am not Richard, he thought, since I know that, there is nothing wrong with saying this. "Prove Richard is dead."

"Ain't I been working on that these past eighteen years?"

"Of course you have." Reisden let the silence hang.

Daugherty sighed. "Well, I ain't found him yet, have I?"

"He disappeared from the place up in New Hampshire—Matatonic. How thoroughly were you able to search there? Are there identifiable areas that were missed, for instance the cellars of houses? How thoroughly were you able to interview?"

Daugherty shook his head. "Early on, when Richard first disappeared, we were looking for a live kid, not a body. I weren't real experienced, either, and I was headin' the search. I got the cellars of houses—but like I say, I was lookin' for him live."

"How about the woods?"

"A lot of woods up there. We done some searching. It ain't easy."

Harry raised his head. "You mean you didn't search everywhere?"

"Son, there's thousands of acres."

"You ought to search every one of them," Harry said. "You could do it with Indian guides. They know the woods far better than the white man. This is important, Daugherty. This is about a lot of money. You don't understand."

When Harry left a few minutes later, Reisden and Daugherty looked at each other. " 'They know the woods far better than the white man.' Someday you'll be working for him," Reisden said.

Daugherty sighed and looked down at his square-toed shoes, slightly out of date. "Trouble is, he's going to talk to Bucky and Bucky'll think it's a good idea."

"Is it?"

"Not the whole woods. You find bodies uphill of where they disappeared if they went on their own, downhill if somebody carried 'em. Or by a stream. Streams draw 'em."

Reisden thought. "Richard disappeared from a hotel. Who owns it?"

"We do." Daugherty cleared his throat. "Owners sold out six, seven years ago. We bought it for Charlie's Children's Clinic. The kids come out to the country, stay at the hotel, swim in the lake. We done a search there, but I'd like to do more, maybe take up some of the concrete in the basement. I actually worked out a whole plan."

"Tell me."

Daugherty opened a drawer of his desk, took out two sheets of paper, and gave them to Reisden, who scanned them.

"This is good. Why not do it?"

"Who's goin' to tell me to? Or pay for it? Gilbert just got his Richard."

Richard Knight was bones decomposing under a bush somewhere. And Richard was all he had. Richard was Reisden's madness, working itself out.

"Richard will," Reisden said.

"What say?"

"Were I Richard, I would be annoyed at how comfortable my loss of memory is for other people. For some reason, Gilbert Knight is very relieved that Richard doesn't remember anything. Gilbert has apparently asked Charlie Adair not to tell me anything. Bucky told me today that he has the same instructions."

"Bucky don't know anything to tell, though. Least-ways nothing he's told me."

"It doesn't matter. Richard would be annoyed and inconveniently curious, if I were he. Look, Daugherty. For the time being, like it or not, we have got a Richard. Either I go away and try to ignore this, and get everlastingly disturbed by reporters—how shall I live it down, I wonder?—or I stay here and be useful. Is the Knights' house in livable shape?"

"Sure, we kept it up. Ain't been used since."

"Very well, then. Like betrayed housemaids we shall take our sorrows to the country. We'll live in the house where William Knight died, and from there, if we can, we shall find Richard. We mean to disgust Gilbert with the very idea of Richard. I cannot think of anything more effectively disgusting than rubbing his nose in Richard's murder.

"And do remember there's another factor." Reisden paused, shamelessly for effect. "Whoever killed Richard knows I'm not him. I wonder whether we can stir him up?"

"Reisden, don't joke about them things!"

"Not a joke. Someone killed Richard. Now Richard wants to know why."

CHAPTER 13

"ARE YOU RICHARD after all?" Charlie Adair asked outright.

"No, of course not."

By all appearances, the South End of Boston, on the wrong side of Massachusetts Avenue, had been built all at once about thirty years before, and not for the people who lived here now. Under their grime the brownstones were still elegant, but their façades were piebald with signs and fire escapes. The old doctor listened for a moment to a child's crying from the Children's Clinic and shook his head. From the first floor at the other end of the building came the sound of a piano and children's voices singing. "We're always open. We sing too, at night, and give the poor kids lessons. So many of them work during the day." Adair opened the door into a classroom that was not being used. "We'll talk here."

Children's drawings, children's little desks. Adair closed the door. He offered one of the half-sized chairs; Reisden smiled no, and stood. Adair sat down as if he were out of breath or tired.

"You know what this is about," Reisden said. "Because of the resemblance, Bucky is obliged to find out whether I am Richard. He would like to be able to conclude the whole thing by finding Richard dead. So would I. I need information about the murders."

"You don't think at all that you're Richard?"

"No. You did?"

"You're very much like him." In the man's kindly, ugly face, his eyes searched Reisden's intently.

"I'm not Richard."

The doctor stood up, wheezing a little, and stood in front of Reisden. "Who are you, then? What do you want?"

"To prove that Richard is dead."

The old man's brown eyes locked on Reisden's and Adair looked without blinking straight into him, as if he could see Reisden's brain and heart: as he had looked on the station platform, facing up to something, with a touch of fear.

"Why do you want to prove that Richard is dead?" Adair asked.

"To finish this."

"Is that truly what you want?"

Yes. No. "Yes." Around the stethoscope half-stuffed into the doctor's jacket pocket was tangled a plain wooden rosary. "Pray for Gilbert to understand I am not Richard."

The doctor's wide mouth compressed and he nodded, as if to himself, warily. "I do pray for him," he said, half to himself, "and for his father, daily. And for myself. And, young man, I think I had better pray for you."

"Oh? And what should I do to be saved, Doctor?"

"You should go away. You know that."

"You don't want Richard to be found dead?"

"Very much. But Mr. Daugherty, who's a more capable man than he shows, and I have been looking for him since you were very young, Mr.—Dr. Reisden, you are a scientific doctor, aren't you. I have no doubt you are a very intelligent young man, and I'm afraid I annoyed you by thinking you were Richard. Perhaps you will succeed where we've done nothing. But you don't consider the effect on yourself."

"None, I think."

"Gilbert Knight is very wealthy." Reisden smiled at that. "You don't think you care for money any more than I do." Charlie Adair gestured about him at the shabby classroom and hooked a hand around his worn lapel. "Ah, Dr. Reisden, but I want money all the time. I only have to go outside this door to want money. Gilbert's been as generous to me as a man can be, all these years—Richard would have been as generous, I think. But I always want more, there are always more kids, and I'd be a mad and a desperate man if I didn't have what Bert gives me now. Harry wants to manage the Knight companies into the twentieth century, and he wants money, too; and he's a fine boy, but a little less fine because of the money. Is there anything you want, Dr. Reisden? Something you deeply believe in?"

Money buys better chemistry. "Probably." But Reisden had always been able to make the stock market pay for the lab, and money didn't in the end buy knowledge. Money wouldn't take the blue tinge away from Adair's lips, raise the dead, or cure insanity. "I have money enough for myself. I want a part of Gilbert Knight's to pay for finding Richard dead."

Screams interrupted them. Adair threw open the door of the room where they had been speaking and half-ran out into the hall.

The Clinic hall was in bloody confusion. A policeman had brought in a child, a little boy, with his mother crying and screaming and the child's angry neighbors crowding in behind. They all crowded into the emergency area. The little boy spilled like a sack onto the examination table, face yellow-white, eyes half-open. "—Dhrunken idiots—" the policeman was saying. "—the two of them going after each other with a knife, the D---l take them, and the child between!" Charlie's heart sank. The child's calf muscle was cut through to the bone, and, God save him, a jackknife was stuck near handle-deep in his chest just above the heart.

"My baby! My baby!" the mother was crying. "Ah, Holy Mary, what shall I do!"

The boy's blood was pooling on the table. Someone wound a handkerchief around the leg above the cut and twisted it. Charlie looked around. It was the young man, Reisden, in his shirtsleeves.

"The boy needs blood!" the policeman called. "Will some of you volunteer, now!"

"I've got good blood!" a man called above the mother's cries. Holy Mary, help the sufferers. Charlie nodded. "Yes, you first." Under his fingertips the boy's pulse was fading.

"No," Reisden told the policeman. "Use the mother or father. Blood types are inherited."

"A little woman like that?" the policeman asked, incredulous. "Get the boy's uncle John from the saloon!"

"Let the mother go first," Charlie said. It didn't matter. At that moment the child died. Charlie held the little, bony, dirty wrist and felt the pulse flutter and sink. No priest had come yet, and the child was old enough to have had his First Communion. He is confessing his sins, Charlie believed, and gave the child absolution, to go sinless before God. "May Our Lord Jesus Christ

absolve you, and by His authority I absolve you . . ."
Father Joseph arrived at last and administered Extreme
Unction, Charlie offering to God as his own sin the
pulse that had stopped long ago; then Charlie pulled out
the knife and a great gush of blood followed it, slacken-
ing quickly. "The child is dead."

When the boy's body had been removed, Charlie sat
in the emergency room alone. His heart hurt. To pray
the Joys of Mary would have been too cruel. He sat with
his hands tangled in the sixth decade of his beads: Mary
meets her Son for the first time since His death and
Resurrection.

"You were wrong."

The young man, Reisden, was standing at the door.
His shirt was red halfway up his sleeves.

"What would be right?" Charlie turned on him.
"Can you tell me what would be right, Dr. Reisden?"
Ashamed of his outburst, Charlie began to move the
beads through his hands, but the mother's cry was still
in his ears, drowning out peace.

"Look," said Reisden, "stop that and listen. You
don't know Landsteiner's work, do you? There are four
different blood types. Give the wrong type of blood and
you can kill the patient. Don't your transfusion cases
ever go into shock?"

Yes, they did, and so did cases at every little hospital
that took emergencies. "I know that there's special new
equipment to test blood, and special chemicals to use.
But we're not Children's Hospital or the Brigham, Dr.
Reisden, and I'm not a researcher like yourself. Which
do we buy, a microscope or another bed in the ward? Do
I buy a journal subscription or send a kid to the country?"

"Ask for more," the young man said, "and read more. Landsteiner published the basic paper five years ago. I'll see you get information in English."

Dr. Reisden went to wash his hands. Dear God, help me to feel grateful to him, Charlie thought, left alone. I ought to be grateful to the man. In the past two years they had had transfusion shock four times, not many for a hospital in a poor area like this. Three of the children had died. Charlie had thought it a good record. *Read more.* The rosary beads seemed slick with Charlie's shame.

Dr. Reisden would think he should pray less in order to research more.

The man was what he was, but he wasn't Charlie's type of person.

Charlie went outside and sat on the Clinic stoop. The brownstone was cracking (but which was more important, repairs or soup?). Through the streets the children were still straggling home from their work, and Maureen O'Rourke pulled herself up the steps tiredly, greeting him as she passed, to pick up her three. Pregnant again, Charlie thought, and only twenty-two. Young Dr. Reisden would have answers for all of this. For the children working in the factories, too young to reach the levers, too tired to better themselves, falling asleep at night over their books in Charlie's schoolroom. For the girls who got pregnant at fifteen and married at sixteen, sobbing through their confessions on Saturday afternoons; you could see the holes in their shoes as they knelt at prayer. For the men who drank because they had no work or because their fathers drank. All the answers young Dr. Reisden would have: scientific schools and Socialism, and research into the causes of poverty, and no Catholic superstitions.

Maureen O'Rourke came down the steps again with her three little ones chattering around her and smiled at him as she passed, a loving smile. The Lord is with you, Maureen. Charlie's heart lifted.

But behind her, down the steps came Dr. Reisden, pale and blank-faced, getting away from the Clinic, uncomfortable with Charlie's world. And with him, going from her volunteer work here as she did every Tuesday night, was Charlie's beloved Perdita. They came down the steps together, Dr. Reisden nodding curtly to Charlie and Perdita not seeing him, and walked toward the corner, talking, until a cabman saw them and stopped by them, and they both got in the cab together. Charlie stared after them, disturbed. Of course they would go together in a cab; Perdita was going to see Harry at Gilbert's. But on the whole, Charlie would not much like her to be acquainted with Dr. Reisden.

CHAPTER 14

WHEN GILBERT HAD SAID he would not talk about the past, he meant it.

In all other matters, Gilbert deferred; he was not a confident man. He would not unfold his napkin at dinner without looking round to see if Reisden, Harry, and Perdita thought it was the correct time to unfold theirs.

But for eighteen years he had believed, against everything, that Richard Knight was alive; and now that he
had got his Richard halfway out of the underworld,
Gilbert took a lesson from Lot and Orpheus. He would
not look back.

It was not only determination, it was fear. Reisden
spoke to him directly about William; indirectly, about
Richard's parents, the house at Matatonic, the Knight
family. But William Knight was completely out of
bounds; Jay French not to be spoken of; and there were
many smaller things as well—even Richard Knight's
boyhood reading was somehow suspect, odd for book-
ish Gilbert. Anything about Matatonic elicited a look
from Gilbert like a horse's look at a glue factory. What
was he afraid of? Gilbert would talk about *his* childhood
and his life traveling with a bookseller's wagon, but
almost anything after 1865 set him to run for cover. "I
wonder, Richard, do you suppose Mrs. Stelling would
be willing to make us a pie for this evening?" or "I have
been reading a very interesting book about clouds."

Why was Gilbert Knight so afraid?

Behind Gilbert's stiff tentative talk was fear. He was
afraid of canned goods, electricity, and bicycles. He
liked baseball games—Harry played baseball—but Gilbert had a fund of stories about catchers whose skulls
had been crushed by bats, people in the stands killed by
home runs. Ballpark lemonade caused cholera, Gilbert
told Reisden and Perdita. And hot dogs—Gilbert had
read *The Jungle*—hot dogs were *unspeakable*. Gilbert
knew that, except for the sausage Mrs. Stelling made in
the kitchen downstairs, all ground meat contained mice
and fingers. He was afraid of traffic, excessively hot days,

the subway, heavy rain, and sitting down in public places.

Sweetly, he was occasionally quite courageous. Daugherty told Reisden the wonderful story of Gilbert and the thief. One night some years ago, Gilbert had gone downstairs for a glass of milk and found a thief in the library. Thief says *Grrr,* sit down, don't you know I'm a dangerous man. Gilbert says Oh dear, and sits down. Gilbert notices the thief's feet are wet, a common cause of cold, and suggests he remove his shoes. Thief goes through the room, trying to ignore Gilbert, looking for something to steal. Gilbert begins pointing out things. "Those vases are very ugly but I think they're worth quite a bit." Gilbert wrestles with his conscience and finally, unhappily, tells the thief that his collection of early North Italian bookbindings is the most valuable thing in the room. Thief begins to swear. "Where am I going to fence those, huh? Don't you got any sense?" Thief goes off with the ugly vases and some silver. Gilbert, safe with his unfenceable bookbindings, goes sweetly to sleep. Only the next morning does he send the butler, Mr. Phillips, to call on the police.

Gilbert was afraid of cats, who smothered even grown persons by lying on their faces as they slept. Gilbert was afraid of little dogs, big dogs, squirrels, comets, escalators, drunkards, and drains. Gilbert knew that slates fell from roofs and decapitated innocent people standing on the sidewalk. According to Gilbert, fearful things might happen, shortly could happen, were known frequently to happen in just the situation that Harry or Reisden or Perdita was now in.

"Parts of Dickens," he told Reisden, "parts of Dickens make me tremble."

Gilbert was afraid of the French Revolution.

But who would be hurt now because William Knight had been killed eighteen years ago? Did Gilbert simply fear to look back at it? Would talking about it make it happen again?

Those who are determined not to repeat the past, ignore it.

When Gilbert had thought Richard knew about the murder, Gilbert had been terrified. Reisden remembered his look, like an animal seeing the slaughterhouse and smelling blood. But when Richard had no memories? Gilbert was only his ordinary self, perpetually anxious as that self was.

Why doesn't he simply believe I'm not Richard, Reisden thought. It would be so much less trouble. But at that game he was no better than Gilbert. He should have believed it himself.

HARRY AND PERDITA, the two young lovers, were much around the house. Though Perdita slept chastely at Bucky Pelham's house, she virtually lived at Gilbert's. Reisden saw them in the garden, holding hands at twilight. At dinner Perdita was the hostess, guiding the conversation from the foot of the table; she would be the one to ask Harry what he had done that day. Harry was taking his school examinations that week, and Reisden saw them in the music room, the girl sitting by him while Harry, breathing hard, made his way through elementary algebra. As exams slackened off, Harry's football player friends came over with their girlfriends, ostentatiously ignoring Reisden. Harry showed off his girl, then sent her to entertain the boyfriends' girlfriends, while the football players talked manly topics in the front room.

It was exactly as difficult to live with such family intimacy as Reisden thought it would be. He thought too often of Tasy. Perdita would sometimes come and sit next to Harry, snuggling up to him as close as a dog, and put her arm around him. It would always hurt Reisden, though that had not been one of Tasy's gestures. He would catch himself looking too long at the two of them, and be relieved when at last Harry took the girl back to her own home.

He spent as much time as he could outside the house with Daugherty, planning everything that they could do to find Richard Knight. He was not good at living in a household. He was a natural insomniac, and living wholly alone for five years, he had set the day to please himself, getting up when other people were going to sleep, working through the night. In the first two weeks in the Knight house he was much worse than usual, because he dreamed of Tasy's death whenever he slept.

My dear Victor,

. . . Do assure anyone who may ask that I am not Richard. But here I am nevertheless, having talked myself into finding the child, and he has been dead for eighteen years. I find, discouragingly, that in the right circumstances a skeleton will disintegrate in fourteen. So Daugherty and I may be looking for a more than usually calcified patch of soil.

I don't feel at all clever.

If you have suggestions for me, please send them. In any case, please send everything you have, or can locate, about the Knights.

Reisden

THOSE FIRST SEVERAL WEEKS, Perdita Halley was working at Schumann's *Papillons,* tearoom music, but complicated. She would run through a phrase again and again, bringing it up to speed, changing her reading. He could hear her when he was in the library, near her practice room. To hear a woman's voice in the house, and then to hear music practiced, the tentative handfuls of chords turning into music: He would half-hear a voice singing with the piano, and it would hurt.

He could not bear this almost-presence of Tasy. Out of self-defense he got to know Perdita.

In clear daylight, in a place she knew, she could see colors and outlines. But what was dusk to fully sighted people was black night to her. For her sake, every piece of furniture in the Knight house was always in accustomed places. Reisden learned to tuck chairs under the table and to leave nothing on the floor.

Blindness was remote from him, whose intelligence had been all his life to use his eyes. He couldn't use gestures with her. She didn't see them. He had to speak to her hearing, or it was as if he had made himself invisible to her. All she could see of him was what he could tell her. He didn't want to tell her anything.

"Would you play the piano for me?" he would ask. More often than not she played the Romantics: Chopin, Schumann, Liszt, storms and distress in a pretty package. She was good to listen to and her technique was dazzling, but he felt she was distant from the music.

"It doesn't seem real to me," she said once to Reisden.

"What does?"

"Beethoven. Haydn. Haydn's very out of favor, my music teacher says." She smiled self-deprecatingly.

With Beethoven and Haydn, with Brahms, she was rougher and less reliable but seemed more at home; but then at night she would slip back into the Lisztian tulle-and-dazzle that young women pianists were supposed to favor.

About this time they began to read aloud in the evenings.

It came about because Perdita had never read *The Winter's Tale,* though she had been named for its heroine. One late afternoon, after he had asked her shamelessly for piece after piece of music, she had a request in return. "Uncle Charlie says that you acted Shakespeare in college. *The Winter's Tale* isn't in Braille. Can you tell me about it? What is it about?"

"Child!" he said. "It's about poetry."

All of Shakespeare was next door in Gilbert's library. Reisden had not read aloud to anyone in five-and-a-half years—to whom, and where, not to think of—and he was so unused to long speaking that he grew hoarse. But the voice doesn't forget what it has been trained for, and suddenly the crabbed late verse found its rhythm and he was back on stage.

> Is whispering nothing?
> Is leaning cheek to cheek? Is meeting noses?
> Kissing with inside lip? . . .
> Skulking in corners? Wishing clocks more
>   swift?

Hours, minutes? noon, midnight? and all eyes
Blind . . . but theirs, theirs only,
That would unseen be wicked? Is this nothing?
Why, then the world and all that's in't is
      nothing . . .

He wondered if she would understand the play. Leontes' jealousy was nothing to her and "kissing with inside lip" had never happened to that long wide mouth. But she was a good audience. When Leontes denied his child, she murmured, "How *could* he?" When the oracle declared Hermione innocent, she clapped her hands together as if Harry had hit a home run. When Hermione and the prince died, she held her hands over her mouth, wide-eyed. By the time the bear ate Antigonus, the room had gone dark; Reisden had to turn on the light by his chair so that he could see the words. The little Sèvres clock on the mantel told the hour with a flutter of chimes.

"Is it that late?"

For the first time in the Knights' house, the hours had gone quickly.

"Will you read the rest after dinner?" she asked.

That was how their entertainments began, he reading Harry's fiancée *The Winter's Tale*. They brought Harry and Gilbert up to the music room after dinner. "I would there were no age between ten and three-and-twenty," Reisden began, and they were off into the festival scene of that magic play and "Perdita, now grown in grace/ Equal with wondering." Gilbert smiled at Perdita and patted her hand.

    I would I had some flowers o' th' spring that
       might

Become your time of day, and yours, and
    yours,
That wear upon your virgin branches yet
Your maidenheads growing. Oh, Proserpina,
For the flowers now that, frighted, thou let'st
    fall
From Dis's wagon—

Harry frowned at the word *maidenheads* and looked meaningfully from Reisden to Perdita, clearing his throat. But Perdita turned toward Harry, wondering—it had all gone by her—then back toward the play. Prince Florizel declared his love for the shepherdess Perdita. King Polixenes confronted Prince Florizel in disguise. King Polixenes disinherited Florizel. Harry bristled. Don't be stupid, boy, Reisden thought.

Florizel and the play's Perdita returned to Leontes' court. Perdita nodded as if she had expected it. She whispered a question to Gilbert; Gilbert smiled and nodded. And Leontes was reunited with Hermione, miraculously restored to him; Florizel reconciled with his father; Florizel and Perdita married as prince and princess of both kingdoms. "Oh, *thank you*," Perdita said, her eyes glowing as if she were looking into light.

"I like that play very much, Richard," Gilbert said, "although I remember that there is something very distressing about a bear."

"Will you read more to me?" Perdita asked Reisden.

"My dear, I'll read you anything."

What he had not fully realized was that, in those dim nights downstairs in the formal parlor, she had been blind. She didn't have much vision for close reading, even in bright daylight, and she saved her eyes for learning music. She had read very little that wasn't in Braille—and, for the next few days, he had a guilty epiphany about how much he read that she could not. Did the Perkins School library have texts on forensic medicine or organic chemistry? Did the Howe Press Braille-print as much as the front page of the morning newspaper?

"I want to know everything," she said.

She knew so little she didn't even know what to ask him to read. That didn't stop her. "I want to know how Beethoven lived. Is there a book about that?" She wanted the lyrics of Elizabethan madrigals and, yes, she wanted the front page of the newspaper, and the baseball scores. She knew so little about the world of words that she had no idea what whole categories contained. "Who are the good novelists?" Sometimes she wanted information, not elementary information by any means. "Why do some concert halls sound better than others?"

He had volunteered to be her eyes, and it was a bigger job than he had considered.

Harry objected that he should be the one to read to Perdita. Why should she want to learn about *sounds?*— and anyway, whatever she was to learn, Harry wanted to teach her himself. "Look at some books on acoustics," Reisden advised.

"Women aren't interested in—what is it?"

Reisden gave him the simplest of the books and Harry soldiered through it for an evening or two, mispronouncing the words, until he threw it down. "I've still got my French exam, Pet, I don't have time for this now. Anybody can read to you."

Without either Reisden or Perdita discussing it, they

considered they had been given tacit permission to go on.

And so, evening by evening, the four of them sat in the music room. Reisden read, while Gilbert and Perdita listened and Harry sulked, just a little, behind his textbooks or his sailing magazine. Perdita played music while Gilbert and Reisden listened and Harry applauded with them at the end. It was a truce of a sort; it was a civilizing way of not plumbing any depths. And sometimes Harry and Perdita sat on the couch together, her head on his shoulder, her arm around his waist.

CHAPTER 15

JUST BEFORE they all went to Matatonic, Reisden had a chance to talk with Perdita about herself.

In that hot dry June there had been hardly a shower; but one noontime on Tremont Street he was caught in a squall of rain and took refuge under Stearns' awning. He turned to look at a beautiful profile and recognized her, different out of the Knights' house. She might have come out of a stained-glass window; her hair stood out in waves because of the rain, and that and the greenish light from the awning gave her the look of a Rousseau animal, stylized and innocent.

"Look," he said, "come have lunch with me."

He took her to a restaurant she would probably have called grown-up. It smelled of fresh-ironed linen and hot rolls; the napkins were starched into complex cornets on the plates. They sat in the full light of the window so she could see. Reisden thought about their visibility to newspapermen and made sure that they could not be seen from outside; Richard Knight was still too fresh a sensation.

She seemed nervous and chattery. She had been shopping. "I don't get to pick out material, of course, just to pick it up. It's for *Scenes from Shakespeare,* the benefit play the Clinic is doing this year. Look at the material; Mrs. Fen likes nice colors. Mrs. Fen is in charge." She ducked for a bag and brought some out, folds on folds of an orange made subtle by the rainlight. The odd color next her face gave her a sophistication she did not usually possess; she made a pose like a tragic actress, all neck and arms, and in a second more she bunched the material next to her and folded her arms over it, staring past him with her dark eyes, throwing the moment away. The angles of the cloth, the shadows, the serious face among its dark hair: tragic beauty in the Morris style, and momentarily very striking.

"Is anything the matter, child?"

"I've never been to a restaurant before," she said, embarrassed.

"Something new, then." He was diplomat enough not to sound as surprised as he felt.

"I'll end up with a whole plate of food in my lap and my elbows trailing in the margarine."

"Child, don't talk vulgarity. They don't have margarine here."

She laughed and ducked her head.

"The two of us will get through somehow. Shall I read the menu?" He read every item of it, including the

descriptions, watching as she got control of herself. She
wrinkled her nose at liver; dishes with sauces disappointed her; she was going to nerve herself up to ask
him for something.

"If I were to have a dish that needed cutting, would
you cut it?" Her cheeks were pink. He recognized that
"were to have" from Gilbert.

He would have done it for her gladly but he wanted
to push her doors a little wider. "Why not have the
kitchen cut it up?"

"*Would* they?" She looked at him in honest astonish-
ment. "They would, wouldn't they?"

The waiter came with his pencil poised. Reisden
began to order for them; her questions flew on ahead of
his. He watched her in amusement. The kitchen would
do anything she wanted, even bone fish.

"Why, I could go out to eat *completely alone,*" she
said.

"Power, Miss Halley," he murmured.

Both her parents were alive. Her father was a school-
teacher and missionary to the Indian tribes in the Arizona territories. Her mother studied the native religions.
"Papa says he teaches the Indians that they should have
no gods before God, but he just tries to ignore the ones
that come after." Perdita had been born with cataracts.
At the age of six she had been sent back to Boston, to
Elizabeth Halley's brother, Bucky Pelham, so that she
could be trained at the Perkins School for the Blind.

"But I didn't go; Uncle B. had me tutored instead.
Uncle B. thought I'd start acting blind if I went to
Perkins, and then no one would marry me. I'd already
learned Braille, thank goodness, or I'd never be able to
read Papa and Mama's letters."

"Is Charlie Adair your uncle as well?"

"Uncle Charlie is Mama's first cousin. Which is a lovely relationship; you can be just as related as you please. I wish I had been sent to stay with him instead. But he was supposed to be very rackety because he's Catholic. I had to sneak round to have tea with him when I was young."

"And were you sneaking out when I saw you at the Clinic?"

She shook her head. "No, I get to help out now, because I'm older, and it's a young-society-lady thing to do. . . ." Her face shadowed. "I don't tell Harry everything about that, like you can get lice in your hair at the Clinic. All the kids that come in have them."

"Amusing."

"Harry would mind. He wouldn't let me go there."

"And you would let him keep you from it."

She looked up, then down. "I love Harry very much."

He didn't say anything.

"He's so unhappy," she said simply. "He wants everything to be clear and plain and simple. And it's always been torment to him that William Knight got murdered. He says they wouldn't take him in the Porcellian Club because of it. Somebody proposed him for The Country Club last year, and he found out that one of Lizzie Borden's cousins belonged to it, and he wanted to hit the man who had proposed him. It's all so silly."

"A gentleman should never have his name in the papers?"

"I want him to be happy," Harry's Perdita said. "I love him so, and I love Gilbert. And whether you are Richard or not—" She leaned forward and touched his hand as another person might have met his eyes. "I like you too."

Their food arrived. He watched her while she ate, telling her where things were on her plate according to the clock system she taught him. The plate was at the center. At two o'clock on the dial of the plate was located the fish; at seven o'clock, the potatoes; peas at eleven o'clock. To the right of the plate, the knife, then the spoon. Above the knife was the water glass. Every part in relation to every other part. At the center of the Knight clock was Richard Knight, where nothing was. Filling that place, Gilbert Knight, but too small. Off to one side, Harry Boulding. Perdita must fit all that into a whole and keep it fitting. So she lied a little to her fiancé and smoothed things over for him. And she had more intelligence, and was perhaps a little more independent, than Harry considered. Reisden wondered how well things fitted after all.

"Why have you never gone to a restaurant before?"

"Oh, Harry thinks—" She blushed. "Harry's very thoughtful for me."

The rain stopped outside their café window with a suddenness that left them speechless, as if they had needed the excuse of rain to have lunch together outside the house. They said goodbyes. One of her bags spilled something; he picked it up to return it. It was a sample of lace and white silk, pinned to a card that had the name of a bride's-shop.

She was so young. She had not even had coffee; she had drunk milk.

She was a fulcrum for the Knights, in all her innocence. Seventeen years old. The big ring glinted on her finger; more than once he had seen her sit with her hands in the light so she could see it. Harry and Gilbert used her to keep themselves together. Reisden used her music to keep himself from thinking. All she wanted was to play the piano, to be read to, and to marry her Harry.

All she wanted was Harry's happiness, and Gilbert's.

And, of course, Reisden thought wryly, now Richard Knight's.

CHAPTER 16

LOUIS DALLOZ saw the newspaper on a kiosk in Times Square. The picture was blurred, taken from far away, but he knew who it was. Hadn't he been looking for Reisden on every street corner for most of the past month? He bought the newspaper; with a dictionary he made out what it said.

What does money do? Louis had never known. Twenty-five centimes bought a *baguette* and thirty-five a *bâtard*, forty a cup of good hot coffee. But finance and stocks, what Reisden did with his spare time, Louis didn't understand them, they were marks on paper. Reisden could afford an apartment with a good address in Lausanne; he drove cars that you didn't pay for with copper money. When Louis asked him whether he was rich, Reisden smiled and said probably not.

This heir was rich; and what had Reisden done?

Louis found the Knights' house at twilight, one of a row in a long rich street, where the housefronts had a formal, secret air, like masks or diplomatic faces. The newspaper article said the Knights' money had come from war profits; it looked like that, a big house built on workers' sweat. A butler answered the doorbell. Louis stared. The butler did not recognize Louis' name, or Reisden's; Louis had to ask for the name in the newspaper.

Louis waited in the rich, dark, faded hallway, by a mirror that reached to the ceiling, next to a cabinet full of multicolored china. One of the other servants drifted in and watched him, as if they thought he was going to steal the silver tray on the hall table. *Solidarity,* Louis thought, nodding at the servant, but the man looked down his nose at Louis. Louis heard men's voices from far away in the big house, polite tones, quiet. One of the voices was Reisden's. It raised in a question, and then Reisden came out into the hall.

He was dressed for dinner, in a dinner jacket, like a rich man. Louis had never seen Reisden do that in his life. While Louis watched, the expression drained out of Reisden's face and left it pale.

"Louis." Just from the name, Louis could tell Reisden was speaking English, which they never spoke between them. He had changed, and the change stood between them like a distance.

"*Sacha, qu'est-ce que tu fous là?*" Louis exploded. "*Qu'est-ce que c'est que cette connerie?*"

"*Laisse. Je viens.*" Reisden's voice was expressionless. He went back through the door and Louis heard a muttering, the high voice of an old man. The butler held Reisden's coat and hat. Was this what Reisden wanted?

A cab was going past the big front door; Reisden stopped it with a gesture and said something to the driver. "Shall we just drive?" he asked Louis in French.

"No." Louis didn't want to drive in a closed cab. He wanted to know where he was. "We could sit and talk there." He pointed to a bench in the long narrow park down the middle of the street.

"No."

"And I can't talk to you in *that* house, hey?" Louis jerked his thumb back.

"No, you can't," Reisden said levelly.

"I embarrass you, in a house like that? Is that it?"

Louis looked at the housefronts going by, one after another after another. Reisden sat on the other side of the cab, saying nothing and not looking at Louis. He was very thin and looked oddly handsome in the gentleman's getup, but wrong, like a waxwork, as if he had glass eyes. "I embarrass myself by being there," Reisden said after a while.

"But what are you doing there? Who is this Richard Knight? What have you done?"

They came to the center of the city. Reisden paid off the cab and got out first, ducking his head as he always had because he was tall. As Louis leaned out he saw a couple of men standing on the sidewalk; one poked the other on the arm and pointed right at Reisden. Reisden got back in without looking; his arm struck Louis across the nose. Louis cupped his hands over his nose. "Sh-t! Sh-t! What's the matter with you?"

"They recognized me," Reisden said, as if it explained everything.

Louis felt a fearful irritation. *They recognized me.* The butler. A bookcase full of old cups and plates, not matching. The look of the house, like a posh hotel, the querulous high voice far away, and no room for his friends. He pinched the bridge of his nose to see whether it was swelling.

Reisden gave the cabdriver a direction. The horse clopped through narrower, darker streets until they reached a hotel, someplace shabby and anonymous.

No one was ever *recognized* there, Louis thought.

At that time of night everyone was in the bar, listening to a singer. Louis wanted a beer. "We'll have coffee," Reisden said. The coffee shop was below the street, muggy, deserted, dark; the coffee smelled like it had been made in a train station. Reisden sat facing the door, his face dim. Down the stairs from the floor above fell bits of laughter and off-key music.

"Tell me what is going on," Louis said. "Tell me what you want from this."

Out of his wallet Louis brought the clipping from the New York paper that had brought him here. The headline was "MISSING HEIR FOUND." With it was the letter Reisden had sent instead of coming to New York. Louis stabbed the two with his finger.

Reisden picked up the clipping as though it had nothing to do with him. His mouth tightened as he read it. "I didn't intend to stay here. You knew that; I wrote you." Reisden dropped the clipping back on the table and pushed it back toward him. He was speaking low, expressionless but hurried. Like a corpse saying, I am so sorry not to tell you what you want to know, but excuse me, I have to be buried now.

"You wrote me a letter *with no return address*. I couldn't read the postmark. I didn't know where you were. You disappeared. I didn't know if you were alive."

"I'm sorry," Reisden said. "But you see I am alive."

Louis handed the letter over as if it were a card he were trumping. "I want an explanation. Who am I, the dog? For the dog you put down a paper. What are you doing?"

"I wish I knew."

"That's not good enough. Are you Richard Knight? You can't be."

"No, of course not."

"Then what are you doing here? Why aren't you in New York talking with O'Brien? He says you and he worked on some very good approaches at the conference."

Reisden turned away impatiently, then back, a little movement, only sketched, nearly impassive. The coffee shop was lit by gaslights; Louis gave the chain of the one nearest them a couple of tugs, and the light wheezed up a little more brightly.

"I told him some things he could do. I am—" Reisden shrugged as if looking for a word, not finding one, or not the best one. "I am pretending to be Richard Knight, for reasons too odd to go into. It will probably take most of the summer. I didn't expect it to. And I cannot possibly explain to you why I am doing it."

"No, you're going to. What the h--l are you doing?"

He had been looking at Louis, and now he dropped his eyes, then looked around the room as if distracted, looking for some face in a crowd that wasn't there. A thin line of muscle set very tight against his jaw, and he wouldn't look at Louis for more than a moment, not even bothering to hide that he didn't want him here. When had Reisden been like this before? Reisden was very capable at being impolite; that was a natural part of being brought up rich. The time before—Louis remembered when. The hairs on his arms rose up from animal cold.

"Reisden!" he shouted, as though Reisden had been about to step over a cliff.

Reisden turned his eyes back with that same odd, cold, breakable politeness.

"I'm going to say this one time in my life. You can't get away with this." Reisden looked straight at him, not seeing him at all. "I'm an old man; you're twenty-seven. You're the Baron von Reisden. Everybody takes you seriously; everybody thinks I'm the man who cleans the floor. I care about chemistry. You do chemistry, you do it very well, but you are not going to waste my time with—" He couldn't say it. "After Tasy died, I watched you losing control of yourself, for months, and you knew it, and you wouldn't talk to me. You tried to kill yourself, but you wouldn't talk to me. You did that to me. Once. No more."

"I did that to you?" Reisden said, very gentle, looking at him for once. "If I knew what the h--l I am doing to myself, I would tell you what it was."

"That's a lie, Sacha. You wouldn't."

Reisden waited too long without replying, staring past Louis; it was hard for Louis to remember the young man once, long ago, who had come to see Louis at his office in London. I came to learn chemistry.

"Come to New York with me. You need to."

"I can't," said Reisden.

"Sacha, you'll kill yourself. Stop."

Reisden simply got up and took his coat and hat, turning away. Louis jumped up and grabbed him by the arm. Reisden put his two hands on Louis' shoulders and shoved him down into his chair and stood over him. He was frightening, eyes staring and remote. *He says he's crazy,* Louis thought, *but he is crazy.* Louis looked up at him. Reisden gave him one more look, a quick, cruel, horrified look like fingers flicking some sort of lint off his sleeve. Then he was gone.

Louis heard change clinking on the bar as he went. Reisden had paid for the coffee.

"That's enough," Louis said out loud. *Ça, c'est fini.* He was not going to forgive Reisden for this. For being the Baron von Reisden in evening dress and treating him like a pig farmer. For paying for the coffee. For— Louis sat at the table and played with the light, turning it down until it popped and went dark.

For what, *ouais,* he knew for what. Louis had run out of ways to stop him.

But he'd never forgive him.

Chapter 17

Just before they went up to William Knight's house in New Hampshire, Reisden leased a car.

Automobiles like the one he wanted were not bought. One knew people and got on lists. One waited until the maker decided to build one's auto, and waited while he did—it could take two years to build a good racing car. Reisden pulled strings. He was introduced to a man who had a car he couldn't drive.

In Brookline, the auto was stabled by itself in a

tree-shaded garage on a big estate. It was a heavy black brute with a long scratch down its side. The chauffeur shook his head. "This one's a bastard. Drives big and mean, throws its weight away from you when you try to take a corner. Fights you all the way. We wanted to do the Glidden Tour this year, but not with this animal."

"It has power?"

"It'll do a hundred on a straight, and Dead Horse Hill didn't even phase the sucker. I wouldn't try Mount Washington with it, though. First time you try a bad curve at speed, bastard'll tip like a drunk." The chauffeur spat. "Go ahead, wreck the son of a bitch. We're insured."

"Gilbert's goin' to be terrified," Daugherty remarked that night.

"For Richard," Reisden said absently. He had the housing off the steering, looking to see what could be done with it.

"Harry wants to drive 'er, too."

Reisden moved him aside and unscrewed the floorboard, playing a flashlight down into the connections between steering gear and axle. Once he'd seen one of these chain drives explode like shrapnel. He saw Harry driving this black brute, with his Perdita beside him. The image stung shockingly. "Harry will not," he said sharply. "That's a bad design. If the chain catches on the housing it'll rip apart."

"Goin' to kill yourself?" Daugherty said dryly.

Reisden wiped his hands on a rag and lit a cigaret, wondering how much Daugherty actually knew about that. The two men's eyes met and the silence lengthened. "No, goin' to cut back the housing," he said finally, mocking Daugherty's accent, which was low of him; Daugherty didn't notice, or pretended not to.

"Just don't want Harry to drive it," Daugherty suggested.

"It's top-heavy as well." Harry and Perdita would never drive together in an auto like this. Not if he could help it.

"If I'd got to live around that boy," Daugherty said indirectly, "sometimes he'd get on my nerves."

Reisden shook his head. "It's Richard gets on my nerves."

When Gilbert no longer believed in Richard, which must happen soon, Reisden would escape in the big black auto. Get away, drive all the way to New York. It would take days, and as long as he was moving between here and there, he could really be neither who he was nor what he had got himself into.

Reisden stubbed his cigaret out.

Methodically he wrapped electrical tape around the wheel and listened to the muffled Boston traffic, trying to forget the sound of the engine and the smell of cold November air, and the feeling of a wheel under his hands.

CHAPTER 18

GILBERT TAPPED THE EGGSHELL with his spoon and fumbled for words, finding nothing to say. A maid pulled the blinds down one by one and cut the morning out of the house. Mr. Phillips threw dustcovers over Gilbert's chair in the library and shrouded the family portraits. Richard's portrait disappeared under linen as it had never done before; in almost nineteen years, Gilbert had never gone even as far as Nahant overnight; and living Richard, whose work all this was, sat taciturn on the other side of the breakfast table, with his coffee cold in front of him. Gilbert reached for a piece of the morning newspaper and gathered it about him. Richard stared over the edge of the world and accepted a second cup of black coffee, but did not drink it either. Harry wasn't down yet.

"We'll miss the train," Gilbert said. He did not want to go to Matatonic; but he didn't want to keep the train waiting. That was another misery. The Knight family owned two railroad cars, in storage since Heaven knew when, and they were taking one of them up to Matatonic. Traveling nowhere, Gilbert had not been so conspicuous since Father died. He wondered if Richard remembered his grandfather's parlor car. Even the upholstery had made Gilbert uncomfortable, hairy plush green cushions round and stiff as limes.

"I wish we didn't have to go," Gilbert said.

Richard seemed about to say something with an edge to it; but instead he made it a quotation. " 'If 'twere done when 'tis done, then 'twere well it were done quickly.' " Gilbert smiled and Richard gave him a half smile in return. *If it were done quickly,* Gilbert thought. The only consolation he had was that Father's portrait was under linen too. But they were going to Father's house.

Gilbert rang the bell. "Could you please tell Master Harry how late it's getting?"

Richard snapped his watch shut and lit a cigaret.

"Richard, I can't get used to your smoking. Don't you think cigarets and all that coffee, and nothing to eat, will make you sick on the train?"

Richard only looked at him, all distance, as if he hadn't even heard him. Gilbert hoped against hope. "Just a little bit of toast?"

In the hall on a tarpaulin were piled a trunk, suitcases, Harry's tennis rackets. Gilbert had not known there was such a thing as a tarpaulin in the house. What were they used for? Tarpaulins were for bicycle trips, tents, a cloth on the ground. When the athletic Farnums down the street left for Cold River, their cab was piled high with tarpaulins.

"Richard," he said desperately, "I wonder when was the last time I left this house."

"I beg your pardon?"

"I wonder why we have got a tarpaulin."

"Pardon, sir," said Lucy, bringing in some of Mrs. Stelling's shirred eggs, "it's to protect the carpets." From what? Gilbert thought, startled. Mr. Phillips went through the breakfast room with a china clock cradled in his hands.

The Sèvres clock was going into storage. It had stood on its mantel since after Father's funeral, when Gilbert had quietly put away the black marble tomb that had told Father's time. The shepherds and all the china figures of fancy threw out their arms on their way to banishment.

"I feel as if I were dead and all the house breaking up."

He said it very quietly and Richard did not hear him. Gilbert desperately drank a second cup of coffee himself.

Muffled in newspapers and excelsior, the Sèvres clock chimed eight. The smell of oilskins and tarpaulins and dust hung over the breakfast table.

ON THE SAME DAY, with much less fanfare, Charlie Adair's children went to the country. As they gathered on the station platform to leave for Matatonic, Charlie watched them. And down the platform, on the same long train, he saw the huge, gaunt private car that William Knight had used. The blinds were drawn, which meant that Gilbert was already there. With him, no doubt, would be young Dr. Reisden.

The children milled on the platform. They looked like so many to go down to the country; but, ah, so many more were left behind. When Charlie had been given the hotel, he was like a man with a big pot of soup in a soup kitchen. He had ladled it out freely to anyone who asked. Yes, this child could come, and that one; they could stay all summer; yes, and their brothers and their sisters too. The first summer had been disastrous. Too many children; they had to sleep two and three to a bed, fighting all night, no bathrooms to speak of at all. Now he knew how soon his ladle scraped the bottom of the pot. Only one child from a family, and that child could stay two weeks only. Only from families guaranteed to be destitute. This morning in the train station, the children who were going laughed and shouted on the platform, but Charlie's thoughts were with their brothers and sisters who stood silently aside to see them off. Only one, only, only.

Just down the country road from his hotel was the Knights' huge estate. Island Hill would have suited the children better than it ever had the Knights.

Father, I confess to the sin of avarice. I want Island Hill for the children. I want my dear Perdita and Harry to have Gilbert's money. I want Gilbert to love Harry as he should.

You want nothing for yourself?

I want my will for myself. God, I don't depend on Your mercy.

What do you want for yourself?

I want to die in peace, Charlie thought.

But he knew he meant something different.

I want Dr. Reisden to find Richard's body, wherever it may be. And to find out nothing else. Nothing at all.

HARRY AND HIS PERDITA, Perdita's aunt Violet and her cousin Efnie stood together on the platform, by the porter's truck with the lunchboxes. Perdita was in charge of the sandwiches, which she and Efnie had packed last night. Aunt Violet Pelham was chaperoning Perdita, which Violet considered put her in charge of the sandwiches too. "You, boy!" her stentorian voice carried down the platform. She poked an enormous lacy parasol at a child who scrambled down off the truck. "If you touch that food I shall have you arrested." She was a small, stout woman with slightly protruding eyes. Her large hat trembled on top of her head as if it were enraged and about to spring.

Daugherty and Reisden watched them from the cool, moldy inside of William Knight's private car. Daugherty was going up at the same time as Gilbert and Reisden, to lead the process of looking for Richard Knight.

"Ayuh, that's Bucky's wife Violet," Daugherty said to Reisden. "And her favorite daughter Efnie. Both of 'em goin' up to Matatonic to keep an eye on Perdita. Perdita's been up to the lake before, helpin' out Charlie, but this time Harry's comin'. And it ain't fittin' an engaged girl should be in the same town as her fiancy, without someone like Violet to come between 'em."

Efnie Pelham turned dewy eyes toward Harry. She was tall, willowy, and athletic, a blond Gibson girl, lusciously pretty; only the wary would see any resemblance to her mother. Harry's eyes were following Perdita restlessly as she supervised getting the sandwiches loaded into the car. Efnie tilted up her little straw boater and began bantering with Harry. Perdita knelt down to have a conversation with a little boy. Harry stepped forward to order the child back in line. Left alone, Efnie compressed her lips into a sudden tight line, then tossed her head.

"Efnie's got a dozen boyfriends," Daugherty went on, oblivious. "We got an office pool goin' which one she'll take."

DOWN IN THE NOISE and jostle of the platform, Harry pulled Perdita aside. He was hot and cross. He didn't want even to ride in the private car; it was out of date and conspicuous. Perdita laughed and threw her arms around him.

"Sit with me in the public cars," he said. "I'll show you off."

"Of course, Harry, if you want."

No, he didn't want; he brooded. She must know he didn't want to sit with an army of children. She wasn't paying attention to him. Just being mealy-mouthed and saying anything to make him "feel better." What he wanted was to sit in the private car with her and to have

Reisden nowhere. "Never mind," he grumbled. "We'll sit in that stupid car with Gilbert, if it makes *you* happy." Immediately he knew he was being unfair to her, but he didn't know what to do about it but grumble. "Then maybe you won't pay so much attention to those kids."

The private car was already crowded with too many people. Reisden was at one end talking with Daugherty, Gilbert talking with Charlie Adair. Violet Pelham had invited herself in. Efnie was waiting for her on the stairs. "Oh, you come in too," Harry told her, "everybody else's already here."

"Pew," Efnie said, "it smells!" Harry felt a little better.

Underneath the dust and the mildew Harry scented a dark, burnt smokiness, a smell of char and old fires.

"Father's cigars," Gilbert said. "It smells like Father."

Efnie shrugged. "I'm going outside to the observation deck." It was a good idea. Harry looked around for Perdita, but she was talking with Reisden. Spending too much time with that man.

"Come along with me, Harry?" Efnie asked casually.

He'd just as soon have gone, although he knew Efnie was flirting with him. It made him feel pretty good right now to have an attractive girl like Efnie flirting with him. But he was engaged to Perdita and he didn't want to string any other girl along, even though there was no harm in it. So he stood by the door while Perdita did just about anything she pleased, sat down next to Reisden and talked with him for minutes on end.

The dark station roof slid away from them at last. Boston gave way to Lawrence and Lowell, smudges on the Massachusetts farmland. As they crossed into New Hampshire, the farms grew sparser and the forest began. Their train steamed through Nashua and into Manchester's morning grime. The cars jerked and shuddered as they switched onto the Short Line, and the train followed the river, the hard-rock bed and the clear race of the Merrimack. Mills gave way to pines and they climbed toward lakes and mountains.

THE BLACK AUTO was going up with them as luggage. Reisden made his way forward in the train, through a baggage car where trunks were piled high behind wire mesh. There were two automobiles on that train, his and an enormous CMG tourer destined for farther up the line. Reisden checked the blocks and the tying-down on his, then talked with the CMG's chauffeur. From the next baggage car they heard thumps and neighs: horses quarreling with each other. "For me, I'd rather work with horses," the chauffeur said, "much less trouble they are, but the future's in the autos. Can't escape the future, eh?"

Reisden thought about a hard-mouthed black horse he'd ridden in Graz. No control at all, but the beast went fast. "They're not so different." Black horses, and Africa, and back beyond that, a thing that the eyes could not focus on, like darkness or absence. If Richard Knight were alive again in Matatonic, might something make him remember?

General amnesia cures itself within weeks or not at all.

There are a few exceptions, but not many; and, Reisden thought, he would not be one of them, because he was not Richard Knight.

The chauffeur had said something to him. "Excuse me?"

"You going to drive her yourself?"

They talked about autos.

CHAPTER 19

LAKE MATATONIC was a great blank clockface of water among low hills. From one to five o'clock was the town center—Leroy's Provisions, the Civil War monument, the public library, the post office, the bank, the white Episcopalian church, Woolworth's, and two or three stores that sold expensive trifles to summer people: bathing suits, candy, and clothes that came from Fifth Avenue and from France. There were a few streets of houses and the town's modern hotel, the Lakeside, with its pier that jutted into the lake. The best houses were tucked into the woods around the lake. Violet Pelham explained all this to Gilbert Knight in a loud voice, and Gilbert murmured at the number of floats, piers, and moored sailboats that he could see, each one marking someone's summer house.

The railroad station was at six o'clock, a pretty little building with a view of the lake. William Knight's railroad car was uncoupled on the siding. The Clinic children poured out on the platform and scattered uncontrollably, some of them clustering around Reisden's black automobile and swarming over it like ants, some running down to the water. Nursemaids ran after them, the ribbons on their caps streaming. Charlie Adair tipped his funny hat to Violet Pelham and rescued Gilbert from her.

Reisden walked to the edge of the lake and looked north, toward the later hours of the clock. Surprisingly far away, a great white cube of a house faced the water.

That had to be William Knight's house, Island Hill; it was in the right location. Reisden didn't recognize it, and something unacknowledged unknotted inside him.

Island Hill. It was a muggy hot day and the haze from the water haloed the house. From here one could see only the largest details, long windows blinded by drawn shades, a dark, top-heavy roof. Bushes came down to the edge of the water and stopped abruptly as if someone had cut them with a knife.

"Yup, that's it," Daugherty said under his breath. "And there's your nearest neighbor's house, Anna Fen's."

He could see only the pier, an Italianate gingerbready thing painted in violently artistic shades of yellow and green. A motorboat with a yellow-and-green sun awning was moored to it. The effect was meant to be springlike, Reisden supposed, but it was overdone, theater trees in a real garden, theater makeup on the street. Gilbert Knight and Charlie Adair came down the path to the dock.

"Michael Fen lived there, I think," Gilbert said to Charlie Adair, pointing out the Italianate monstrosity.

"His widow still does," Charlie replied. "She puts on a benefit play for us every year, Anna Fen does. It's *Scenes from Shakespeare* this year. It would do your heart good to see the children playing fairies."

"Why, Richard, you might like that."

Scenes from Shakespeare. Perdita Halley had mentioned it earlier. Children playing fairies, directed by a woman who put an awning on a motorboat. "Perhaps," Reisden demurred gently.

"You must want to get settled in your house," Charlie said to Gilbert. "Come over to the Clinic for dinner."

Perdita was staying at the Clinic. Harry had her trunk on a handcart, bringing it there for her. Roy Daugherty and the servants they had brought—Mrs. Martin the housekeeper, Mrs. Stelling the cook, the head kitchen-maid, and two housemaids—went off to find the luggage.

Two fat ponies were cropping the grass in the fields by the Clinic; they looked up nervously as the black auto started up with a roar. Gilbert climbed into the passenger seat, settling himself nervously. Down Island Hill Road, past the station and away from town, Reisden drove the automobile slowly by the Clinic and the fields and playground. On the other side of the road, the lake side, was a short side road leading to Mrs. Fen's green-and-yellow house. A substantial fence, reinforced with fieldstone, walled the Clinic fields and Mrs. Fen's green lawns off from the race of the Little Spruce River. Gilbert peered over the edge down into the Spruce.

The bed of the Spruce ran deep but narrow and twisting, jammed with rocks. Even in the somnolent summer, the river water slammed so hard against the boulders that spray rose up in rainbows of mist. You could climb up one side of it, up to the Devil's Kettle miles upstream, but you couldn't fish it, boat it, or float logs down it. The Spruce was good for one thing only. It was a barrier.

William Knight had built an iron bridge over the Spruce, raising it high and humped to keep it above the spring runoff. The bridge was narrow, with a low rail, and had granite pillars at either end. Gilbert looked at the bridge nervously.

"I never liked those gates."

Reisden geared the black car down and drove over slowly. The bridge groaned solidly, a long, eerie sigh of iron. The river rushed and splashed below, and the spray rose up and sharpened every smell, but dampened sound. They had driven through some invisible wall, changing every sense but the eyes. They drove into woods. The cool air smelled of pines and mold. Branches were tangled overhead, confused, and in the narrow roadway it was so dusky that the songbirds were quite silent. Long pines had fallen at the side of the road, fallen and rotted and rooted again.

"Why are these woods so thick?" Reisden asked Gilbert.

"Father never had them logged. He wanted his privacy."

The road bumped under the wheels, never having been graded or dragged; it was a carriage road, not for autos, rutted by wagons long gone to scrap, hummocked by time, and so long disused that the grass and the moss had grown over it. Gilbert pointed out a great black cherry, dead and uprooted at the side of the road. New shoots from it had taken root just at the verge, and the tree spilled late blossoms and bumpy black twigs into the road itself. "That tree fell the last summer he was alive, Richard."

"A long time ago."

They turned a last corner and came out, abruptly, onto the lawns of the house itself.

The house was wrong.

It had been meant to be something like the Federal houses of William Knight's early years, a proportional cube. Reisden had seen houses like that in Cambridge, clean and balanced as a chemical formula. But this roof was too tall, the windows were gaunt, blank sheets of glass, and the doorway had been pushed to one side, marring all balance. Reisden felt instinctively uneasy at it, tight and nerve-ridden at the back of the neck, the way he did in the lab when he knew something was wrong but didn't know what.

Across the lawn was William Knight's rose garden, a close-packed acre of bushes. The service road wound around the back of the house past the summer kitchen to the outbuildings and the Knight barn, behind a screen of elms. The barn was four stories tall, as if it had been built for the hugest of working farms.

Reisden parked the car by the corner of the house, under a maple tree that must have been young in the American Revolution. As the motor died the silence swooped in on them.

They both hung back for a moment, looking at the grey walls and the unbalanced door. Reisden felt as if he should take something inside the house with him: a flashlight though it was hot noon, a weapon. How appropriate, a gun. The auto had demountable acetylene headlamps; Reisden unclipped one and gave it unlit to Gilbert and took the other one himself, feeling a fool.

I am not Richard Knight, he reminded himself.

Reisden climbed the granite steps and tried the knob. Gilbert handed him the keys silently. The keys turned, scraping in the lock, and the thick black door swung open.

Amazed and appalled, Reisden gazed back twenty years.

It was as if the air itself had not moved in all the time since William Knight had lived here. William Knight's door opened onto a vast funeral hall smelling of carpet mold, old fires, old food, old damp wallpaper. After the sunlight outside it was green-tinged and dark. They could see shadows of a wide staircase, doors into rooms on either side. All the doors were closed, and the only light in the hall came from a meager window on the second-floor landing. Reisden felt along the wall, then swore when he saw the hall lights.

"Of course there's no electricity."

He had forgot the rituals of gaslight, how fragile light was. Raising the glass shade, he jostled the fragile Welsbach burner, which fell to bits against his sleeve. Gilbert lit his acetylene lamp. Dust danced in the burning cone of light. Underfoot, the carpet was patterned in small diamonds, optically the wrong size so that in the uncertain light the carpet seemed to be moving.

The door to the murder room was the first on the right; Reisden had learned the layout from Daugherty. He turned the knob and pushed, and nothing happened. It was locked.

"Richard! We don't really need to see inside."

"There's an office behind that room, yes? We'll go in through there."

The office was farther down the right-hand side of the hall. These shades were pulled down too. In the dimness it smelled like old papers and the same tarry cigar smoke familiar from the train. The door to the murder room was toward the front, beside a black marble fireplace. Reisden twisted its knob. Locked too.

"That room was cleared out," Gilbert said desperately. "There's nothing there."

"Later, then." He was half willing to give up seeing the room, half unnerved because he couldn't see it now.

"It was a room very like this," Gilbert said.

Reisden pushed back the swagged window curtains and carefully raised the rolled shades. Flat light sliced into the room. Two desks dominated the office, one enormous, simple, stark as a pyramid, the other exactly matching it but much smaller. "Jay French's?" Reisden asked, surprised.

"No, Richard. That desk was yours." The desks had matching uncomfortable chairs, wooden-seated.

"Mr. Pelham said it was habitable," Gilbert said doubtfully. "I suppose it is. He said nothing had been changed."

Every room had a fireplace, all in black marble. The pictures over the mantels ran to Biblical subjects. *The Presentation in the Temple* in the library, *The Sacrifice of Isaac* in the dining room. All over the first floor, like some skin disease on the walls, were little dead-white china plaques painted with Biblical quotations. WORK FOR THE NIGHT IS COMING. THOU GOD SEEST ME.

Upstairs the hall was angled to avoid the chimneys. William Knight's bedroom took up the front of the house, a huge shadowed bedroom with another black marble fireplace and a bed like a sarcophagus. Jay French's bedroom, adjoining, had the impersonal look of a servant's. On the other side, guest bedrooms that looked as if they had never been used: pompous, heavy, comfortless, with more Bible-leprosy on the wall. NO MAN KNOWETH THE HOUR OF HIS DEATH. I DEPEND ON THY MERCY ALONE. White marble fireplaces here, looking as though they had been carved out of old ice.

Richard Knight's bedroom was at the back of the house, past the uncomfortable turn of the hall. Reisden paused with his hand on the doorknob; he didn't want to go in, as if this would be something bad.

FEAR GOD AND KEEP HIS COMMANDMENTS. A BROKEN AND A CONTRITE HEART. A small, narrow bed, cheap white iron, with a shelf of books by it. A single gas jet, fixed to the wall. No fireplace or stove. No toys, not so much as a rubber ball. Reisden opened the closet door. There was still a boy's jacket hanging there, black serge alone in the closet, and a pair of scuffed black boots on the floor. Reisden closed the door and on an impulse went over and opened Richard Knight's window as if he could let the child out of the house. Outside the window, pine boughs brushed the house and filled the room with a bitter resinous smell.

Reisden looked down Richard Knight's pathetic row of books. American history. An algebra text, an atlas, and language texts in French and German. *Hast du denn Deutsch gehabt, Richard?* Poor Richard Knight, if he had been anything but the small-sized articled clerk William Knight had been training. World geography, with the principal trading routes drawn in by hand. A handwritten, sewn book on the essentials of accounting, "Written by William Knight for his Grandson Richard." Edifying stories of repentence.

They went upstairs to the servants' quarters. Tiny featureless cubicles: one bed, one dresser, one hook on the back of the door, one dead-white motto. It would be cold here in winter; there were no fireplaces at all. Gilbert tried to open one of the windows.

They didn't open; they were only panes of glass.

"We will board Mrs. Martin and Mrs. Stelling and the maids in town," Gilbert said with an un-Gilbertish determination. "They cannot possibly stay here; I would be ashamed."

"Yes," Reisden said. "Come outside."

Outside the house, Reisden breathed the outdoors smell of the hot grass, conscious again of the chill and moldiness inside. Gilbert looked around as if he had forgot something. "It is all so very strange. Not a nice house. Richard, how does it seem to you?"

Reisden shook his head. "I've never been here."

Gilbert took a few steps away from the house and looked back at it. Outside, in the heat, he took off his coat, folded it, and draped it across his arm as though he had no closet to call his own. He looked back at the house doubtfully. The corners of his mouth turned down and he shook his head, as if to himself. "Father is not here anymore, of course," he said half aloud. "That makes a great difference."

"Gilbert, he is dead." Underneath the locked window of the front room, the murder room, was a spill of stones across the dirt where water from the gutter had washed away the soil. The long windows reached almost to the ground. Reisden picked up two hand-sized stones. Deliberately, he tossed the first through the windowpane above the lock. With the second stone he chipped away the jagged edges of glass, then turned the window catch.

The room was empty. White walls stripped of all paper. A few lighter patches in the plaster. White ceiling. Plain whitened board floor, boards washed and scraped and holystoned. The black marble fireplace had a single long score across it where a bullet had ricocheted.

"Look," Reisden said. "There's nothing."

Gilbert pushed the window up and awkwardly stepped through, still holding his jacket. He laid it down on the floor, still folded. The rock was on the floor in the middle of the room; Gilbert picked it up as if absently and stood in the middle of the room, hefting the rock, staring all around him as if he were trying to take in all that emptiness. It was a good-sized granite rock, like a weapon or a talisman.

CHAPTER 20

HARRY HAD ARRIVED at the house while Reisden and Gilbert were still looking at the blank white front room where William Knight had died.

"Who broke the window?" he asked, looking at the gloomy house. And, after he had been upstairs and come down again, "Where's the bathroom?"

There was none. No inside W.C., though Gilbert said, stricken, that he believed there was one behind the barn. No bathtub. No shower. No hot water. No running water at all except through the pump in the kitchen. Reisden looked at Gilbert. Gilbert looked at Reisden.

"I really think we should stay with Charlie," Gilbert said with extraordinary firmness, "and have the plumbers in."

Within the next day or so Gilbert had decided how he was going to deal with his father's house. The plumbers came in, and the carpenters, and the painters. Two male decorators wandered through the rooms muttering darkly to each other and left samples of paper and paint. Gilbert walked through the house with a sturdy wooden box, took down each white china motto, wrapped it in newspaper, and stowed it in the box, murmuring with each one, "Forgive me, Lord." Workmen carried heavy furniture, drapes, and some very large pictures out of the house.

"We will make it quite modern," Gilbert said nervously.

Charlie Adair offered them two of what had been the Federal Hotel's suites; amusingly, at the opposite end of the building from Perdita Halley's room. Charlie Adair took his duties as chaperon very seriously; Harry and Perdita could not go out for a walk without Charlie's knowing where.

Perdita's piano was in the small parlor on the first floor of the Clinic. Reisden, wakeful in the early mornings, heard her practicing softly downstairs, well before anyone else was awake. Often at other times of the day he heard her practice: while Harry was out working on his sailboat, playing golf at the small links behind the Lakeside Hotel, or playing baseball with a scratch team. Harry dealt with tension by being athletic. Perdita by practicing early in the morning? No, she said when Reisden casually asked her, she always practiced then, she had since she was a child. Reisden wondered if Harry knew how close his sweet young girl came to working professional's hours. For that matter, did she know it herself, or realize how well she avoided making it plain to Harry? It would not work forever. Reisden could not imagine Harry happy alone in a cold bed at five in the morning while his young wife practiced piano.

Adair added himself to their evenings of reading and talk and piano playing, speaking mostly to Gilbert. As if by mutual agreement, Reisden and he never spoke.

TWO DAYS after they arrived, Reisden met the mistress of the green-and-yellow house, the redoubtable Mrs. Fen.

It was at a party for donors to the Clinic. Perdita was playing the piano in the corner of the Clinic's big reception room; Harry was telling someone else, in the middle of her playing, how well his girl played. Standing in the corner of the room was a tall, handsome woman in a red hat. She had her finger to her lips, half kissing it, and her eyes on Harry.

Amused, Reisden watched the byplay. The woman looked away for a moment, as if thinking, then looked back into Harry's eyes. Harry reddened angrily and looked away. When Harry looked back the woman was still gazing at him, her long frank gaze under the brim of her hat defining the situation as pointedly as a pin through a butterfly. Harry went red down into his collar and turned to face in the other direction, holding Perdita's arm. Lay off, darlin', Reisden thought at the woman; he's virtuous.

She turned around as if she had heard him, and her face froze in shock. Reisden knew the reaction. He wondered which of the Knights he reminded her of. She was in her late thirties perhaps, too young to have been acquainted with any of Gilbert's brothers.

Gilbert, perhaps?

No. Of course. Jay French. The back of Reisden's neck chilled.

Someone introduced them. "Richard Knight?" She

had a low, gravelly, intimate voice. She tried a long sexual look on him. He'd no intention of being taken for Jay French, but he held her hand a little too long, for the experiment's sake. She blushed red.

The question was how well she had known Jay.

"We must talk over old times, Mr. Knight," she murmured.

It was a certain offer to let him find out.

"MY DEAR, the scandal!"

Perdita's aunt Violet paced up and down the parlor in the Clinic. Perdita's cousin Efnie, Violet's blond daughter, yawned idly on the window seat. Perdita herself sat on the piano bench, the uncomfortable object of Aunt Violet's interest, and Charlie Adair stood at the door.

"Charlie, I blame you completely. A man cannot look after a girl." Aunt Violet laid down the law with one gloved finger, as certain as the *Women's Manual of Good Sense and Etiquette*. "The only proper chaperone is an older female relative. Perdita is an engaged girl, and as such she is at a particularly delicate time in her life. Her reputation is at stake. What does it look like when she is living here, practically out of town? And her fiancé living *in the same building?* She must pack her bags and come to us at the Lakeside at once."

Efnie yawned. "Mama, thank heavens you don't spend so much time worrying about me."

"Euphemia, I will thank you not to take the name of the Lord's judgment seat in vain."

"Pooh."

Perdita had sat through many of Aunt Violet's discussions before. "Aunt Violet, it's only until Island Hill is repaired. Then Harry will go there, of course."

"We'd be honored to have you here, Mrs. Pelham," Charlie said. "It's not as fine as the Lakeside, there's no elevator and you'd have to share a bathroom, but it'd be no problem for us. We could find a room or two right up at the top of the house, with a fine view."

"I blame Gilbert Knight for this. I blame Harry. Imagine considering only their creature comforts, instead of Perdita's reputation!" Aunt Violet swooped magnificently upon another subject like an eagle upon a mouse. "Perdita, it's not merely that you are living here, in a rackety way, on the edge of town. Or that your nearest neighbor will be your own fiancé—when he has the decency to move out of this very house—and Gilbert Knight's *supposed* nephew, whom I certainly don't believe in. *And* Anna Fen, the least respectable woman in town." Aunt Violet paused dramatically. "It is this diversion that you intend to engage in this summer. Playacting. *Scenes from Shakespeare.* An engaged woman painting her face? Spending every afternoon in the company of a woman known to be utterly without reputation? Displaying herself on a stage? Perdita, an engaged woman should be quiet, enclosed, like a walled garden, contemplating the great responsibilities of her married life."

"Mama!" Efnie jumped up and shrieked. "Don't be a prune! I'm going to play in *Scenes from Shakespeare.* All the good boys in town will be in it. And Perdita hasn't even got a real role, not half the one I have."

"You are not engaged yet, my love. But Perdita, your reputation—your reputation!" Aunt Violet added, "Anna Fen had her eyes *glued* to Gilbert Knight's so-called nephew yesterday. I knew her when she was young. She was nobody from nowhere, and she and

Susan Crandall used to hunt men in packs."

When Aunt Violet had gone, Perdita stayed behind a moment to talk with her uncle.

"Thank you, Uncle Charlie, you were wonderful. I didn't want to go stay with her at the Lakeside."

"Me neither, you'd have to share my room." Efnie yawned.

Charlie Adair chuckled. "Ah, she's a good woman and she has your best interests at heart."

Efnie giggled.

"Oh, I know, Uncle Charlie. But she worries about such strange things." Perdita hesitated. She knew she could trust Charlie not to laugh at her. "Uncle Charlie—Efnie—I didn't even really know what she was worrying about."

Efnie stared. "Perdita, you're such a muff."

"I believe she thinks that Harry might mistake being engaged for being married," Charlie Adair said bravely.

"What does that have to do with living in the same house?" Perdita said, still puzzled, and then understood what he meant. "Oh."

"You're a good girl." Charlie patted her on the hand and left the room.

"We would never," she said, distressed that Aunt Violet—who knew her!—would think such a thing.

"You wouldn't," whispered Efnie maliciously, "but Harry might."

"Efnie! Harry and I don't think about that," she said. "We're not married yet."

"Pooh."

But what if Harry did? Half of being blind was not having opportunities to learn. She knew quite well where babies come from; she had held the hands of women in labor in the Clinic, which certainly gave her some experience. But she didn't know how babies were got. How were men shaped, what did they do? What would she have to do when she and Harry were married? Other girls learned by looking at animals, hearing things on the street, asking their friends at school, looking into their father's or brothers' books. But she had been tutored and her brothers were out West. She could write her mother. *Dear Mama, Please tell me all about sex. Yours truly, Perdita.* But it would take weeks to get a letter West and back.

And in the meantime, Harry and she were living in the same house, away out of town, practically together.

CHAPTER 21

ROY DAUGHERTY, standing at the edge of the cleared fields behind the Knights' barn, passed his handkerchief over the stubble of his short hair. Harry stood by with his arms crossed, looking out at the woods. "I was a logger," Daugherty said, "winter or two, when I was a kid. Woods're a bitch."

The Knights' hayfields ended at the first trees. The hay grew tall and green among a tangle of bushes. Spiky old roses, still in bloom and fragrant, wove a curtain of thorns over a dead apple tree. Nameless bushes gave way to trees, vines tangled around saplings and branches. Farther into the woods Reisden could see the shadowy verticals of the old trees, leaning deadwood precariously balanced against still-living trees, and the occasional white line of birches.

"Remember a story from when I was a kid. Farmer goes out huntin' one day in November, in old woods not too much different from this. Don't come back. Whole town goes out lookin' for him, covers all the woods like a hat, don't find him. Winter goes, spring comes, wife carries on with the farm. Few years later she decides to have the land logged. Loggers find him, what's left of him, not more'n a hundred yards from his own place, dead and covered in ferns. Woods," said Daugherty, "they cover everything. Even take the smell away, less you get close. Richard, if he'd a got killed out here, he would have stunk in August—I remember it was real hot—but who'd a smelled it? We didn't start lookin' for a dead boy for a couple of weeks, and he would a moderated a good deal by then."

Harry kicked a rock and looked out at the woods. "You're not just going to lie down and not look for him, are you?"

"Sure, son," Daugherty sighed. "We'll divvy these woods up with surveyor tools and search by squares. We're going to look in every old cellar in town. We're double-checking all the records of found bodies any-where, 1887 or '88. We got a man in Charlie Adair's Clinic, tappin' the walls for Richard's body there, which I don't think it is. We're doin' a lot more that I won't bore you with. And maybe we'll get lucky and find a body. Or maybe Jay French'll call us on the telephone and say 'I know Reisden ain't Richard, I killed him and I buried him such-and-such a place.' "

"Maybe," Reisden said absently, "he'll simply come back and shoot me."

Daugherty sighed. "You gonna talk with Anna Fen, Reisden?"

"Yes, and with the rest of the list you gave me."

"Well," Daugherty grinned, "mind you tell me how it goes with *her.*"

"What if you don't find anything?" Harry said, and answered his own question. "You're going the fifteenth of August"— Reisden had set a time limit.

"Yes, in seven weeks." Reisden looked across the field to where the black automobile was parked.

"Daugherty, you have until August fifteenth to find Richard. If you don't, then, Reisden, you're going to tell my uncle you're a fake."

Harry invested the last word with startling venom and stared belligerently at Reisden. Harry wanted to make quite sure Richard was dead, and Reisden himself was the only Richard Harry had. The dead make bad enemies. If Harry said Reisden was a fake, Gilbert might not believe him, and that was not to be acknowledged between them, except in the pleasure that Harry took in antagonizing Reisden.

"I most certainly will, Harry," Reisden said equably, "Gilbert Knight and all the world; for I want no one to imagine that I am Richard Knight."

Later that morning Reisden overheard Harry being angry at Perdita because she was going to a piano lesson in Boston and would be gone all day. "You don't pay enough attention to me. You don't spend enough time with me." If Reisden was Harry's Richard, was Perdita his Gilbert? It would not do for that to go on, either for the boy's sake or for hers.

CHAPTER 22

ONE RAINY DAY at the Clinic, Daugherty had come over with his search records. He and Reisden occupied a visitors' parlor, the room next to the one where Perdita practiced her music. They pulled together two tables into a space twelve feet long and spread papers over it. On a large-scale map Reisden crossed out all the areas already searched. The Knights' house and barn, all but the barn attic, which held several tons of moldering hay that would have to be moved. The Clinic itself, which had been the Federal Hotel from which Richard Knight had disappeared. The area around the Clinic. Daugherty rolled out a map with a larger area, and the portion that had already been searched dwindled to a dot among miles of woods. Daugherty had hired a mixed crew of loggers and college boys. "College boys for in town, to be polite to folks," he said, "and loggers for up in the woods, where they got to know what they're doing."

Gilbert Knight wandered in during the middle of it. "To look for a body . . ." he quavered.

"You're the only person who really thinks I'm Richard," Reisden said, heartlessly gentle. Gilbert turned his eyes from their records and file cards as if they were soaked in blood.

It was late June already, little enough time to find anything.

Eventually Daugherty cleared away his papers and went for lunch, and Reisden had the parlor to himself. The rain increased until it was soaking and wind-blown, tossing the leaves of the trees by the lake and flattening the grass into green rivers. Reisden opened the window to get air and stood with the wind on his face, watching the storm. Gilbert would worry who would be hurt when the trees around the Clinic fell. Reisden went to the door and propped it a little open so that the draft would stir the air.

Because of the rain he heard Perdita crying.

It came from next door, her piano room. She was crying very softly, in little moans, as if she had fallen and was hurt. But as he opened the door, she was sitting on the sofa, in the half darkness of the rainy day, with no lights on, her head thrown back and a paper in her hands, crying like an abandoned child.

"Harry?" she asked.

"No, only me."

Harry would not be back until the afternoon, something she wouldn't usually have forgot. He sat beside her. Her hair was damp from the rain and her cheek was damp, like a little girl's.

"Tell me," he said when she had quieted.

"Mademoiselle——" Her voice broke and she leaned against him again. "Mademoiselle Brin writes that she won't give me piano lessons anymore, because I'm going to be married."

"What?"

Mademoiselle Brin was Perdita's piano teacher, a formidable French virgin who had studied at the Paris Conservatoire. "She says that I should go on with my music, but that I could never do it and be married. I would have to study in New York or Europe, not just in Boston, and go on tour, and my husband would never allow that. So it isn't worth her time to teach me—" The last sentence ended with a gasp.

"Nonsense." He gave her his handkerchief. "Stay here a moment." Adair kept liquor for guests in a cabinet by the fireplace. He came back with a glass. "Drink this. Not all at once," he warned as she obediently drank and choked.

"What is it?" She tasted it again. "Is it sherry?"

"Port wine, child. I am going to get you drunk and disorderly. Then we shall send you to visit her and you'll spit in her eye. First we'll talk, no?" Turning on the light, he sat down on the couch again, this time at a distance from her. In the light the wine shadowed her white dress red, and her two slim hands held the glass cautiously like a beaker of blood.

"She sent you a letter?" He looked at it. It was a particular cruelty to tell Perdita any news by letter. Her magnifying glass was on the piano bench. He could imagine how she had read through that letter, two inches of blurry writing at a time.

"First," he said. "What is required of you is to play the piano." She nodded. "You have skill; you practice; you think about music. You're very young, and of course you may stop caring about music, or not be good enough to want to go on. But it seems to me you are good enough to try."

"I'll always want to go on," she said in a trembling voice, too young to know about change.

"You also have other wants, which may conflict with your need to do music. You want to marry Harry, to be a daughter-in-law to Gilbert, to be a good wife. Yes?"

"To have children," she said, barely breathing, and blushing all the way down into her high collar. A fully sighted woman would have lowered her eyes. Hers were focused on him. He had the sensation of intimacy he remembered from the garden: he was intensely alone with her. Girls' clothes were designed to disguise the body, and one never knew what one would find under all the whipped-cream of white lace and cotton, but he had the distracting thought that if he set his imagination loose for an instant he would know what she looked like naked.

"Do you want children for yourself, or because Harry wants them?"

She spoke even lower: "For myself. Harry doesn't, not *so* much."

Oh. When he thought of it he was not surprised. "Children and music, then." Children and music, he wondered, or sex and music? One of the few thousand things one could not discuss with virgins. He wondered if anyone had told her that it was possible to have sex without having children. He didn't think so. This was America, with one of the least civilized attitudes in the world.

"Do you think that children and music are incompatible?" he asked her.

"I don't know." She added, "Harry says that—" and blushed deeply.

He could only imagine what misinformation Harry had. America had the Comstock laws and Boston had the Catholic Church, and young men like Harry got most of their information from the walls of urinals.

"Is it true," she asked, barely loud enough to hear, "that women who work—and think—can never have children?"

"Good G-d." He stared at her. "S. Weir Mitchell's work, and I thought he was dead. Don't believe it." Now he was on ground he knew. "Mitchell treated women who were physically exhausted and underweight, which *will* interfere. He put them on a regimen of bed rest, good diet, and no reading or other intellectual work. He got results. Conclusion: women should not read or write. If he'd done a double-blind—" He rephrased the jargon for her. "If he'd taken a similar group of women, given them rest and diet, and let them read and write what they pleased, he would have had something approaching an experiment. One of Mitchell's unpublicized results, by the way, was the complete nervous breakdown of one of his patients. Don't let it happen to you."

"He kept them from reading or writing?" said Perdita, shocked.

"Just so. Tell me about your mother. How many children does she have and what else was she doing when she bore them?"

She opened her mouth, then closed it again and grinned at him.

"I have six brothers and sisters. Three of each. They're all older and out in the West. And Mama was going up and down ladders on pueblos and riding donkeys and helping Papa with his books about the Indians all the time. She would explode without a pen in her hand. I suppose I don't have to worry about Dr. Mitchell."

No, just use your brain. He filed away for reference

that Perdita's mother did scholarly work. Hereditary professional woman: very promising. "How does your mother handle having work and her children?"

"I don't know."

"Ask her. Tell me, what do you have to do to be a professional musician?"

"Practice, first, and learn music."

"How many hours a day?"

"Seven or eight."

"Do you do that much?" he asked, surprised. He would have guessed five.

She nodded. "Most days."

"And you take lessons? How many times a week?"

"Twice."

"Do you give concerts?"

"Yes, of course! Maybe ten a year."

Once a month or so. "That's very good. What else will you have to do to develop yourself?"

She hesitated. The port glass was still in her hands. She seemed to want to gesture, but—no, he realized suddenly, she didn't know where to put it down, though the table was hardly four feet away. In the grey storm-light she was blind. He reached over. "Do you want your wineglass anymore? You don't have to drink it; it was to get your attention." She gave it to him gratefully. Her hands were freed, eloquent like most musicians'; they gestured angularly, gestures of dismay.

"I would have to go to other places, just as Mademoiselle says." Her voice was still very low. "I mean not Boston. I've learned almost what I can here. I would have to be away from Harry, really away, perhaps to Europe. I wouldn't know where I was. I'm not really sighted. I can't read street signs. I would always be lost in strange cities. Harry wouldn't like it if I ever left him to go away even for a night."

"Don't blame Harry."

"No," she said, her voice an edge of glass. "It's me. I'm afraid."

"Of going to strange places. It's odd you aren't afraid of giving concerts."

"Oh, no, I can do that." It was childish certainty. "I mean," she said, "it might go awfully and I might get a half bar away from the orchestra and the audience might like me only because I'm little and blind. But I can still do it. Once I find the piano bench and middle C, I'm there."

"All right, then. What do you need not to be lost?"

"Eyes," she said bitterly.

"Hire some."

She absorbed this in real puzzlement.

Among the other few thousand things one cannot tell virgins is that they are economic beings. "Don't tell me you can't. You have already told me who you are: You're a musician. Act like one. When you are married to Harry you'll be a rich woman. You'll have a personal maid. You'll want to go somewhere for lessons, perhaps New York. That's a few hours on the train. *Take her with you.* When you give concerts, the same."

"Harry wouldn't let me go to New York," she said. "He would think it'd be so wrong—a wife traveling without her husband."

Reisden sighed in exasperation. "Does he know you?" he asked patiently. "Does he know that you want to play music?" She shrugged, as if her wants in the matter had not quite come up between them. "Would you love him as much if you played music?"

Yes, her nod said.

"Would you love him as much if he helped you?"

"I would love him even more!"

"Do you think that will change when you marry him?"

She shook her head but didn't speak.

"Does he?"

Neither yes nor no. Her hesitation told it all. "As it happens," Reisden said, "you are right and he is wrong." Her dear Harry, who had minded when she had left him for a single piano lesson.

Reisden got up from the sofa and went over to the window. "I know how Harry feels," he said. "It is survivable." He didn't know whether he wanted to say this to her. It was more suited to Harry, and there was no way to say it without talking about his own history, which he had not brought into this affair and didn't want to. But she needed to know how Harry felt.

"She went to Glasgow. My wife," he began. "Just a week after we were married. You don't know, I think, that I was married. Tasy—Anastasia—was a professional musician, a singer in the chorus of an opera company. Only in the chorus, so she didn't actually have to go to Glasgow, they'd have found a substitute. But she went. I was very noble: Of course she had to go, it would help her career, I was busy at the lab anyway, I'd hardly miss her. My G-d, I was jealous. I'd been stung. She'd gone off and left me. I was alone without her. I'd never been so close to anyone as to be lonely without them. And I didn't like it. I was furious. Women shouldn't go off like that."

"What did you do?"

He was still looking out the window, remembering

Scotland in winter, the coal-black trampled slush and the lashing rain. "I went to Glasgow. I didn't think I should. Men don't act like that. I didn't think she'd respect me for it." He had wondered if she wanted to see him, if the whole company would laugh at him. "It turned out . . . very well." Tasy and he had made love in the manager's icy cold office, in their clothes, she in costume, between the second and the third acts of *Lakmé.* After that they really had not needed to do much explaining; and after that, too, Tasy had begun to get roles: one only needs to be noticed. She missed me too. So we never had to have much pride over wanting to be together."

"You loved her very much," Perdita said.

"She's dead," he said, closing the subject. "So. When you tell Harry that he is marrying a musician, expect him at first to be unsure what he is to do about it. Make him feel welcome in whatever you do. And make him do some of the work. Do you know what you will say to your music teacher now?"

"Yes, I think so."

He took both her hands in one of his. "Excellent. Can you get to Boston and to her house?"

"I always do. I take cabs."

"Of course you do. Get your coat and hat."

They smiled at each other.

And at just that unfortunate moment, Harry opened the door.

The two of them, Reisden and Perdita, stood frozen, for all the world like illicit lovers in a Victorian tableau. The room had all the elements: closed door, dimmed lights, and even a sofa on which the two of them had all too clearly been sitting.

"Harry!" Perdita said.

Reisden and she dropped hands and moved away from each other. Wrong move, Reisden thought inwardly; take it more slowly.

"Pet!" Harry groaned.

Reisden took charge; he had no interest in acting in French farce. "Miss Halley, you're going to the station?— Yes, you are. Go. Harry, I'm glad you're here; I want to consult you about the search. Sit down. Would you excuse us, Miss Halley?— Go," he murmured at her. "We shall talk again," he added for Harry's benefit, "when you have had a chance to consult with Mademoiselle Brin." He walked her to the door, not trusting that she knew where it was, and opened it for her. "I'll explain," he said for her ear.

"Oh my."

"He loves you," Reisden reassured her, still low; "but I will not if you don't get yourself a teacher." He closed the door behind her.

Harry was standing up, fists clenched. "What were you doing embracing my fiancée?"

Embracing. "Raping and pillaging, actually. We'd just done the rape part and I was trying to remember how to pillage."

Harry went completely white, as if Reisden had hit him in the stomach. Wrong move. Very wrong move. Harry brought his fists up. "Hit me, Harry, if you believe me." Reisden sat wearily down on the sofa again. "Miss Halley was upset and I calmed her down."

"You were holding hands."

"She was upset." Perdita would shake hands with both hands, kiss someone when meeting them. She held hands with Gilbert, which, when he'd first seen it, Reisden had thought peculiar. She was a person who touched. If Harry intended to be jealous of Perdita, he would have no trouble fulfilling his intentions. "You don't ask why."

"I know it's about Perdita's lessons," Harry said. "Miss Brin asked me awhile ago whether Perdita was going on with concerts after we were married. I told her of course not. She said she was going to stop giving Perdita lessons."

I told her of course not. "You told her Perdita was giving up music," Reisden said flatly.

"Of course. She won't have any time for it after we're married. She'll have to go on visits and give dinner parties. Her music isn't important and she spends too much time on it."

"You did expect her to be upset."

"She'll get over it."

Fool. Fool. Who was the fool? Reisden had known essentially what kind of person this boy was. Not unkind. Too unimaginative to know when he was being cruel. Harry could be changed, but it wouldn't be a day's work.

"Girls have time for things like music. Wives don't, Reisden. And Perdita will never give up me."

Harry said this with absolute certainty. And no, she wouldn't. Harry stood by the window, blond, tall, and handsome. Between their children and her Harry's love, Perdita would be very near happy. Unless she was a real musician—because what Harry proposed to deprive her of was all she really wanted. If she was real.

Perdita came back very late, by the last train at ten o'clock in the evening. They were waiting for her, all three downstairs in the Clinic parlor, Gilbert peering out the window and murmuring wretchedly about derailments.

"I didn't go to Mademoiselle Brin's at all," she said quietly, still in the doorway. But in the dim front hall she shone. Her girl's flat straw hat was pinned on crookedly; she pulled out the pin with one hand and simply let pin and hat fall on the floor as she shook out her hair. Unheard of. In her other hand she held a thick roll of music, nothing like the slim piece of Schumann she had been working on.

"Mademoiselle Brin is the best teacher in town who will take women students. But there is a man I wanted to work with. As long as—well, never mind. I went to him." Her face was lit inwardly. "I went to his office at the Symphony and said 'I need to be your pupil.' *I've been in Symphony Hall, playing the piano with him, for two hours, in Symphony Hall.* Harry—oh, Harry—" She held out her arms. Harry walked into them stiffly. "I am happier than I have ever been in my life," she said. She lay her head on Harry's chest. His eyes and Reisden's met over her head.

Remember who she is, Reisden thought at him. Isn't she worth more to you like this?

"Sure. That's great, Pet," Harry said.

CHAPTER 23

ON THE MONDAY before July the fourth, Gilbert, Harry, and Reisden moved back from the Clinic to Island Hill, and Gilbert took them on a tour of the house.

"Oh, Uncle Gilbert, it's really pretty!" Perdita said.

No, child, Reisden thought, nothing could make Island Hill pretty except being seen in a blur, but it was comfortable. Pale rugs on the old dark floors, wallpaper in shades of cream and leaf green, wicker settees and painted pine dressers. Harry thought the painted pine was embarrassing because one of the Knight factories made it. Reisden thought, but did not say, that it was rather Gilbertian furniture, painted to blend with the wallpaper, shy furniture. The dark paneling and black marble fireplaces had been texture-painted by an artist from the same factory, so that they seemed to be made out of curly maple. Harry said nobody but a man-decorator would paint marble. Reisden could feel the black stone glowering underneath, like a vibration or the memory of a lie.

One of the downstairs parlors had been turned into a music room with a piano. A pale, splendid Steinway dominated the room; everything else was delicately cream and ivory. If Gilbert were a man-decorator, he would have a future in it. Harry took one look around the room and frowned. Perdita sat down and made the piano speak, and was lost to them for the rest of the tour, but her piano music followed them into the other rooms.

Nothing had happened to the murder room. The same white plaster, the same black marble fireplace. "You ought to have done something to it," Harry complained. Reisden glanced at Gilbert.

"I just didn't have a good idea what to do," Gilbert said, distressed, as if forgetting were a matter of paint.

Harry's eyes met Reisden's over Gilbert's back, trying to stare Reisden down. "Do something," Harry said. *Give me Richard's body.* Reisden raised his eyebrows slightly and shrugged. Harry wheeled abruptly out of the room, and a moment later the piano music stopped.

THE FOURTH OF JULY was a Wednesday, hot and dry. Harry picked up Perdita at the Clinic before the parade. She was wearing pure white, and that irritated Harry. "People will think you're a suffragette."

Women voted in Arizona, Perdita objected mildly. Her own mother and her sisters voted. (She wanted to wear the green-and-purple VOTES FOR WOMEN button one of her sisters had sent her, but she knew it would irritate Harry. Secretly she had pinned it on the inside of her hat.)

"The Arizonans will stop that soon enough if they want statehood."

"Some of the Arizonans are women."

"You have a lot of opinions right now," Harry said. "You don't know anything, though, Pet, so you just make yourself look foolish. Don't you know the sort of women who started that movement? Don't draw attention to yourself; go up and change your skirt."

"Oh, Harry, I've only got this and the brown one; the rest are at the laundry." That was true, but she could have got them the day before.

"The brown one is fine. Come on, Pet, everyone's waiting for you."

She did change the skirt. After all, she had no political opinions, she didn't read the newspaper, she had no right to take part in discussions. Her degree of independence was going out to lunch alone. She honestly didn't know whether women should have the vote, or what the arguments might be against it; but she knew that there were women who did have opinions about it, and by not being one of them she felt herself in a smaller sphere. Harry was probably right, but it wasn't because she knew he had right on his side; she just had nothing to set against him.

Heavens, what would Harry think if she asked Richard Knight to read to her about women's rights? She laughed.

To be honest she ought to take the pin out of her hat. She thought about it until she knew Harry would be irritated that she was late. But she left it there, pinned underneath the hatband where no one would see it. It was not precisely an opinion. It was a question in her head.

She did not feel either good or brave.

The parade was in full swing when they arrived. Bands blaring, streaks of scarlet, hooting explosions of brass-colored light from a tuba or a trumpet, *bang bang bang* from the big bass drum. Flags thumped on flag-poles, blurs of salmon and pink. Perdita shaded her eyes from the glare. Harry hummed along with the Sousa marches. A string of firecrackers stuttered behind them.

"Hope they don't set off much a them firecrackers. Morning, Miss Perdita. Morning, Harry."

Perdita liked Roy Daugherty. When she was little and visited Uncle Bucky's office, he had always had a few pieces of some kind of old-fashioned candy in his desk.

"Woods are dry as paper. We ain't even had mosquitoes up where we been searchin'. I ain't been letting my men much as smoke up there. I'd be purely disgusted if anyone sets off a box full of fireworks in all them dry leaves."

"But they will certainly try it," Gilbert Knight agreed mournfully, "and the most appalling accidents happen with fireworks. Mr. Daugherty, I heard of a young man who set off what he thought was a very small one, but the manufacturer had put the wrong kind of powder in it and it blew his face completely off. I expect it happens all the time."

"I bet you'd like us to stay inside with the windows closed during the fireworks," Harry said sourly.

Perdita squinted to see whether Richard Knight had come with Uncle Gilbert. He had made a practice of not coming into town because of all the notoriety around him. But there he was, a tall shadow. "Good morning, Miss Halley."

"Good morning—" She made her own practice of not calling him Richard, since he didn't like it. "Do you like the parade?"

"Yes—because for once I am not it. Do you?" A trumpet blatted off-key. She made a face; they laughed together and fell easily into conversation.

"There is our neighbor Anna Fen," he said. Perdita

saw a tall white dazzle—oh, good heavens, Mrs. Fen was wearing white! And even her eyes could make out the huge green and purple cockade on Mrs. Fen's shoulder.

"There's an association I've saved you from, Pet," Harry murmured.

"Votes for Women!" Mrs. Fen's low, carrying voice sounded like someone on stage. "Mr. Knight, wear a button for the ladies. Mr. Boulding, will you take a button from me?"

"What does it say?" Harry gibed. " 'Free Love'?"

"Harry!" Perdita hissed.

"Miss Halley, will you wear a button for yourself?"

Perdita flushed and took a step back. "I—" She shook her head. Under her hatband her own button pressed against her forehead. Her own sister's button, but if Harry ever saw it he would think she had got it from Mrs. Fen in secret. Better to disagree with Harry openly once. "Yes, please, Mrs. Fen," she said, louder than she had meant to. Harry would be furious.

"Very good, Miss Halley." Anna Fen pinned the button on her. She was surrounded by a cloud of perfume, a thick, complex odor. That choke of sweets and flowers was the best argument Harry had, it was insistent, like the rest of Mrs. Fen: that flaunted, purring voice and the hands that moved around Perdita's collar. Perdita felt panicked, as if she had agreed to much more than she knew. "Mr. Richard Knight?" Mrs. Fen said.

"Not Richard, nor American, Mrs. Fen: I don't vote here."

"Neither do we," she purred back at him. "So you must take a button. Here, I'll pin it on."

Would she pin it on the same way, Perdita wondered,

and would Richard Knight smell her perfume while she did it?

"Well, then," Roy Daugherty rumbled, "I'll take me one of those buttons too. Mr. Knight, you want one? Harry?"

"Yes, I believe I will," Uncle Gilbert said. "No, thank you, Mrs. Fen, I'll pin mine on."

"Free Love!" Harry muttered.

The four of them spent the day together: Gilbert, Richard, and Harry and Perdita. It was awkward. Gilbert did not at all like being out in society, not even informally at the parade, since it brought up the dreadful strangeness about Richard. Gilbert tried to introduce him to some people, but Richard smiled and asked him not to: "What name would you give them?" So they kept themselves to themselves at the parade and at the town picnic afterward, and Gilbert stayed a distance away from Richard so that he would not be caught in an introduction, and when people came up to Richard and introduced themselves, Gilbert saw Richard shake his head: *no, I'm not Richard,* saying it with exactly Tom's smile.

It was worse, if possible, with Harry. Away from his friends down in Boston and Nahant, Harry carried Perdita with him everywhere like a toy he had to have. At first Harry made Gilbert introduce him and Perdita: "This is my adopted nephew Harry Boulding and his fiancée, Perdita Halley." But that was not good either, because so many people asked where Gilbert's other nephew was, and once, terribly, asked for his *real* nephew. So Perdita and Harry went around the crowd by themselves, Perdita introducing Harry. "This is my fiancé." Gilbert finally hid in the Clinic and played a game of chess with Charlie.

That night the fireworks screamed and banged over the lake like old battles remembered. Gilbert went to bed and dreamed disjointedly of flares spattering red light into the sky, Verey flares, window-shaking guns and gunfire. In his dreams he fled through burning orchards. Gilbert was an ambulance man again, but Charlie was driving the ambulance and somehow the war was mixed up with Father and Richard. In the dead hour of the night Gilbert shivered and woke, dreading something undefined. He took the candle by his bed and went to check on his nephews.

Harry was asleep soundly, muttering and snoring under the covers. Richard's door was half-closed and the electric light still on. Gilbert peered around the door. The papers Richard had been studying had fallen on the floor. Richard had never gone to bed but had fallen asleep uncomfortably in his chair, his long legs stretched out in front of him and his arms crossed. He looked much more tired than when he was awake, all the animation gone out of his face, shadows under his eyes and the beginnings of lines around his mouth. His head had fallen against the chair-back awkwardly so that his reading lamp was shining into his eyes.

Gilbert hesitated by the door for a long time. Even though Richard was asleep, the light in his face must be uncomfortable. Gilbert thought of waking Richard, of getting him a blanket, of doing anything that would make him comfortable here. It was the light that he wanted to change most, it made Richard seem so helpless, and after a moment he entered Richard's room and carefully turned out the light. He stood in the half-dark.

But Richard would know he had been here. Was he interfering in Richard's privacy? In panicked shyness, Gilbert swung the heavy bronze lamp around so that the shade was at a better angle, then, shadowing it with his arm, turned the lamp on again. As if by accident Richard's face was shaded from the light. Gilbert backed very quietly out of the room.

He lit his own reading lamp and read Dante's *Purgatorio* to settle his mind. Eventually Dante wrapped him round with sleepiness like grey cotton wool. He had half fallen asleep in his chair when there was a sudden rap at his door.

"Gilbert."

"Richard? What is it?" He panicked for a moment because of having moved the lamp.

"Will you come here, please?"

He swung open his hall door. Richard was outside, as self-possessed as if he had been to bed and dressed again, but looking pale. Beside the little light they always kept burning, there was a strange red tinge to the darkness in the hall.

"What?" Gilbert said sleepily.

"Look toward the town."

He came out into the hall. Behind Richard he could see through the big new window on the staircase landing, all across the lake. The town buildings were silhouetted across the water in a red waving light that reached in streamers into the sky. "Oh, that cannot be," Gilbert said, because whatever he had said and believed about the danger of fireworks, he did not really believe that fireworks would do anything more than frighten him. No more had he really believed that Richard would come back, except in his desires.

As he watched, one of the silhouetted houses crumbled, just like a log in a fire—he knew the people there, one of the housemaids boarded with them. He rushed to the window and looked out, over the whole lake. In the terrible glow and sparkle of the fire, everything was dissolving in the light; there was no land, only water, smoke, and flame.

"It's coming toward the Clinic," Richard said.

CHAPTER 24

WHEN GILBERT, Harry, and Richard got to the Clinic, the children were already streaming outside, into the fields, running toward the lake. Charlie came out of the house, still dressed in his bathrobe and pajamas, leaning on Perdita's arm.

By the lake three trees were burning. At this distance the flames made no sound, wavering quietly in their own heat like giant candles. Through baroque gauzes of smoke the station was aflame. The fire was coming fast, moving up the road in a fan past the Clinic fields. Gilbert stood openmouthed. Shockingly, Father's railroad car was burning in the siding by the station, as if the fire did not know who Father was. Let it burn, Gilbert thought. And the house too—but to get to Father's house, the fire would have to take the Clinic first.

"Richard, I'll stay with Charlie."

"Yes. Be careful."

"Be careful," Gilbert said to both of his nephews, but it was Richard's words he was repeating. Apprehension balled in a lump at his throat. Richard, be safe.

Reisden and Harry plunged into the smoke. "We need men for the bucket brigade, men and women for the bucket brigade!" a lank voice droned in a background of shouts. A woman in an apron waved her arms and sobbed. "There are six horses in my barn," an old man cried. "I need help with my horses."

Harry and Reisden led the horses out one by one, draping saddle blankets over the horses' heads so the animals could not see the flames. Harry was trembling almost as much as the first horse he led out. "Don't be afraid. They won't rear," Reisden said. "They won't move unless you lead them." It wasn't entirely a lie. Reisden in his shirtsleeves, manhandling the horses out between burning timbers, thought calm at them. The horses stepped out quietly and stood under the trees in the dawn.

They got out five; but as they tied the fifth's lead rein, the barn swayed and leaned to one side. A great blast of heat puffed into their faces. A fireman shouted and waved them back. Some joint gave, burned through. Half the barn sagged and sighed inward; the fire reached up to explore the air half a story above where the roof had been, and finding nothing, runneled back over the still screaming and collapsing timbers, cracking and digging at the wood. Over that hideous noise came another scream, and out of the fire for a moment rose a living head, all fire, all mouth and burning mane. The cry seemed more noise than a horse could make. "Can't someone shoot it?" a woman quavered, but the barn sank slowly down over it. The old man moved among the living horses, patting their heads; they huddled in a circle by him. Someone had rescued a handful of tackle, and he stooped and picked up a bright new bridle and held it awkwardly to his chest.

The Children's Clinic had an engine to itself. Channeled by a long hose from the lake, the water pumped through the smoke and played over the windows. On the long verandah, it blew over the potted plants; they lay with limp leaves and mud spilling from their pots. The nurses held the children back. Charlie Adair watched the fields burn below the Clinic. *Hail, Mary, full of grace, the Lord is with thee, don't let the Clinic burn* . . . Mother of God, think of the children shut up in tenements in Boston. Hail Mary, full of grace, the kids need us. The fire crept up the fields toward the ramshackle white building, and the carved gilt eagle screamed on its cupola like a trapped phoenix. Charlie Adair watched the sparks land on the battered shingles of the Clinic, and char the shingles and the first planks of the porch; and then the wind changed, and the fire rose back up over the black fields, and finding nothing left to burn, guttered and fell harmlessly away. The children played in the puddles on the lawn, then demanded their breakfast.

Perdita and Gilbert were in the bucket brigade, passing galvanized buckets until their arms were half pulled out of their sockets. They were pushed and led from one place to another as the fire grew, spread, and was beaten down again. Perdita held Gilbert's elbow as they shuffled along in the crowd through the smoke; Gilbert gave her news. "Five houses gone! Everybody safe, though, that's the important thing. Charlie's safe—all the children—the Clinic is safe—no one hurt."

The fire took its toll among the farms north of town, then veered in a gathering wind out into the woods. The biggest battles were fought there. Reisden's black automobile was commandeered since it was the fastest thing in town. Reisden drove through the morning woods down obscure logging roads, with Roy Daugherty in the passenger seat and on the floor a case of dynamite. "Sure hope I remember how to blast a firebreak," Daugherty commented. Going around curves, the black car bucked and fought, slewing over the ruts. Daugherty clutched the dynamite. They stopped near the edge of the fire while Daugherty threw sticks of dynamite, apparently at random, into the edge of unburned woods. Trees crashed nearby, dirt rained around them. "Want to try one?" Daugherty asked him. Reisden threw and they ducked as branches flew over their heads. The firebreak was beginning to make sense: piled green trees, then a cleared area.

"One could get to like this," Reisden said.

Anna Fen's green-and-yellow barn burned, with all the *Scenes from Shakespeare* costumes inside it; but her house and all her animals were saved. Seven houses burned in all, eleven barns and other outbuildings, one wooden roof with an ornamental cupola where the owner kept pigeons. A fireman smashed shutters just in time. Back in town, in front of the house of a Mrs. Bartarin, Reisden saw the pigeons fly free, wheeling in the hot air. Mrs. Bartarin's housemaid and her two daughters made lemonade inside the house; Mrs. Bartarin, smiling on the porch, ladled it out for the firemen. She was a fat woman with a sooty hospitable face. She handed Reisden lemonade in a cut-glass tumbler as elaborate as a vase.

"Don't you find it quiet in our little town, after the big city?"

"Do you do this often?"

She chuckled. "My husband just came by, he said the worst's over and done with, thank Heaven!" She talked on comfortably. Her family had spent the summer at the lake for more than thirty years. (Reisden made a mental note: Emma Bartarin, here when the Knights died.) Her husband manufactured candy. "I used to be thin as a new moon before my Walt spoiled me." Reisden watched a grey house down the street. Earlier the fire had blackened its outbuildings and now, from the wet, charred back of the house, smoke was creeping out again. As they watched, a window exploded outward with a great bang of smoke and they saw the fire inside.

"Land, another one." Mrs. Bartarin's round face furrowed. "The Yeos' house. They have a little one, Nellie, only three years old; I hope her parents are looking after her." The firemen were nowhere to be seen. A woman with an older child in tow was standing in the front yard, looking around, calling out sharply. Mrs. Bartarin sucked in her breath.

Two figures came into the front yard, a man and a girl. The older woman was protesting wildly, shaking her head, pointing at the burning house. The man ran inside. He was tall and muscular with blond hair. The girl stayed for a moment with the older woman, then—In the yard of the house was a pump; the girl backed up against it, pumped the handle quickly, and stood while the spout soaked her dress, then bent down to wet her long hair.

Mrs. Bartarin's glass crashed on the ground, lemonade and splinters of glass. "Is Nellie still *in there?*" she cried out.

Perdita ran inside the house after Harry and the woman's child.

Nothing, nothing at all for about thirty seconds. The fire was taking the back of the house. They'll both die, Reisden thought quite calmly; he was already running toward them. The screen door at the front opened but only Harry came out, coughing and retching from the smoke. He straightened up and looked around, kept looking around, expecting Perdita to be there.

Air was being sucked in through the open door. The porch floor was smoldering. Harry made a rush at the door but the heat drove him off it, coughing and retching from the smoke.

"Go get help!" Harry shouted at Reisden. "What are you doing?"

"Get the bloody ladder." There was one standing against an apple tree in the garden. Reisden hit at the square porch pillars with a shovel from the garden; pillars and porch and tin roof fell over the burning steps. The ruined door fell; in the short protection the porch gave, Reisden climbed over it and jumped down inside.

PERDITA had been in the Yeos' house often when they had hosted musicales for the Clinic. "Nellie, Nellie, where are you?" The heat hit Perdita's face, in her eyes, her throat, and then the smoke. Nellie would be upstairs in her room, with her dolls. Perdita held her arm over her nose and face, trying to breathe through the wet cloth of her sleeve, and felt with her other hand. Five steps forward, then turn and up the stairs. Her foot found the first step. In the upstairs hall the carpet ticked and crackled beneath her feet. The oily smoke choked her. She groped forward, arm over her nose and mouth, eyes burning and half-closed, feeling her way with her feet. "Nellie!" she shouted.

Somewhere behind her the little girl shrieked.

Perdita turned around. The hot dimness pressed on her eyes like dirty cotton wool; she could see nothing, nothing, but here and there and nowhere a dim red light, smarting red. Somewhere in front of her she saw sharp redness, a flame, close, too close. In a blink it was gone. She touched the wall to spot herself, then coughed as she snatched her hand back; she had touched something hot.

Nellie was crying, somewhere close. "Mama! Mama!"

Back farther along the hall. Three doors on the right, she thought, two on the left. The house was full of noise, creakings and groanings. She found a doorknob and opened it.

Paler, dim, blurry light. She felt the head of a rocking horse, bumped against a little girl's dollhouse. "Mama!" She shouted. "Nellie!" The smoke was coming in after her. She shut the door. The little girl's voice was muffled by something. "Nellie, where are you? I'm taking you out to your mama!"

She blinked desperately, trying to see motion. Nellie was scared and hiding. Under the bed, maybe; but where was the bed? She groped forward, fanning out both arms to find it. "Nellie, please!"

"I can't! My dollie doesn't want to!"

"Where are you, honey?"

Only a shriek. Where was the closet? She could not even find the bed. There was the slightest sagging in the floor. She crouched down, touched the floor with her fingers; it was hot. She felt her way forward, trying to find the closet door, a window—

She had lost the door to the room. She didn't know where it was; she had let its position get away while she was looking for the bed.

She didn't know how to get out of the room.

Downstairs someone shouted. "Here!" she cried out.

"Stay there! I'm coming."

Not Harry, but Richard. She stood stock still on the hot floor, waiting until she felt his hand. He took her by the arm, holding her tightly.

"This way—" He was coughing too. "Quickly. The stairs won't last."

"Nellie's here! In the closet!"

"Right." She heard a door bang open. Nellie shrieked in panic; Perdita held out her arms and he thrust the heavy little girl into them. Nellie kicked and twisted; Perdita held tight. Reisden pushed her forward. Perdita's shoulder scraped against the doorjamb. The hall floor shook delicately, like a dance floor; the house creaked; the smoke streamed past them. She felt the knob of the stair rail, and then quite suddenly the smoke cleared and she felt a sudden shock and saw a bright red and yellow light. She stared, fascinated, over Nellie's head; there was a rumble overhead, she flinched—

"Back, *fast!*" he shouted and pulled them back with him; he pushed her into the shelter of a door and slammed it shut between them and the stairs. She heard a screaming like nails pulled loose from wood, and a buffeting, and a moan.

"It's the stairs," she choked.

"It's the stairs."

"But there's no other way to get out—"

The smoke was less thick in this room; for a shade of a moment too long she could feel him, through it, only looking at her. "But we have to," she said, "can't we get out?" and she felt him give a great gasp, and he said, "Oh no. Not you." She screamed out because she did not understand it and because he sounded so strange and desolate, and she ran at him pounding with the fist of her free hand at his chest and arms, as if he were some sort of machine that did not work, and he caught hold of her and held her awkwardly while she struggled, and Nellie threw back her head and screamed in panic.

"Not you," he said, coughing, "I'll get you out, I promise it. I *promise* it, both of you."

Outside the door, the wind of the fire screamed.

"Window," he said against her ear. "Find it."

The room was crowded with hot dim objects they bumped against in the smoke. They knocked against a brass railing, something that careened crazily away from them, and finally something hard with a smoldering cushion over it. He kicked it out of the way, and knelt, and felt along the floor for something to throw through the window, but it had no lock and no catch; he reached out through the smoke and slid it up. The cold air blew into the room. A great yellow fan of sunlight made the smoke misty; then it was quite thin and he could see.

The ground was too far. Four or five people were huddled in a group in the yard. Down below was the stone carriageway of the house, hard grey blocks fitting smoothly together. The figures down below waved and pointed and all turned at once, away from them, looking at something else. Two men came around the side of the house carrying a long ladder. One of them was Harry.

"You'll go first with the child," Reisden said. "You

can carry her?" Perdita nodded. The end of the ladder scraped against the house and crumbled away paint with it. It rested below the sill. "Out, now." He held Nellie awkwardly while she clutched at the side of the ladder. It was so long it was springy; it bent under Perdita's weight. He passed Nellie to her, then held the end of the ladder. Nellie held her around the neck; she had Nellie around the waist and only one hand for the ladder.

Perdita felt for each of the rungs. The bushes by the house were burning; the heat and smoke runneled up; she lowered herself and Nellie from rung to rung. The ladder would char; it would burn. Halfway down she looked up and she could no longer see him; there was what seemed like smoke pouring out the window, and he was still inside, with the flames. She slid and stumbled down toward the bottom, almost falling. Hands reached up to her, she gave Nellie to someone familiar—she blinked, it was Uncle Gilbert—and she jumped from the last rungs off the ladder and looked up.

Reisden felt through the wood the jar of its sudden lightness, and almost at the same time felt a larger jar that shook the frame of the house. The window shuddered and slid an inch or so downward. Below, at the foot of the ladder, he saw a crowd of people. He ducked under the window and steadying himself with a hand on the sill, found his foothold. Just off balance on the ladder, he felt another jar go through the building. The sill had cracked from end to end; he looked up, at the top floor and the overhanging roof, and saw them move.

The ladder began to fall in toward the flames; he threw his body backward and hit out at the wall, trying to overbalance the ladder in the other direction. It balanced, hesitated; in front of him the whole window, frame and glass, cracked and disintegrated into splinters; he flung his arm up to protect his face and felt himself falling, he didn't even know which way. By instinct he kicked the ladder away from him and simply dropped. Something hit the ground inches from his skull; he rolled and ended up on his back, stunned. There was sky; there was grass under his face and fingers; nothing he moved seemed to be too much damaged. He sat up dizzily. The ladder was on the ground, broken-spined, one end burning merrily. The lawn and carriageway were littered with burning debris: shingles, a broken rocking chair, part of the roof, every sort of wreckage; but he had landed clear. The grass was singeing brown. He stood up and got rather uncertainly as far as the fence that ringed the yard. He leaned against the gatepost, watching the house burn down. He could hear the little girl coughing and crying. That was all right then. Someone touched him on the arm; he recognized Perdita, who was looking at him with a mixture of horror and shyness and concern. When she saw he was all right, she hugged him and burst into sobs. Perdita wasn't dead. He put his arms wordlessly around her and held her. The straight parting of her hair was tousled and her hair was wet; that seemed to him very touching and important, that she had thought to wet down her hair. The fire belled up from the wreckage. He watched it as if from a very great distance. How had he got out? At best, he knew, they should have got out her and the child.

Gilbert Knight stood in front of him. Eyes like the stare of a tragic mask, wild white hair sticking up. Brown liver spots stood out on his face. Richard, he said soundlessly. Reisden saw the scene through Gilbert's eyes. *I nearly killed your Richard, didn't I?* The burning beams of the house cracked and a part of the wreckage swayed lower. Gilbert was flinching with his need to be reassured. Reisden would not look away from him and would not reassure him. Gilbert's eyes filled and he blinked. He groped for Perdita. "You're all right, my dear?" he asked, safe to ask. She soundlessly put out an arm to hug him too. She was still trembling against Reisden. "My dear, you aren't hurt?" Gilbert quavered. "You mustn't cry?" He put an arm around her, and as if it were an afterthought, put the other around Reisden. Something broke in Reisden and he reached out and put an arm around Gilbert too.

"I'm all right, don't worry," he said.

"Oh," Perdita said, half laughing, crying as unself-consciously as a baby, and still holding on to them both, "oh, I'm so scared *now.*"

"Don't," Reisden said. "If you're scared I will be." True. He could be terrified if he thought of it. One of the last windows broke with a pop, flinging glass. He held up his arm to protect her. "We'd better move back." They retreated, still in a huddle. None of them would let go their unlikely triple knot, clinging to each other. Reisden was afraid that if he let go of her, stopped looking at her even for a minute, she would not have got out, she would be crushed under the smoke-steaming beams, screaming like the dreadful horse they had not saved. He bent his head over her and they held each other so tightly that he felt the press of her breathing against his own. He was intensely grateful to her for being still alive. "Richard saved you, you know!" Gilbert was saying, laughing a little, patting them both on the arm, making a little joke.

Richard?

"Not Richard," said Harry behind them. "Pet, come away." But for a moment she still clung to them; and Reisden, looking up at the big blond boy, saw something crack in his assurance, his certainty that he was everything to someone. Idiot boy, your woman is alive, you have someone to love, don't ask for hostages. But Harry stared back at him, flat-eyed.

CHAPTER 25

IN THE AFTERMATH of the fire the whole landscape seemed black, skeletal, ghostly in smoke. The fence that had kept the Clinic children away from the road was twisted metal in blackened grass. The children touched the hot fence and stepped gingerly in the hot grass, feeling the crackling and pricking of the lawn that had been soft.

Everything smelled like caramel with a nauseating underodor of char. Perdita did not know how to deal with the change in her landmarks, fences that had melted, trees that had disappeared in an afternoon. She clung to Harry. But all the time she felt Richard's arms around her. When the ladder had fallen she had screamed out so loud that she was hoarse afterward. She loved Harry, but Richard had been about to die.

"I saved you," Harry said. "I brought the ladder."

She said nothing for a moment, rationalizing that her throat still hurt. "Yes, that's true."

"I always do the right thing," Harry said quietly, "and nobody ever gives me credit."

Two months, a month ago, she would have said, "That's right, poor Harry," and she wouldn't have done it out of loyalty to him but because it was true. And it was still true, but Harry didn't have to say it. She broke into tears, she clutched at him, weeping in futility against his muscular arm. She didn't want to find Harry imperfect.

"There, Pet, you're just tired out," Harry soothed her, and she took refuge in that, womanly and weak, and cried harder.

REISDEN was unable to stop noticing Perdita.

It was a plague of noticing, of common unsensual things like the shape of her hands and her eyelids, the way she sat down at the piano bench or gestured or laughed. He could not be in a room with her without being drawn to her, his eyes and ears attached to her on short strings. It was a common malady among those who had gone through the fire. Reisden saw Mrs. Bartarin once on the street, the neighbor of little Nellie Yeo, whom Reisden and Perdita had got out of the house. "When I see Nellie now, I just go straight up to her and hug her. I'm so happy she's alive," Mrs. Bartarin had said, and hugged *him*. Reisden had no desire whatever to hug little Nellie Yeo. But he could have stood for hours with his arms around Perdita, learning how to believe that the world was not as fragile as it had seemed.

And so, perhaps because so, he went to see Mrs. Fen.

He actually had business with her. With Mrs. Fen's barn had burned not only the Shakespeareans' costumes but their rehearsal space. Barn space was at a premium this summer, and almost the only barn not being used was the Knights'. Perdita had asked Gilbert for it on the Shakespeareans' behalf.

Anna Fen kept Richard Knight waiting twenty minutes, and came downstairs holding a hat, wearing casual white cotton, as if she had just been interrupted at her garden; but the dress was unrumpled and very attractive. He would have been flattered to be so dressed for, if she had dressed for him. She stood for a moment at the door, looking at him with the shadows of old thoughts in her eyes.

"Mrs. Fen?"

She sank down into a cushiony chair as if it had been her bed. "Anna Fen," she said; call me Anna, the tone of the throaty voice suggested. "Please sit down."

He did so, and made the offer of the Knights' barn, which she accepted. "You are so kind." Her eyes looked up at him. You are so kind.

She served him tea. They sat on either end of the same long sofa. "My gardener says that you are putting on a search for yourself, Mr. Knight."

He smiled. "I'm not Richard."

"How extraordinary."

"Much more extraordinary if I were, after all this time."

She bit a cookie, looking over the edge of it at him. "You don't remember me."

"Another proof I could not possibly be Richard." He wondered what precisely about her, and about Jay French, Richard was not supposed to remember.

"I didn't know the Knights well," Anna Fen continued. "William Knight wanted privacy. We could see Island Hill only from our wharf."

"Did you ever visit the house?"

"I don't think so," she said after a hesitation.

"Did you know any of the household?" he asked

quite bluntly, wondering what answer he would get.

"No. Of course not. They were a household of bachelors. They didn't entertain."

She got up and fiddled with some peacock feathers in a vase, looking at him all the time, wanting to see how she affected him. She kept her parlor feminine: a universal ruffle of flower-printed chintz, lacy furniture scarves and potpourri, frivolous and complicated. The couches were deep and covered with pillows.

"My late husband knew Jay French slightly, because of the suit."

"Suit?"

"William Knight sued Michael over our dogs. They fouled his footpath. So he said."

"Were you here the evening of the murders?"

"I was here by myself. Michael was away. I didn't see anything or hear anything until the police came. It's so long ago, I was very young."

He phrased the next question carefully. "Were you in any way unsurprised at the murder?"

"I was very surprised," she said sharply. This bit of the conversation was real, Reisden thought. "Jay was very fond of William Knight, very devoted to him. My husband always said so. I was very surprised that he could murder William."

"Charlie Adair saw him doing it," Reisden said.

"Come outside with me," she said. She pushed open the French windows and they walked through her garden and down a short gravel path. They crossed the road and cut through a screen of trees to her dock. Her motorboat with the ruffled sunroof bobbed in the water by the dock, looking unused. She stood on the wharf and pointed across the water.

"Charlie saw *someone*. You can't see much of Island Hill from the road. The woods are in the way from this house onward." She pointed in a swath along the edge of the lake. The ugly bulk of Island Hill was visible across the water. It was a bright day and the house was a white block against the green of the lawn. Jay French would have been a little figure from this distance.

"Charlie thinks it was Jay," she said. "That's all."

"Who killed William, then?"

She shrugged. "Who killed Richard?" she asked. "Since you're not Richard?"

"Then Jay didn't do that either?" he asked.

"I don't know," she said, and her eyes were shadowed again.

He watched her. She smiled and lowered her eyes. She leaned against the handrail of the dock, jiggling one knee under her thin cotton skirt. There was a little breeze blowing; it flattened her skirt against her thighs and long legs. Reisden smelled the heat of the lake water, waterweed, and Mrs. Fen's mixed perfumes. Anna Fen had called Jay French repeatedly by his first name without remarking on it. "It's warm," she said.

"Very warm," he said.

She looked up at him. "Come in the house. It's cooler there."

She was the sort of woman he knew all through. He would perform very well for her and she for him. Neither one of them would be disappointed, or very much surprised. It was far too much to say that he was bored before the thing started. Rather he was bored with himself in it. How much extra work would it be to get the information without the woman? He could see her when he needed to; she would be in the Knights' barn every afternoon rehearsing *Scenes from Shakespeare.*

On the whole, he thought he would let himself be a little courted before he gave in.

He made decent excuses. She tossed her head and turned away down the path. "Come see me again," she said.

"I will."

CHAPTER 26

PERDITA FELT LEFT OUT of *Scenes from Shakespeare.* Mrs. Fen asked her to do the music, which was good; but the place to be this summer was around the actors. Like most blind people Perdita had never acted in any kind of theater, because actors must position themselves on visual marks. But she could have found her position by counting steps or watching large objects, the way she did on the street, and she could have said the words well. Blind people know words. But no one thought of her.

Richard Knight was all taken up with the actors and Mrs. Fen. Obviously he knew about plays and acting. Mrs. Fen had got together a list of the scenes they were to act, and he only looked at it and said, "No, this probably isn't what you want to do." Before Mrs. Fen could take offense, he was talking with her about having a theme and pacing, moving the action around on the stage, giving time to change costumes. Mrs. Fen's voice went all soft like overripe fruit. "Oh, Mr. Knight. Of course, Mr. Knight." She stuck to him like glue.

He came in every day toward the end of the afternoon; Perdita could feel his arrival because every voice in the barn would stop a minute, then shift, and all the people hurry toward him. They wanted to know how to read their parts, where they would go on stage. The man who was building the sets wanted his advice on something. The two boys who were learning the sword fight wanted him to show them how. Mrs. Fen wanted everything, and she would stand at his elbow and talk to him while he did it all. There was something entreating in her voice when she talked to him, something confident too.

No answering sweetness in his: only tired, competent, amused. Perdita listened hard and heard no more than that.

"Mrs. Fen goes after any man," Efnie gossiped casually. "Mama says that she's closer to Richard Knight than his own trousers."

"Oh, Efnie, no!" Perdita gasped.

"At least Richard keeps her away from your Harry."

Perdita could not bear these things. "Efnie, Richard Knight was married to a woman he loved very much, and Harry is going to be married to me."

"Oh, excuse me, then!" Efnie laughed at her. "I didn't know we were talking about marriage."

She couldn't talk to Efnie.

WHAT DID MEN and women do?

The subject of sex began to obsess her. She thought about it early in the morning, when she was practicing scales and doing exercises. It crept into Beethoven. Dr. Frosch praised her reading of the music, and she wondered what Beethoven had thought about sex. She did not know how to become better than ignorant. She had hardly had a chance to get to know girls of her own age; and girls of her own age probably would not know. Her closest girl acquaintance was Efnie, and she wouldn't trust Efnie to know that ice melted.

What was sex, and who knew about it best?

Who would tell her?

Uncle Charlie would think badly of her for asking. Uncle Gilbert—for the first time in her life, she wondered if Uncle Gilbert knew. Aunt Violet would scream. She couldn't ask Harry. It must be a married person, one she could trust, and she hardly knew a married person.

Except one—

The idea appalled her. That would be much worse than even women's rights.

But practically every day she was given some hints of the mystery that she could not see. Mrs. Fen occasionally slipped and called Mr. Knight "Richard." The plans for Perdita's own marriage were going forward. Efnie hinted about the honeymoon. "Oh, the honeymoon! Don't you wish you knew!"

She most certainly did.

No, of course she was not jealous of Richard Knight with Mrs. Fen; she was jealous of his time, the afternoons they had had in Boston and didn't have anymore. She wanted, simply, to be alone with him once. Not to ask him anything—no, certainly, not to ask.

She sat next to him at a Clinic musicale, and said not a word to him, because Harry was on her other side. But all that evening, the side of her next to him was sensitive and hot, as if she had burned herself in the sun. His arm brushed hers once, casually, and she blushed. It was as if anything around them reminded her of the subject.

Toward the end of that evening's music, Mrs. Fen came by and sat next to Richard. Harry took Perdita's arm and carried her off to see her aunt Violet and Efnie. She wanted to stay and be his chaperone . . . she could have killed Efnie for that phrase. She hadn't thought of Richard Knight as—with trousers—but wasn't that why she thought of asking him, because he had experience?

She felt she would never be so self-unconscious as she had been when she knew him first, or so unaware that Richard Knight had a life outside of her and them.

"Come away with me, away from the music." Harry took her arm and steered her into the darkness of the garden. He walked with her down the paths, then onto soft grass. She heard the whispering of the river, the Little Spruce, and felt the moisture of its spray on her cheek. Her heart beat hard. She knew they were quite alone, and she wondered if he would do anything about it, and if so what she was supposed to do back. Women were supposed to know by instinct. She didn't.

"Oh, Pet, I want you so." Fumbling, he put his arms around her. He kissed her hard on the lips. "Put your arms around me," he urged her, "hold me." She was caught in his arms. He touched her under the breast. She jumped.

"No, Harry! It isn't right."

"I don't want to wait to marry you," he said breathlessly. "Run away with me. Let's get married right now. I want us to be all alone together, us two, my Pet." He kissed her; his lips were warm and wet and rubbery.

"Harry, don't!"

He laughed at her but he let her go. "What's the matter, Pet? I'm just kissing you. Are you frightened?"

They had certainly kissed before, but not away from everyone else, here in the dark. She was indignant that she didn't know anything, ashamed because she ought to. Tears streamed down her face. But she didn't know if she ought to feel bad.

"I only want us to get married early." He was a little sullen. "Not wait all the fall. I love you."

"I love you, Harry," she said obediently. That much was clear. But get married? She was still six months from being married, and it hardly seemed enough time to dent her terrible ignorance. She didn't want to get married now, she wanted to wait until Christmas.

ON THE HOTTEST DAY of the year so far, the dressmaker came up from Boston to fit the wedding dress that Perdita would wear in December. Aunt Violet and Efnie took over the Clinic's parlor for the fitting because the train of the dress was so long that it would not fit into their rooms at the Lakeside. Perdita held her arms out from her sides, and they buttoned her into what the dressmaker called the Garment, a scratchy damp camisole with thick cotton pads sewn under the arms. "We ask all our young ladies to do their fittings with *the Garment*. We don't want to soil *the Dress* during your fitting, do we, dear?"

Pounds of silver lace weighed down Perdita's shoulders. White lace, white silk, white pearls. Aunt Violet and Efnie *oohed* like doves. "You look so grown up, Perdita!" Across her back and neck she felt the little catching scratch of crusted lace, lace from France, sewn with pearls. Her hair was up for the first time, pinned in a great weight at the back of her head, giving her headache. "The pearls will be real on the day," Aunt

Violet murmured in satisfaction. "Ooh," Efnie groaned. The dressmaker cooed, "Ropes of pearls are so tasteful." Perdita had to wear a corset with the wedding dress, steel-boned and tight so that she had to breathe up at the top of her lungs.

"Getting married," Efnie whispered. "Walking down the aisle—and toward Harry Boulding!"

The assistant dressmaker patted her back. The woman's breath smelled like old meat and peppermints. The smell of faint rottenness made her stomach queasy. "Can't I sit down?" she asked the dressmaker.

"Five more minutes, dear. You look so beautiful!"

She held her arms out from her sides, taking hot short breaths, while the dressmaker prodded her with long-nailed fingers. "And then the *honeymoon*!" Efnie breathed. Perdita could not imagine it. In her mind she walked down the aisle toward Harry, and after that the rest of her life was a great blank. She balled her hands into fists, she was so afraid of what would happen to her, it was like dying.

The box on which she was standing teetered; she reached out to grab something and fell over the edge.

The door opened. She heard Richard's voice in the hall. She could not find her feet, they were tangled in all the whiteness. She tried to take a breath to cry out, breathed in the smell of rotten meat, and choked. She was lying in a snarl of silk and heat, scratches and prickles against her cheek from the lace.

"—fainted from the heat," Richard was saying. He touched her cheek and her forehead with his hand. She broke out in a hot sweat as his skin touched hers. She thought, embarrassed and frightened, he knows exactly what is going to happen to me.

"—a man should *never* see a bride in her wedding dress before the day, it isn't proper."

"Nonsense. Fit your dresses on a cooler day. Look, the child is red."

Perdita tried to struggle up, thinking of Richard seeing her on the floor. *Look, the child is red.* But she could not even move her feet; the stupid skirt was wound all around them. Richard lifted her and freed the big train of the skirt from around her ankles. "I only fell," she said, trying for some shred of her dignity. But he carried her over to the sofa. She thought of Harry and being carried over the threshold, and wanted to gasp or sigh, but the corset was too tight, like an iron fence wrapped around her. "Take this silly dress off!" she whispered to the dressmaker, ashamed that Richard should see her in her wedding dress.

Richard said he would send ice water. "We have water here," Aunt Violet said grimly and closed the door behind him.

"Please, take the dress off," Perdita gasped. "It's too hot."

"We will keep you till this evening, since it is *too hot* to fit this dress," Aunt Violet said to the dressmakers. They bowed themselves out.

Efnie helped her out of it. "*I* would wear it on the hottest day there is," she sighed. Perdita slipped on her ordinary blouse and skirt and fumbled the pins out of her hair. Aunt Violet braided her hair back from her face in a series of small sharp tugs.

"You're only a child," said Aunt Violet grimly. "Nothing but a child after all. 'Silly dress.' I don't see what Harry sees in *you*. This evening, girl, whatever the heat, you will have the most fashionable dress in Boston fitted to you, and you will say nothing about its being too uncomfortable or too tight. Too tight! And you will *never faint again,* Miss, do you understand me? Girls who faint before they are married lay themselves open to criticism! And you are so unconventional, so—uneducable, so— You're my sister-in-law's child and I try to do my best. But I will not have any girl in my household spoken of."

THAT EVENING Perdita and Harry sat together in the parlor of the Children's Clinic, with the door open so that Aunt Violet would not suspect them of doing wrong.

"Your aunt Violet is very disappointed at your behavior, Pet. She told me so."

"Oh, Harry, please don't throw Aunt Violet at me," Perdita said in a low voice so as not to reach Aunt Violet's ears. She had been through another hour of standing in that dress. It seemed to her as though the dress was getting married and she was just going along inside it.

"This wouldn't have happened if you hadn't changed piano teachers," Harry said. She stared at him. "Dr. Frosch isn't good for you. You've been strange and snappish since you started with him. You're overexerting your intellect, Pet, and you're taking it out on me."

That was S. Weir Mitchell's unscientific nonsense. She knew not to say anything of the kind. "I work hard with him because he makes me work hard, but I like it."

"I don't," Harry muttered. "You don't have to be like this, Perdita. Be more like Efnie. Efnie is fun, and she's a real girl."

"Efnie is silly!" protested Perdita in a whisper.

"She knows what's important. The way you act, you'd want to take your piano along on our honeymoon."

She laughed at that, but just a little guiltily.

"Harry," she said, "do you think I'm going to change a lot when we're married?"

"Of course you are," Harry said.

"Why?"

"Everybody changes when they get married. You're supposed to. Oh, Pet, how do I know? You sound as if I know everything. I've never been married either, honey."

"Are you going to change a lot?"

"Of course! Yes. Sure."

"But what if we don't? What if you're exactly the same person you are now? And what if, when I'm Mrs. Harry Boulding, I'm still me? What if I want to be married to you, and to love you, but the only thing I really want to do besides that is to play the piano? Because, Harry——" She clasped her hands around his and leaned forward, to sense what he was thinking, who he was—"Harry, you know about me, don't you, that I really want to play the piano? I always have. I don't know how to be different."

He laughed. "You're going to be different. You'll see."

He kept tight hold of her hands and moved closer to her on the sofa. The Clinic children were in their beds; they had the first floor almost to themselves. He put his arm around her and put his lips to hers. She kissed him back, a chaste, doubtful, Aunt-Violet-is-watching kiss. She had known him for so long. In six months she would be married to him, in the white dress.

And what would happen then?
Would she really be different?

AND THEN, finally, she got to talk with Richard Knight.

CHAPTER 27

ON A SATURDAY, they went boating on the lake: Uncle Charlie and Uncle Gilbert, Richard, Harry, and herself. Uncle Charlie sat in the shade on the shore. Uncle Gilbert took the boat and pushed around in the shallows for a bit, getting his paddle caught in the irises and waterweed. Richard sat on the shore by himself.

Harry and she went for a long ride in the rowboat. Harry didn't say anything to her, but just breathed hard and grunted with every stroke, driving the oars through the water, as if he hated and enjoyed the effort all at once. She could only think of Richard, there by the lake, alone and approachable. She sat by herself at one end of the boat; she put her hand gingerly over the side and let the lake water slide through her fingers, catching at her with slime and weeds, with ropes of hot currents and cold.

Finally Harry let her off at the dock and cast off with his sailboat; and she walked over to Richard and stood by him.

"Hello, Perdita," he said; and she sat down and asked him.

"You want me to read you what?" he asked. She

listened for amusement in his voice or anything that would make her ashamed. There wasn't anything.

"I thought, actually," she said, "you would know without reading."

"Yes, I would," he said. "Do you mean the mechanics? Are you sure, Perdita, that you want to ask me?"

"I don't have anyone else to ask. I wrote my mother, but it takes a long time for her to write back. I don't want to ask Aunt Violet."

"Oh no," he said, "not Violet."

He told her. They both pitched their voices very low, to avoid being heard by Uncle Charlie or Uncle Gilbert. She asked questions. She had never known for certain what shape men were, down below, though she had changed naked little boys often enough at the Clinic. She had met another blind girl, once, who said that *she* had felt a statue; but Perdita couldn't have imagined doing that.

"Efnie says it's dirty," she said.

"No."

They were both very embarrassed; he told her he was, and she said she was too. She hadn't thought of his being embarrassed, or being unembarrassed enough to tell her. But she was relieved to know what it was about; and all of a sudden she could talk with him again.

"When a person starts, I mean to . . . starts, does it hurt?" she asked.

"It can." He told her how it might hurt, and how she could prevent it hurting.

"Do babies always come, after a man and a woman do it?"

"Not always."

"When do they come, and when not?"

He told her about the cycle of conception: the menses, the ripening of the egg follicle, the release of the egg. At the right time of the cycle, unless the sperm were prevented from reaching the egg, the two would fuse and a baby would develop.

"Unless they are prevented——?" she asked. "How could you prevent that?"

"Hello, Adair," he said, and she jumped; and they made conversation about nothing until Charlie had gone off again.

He didn't know what to tell her. In Holland and England there were the Neo-Malthusian Societies. In America the situation was very different.

"There are devices to prevent the sperm and the egg from meeting," he told her, feeling shamefaced about telling her no more, but certainly not willing to explain the exact operation of a condom to a seventeen-year-old girl. In any case that wasn't the issue. "They're hard to find in America. I don't know where you would go." The prostitutes always knew; he couldn't tell her that.

"Just as well you want children," he said.

"Yes," she said, "of course I do." It seemed so odd, though, that babies came all the time even if you didn't want them. Four children in four years, like Maureen O'Rourke? She very much wanted children, but she hadn't thought of Maureen and herself in the same breath. Mama had had seven. For the first time Perdita thought about that. "If I ever did want to know," she half-questioned him.

He took a long deep breath, then let it out. "Look, child: a word of warning. In the eyes of people like your aunt Violet, by telling you what I have told you today, I have thoroughly debauched you. You want to know, and I've told you, but it isn't done. Don't tell Harry, or anyone else, that we have had this conversation. Do you understand that?"

No, she thought. She didn't understand why it should be wrong to learn. She could understand why Aunt Violet thought so, because she knew Aunt Violet. But it was not wrong.

"Isn't it possible to be honest about it?" she asked. Honesty would be simple somehow, not like the hole-and-corner way Aunt Violet was always looking over her shoulder to see what the world thought of her.

"Child, child—" he said.

She wondered if he wanted to laugh at her. Then it was dirty, or sounded that way, if it wasn't possible to be honest.

"No," he said, "I don't want to laugh at you. To hug you. And to be frightened for you. But your Harry is looking at us; you'd better go over and reassure him."

She scrambled to her feet. "Just one more question."

"Oh?" he said.

"Would you find me a role in the play? I want to act too."

He laughed explosively. For the first time she understood that she had really embarrassed him. "I'm sorry," she said, "I just didn't know who to ask."

"It's all right. And I'll find you your role."

My dear Victor,

. . . The Knight case is more involved than you thought. Gilbert Knight is afraid of something that Richard knew, and won't tell me about it because of course I am Richard. Opportunity and motive he certainly had, though I don't think he did it. As you say, if nothing else, he is boringly obvious. But what does he think Richard knew?

A Mrs. Anna Fen, a near neighbor, apparently had an affair with Jay French. She is convinced that Jay is innocent. Meanwhile—

Reisden broke off and looked at the sheet of paper.

Can you imagine a child like that, seventeen, asking the things she had, and of him? He hadn't known what to tell her but the truth, and still didn't know if he had done the right thing. Telling her fictions would have made him feel exactly as uncertain and involved. The truth is he should not try to be Dutch uncle between Perdita and Harry.

Even supposing Harry knew what to do, contraception was cumbersome, like making love with gloves on. And, whether or not Harry wanted children, he would certainly see the advantages of giving his Perdita a child. Reisden continued in a rush of anger:

Meanwhile Perdita Halley continues to give us music. She is good, and getting better; she has found a teacher who challenges her. Remember her name. You will never hear of it again; she is going off to be married and become domestic.

Reisden

IT WAS THE EVENING of the sixteenth of July. From a logging camp, several miles down the road, two loggers had brought a boy of about seventeen into the Clinic, bleeding badly. Reisden and Gilbert, visiting, were pressed into service. A nurse held a pressure bandage against his head, and Gilbert, kneeling on his other side, put a tourniquet on the boy's arm, which had been cut to the bone with a saw. Gilbert had the air of having done such things often. Having had more of this in Boston than he wanted, Reisden stood back.

Charlie Adair knelt beside them. "There, we'll have you better soon." Behind him, a younger doctor and three nurses had appeared, moving with the controlled fast movements of people taking charge of a medical emergency. They rolled the boy onto a stretcher and Adair went with them.

The rug where the boy had lain was splotched with blood. Twice now, Reisden thought, remembering the child at the Clinic in Boston. At least Adair had the Landsteiner information now. This one wouldn't go into shock.

Reisden helped Gilbert to his feet and, giving him his hand, felt it was slippery. Gilbert's hands were covered in blood, red up as far as the wrists. His shirt cuffs were wilted with blood. There was an overstuffed chair close to him, covered in chintz; Gilbert sat down in it heavily, holding his hands away from the fabric. A nursemaid had come with a pitcher and ewer of water. Gilbert plunged his hands into the water, and they bled into it as freely as if he had cut his wrists. Reisden's own hands were bloody from having touched Gilbert's; for a moment he saw flickers of Tasy dead among the leaves. He shivered and used his handkerchief to wipe at the stains.

Gilbert rolled back his cuffs and found blood underneath them. He thrust them out away from him, looking afraid of his own hands. Then he grabbed up the washcloth and scrubbed and scrubbed until the skin looked scraped beneath the washcloth. It went on far too long.

"Gilbert." Reisden laid a hand on the old man's.

Gilbert let the washcloth fall. There was still blood rimmed under his neatly trimmed fingernails, not much. "Stop."

Gilbert's eyes met Reisden's and Gilbert obediently kept looking, but the sense behind his old grey eyes hid again, like a frightened fish hiding in the depths of its bowl. Gilbert held his hands in their bloody sleeves away from himself.

The blood was still on Reisden's own hands, on his shirtcuffs. It was still on the carpet, gouts of it. On the windshield of the car, pooling into the leaves.

A nurse had come into the room and was asking them if they had seen the relatives, for the blood. Gilbert was still looking at his hands as if they frightened him.

Gilbert, what do you and Richard know?

"Richard," Gilbert said, as if trying to interrupt both their thoughts. "Blood types? Would you and I have the same one?"

"You and Richard would have the same one," he said automatically. "You and I might. But there are only a few types, it doesn't prove anything."

"Oh." Gilbert shook his head and sighed. "I must change my clothes."

Change them, the way you have changed the house. Reisden wanted to say, "Wait a moment," to ask him about his fear. He didn't do it. Talking about blood types, they had already got away from what he had barely sensed.

And the moment passed.

It was the eighteenth of July, over a month since Gilbert Knight had recognized Richard in the lawyers' offices, less than a month to go. No unidentified children's bodies had been found on trains, August 1887 to as far as early spring 1889. No unidentified bones had been found in the woods. The town had been discreetly and systematically searched by Daugherty's crew of college boys. Island Hill had been searched during the renovations. In the Knights' summer kitchen, which was his office, Roy Daugherty had crossed out about half the squares of woods on his map. Each of those small squares was a patch of woods fifty feet by fifty, a day's work for a man.

"Bucky's real concerned about how little we got."

"I wonder what he expected."

Daugherty passed a bandanna handkerchief over his cropped hair. The summer kitchen, a single large room with a stone buttery on the north, was meant to be cool, but no place was cool in this July. The grass was crisping on the front lawn; the catalpa tree opened all its orchidlike flowers at once, then spread limp white blossom across the grass. The day lilies wrinkled in the late afternoon heat.

"Daugherty, do you like melodrama?" Reisden asked. "Do you know the scene when the eyewitness talks with the detective, and says, 'I'm going to tell you everything—but not now!' and puts it off, and gets shot because he knows too much?"

"Sure, and the detective sits there, no more use than a moldy turd."

"I've got two witnesses. Neither one wants to talk."

"You been holding out on us?"

"Neither one has actually said anything."

"Going to tell me who they are?"

"Do you have to tell anyone else?"

Daugherty blinked slowly, like a frog in a hot pond.

"Depends. How soon they tell you, how desperate we get, whether it has anything to do with where Richard is."

"I don't know."

Daugherty massaged the back of his neck. "Do what I can."

"All right. This is bad evidence and I'm not sure I should bother with it. But never mind. One of my witnesses knew Jay French well and is insistent he didn't do it. I've spoken with this person several times. When we last talked the witness purported to have evidence— facts—to clear French."

"That ain't no good. We know he was there and shooting at people. Charlie saw him."

"The witness says Adair was too far away to see anything."

"Why didn't he come out with this back in '87?"

"She."

"Oh hoh." Daugherty smiled. "Jay French was a pretty fella. Who is it, one of the housemaids? No, I won't ask. They was all shocked and teary when they heard what he'd done. He had 'em pretty much all, I heard tell. But I never heard of no evidence beyond that."

Reisden shook his head. "Very likely there is none."

"If it's Annie Fen, you tell her she ain't never had no reputation to speak of, so she might as well trot out whatever she thinks happened."

The two men looked at each other like two men who are not discussing a woman's reputation. Reisden shrugged.

"Between ourselves? I would guess they were still

warm from each other when it happened. That will be her evidence."

"That's no good. I seen that happen before." Daugherty added, a little wistfully, "Is she as good as they say?"

"I haven't actually tried yet, but"—Reisden dropped into Cockney "—me virtue's 'urtin' somethin' 'orrible."

Daugherty wheezed. "Who's the other witness?"

Reisden picked up a pencil and began idly shading the crossed-out areas of the map. "Gilbert Knight."

Daugherty's wheeze stopped abruptly. The two men exchanged looks.

"I don't make these things up," Reisden said.

"Gilbert *ain't* got nothing to do with it," Daugherty said. "I ain't kidding. Bucky's looking for Gilbert to be Richard's heir. He don't want no complications."

Reisden stopped drawing. "You hired me to find the truth, not to talk to the newspapers."

"We'll do without truth if we got to, and we know where he was. He got an alibi. He wa'n't nowhere near."

"Why doesn't he want Richard to remember anything?"

"Goodness of his heart. That ain't evidence."

"He was terrified of Richard when he thought Richard knew something. I'm not accusing him of the murder, Daugherty, he already knew Richard didn't know the answer to that. It was something else that Richard knew." He wouldn't have put forward a lab result on so little evidence. He hit the table with the flat of his hand. "Yesterday a hurt young man was brought to the Clinic." Gesture is nothing; gesture is not evidence, it is intuition. Actor's intuition. "Gilbert helped with the bandaging and his hands were bloody. He did *this*," Reisden said and sketched the motion: a man afraid of his own bloody hands, widened eyes, lips drawn a little back, shoulders squared as if to ward off a blow.

Daugherty closed his eyes. Bucky would have made the same motion: *I don't want to see, I do not see.* "Reisden, quit it. You know he's just afraid a things."

He had told Daugherty out of a need to check what he thought, and he was not usually stubborn about holding on to a theory. Eyes do not want to believe that there is nothing to see: Put in complete dark, almost everyone hallucinates some light, however dim. But there was something; he could sense it.

"One way or another," he said half to himself, "I will make Gilbert tell me what he thinks I know."

CHAPTER 28

"I AM SO CONCERNED," Gilbert said. "Charlie, you know Harry is inclined to be positive, and he doesn't much care for Perdita's music."

Charlie Adair turned down the corners of his mouth. They were playing chess. It was a sin to play against the man, Charlie thought; Gilbert had just moved a bishop so that Charlie's queen could slide all the way across the board.

"Isn't it one man's opinion you're giving me, and he doesn't know her?" Charlie asked.

"It is Richard's opinion, yes."

Charlie's hand hesitated over the board. It's not Richard's opinion, he thought. Richard is dead and we've got this young Dr. Reisden to torment us.

Gilbert blinked down at the chess pieces. "Charlie, I think you had better look hard at the board before you move."

Charlie resignedly slid the queen across and captured Gilbert's bishop. "The man has his own opinions. But I don't agree with him."

"Charlie . . . you know, in spite of how painful this is, I am happy—very happy. And Richard— I don't believe, Charlie, that he has forgot quite everything. Once, the other night, I was quite sure he remembered something. When the time comes, I think he—will be able to think about it—and talk about it— I hope I shall too. With him I shall. And then, God willing, we will all be happier than before."

Hail, Mary, full of grace— "What did he remember?" Charlie said sharply. What did the man mean to put over on poor honest Gilbert?

"It was when the young man was hurt at the Clinic."

"What did he remember?"

"Why—he was looking down at the carpet, which was all over blood, and then, Charlie, all of a sudden he went pale, dead pale. Then he started to ask me something, but he didn't."

"Perhaps he doesn't like the sight of blood," Charlie said shortly.

Charlie picked up one of the pawns and ran his thumb across the top, counting the bumps as though they were rosary beads. His thoughts pinched him like little demons.

Once I was full of Grace; I saw the man across a railroad yard and I knew he was Richard, knew it for a moment at least, back from the dead or wherever that hideous man Jay French took him. And I was wrong. But is it possible to blame Gilbert when I thought myself I'd found the boy? Lord, was it You who gave me that sight?

What did the man mean by trying to interfere with Perdita's marriage? Once in the afternoon, trying to take the nap that eluded him, Charlie had seen the man leaving Anna Fen's house, the way so many other men did. Charlie had let the hedge grow up so the children wouldn't see. The woman sinned because she wasn't able to help herself. The man, out of policy—Charlie had seen his face well, glad enough to have taken what Anna Fen offered, no doubt, but more glad to be out of her house. Even Our Lord had valued the thing if done in love; though that was no lesson for children.

Charlie stood up and went over to the window, and the twinge and congestion in his chest as he moved reminded him of how little he had to fear from this earth. Every day for many years he had gone to confession and communion in the next town; a long time ago he had walked, now he had himself driven. I think I have been faithful. I have confessed my sins, I have not lied to God, I am at peace with Him.

Then why did He send me this man who was not Richard?

Pray for us sinners, now and at the hour of our deaths . . .

Charlie sighed. If the man were not Richard, he might speak with Gilbert.

But if he were Richard, and remembered anything at all, it would be Charlie he'd come to.

· · ·

IN THE CLINIC PARLOR the next morning, Charlie interrupted Perdita's practice to speak with her. She sat at the piano bench with her hands in her lap, an obedient girl in looks, but casting glances toward the piano.

"I hear that man has taken to telling you that you should work at your music more than at your marriage! That's wrong, my darling."

"He hasn't said that," Perdita protested in a small voice.

"Listen to me, now, and don't go looking toward your piano. This is serious. You'll be eighteen soon; you're almost a woman. You must think and feel as a woman does, not as a child, my love."

She closed the cover and turned her back to the piano. "Uncle Charlie, I'm sorry."

"The man comes from another country and from a very different way of life. There's no solidity in him, no commitment. A person can get married, in the kind of life he leads, and then simply go off, as if there were nothing special about two people together. A woman who did such things here would be very wrong."

"He tells me I could go to New York and take music lessons, and not hurt Harry at all."

"Do you believe him? I see your young man moping about every time you go as far as Boston. Perhaps you think you won't hurt Harry very much, or that, however you might hurt Harry, it isn't so important as making music? It seems to me that'd be unfaith to Harry and to yourself."

She began to speak, defensively, then stopped, finally began again.

"But Uncle Charlie, making music isn't selfish. It's

something that people must have, the way they have food."

"But must they have it from you, my darling?"

"*I* must!—" she cried out sharply, then folded her hands. "Uncle Charlie, you're right to speak to me. But what shall I do, how shall I change? It is so much to me—it's not like growing up and putting away toys. It's my own self I would give up."

Charlie Adair patted her hand. "Child, child, it's always 'my' self. Learn to do what you must."

He left her silent by the piano.

It was silent a long time. Then she brought her hands down in the opening forte chord, and melted into the depths of the music; every note rightly proportioned, articulate, a long and sorrowful cry. Dark chords in the left hand, in the right only the questioning theme. They mingled into silence. She held her hands still on the keyboard, waiting for the long silent measure to end. The sunlight fell across her hands, the black and white of the keys, the shadows of her hands on the keyboard. Harry's ring dazzled in the sun. *Oh, Harry, what shall I do?* On the one side everyone she loved, Harry and Uncle Gilbert and Uncle Charlie, pleading with her to love them and marry Harry and be with them forever; and on the other only this stillness, the passion in music, and how could that break everything apart?

The silence of the measure went on and on, longer, far longer, than Beethoven had written it; and she sat still with her hands on the keyboard. People must have music; *but must they have it from you, my dear?* People must have love, and so must she; and must give it; music is not love, it is something else, it is not the comfort of a peaceable home, it is not children. Blind girls don't marry, no one wants them. Women who give piano lessons don't marry, they are like Mademoiselle Brin, alone in a room with a piano, with pictures of their students instead of their children, old women smelling of dried flowers. What about a girl who is loved, who wants children, even wants what Richard had spoken with her about?

And while she had thought, her fingers had taken up the keys again, and the insistence wove into the question until she could not tell them apart. She played the sonata straight through; and then she sat again, silent, breathing the air, and peaceful and all whole, as she was when she had played well. And then she stood up, and with desperately steady fingers she closed the piano lid and turned the key in the lock.

Harry, and children, and all that she had been raised to be, and was meant to be; and music too, please God! but only if Harry said so.

She groped her way from the room in confusion, feeling as if she had caught in the closed lid some part of her dress, or herself; there were strings between her and it, she was unraveling as if she had left under the lid all of her senses and heart, everything that belonged to her.

Oh, Harry, Harry, I hope you know what I am doing for you!

And to herself she sounded already strident and unhappy, as though she were accusing him.

CHAPTER 29

"WE DONE ALL THE SEARCHING in this town that there is to do. We been over the Clinic with a comb. We got Island Hill covered." Daugherty chuckled. "I sent some guy down the outhouse hole with a flashlight. He wa'n't best pleased, I can tell you. Standin' there in his undershirt and waders, plowin' up old lye with a stick." Daugherty sighed and went over to the ice chest. "Beer makes you hot," he commented. "Think I'll have another. Want one?" He grunted as he knelt down to get his beer.

Reisden shook his head. Daugherty took a long swallow, sat down at the table again, scratched his neck, and began making circles in water on the table with the bottom of the beer bottle.

"You been talkin' to people," Daugherty mused out loud, "and not come up with anythin' yet. Anythin' from Anna Fen?"

"In no way. Is there any place you haven't tried except the woods?"

"Got to get to the barn attic this weekend. I sent a guy up there beginnin' of this summer, he come back and said there was about four tons of moldy hay and the floor was crunchy with mouse droppings, and could we please leave it till last? You know that hay, underneath the top, it's going to be pure compost. Four tons a mice and compost." Daugherty took another swig of beer. "I do purely hate mice, Reisden. Anyway, we got to do it this weekend, 'cause all the little Shakespeare Club folks are going off to some dance and we can tromp around and make a smell. Bob Gosselin and his crew goin' to come in and start shiftin' it Saturday. I'd find someplace else to be if I were you, 'cause you're going to have mice sittin' on the edge of your plate come breakfast Saturday."

"Send the mice to the dance."

"They roped you in for dancin'?"

"I'm afraid so."

Daugherty swabbed his neck with his handkerchief. "Me, I'm goin' fishin' with my boys." Daugherty was a divorced man and had two sons in Massachusetts.

"Reisden, when's your man going to write back with his information about the Knights?"

"Victor Wills? I don't know. I told you he was interested; he even wants to write about the Knight case, assuming we find something definitive and interesting. But he hasn't written me at all this summer, which isn't like him."

IN THE NEXT DAY'S MAIL, the last day of July, came the news that finished all news of Victor forever.

Il mio più respettato e caro Amico è morto— Victor's Italian waiter wrote with a sputtering black pen, on the kind of black-bordered mourning paper that Victor would have called simply deliciously Catholic. The spelling was uncertain and the paper was scented; but this last of Victor's waiters had nursed him, and stayed with him, while he died.

Victor was dead. They had never been as close as

they should have been. In the beginning Reisden had been drawn to Victor's literary talk but put off by Victor's only too obvious other interests. But Reisden had got from that relationship so much more than he could give without being misunderstood. Victor had widened his horizons, teaching him that being creative was important, whether it was in bad poetry or chemistry. If it had not been for knowing Victor at fourteen, Reisden would not have started acting at sixteen, and he would never have joined Louis and done chemistry. When Reisden had known him in more recent years, Victor had diminished into a charming, gossipy old man who had barely known Tasy, and Reisden had been so sunk in his own unhappiness that he had paid little attention to Victor's. Victor had suffered from heart disease for several years, the waiter Marco wrote; but the end had been very quick, a stroke, a few days when Victor had struggled to stay alive, then reconciliation with the Church and death. *He spoke con gran'Amore of a man named Oscar,* the waiter Marco wrote; *but what he said to me contented me.*

Victor had been dead nearly a month.

I should have given you what you wanted, Reisden thought, knowing that in that way he had never been capable of being either loving or sincere.

The letter from Reisden, asking for Knight materials, had come during Victor's last illness. Marco had gone through Victor's files and was enclosing everything that related to Reisden or the Knights, since that was what Victor had apparently wanted.

There was a heavy box of materials with the letter. Half of them were Knight materials; but there were letters from him to Victor as well, the two mixed together.

Reisden took the box and letter up to his room and spread the Knight material out on the floor. He kept finding bits of his own life mingled with them: the same stack would contain newspaper clippings, a copy of the coroner's report on William Knight, and then a letter from him to Victor, describing an experiment or a visit to a play. The letters dated from his public school and university days and sounded as if they had been written with a cigaret dangling from one corner of the mouth, offhand and scornful of everything that didn't match his eighteen-year-old high standards. Reisden remembered polishing some of the phrases to what seemed now an excessively high buff. He put them off in a corner by themselves, to be burned.

He found a photograph of himself as a schoolboy in England, very young, thirteen or fourteen. He didn't remember its being taken (and how had Victor, of all people, got a photograph of him at that age?). He was dressed in the school uniform and looked appallingly dewy and charming. That was embarrassing; otherwise the picture interested him, because Reisden had thought no one had bothered to photograph him before he had started acting in earnest; the schoolboy was a stranger. Could Victor possibly have got the photograph from him? Reisden hoped not. He hesitated, then took out his billfold and put the small photograph in it, feeling as if he were keeping pornography.

There were drafts of some of Victor's poems. One he knew from *Les Amourettes;* it had been dedicated to

Tasy and the draft was fairly complete, written in Victor's spidery hand and violet-tinged ink.

> *Une des voix qui muent et qui volent,*
> *Mouette jouante au grand ciel*
> *Belle des belles . . .*

Beauty of beauties, who is all beauty, and not beautiful for me or for yourself . . . Victor had written that on meeting Tasy once, in London for a weekend, fussing over every line.

Would there be a picture of her? There was. It was the two of them on Brighton Pier in March. A Sunday, it must have been; she had been down there singing in the chorus of something, he forgot what, and he had taken the train there to see her. They had their arms around each other; she was clutching a stick of Brighton rock and her brown coat was blowing in the wind. She looked young enough to make one cry. Since her death she had grown a little older in his mind, but there she was, eight months before everything would end for her, her hair whipping like flags in the sea wind, round-chinned as a child. He had burned all her pictures after she died, because he had needed nothing to keep her alive then. He held the picture over the group of letters to be burned, and then held back and slipped the picture into his pocket with Victor's scrap of poetry. Someday he would be an old bachelor of forty, and he would think his wife had had grey in her hair when she died.

The next photograph—

He took one look and turned it picture side to the floor, sickened and angry. It was Tasy, dead on the leaves by the car in the New Forest. He remembered exactly the position of the body. Her head had drifted, somehow, behind the body, sunk on her left shoulder, so oddly angled that he had knelt down and turned her over to see what was wrong. "No," he said aloud, the way he had then; but it was too late not to remember everything, the blood from her smashed face all over his hands, feeling through the blood the little sharp splinters of bone. He could never stop realizing that she was dead. *She is dead, she is dead still, she is dead.* And he had been glad. He clamped his hand over his eyes to shut it out, but everything was still with him, he felt he had smeared her blood on his face.

Victor could not have that photograph. He took his hand down, still smelling blood.

He had seen her on the ground and turned her over. What photograph could there have been?

Reisden set his jaw, gazed at its blank back, flipped the picture over, and looked.

Not Tasy. Of course it had not been. He recognized the downstairs carpet with its clashing diamonds. William Knight lay on that carpet. His head was bent ludicrously on his neck at the same eccentric angle that Tasy's had been, so that one wanted to protest and straighten it out. The face was turned away. The top of his head had been scratched out on the photographic plate, as was done sometimes when a very unpleasant picture was to be shown to laymen. The left side of the head looked curiously flat and under it the carpet was discolored to an uneven, white-speckled darkness. William Knight's left hand was under his body, but the right was flung out in an almost comic disarray on the carpet. Reisden looked at that photographed hand for a long minute, recognizing from other photographs the long fingers, big knuckles, and spatulate thumb. They had always grasped something firmly; now they lay loose. William Knight was dead.

Reisden took the photograph downstairs into the murder room. In the photograph were the sprawled body, a section of carpet, and the leg of a chair, and in the white room now were only holystoned oak boards and plastered walls. He stood in the white room and mentally fit the body into various places in it. He took the photo out into the hall and gazed at the long flight of front stairs going up into darkness. Richard would have come out into the hall and stood looking over the banisters. Reisden climbed halfway up the stairs and looked down through the door of the white room onto its plain scrubbed floor. Richard would have seen the front half of the room, the windows and whatever was near them. Where had William Knight been shot? Would Richard have seen William dead?

The picture still looked like Tasy.

In the dimly lit hall it was easier to see: the lifeless angle of the neck, one hand flung wide.

Reisden sat down on the stairs, swept by anger and desolation. He wasn't the right person to investigate William Knight's death. He didn't want to suffer for it by seeing Tasy here.

The picture still looked like Tasy.

It was the angle, and more than the angle; he could almost see one in the other. He closed his eyes, trying to clear them of what was after all only a coincidence; but it was in his eyes, he couldn't stop seeing it. In a moment he would think it had been Tasy down in the white room, dead on the floor.

But it had been the other way around, hadn't it?

He sat on the stairs, shocked out of thought, waiting

for the moment to pass, the way it had when he had seen Gilbert's bloody hands, or before that, much before, when he had seen Richard Knight's face in a photograph. Just a moment ago, upstairs, he had seen Victor's files, with Richard Knight's materials and Alexander Reisden's mixed together, as if they had always been together. He remembered Victor's nervous chatty trivialities the last time he had seen him. Victor had kept the Knights out of *American Crimes,* Victor had said. For Reisden's sake, he had said; and Victor had not known whether to tell him to go to America or keep away.

He held his head in his hands, dizzy, not daring to touch or hear or see what he thought he knew.

Not Tasy dead on the floor downstairs. William Knight dead on the leaves in the New Forest.

Sitting on the stairs, he was back in the New Forest again, on a cold November morning, kneeling by a smashed auto. But he was looking this time at someone he couldn't focus on, only a scrawled dead agony among the leaves. And he let himself feel what he had not dared to for years, exactly what he had felt then, a wild and almost hysterical relief, because everything was all right now.

Because he was Richard Knight.

There, on the stairs, he knew for certain who he was. And it was the wrong answer.

He could not possibly be Richard. How could it have happened? Richard would have had to get from New England to Africa. Graf Leo would have had to adopt Richard.

And he would have known; oh my God, he would have known.

"You are *hoffähig*. To be court-presentable opens doors," Graf Leo had said. That was all. The Loewensteins had never made a secret that presentability was important, descent was important. When Reisden had married Tasy, outside the court circle, he had lost all value to the Loewensteins until Tasy died.

Reisdens don't adopt. No. Not even if he were the last male Reisden; not if he were the one after the last, Graf Leo wouldn't have adopted an unknown boy as a Reisden. Reisden hadn't been close to his guardian, but that was true. No one had more of a sense of family than Graf Leo, or had tried harder to give it to Reisden.

He was Alexander von Reisden. Baron Alexander Josef Jászai von Reisden. His father was the Baron Franz Eugen Joachim von Reisden; his mother, Charlotte-Elisabeth Adelaïde von Loewenstein, cousin of the Graf Leo von Loewenstein. He had had two aunts who lived in Salzburg; they were both dead now. He had gone to university and got degrees. He had published articles. He had a profession and a stock portfolio and an address in Lausanne.

He knew who he was.

And after a moment Reisden took out of his billfold the first picture, the one of himself at thirteen or fourteen, which, far more clearly than himself now, was Richard Knight.

General amnesia cures itself within weeks or not at all.

Could Graf Leo have foreseen that Reisden would meet Charlie Adair on a train platform in Lausanne, at four o'clock in the morning, a lifetime later?

It is not true, Reisden thought. I'm not Richard Knight.

An elephant trumpeted and spread its ears. ". . . the son of my friend Franz von Reisden. That is who you are. You understand that." Graf Leo's remembered voice went on inexorably. "You are Alexander von Reisden."

He had been named that day.

The house was very quiet and he sat for some time in the near-dark, drained and empty, missing Victor, whom he wanted to talk to more than he ever had in his life. He felt bad physically, punched-out and tired. He didn't want to go upstairs; he would have to clean up those papers before he went to bed, and he didn't want to face any of them. He wanted to burn them all without touching them again. Victor had left him a legacy, Richard Knight, for whose story Victor would have got three hundred pounds. How many months' salary to Victor? It would have been a big book, and Victor would have wanted to write it; look at the way he had told it. Reisden knew exactly what Victor's temptations would have been.

And you didn't do it, did you, Victor, and left me with the questions.

Now what?

The long clock in the downstairs hall rattled like bones and chimed midnight.

And Gilbert Knight came out of the door from the library, carrying a wooden crate of books, and moved somehow furtively down the hall to the kitchen.

Unseen behind the banister, Reisden watched him. The box was piled high with books. Gilbert had trouble with the kitchen door, which was set at an awkward angle behind the dining room. Reisden heard the creak of one door, the rattle of a knob, and a startlingly loud

wooden clap as the swinging kitchen door hit the dining-room door. Gilbert was in the kitchen at midnight
with a crate full of books.

Through the door Reisden heard the heavy crate
being put down. A minute later he heard the distinctive
sound of scraping. A shovel, scooping the ashes from
the firebox of the kitchen stove. Gilbert was unbanking
the fire.

Coal stoves were convenient for getting rid of awkward objects. The fire was never out, not even in summer, because everything hot in the house depended on
it, from coffee to bathwater. At night the fire was banked
down to coals under ashes, but one needed simply to
remove the covering layer of ashes, add newspapers and
pine kindling, and then add more coal. The fire was
ready in a few minutes.

Reisden heard the scrape of the shovel, then a little
ripping sound, then a dry snap as Gilbert broke some
kindling. The kindling crackled as the fire caught; Gilbert rattled coal into the firebox.

Books? Reisden had once seen him rescue a book
from an empty lot, smooth the pages, and carry it until
they passed an open-air bookseller's, when Gilbert had
slipped it apologetically among the five-cent second-
hands.

Gilbert would not burn books.

There was a small glass window at head height in the
kitchen door. Gilbert had not turned on any lights and
the roller blinds were pulled down over the windows.
He had built the fire up high, so that flames were shooting out of the top of the stove. Gilbert's pale, dim face
was shiny from the heat. He had his reading glasses on,
and in the red blaze from the stove, he took one book

after another from the crate, read each title page, and put the book into one of two piles, a very small pile of books away from the flames, a large one close by the roaring stove. In his pale suit, with his pale hair, Gilbert looked like H--l's librarian sorting the saved and d--ned. He took the top book of the pile, ripped the pages from the cover, and threw it into the stove.

"Gilbert, what are you doing?"

His voice was much sharper than he had meant it. Gilbert jumped, stared at Reisden stricken, and sat down in a chair. Still, he put his hand on the top of the large pile of books, as if to say *These are mine,* and he edged forward in his chair as if to put himself between them and Reisden.

"Let me see."

"Richard—"

"Let me see, d--n it." Reisden took Gilbert's hand from the top of the pile. Gilbert's eyes widened; he stammered something.

"You don't tell me anything; don't you think I have a right to know when something odd goes on in this house?"

Gilbert's hand dropped and he sank down in his chair, his eyes following Reisden, like a rabbit mesmerized by headlights. Reisden flipped open the first book and looked at the title page, but he had already recognized it. It was one of the books that had been shelved next to Richard Knight's desk.

True to the End, a Story of School Life, by a Rev. Theodore Peter Codlington. The flyleaf was inscribed "To His Beloved Grandson, Richard H. Knight, from William H. Knight, October 6, 1885." *Pluck and Luck,* by Horatio Alger, "to His Grandson, Richard H.

Knight—William H. Knight, March 1886." *History of the American Settlement; Elementary Mathematics.* To Richard, to Richard, to Richard. Gilbert was burning all Richard's books.

Gilbert the librarian angel had saved only two undistinguished collections of Bible stories, *Through the Looking Glass,* R. M. Ballantyne's *The Coral Island,* and *Huckleberry Finn.* The last three had been given Richard by Gilbert.

Gilbert had put the stove lids back on the stove, closed the damper, and opened the windows. He had set the lids back on too soon; one cracked with a loud ping from the heat of the fire below. Gilbert fussed and, using the lifter, moved the broken pieces to the back of the stove.

"Why?"

Gilbert pushed the two broken pieces with the lifter, trying to fit them back together.

"Stop that." Reisden threw the book he was holding into the crate again. He took Gilbert by both shoulders and shook him. Gilbert stared up into his eyes, hypnotized by fear. "I'm not eight years old, Gilbert, I came here to find out and not to be lied to. What's in these, that you want to burn them rather than let me see it?"

Gilbert shook his head, flinching.

"I won't hurt you." Reisden let him go. Gilbert dropped back into the chair. "Please. Gilbert. *Please talk.*"

Gilbert kept on shaking his head, but his cheeks flushed. "You say you aren't Richard," he trembled. "If you aren't Richard then it is of no consequence to you. You don't want to remember any of this. Don't make me tell you. Richard, please."

Gilbert turned and almost ran out of the kitchen.

CHAPTER 30

REISDEN TOOK THE BOOKS upstairs in their box. He had a pure research problem; one box of books is one set of data to make sense of. He did what he usually did when the paper mounted up: declared himself sick for the duration, stayed in bed with coffee and cigarets, and went through everything.

Why did Gilbert want to burn Richard's books?

It took him until the middle of the morning to read them.

Horatio Alger wrote six books about Mark the Match Boy, "a timber merchant in a small way." William Knight, who had been a timber merchant too, had given Richard all of them. Reisden riffled through the pages of two, then put all six back in the crate. They were just boring; the rest were sadistic in the peculiar style of Victorian children's books. In *Jack Saunders, a Tale of Truth,* the twelve-year-old hero told a lie, was horribly burned in a fire, and expired repentant. *Sin and Redemption* collected no less than forty-two stories of youthful sinners. Lying, swearing, and cheating on exams caused them to be run over by horses, felled by tuberculosis and smallpox, imprisoned for debt, maimed, and in one case buried alive. They died with a prayer, a hymn, or their mother's name on their lips, at ages from five to eleven. F. X. Farrar's *Eric, or Little by Little* followed Eric

Williams through a career of crime: irreverence in the school chapel, swearing, smoking, and the intemperate use of spirits. For this the child was expelled from school, shanghaied into the navy, and flogged almost to death by his captain. (The book opened by itself to the flogging scene, which sounded as if Farrar had whipped a schoolful of boys for research and enjoyed it. William Knight had written in the margin, "The way of the transgressor is death!—Take this to heart!") Reisden skipped a hundred pages of broken repentance, threw the book with all the others back into the crate, and leaned back, massaging a headache out of his eyes, feeling as if he had spent the morning being raped by Christians.

The books were bad, but no worse than others. Why would Gilbert burn them?

So Richard wouldn't see them.

Reisden took another two hours and examined each one minutely as a physical object. Nothing between the leaves. No missing pages. No codes created by underlining certain letters. No pages soaked in mysterious poisons or treasure maps written in blood on the flyleaves. A few more annotations in William Knight's hand, mostly in the history or mathematics texts. In the back leaves of a German text, someone had penciled in a child's blocky picture of a black-and-white dog with a big smile. Underneath, in staggering script, "This is Washington a Dog. I love him." Richard's dog, the one in Richard's picture. (My dog? Reisden thought. But he had never had a dog. He knew this the same instinctive way that for twenty years he had known he was Alexander von Reisden.) He wondered what had become of Washington.

In the morning light, his old photograph looked far more like himself than like Richard, and the gruesome photograph of William Knight had nothing to do with Tasy. What was he doing in Richard Knight's house—understanding something, or making it all up? He distrusted his insights and distrusted the distrust.

He could spin a story that would make himself sane, but it didn't answer much. Richard Knight hated William. Why? William had terrible taste in books and kept Richard under his thumb. Very likely William had flogged Richard, F. X. Farrar–style. The books indicated that much. Then William died. Richard was happy, very happy. Relieved. He would never be hit again and he would never have to read Horatio Alger.

What nonsense.

He took his own letters downstairs to the kitchen and burned them in the stove, disturbing the kitchenmaid, who was cleaning. The two broken pieces of the stove lid were still on the back of the stove. He took a walk outside, through the fields behind the old barn and into the woods. In the fields it was hot, itchy, and buggy; in the woods, humid, smelling of mold and leaves, far more buggy. He sat in the old damp gazebo staring at the lake, smoked far too many cigarets, and felt dissipated and disarrayed. It was Friday, August third, and he had no ideas at all.

Perdita was downstairs in the music room, sitting on the piano bench with the piano lid closed, deep in thought, and with her hands outspread on the lid.

"Perdita, do you know why Gilbert should burn Richard Knight's books?" he began.

It took her a moment to come out of her thoughts. "Burn them?" She seemed as distracted as he was.

"Am I in your way? Would you like to practice?"

"No," she said vehemently; "please stay. I'm not practicing."

It was hot. They fell into silence, he thinking his thoughts, she thinking hers. She ran her fingers through her long hair, lifting it up away from the back of her neck, then twisting it absently in a knot. Not quite a grownup's style, but as she let it fall, it struck him that this was almost the last time he would see her in her childhood. She would be eighteen on Sunday. Her skirts would lengthen and her hair be put up, and officially she would be a woman. In her distracted mood she seemed older.

"Are you going to the dance tomorrow?" she asked.

"I suppose I'm required." Because dances required a four-to-one ratio of men to women, men were in desperately short supply.

"Oh, please. I'd like to dance with you," she said. "You're the only nice thing about this summer."

"Then of course." The last dance he had been at was a Communist Party Bastille Day celebration in Hampstead. He remembered Tasy in her striped skirt, dancing with a fan in her hand. It had been hot and she had fanned them both while they waltzed, cheek to cheek, comfortable, domestic, and married.

Tasy dead on the leaves. William Knight and Richard Knight.

"Have you ever been to a big formal dance?" she asked.

"Yes. And you haven't?" Of course not; she wasn't yet eighteen. "But you've had dancing lessons. It's very much the same."

She shook her head. "Harry doesn't care much about

dancing. I made Uncle Gilbert teach me to waltz."

He could imagine the results. "Waltzing may have changed somewhat since Gilbert learned to dance," he said cautiously.

"I don't want to ask you about everything," she said.

"I do know how to waltz." Vienna taught one that. "Would you like to practice?" He got up and moved the sofa and chairs to the sides of the room. She scrambled up, almost as if she were eager to get away from the piano. "Here, we have a little room."

"Uncle Gilbert says I should stand like this." She stood at arm's length from him.

"Not since the 1830s. Stand close by me. You rest your hand on my shoulder, I put my right hand on your waist. Your right hand clasps my left hand, so. Now, dancing is like being led by a guide. I guide your path, so, by suggesting it to you with the pressure of my hands. You know how to do that; you should be good at dancing." He counted, one-two-three, one-two-three, then thought of her metronome and set it ticking. They danced a simple box step in the space between the chairs and the piano. The blinds were down against the heat; the room was dim. Her back muscles were rigid against his hand. Right-left-right; left-right-left. They danced for a while in silence. His legs were longer; he experimented with how large the box should be so that they would both feel natural. The metronome kept up its rigid ticking. They fell into a rhythm together, but it was odd to dance with this strange skeletal clacking, no music at all. Suddenly she began breathing too deeply, in gasps under his hand, as if she were trying to control herself. He set her down on the sofa and sat down beside her.

"Is anything wrong?" he asked.

"It's so sad without music."

"What?"

She wasn't going to cry. She turned away her head and put her knuckles to her eyes. Her voice trembled. "It's so silly. Harry can't dance."

She held her long fingers in front of her, put them down in her lap, clasped them, as if she didn't know what to do with them. "I don't know why I should mind it so much. Harry can't keep time. Harry can't sing. Music doesn't mean one thing to him." In her lap her hands kept turning like trapped things. "I did something, I made a promise. Yesterday——" Her hands flew up and hid her face. Reisden took them gently. She half drew away from him; he let them go. "I told Harry that I wanted to be married to him, more than anything, and that I wouldn't play the piano if he thought it was wrong."

She was trying to look at him, but blindly; she reached out her hands again and he took them.

"You made that promise? And Harry took a promise like that from you?" he said.

"Harry was glad," she said simply. "He wants me to be his wife more than anything else. I want to be completely faithful to him."

He said nothing and only held her hands.

"But I don't know how I can do it!" she said in a sudden high, clear voice, almost a shout. She stood up, withdrawing her hands from his. "There's music everywhere. I can—not do it—but I can't ignore it—I would listen to a hurdy-gurdy if there weren't anything else.— How can I keep my word to Harry?"

She dropped down on the sofa, sitting stricken, like someone shot.

"You can't," he said.

She swayed back and forth like someone grieving, soundless. She grimaced as if she wanted to cry, soundless, as if not having music had deprived her of any voice. Creative work requires, at some level, perfect lifelong attention; and Harry had told her not to pay attention at all.

"Fully, and sincerely, and with your whole heart, you cannot, ever."

"Uncle Charlie said I could," she whispered.

"And so you asked someone else," he said, not being cruel to her, "who would give you another answer."

She bowed her head miserably.

"You are a musical person and you have given your word not to be. That was stupid, like locking yourself in a closet. You're not the sort of person to kick down the door or scream for help; but you can't spend your life there."

She looked up at him, wide-eyed and pale, as she would have looked at the edge of a precipice.

"He'll like who you really are, you know. Anyone would." He hoped it was true, since it had to be.

"He doesn't like my music. And I love him."

"*You* love him. Not the girl he's made up and put in your place. She doesn't feel anything; she doesn't exist. He'll be able to tell the difference. He'll resent you if he doesn't get the real thing."

She looked at him dubiously.

"You will have to tell him callously and repeatedly, I should guess. But you have got to, Perdita. End of sermon. Would you like to take a walk?"

The afternoon heat hung like sweat in the air, smudged with convection over the rocks. He took her out in the rowboat. The lake absorbed sound, or it was only that the whole lake valley had filled with a hot silence. The water moved slowly past their boat with an almost inaudible creaking, so close to soundless across the bow that they might have felt it in the skeleton of the boat, and heard it only in the imagination. She said nothing. She turned and put both her hands in the water, then held her cold wet hands over her face and neck. She moved down the boat toward him, held her hands in the water again, and held both her hands over his forehead, cooling him. Harry would have disapproved. Still she said nothing.

Reisden remembered the first time he had come up against something that he could not do. It had been just after he had graduated from university. Reisden's future had included a post in the diplomatic service, on the staff of an influential member of the royal family, and marriage to his cousin Dorothea von Loewenstein, who was rich, beautiful, and clever. He had been missing chemistry day and night, and he and Dotty both knew that they were in love with other people, but it could well have worked out; less promising matches were made every day. So he had argued to himself.

He shipped the oars and looked at her, the child Perdita, to memorize her face before it became a woman's. Oval chin, straight nose, eyes lidded by shadows. Her mouth was full and wide, a woman's almost, drawn with seriousness. Her hands moved against each other in her lap, the fingers folded together, as if they had been put away, things with no use. *This is my hand;*

why does it move? The obvious questions are the hardest
to take seriously. He wanted some sound in the bowl of
the valley for her, something that she could make into
music.

Suppose that he had loved Dotty; would he have been
able to let her and his well-planned future go?

Reisden bumped the rowboat against what had been
William Knight's landing stage, below the half-ruined
gazebo covered in bittersweet. The old rose garden lay
between them and the house. The roses were gone to
fruit and desiccated leaves. In the elm trees by the barn
a mockingbird had nested. As they walked under the
trees the bird began to sing. She held up her hand. They
stopped. She listened, and he watched her while the
mockingbird sang, a girl in a white dress with her head
tilted up toward the music, her hair down her back and
her hands clasped in front of her, enchanted while the
music lasted.

Please, he asked whatever balanced the universe, turn
her way.

"I think I want to learn some more about dancing,"
she said when the bird flew away. They were near the
big front door of the barn; he led her inside into the
coolness and the long shadows, thinking that they could
dance on the second level.

But on the second level the Shakespeare Club's big
background flat, a forest scene, was spread out to dry on
the floor, and there were no west windows. At four
o'clock it was just barn-dim, but for her it was almost
dark.

The attic stairs were blocked by a wooden door. The
afternoon light would be stronger up there. "Are you
afraid of mice?" he asked her.

"Little barn mice? No."

"Lots of little barn mice. Let's try."

He went ahead of her. The air puffed out as he opened the door: hot air, old, complex, smelling of grass and decay. He smelled the sweet rotten smell of hay, something like manure gone bad, and the ammonia smell of mice. She wrinkled her nose. The hay filled half the big room, mostly baled; but mice had eaten the twine on the outermost bales and the hay had drifted down, half covering the floor. Hay drifted under their feet and whispered underfoot.

"I'll open the windows," he said.

She stood still in the middle of the floor. The thumb-rule of the partially sighted: when in doubt, don't move. "I can see to sweep if you can find a broom."

There were five windows on one end of the loft and, on the west end, four and the low, broad hayloft door. An antiquated broom stood brush-up against one wall. It looked usable. "Can you sweep some of this into a corner while I open windows?" he asked.

"Yes." She started at the east end, brushing methodically, while he pushed open the windows on the west end. They hadn't been opened since William Knight had died, but they screamed open reluctantly, letting in cool air and a fly that buzzed aimlessly around the ceiling. The hayloft door was partly open, probably why the smell wasn't worse. He saw owl scat by the door. He braced himself against the doorframe and forced the door the rest of the way open. Through its frame he saw the east side of Island Hill beyond the rose garden: the windows of the office, Jay French's bedroom, and the murder room.

"Be careful of the hayloft door," he called to Perdita.

"I can see it." She was efficiently brushing the dirt and hay into piles, which helped her to see where she had been. He started on the east windows, making a cross-draft. They were harder because higher on the wall. By the time he had opened three, she had cleared the floor and was brushing the piles up against the wall of hay.

"Where did you learn to brush like that?" he called to her.

"The Clinic! It gets dirty all the time. This is easy!"

He decided to give up on the window half buried in the hay. The one over the stairs looked easy, but he would need to stand on the stair rail and it was starting to give. He looked for another way up.

"Excuse me? Would you come here?"

Her tone made him turn around quickly. She was standing by the wall of hay with the broom in both hands, not brushing, but holding it like an extension of her fingers, as she would have used a cane. She was feeling at something that was hidden by the drifts of hay.

"There's something here," she said, her voice high and nervous. "Will you come and tell me what it is?"

He took the broom from her and felt where she had. There was something in the hay, as if some of the hay had adhered together in a lump. "It may be a mouse nest," he said.

"No." Her top lip was drawn a little back from her teeth; she shook her head. "It doesn't smell right."

He smelled powdery sweetness that caught in the nose. The back of his neck chilled suddenly. He took the broom and began to brush the hay methodically away from whatever it was.

The hay was tangled, old matted fieldgrass; it came away in lumps, but as it did the hay above it slithered down. He climbed up the hay mound above and moved the old, disintegrating stalks in armloads, carefully as armfuls of glass rods, until he had brought the pile back to hay that was still baled. A low mound of hay covered what Perdita had found. She gave him the broom and, as carefully as an archaeologist, he began to clear away the layers.

The topmost hay brushed easily, old, fragile layers of grey-tan stalks. Below that, it was as if the hay had been wetted and then allowed to dry again; it was flat crumbly stuff, nearly topsoil, in places stuck together like mud-brick. Reisden looked up at the roof for a leak, but there was nothing. The discoloration was quite large, an ir-regular oval perhaps a meter long. Reisden used the broom bristles to brush down into it. The smell was stronger. He could see, down almost at floor level, some even darker patches, almost the color of charcoal, a rusty brownish black. A fire? Some sort of acid? The smell was very strong now and unmistakable, the smell of cemeteries in the summer, the sweet choking powder of decay.

At one end of the pile there was some sort of hum-mock or lump, not a big thing, perhaps the size of an owl. An animal's body, Reisden thought, an owl or a dog; but when he uncovered it, it was the same charcoal-colored substance, only in a hard ball. Something very peculiar, almost the size and shape of a coconut, with a fibrous matted outer layer. Reisden knelt down. He held his breath against the nauseating smell while he felt around it. The fibrous spiky surface gave way to some-thing almost like leather. The thing was stuck to the hay underneath it. It shifted as he rocked it back and forth.

Gingerly, he picked it up—it came hard—to separate it from the matted hay.

He had it in his hands, and had felt the bones of the neck, before he realized what it was.

CHAPTER 31

HE HAD THROWN THE SKULL away from him. It rolled a few feet into the drifts of hay, facedown, only the unspeakable matted hair visible. Reisden clenched his jaw, tasting coffee at the back of his throat.

If he didn't get away from it he would be sick. "Come out," he said to her. They stumbled down the stairs together.

Out away from the barn, by the elm trees, they stopped, both leaning against a tree, arms around each other. Perdita was shaking and he could feel her heart pounding as hard as his own.

"Who is it?"

"I don't know."

She hesitated. "Is it Richard?"

"I don't *know*."

No. Yes. Who else's body would it be?

For a few hours he had had some of Richard Knight's memories, and they had made him sane.

It can't be Richard.

He held on to her. He could still smell on both of them the artificial pink-powder odor of decay. He wanted to cry out, pound his fists against a tree, go back inside, and rip that skull apart to know whose it was.

"Perdita. Get Roy Daugherty." No. Roy had gone off fishing. He needed help and information and somebody else to be in the barn while he looked at that horror again. "Get Gilbert." He added, "Keep Harry out of our way."

The light was fading rapidly in the barn. While he waited for Gilbert, Reisden looked for a lantern among the litter of Shakespeare. It took him five tries to strike a match; his hands were shaking. He stared at the lantern flame, not thinking, until he heard Gilbert at the door.

"Bring the light."

Reisden went up the stairs ahead of Gilbert, looking back to see his long, distressed face lit by the lantern. *This lantern is the moon. And this dog my dog. This is Washington a Dog.* What was the blood on Gilbert's hands? Gilbert held the lantern high, looking, not sure where or what to find, and Reisden stepped out of his way.

Gilbert's eyes widened past the diameter of their irises, white on every side. He put the lantern down next to the horrible black thing and knelt beside it. His mouth turned down in a perfect Greek tragic mask. Moved to his soul, distressed, revolted, Gilbert looked up from the horror. The two men's eyes met: and there was no guilt in Gilbert's face at all.

"What is this?" Reisden asked.

"Is it Jay?" Richard's uncle asked.

Gilbert got slowly to his feet. The skull was still where it had rolled. Gilbert held the lantern near it and the light cut raggedly into matted black hair and the old-tea color of bone. Shadows for eyes and nose, some of the front teeth gone, and one side of the head matted with what it had lain in. Gilbert set the lantern down carefully, well away from the hay, took his handkerchief out of his pocket, and wrapped it around the skull before he picked it up and gently set it down where it belonged. He left the handkerchief over the head, as if the man had been newly killed, and the outline wavered and became what it must have been. A man curled up in agony, legs drawn up, arms crossed over his side.

"Yes," said Reisden dully, "that's Jay and he is dead."

Gilbert knelt in the hay beside the dead man. His lips moved.

Reisden knelt beside Gilbert. Jay's body. Not Richard's. He didn't know anything. Only that.

"Gilbert. Now you are going to tell me everything you thought you had better keep from me."

"WE WERE HAPPY ONCE," said Gilbert. "All of us boys and Isabella, all of the Knights."

He said it half defiantly, half wistfully, as if there needed to be some great fall to explain the horror of what had happened later.

Harry was not in the house, the servants were gone for the night; the two men were alone in the library. One of the lights in the electric chandelier was buzzing; Gilbert got up and turned it off, then went around the room turning on other lights. He sat down in a chair not too close to Reisden, not too far away, and sat looking at the carpet.

In his childhood, Gilbert said, the Knights all lived by the sea. Gilbert was the youngest, a little boy in kilts and long stockings. When Father came home from his office in Boston he would bring presents, carved pieces of whalebone, China fishbowls with beautiful multicolored fish painted on them, tin toy sleds and toy stoves from England, wooden goblin masks with great staring eyes. Father would march his sons down to the wharf—"all my sons! Look at 'em!"—and show them around to his captains, and then they would all stop in at the doughnut shop on the way home. Father looked something like a goblin mask himself, long-faced, with staring eyes, coming among them like Jove in broadcloth, in a shower of presents. At the end of the day they would all cry in pleasure and exhaustion; and then Father would go back to Boston for another two weeks or three to make money, so that all of them would be rich. Gilbert never wondered why Father was so seldom there, and never knew to this day whether, so long ago, there had been reason for the children to be kept away from him.

"I have thought a great deal about those masks, Richard. Father never took a ship to Africa, nor dealt with Africans as one man to another. I don't believe he respected the African, or thought of them as—anything more than labor." When the war came, most of Boston was Abolitionist. Father publicly believed as his business friends believed, of course. But Father was a Southern sympathizer.

"All us boys were old enough to fight in the War (all but your father, Richard, who was just a baby then). My brothers fought. I believed the cause was right, Richard, but I saw so much death in it. . . ." He held out his hands in front of him, half as if to stop something coming toward him, a tiny gesture, quickly suppressed. "I was with the ambulances. I got splinters in my fingers from the stretcher poles, and that was all my war wounds.

"My brothers died. Three of us five brothers. Billy, John, and Al.

"My last brother, Clem, came home from the war before me. He was a hero, decorated all over. He walked down from Park Street, in his uniform with his medals, but no one would speak to him; shamefaced, as if they didn't know whether to say something or not; and he said someone asked him where he was going, but when he said 'Home' they told him not to go there. People used to throw garbage on the steps of our house. Father had helped the rebels.

"When Clem heard what Father had done, he moved down to New York and drank himself to death. He wrote me to come to him, at the end—I was still down in Washington, working at a hospital—and I moved up there with him in New York. I didn't stop him, I couldn't.

"I came to Boston afterward. Forty years ago this spring. Father was alone in the house. I told Father that Clem had died." Gilbert took off his glasses as if not having them on would help him see better. He turned them in his hands, staring at them with a lost, unfocused look. "Father took his cane and whipped me out of the house."

He had a little dismayed twist around his mouth, as though he were still a grown man being caned from parlor to door.

"What was I to do?" he said finally, gently. "He wasn't well. I could have nursed him. But I—I don't suppose I wanted to. Not after Clem. So . . . But it was more cowardly than not having fought."

"I had a little money, and I wanted to see the country, so I bought a wagon and some stock and began trading in things. I had some pots and some pans, needles and thread, fishhooks, things not worth going to town for. I always had some books. I didn't paint my name on my wagon, and Knight's a common enough name anyway, so I was just Bert the bookseller: It was a very good time, Richard! Your father was at school and I'd stop by whenever I could. When I'd leave, Tom would ride on the wagon with me for two or three miles down the road. He always wanted to go on the road with me. Tom thought being a peddler-man, why, that was as good as a circus.

"Tom said Father was peculiar. But of course Father always had been. I didn't know any more," Gilbert said with a strange intensity, "because I didn't ask him. He must have thought I knew.

"Tom had a sort of a temper, like Father, but nothing near as bad. And he was the sort of man who—" Gilbert paused and pinkened slightly "—ought to get married young. He fell in love with Sophie when he was sixteen and she fourteen, and told me then that he was going to marry her. Sophie Hilary from New York . . . She was a beautiful girl at a dance. Tom wrote me just after he was eighteen and said I was to come up to Boston because he and Sophie were getting married. I hope I don't shock you: there was a real necessity for them to be married. I have to say that, because, Richard, Tom spoke to me of you."

This time, a pause so long that Reisden thought of prompting him. Gilbert stared straight in front of him. The glasses hung unnoticed from Gilbert's hands.

"Richard," Gilbert said suddenly, anguished, "he told me, if anything ever happened to him, not to let Father have you."

He stopped as if all his confession had been finished in the single sentence. Reisden waited.

"The evening before he was married, Tom said that he wanted me to take you and raise you, if it should ever come up. He said it was important. I said I would. And he wrote to me about it after too, but I didn't keep the letter. And I didn't think anything about it, Richard!"

He seemed to be pleading for himself, and then made an impatient gesture and put his glasses back on. He didn't look at Reisden; he was still looking inside himself, where he had been judged and found wanting all those years ago. He didn't want forgiveness from Richard; Reisden could not have given it to him; forgiveness would have hurt Gilbert. His pale old eyes blazed; he was the Angel of Judgment in a mirror, staring at a foolish old man and telling him that, once, he should have been strong.

"I thought Tom was talking nonsense," he said finally. "He was just eighteen.

"So Father got you when Tom and Sophie died.

"People don't remember where money comes from, do they, Richard? By the time you went to him, no one seemed to mind that Father had grown so rich from the War. Father was so very well off. He was eccentric, of course. He would hold prayer meetings in his office and read out of the Bible for quite long periods at a time. All the professional staff could sit, but the clerks had to kneel. He prospered so much, Richard, that I heard several other firms held prayer meetings too! But no one could bring it off like Father."

Gilbert said it in a sad sort of way, almost proudly.

"I didn't see him, of course. . . . I heard that Father was training you to take over the business. I sent you books, but never a letter. You wouldn't have remembered me anyway, you were too young. I hoped Father would send you away to school, then I could come and see you there. But Father was raising you under his hand." Gilbert's shoulders squared as if he had shivered. "Raising you himself.

"One evening in March, a man came to the lodging house where I was staying and asked me if I were Richard Knight's uncle. He was a very elegant young man, a doctor with curly red Dundreary whiskers— Charlie was grand in those days. He said he was Richard Knight's doctor, and he needed my help, because something was very wrong with Father." Gilbert's voice abruptly trembled. "With Father's mind. Charlie gave me to understand, that evening, that what—"

Gilbert's voice stopped abruptly.

"What Father had done to me, when I told him about Clem—"

Gilbert's throat closed up entirely. He got up and paced around the room. The box of books was downstairs again, here in the library. Gilbert stopped at it and rummaged through it until he found the big book, *Eric, or Little by Little,* that Reisden had read that morning. He brought it over to Reisden and let it fall open. "This!" Gilbert said in a choked whisper, and tapped the text underneath. "He did this!" *The blows fell on him like rain, and the child screamed and writhed* . . . Reisden reached out and took the book, and read, and kept it open a minute, because, after all, it was truth at last.

Flogged him, F. X. Farrar–style. Exactly.

"He beat—" Reisden could not say 'me.' "He beat Richard."

"Richard," said Gilbert, "he would have beaten you to death."

He thought of Gilbert, the day after they had arrived, taking down all of William Knight's mottoes from the walls. THOU GOD SEEST ME. I DEPEND ON THY MERCY ALONE. There was one, he remembered, BE YE PERFECT. Charles Adair cared for children at the Clinic, where battering was as common as dirt. Richard Knight's doctor. Gilbert was afraid of physical harm to anyone out of his sight. Gilbert had washed blood off his hands, horrified, in Richard Knight's presence.

He thought of himself.

Reisden had gone to an English school, where the headmaster beat the boys who got in trouble; and since he'd never been very good at staying out of trouble, his time had come to be caned. He had given the headmaster a black eye. One didn't fight back, ever; it was a cowardly and vulgar display; the headmaster had right, such as it was, on his side; but— "I never let anyone hit me again," he told Gilbert. It was that moment when the evidence shifted and he felt he had been Richard all along; through something meaningless; through something he said.

"Oh," said Gilbert, and looked at him as if he had said something utterly characteristic. Reisden gritted his teeth, flooded with more than he could feel, anger and desolation.

Gilbert took a long shaky breath. "Proving harm against children is very difficult. Against a relative, in possession of the child . . . and Father was very well off . . . very devout. Charlie and I talked about what to do. You and I would have gone very far away. That was our only chance, to run away someplace where Father couldn't find us." Gilbert smiled sadly. "Charlie sent me telegrams every week. He told me that he had talked to you, that you were willing to run away. . . . You thought it would be an adventure. Richard, you were very much like Tom."

"What did you do?"

Gilbert shook his head. "I didn't do anything. Father died. And we were so glad."

"Yes," said Reisden. "Of course we were."

CHAPTER 32

GILBERT NERVED HIMSELF UP to use the telephone and leave a message at the Lakeside desk. Roy would call Reisden when he returned. Reisden found somewhere in his head the name of the man who had been going to clear out the barn and left a message to stop it. He thought of calling Perdita to keep Harry out late; in the end he got Gilbert to do it.

Gilbert had also called Charlie. Would Charlie come round the next day and look at something they had found?

"I didn't tell him that it's a body, Richard, but I will before he looks at it."

They did not want to startle Charlie's heart. "I don't think he can identify much. I suppose it's worth trying. He's a doctor and he knew Jay."

"He should be told."

Reisden nodded.

They sat outside. It was full dark by now. Reisden sat down on the steps, leaning against a porch pillar. He lit a cigaret and blew smoke into the night air. A wakeful frog chirred from the lake, sounding like a cricket. A mosquito keened around his neck and he slapped at it.

As flies are to wanton boys, are we to the gods. They kill us for their sport.

"I don't suppose I have to ask you why you didn't want the money."

"No," Gilbert said.

"Or why you burned the books. Why all of them?"

"You didn't remember. I thought I could," Gilbert looked for a word, "confuse you, Richard. They had things in them."

Perhaps confusion would have been better after all. He felt as if he had been in an accident and didn't know yet what was unhurt, what broken, what gone forever.

"Why did you refuse to inherit the money for Harry? Surely that would have been all right."

"But you were still alive."

He didn't understand that. "Why?"

"I don't think I have good reasons for most things. I—it seemed to me that if I could only believe enough . . . Richard, did you think in all those years . . . I know you don't really remember what happened, but did you think that there was something that couldn't possibly be over? I thought of that whenever I thought of you."

"As long as I was alive, everything was all right?"

"I suppose it wasn't, Richard?"

"I don't know whether it was or not."

"Richard," said Gilbert, "who killed Father, if Jay didn't? Who hurt you?"

"I don't know."

"Might whoever did it feel threatened?" Gilbert leaned forward. "You might be in danger."

Reisden looked at him, innocent Gilbert in the moonlight, already preparing to find something else to be afraid of.

"Richard," Gilbert said timidly, "there might be some way you could remember."

General amnesia cures itself within weeks or not at all— "There's nothing left of Richard." Instinct and hallucination. "You should have made me tell what I knew."

"You had been made to do enough." Gilbert looked out over the moonlit lawn. "There was time."

There had been time for everything then. It was Friday, August third, twelve days until Reisden stopped being Richard, and he had only started, with no idea of what to do and a crime that had suddenly become unsolved.

Reisden breathed out smoke, breathed in night air and the smell of pines and the lake. With the match he drew a black line across the grey-painted porch boards. He would need to talk with Daugherty, Harry, Anna Fen; arrange for identification. He would need to find out what he felt. He didn't know that at all.

"Gilbert, I want to get drunk. Will you get drunk with me?"

"I don't think I've ever been drunk, Richard."

"One doesn't need to practice."

"Can I do it on sherry? I've never drunk anything but sherry."

"You could, but I won't let you." The liquor was in the kitchen, since liquor didn't form part of Gilbert's entertainment scheme. Reisden brought out two glasses and a bottle of Scotch.

"I believe Scotch is quite strong, Richard."

"I want to get paralyzed drunk." On an empty stomach he certainly could, though he almost never had. "Tomorrow we decide what to do, Gilbert. Tonight we don't think about anything."

The Scotch was a single malt, very dark, peaty, and smooth. Millionaire's whiskey. Gilbert took a tentative sip.

"Oh, Richard, this is not so bad."

It was thirty-five years old. Reisden poured himself a glass and drank half of it. An injustice to the whiskey. The liquor heated him and blurred the edges of that thing in the barn. He shivered.

"Tell me about yourself, Richard."

"What would you like to know?"

"Mr. Daugherty said you were a kind of chemist," Gilbert prompted.

"A biochemist." The clear distinctions between Reisden and Richard had blurred away. He was afraid of that, but it was a relief tonight to talk about Reisden and not Richard.

"What do biochemists study?"

Reisden moved his glass from his right hand to his left, held up his right hand in the moonlight, flexed the fingers. " 'This is my hand. Why does it move?' That's what I try to find out."

"Why does it, Richard?"

Reisden shook his head. He moved his hand in the moonlight, switched the drink back and forth from hand to hand. "If I knew I wouldn't be interested in it. I'm sorry, that sounds flip."

"No, I understand."

He bent down and picked up a handful of bits of gravel from the drive, and began throwing them back in the drive, one by one. Motion without result. Perfect futility. What moves me?

"Why did you come here, Richard?"

"Because," he took a breath and let it out, " 'because because because,' one must always have reasons, no? Because I couldn't help myself. I couldn't stop thinking I was Richard and I thought I was crazy."

Gilbert nodded.

"I don't want to be Richard," Reisden said. "I know who I am; it's not Richard. I am who I have been. Gilbert, this is all acting. All pretense. Someday soon everything will change back and I won't be Richard anymore. That's a decision." He sketched the gesture of a toast. "Here's to the rational world. I wish I were there."

He was holding the glass very tightly between two hands, so tight that he was afraid he would break it; he put it down and clasped his hands together between his knees. His fingers ached from their pressure against each other, and the webs of flesh stood out between the fingers.

"When I was very young," Reisden said, "I found out what chemistry was. The family I lived with, the Loewensteins, had a country home outside Graz. There were a lot of cousins; we all had tutors during the summertime. The chemistry tutor had just taught us how to add up molecules during a reaction. Very basic stuff." He drank and pressed the glass against his cheekbone because his hand was shaking and he was ashamed of it. "Nothing was created or destroyed. Nothing was ever left out, nothing was unaccounted for. The tutor took us for a walk. *'Meine Damen und Herren,* the smell of the grass, that is chemistry! The grass is chemistry! The cows, and the ducks, and your own bodies, that is chemistry!' I thought, how splendid to understand."

How very splendid to understand.

"I wanted to be angry," Gilbert said suddenly.

"What?"

"Richard, I wanted to be angry, but I never could. Father was so angry, I— There was never enough room for me to be angry. I wanted to do wild things. To yell and insist and look down my nose at people. I wanted to be a riverboat pilot and wear a big hat. But I was always afraid that if I let go, I would end up like Father."

The woods came close to the other side of the gravel drive, and near to the house there was a magnificent old maple, a giant a hundred years old. Reisden unlaced his hands and pointed a finger at the trunk. "Throw your glass at that tree," he said.

Gilbert looked at his whiskey tumbler in surprise. It was a good lead-crystal tumbler, plain and heavy, probably one of William's.

"You wanted to get angry. Throw your glass at the tree trunk. Break the glass."

Gilbert held the glass away from him as if it were a bomb. "I couldn't do that, Richard."

"Of course you can. You know how to throw."

"But I don't have a reason."

"Don't you?"

Gilbert held the glass in front of him, repelled and fascinated.

"If you don't think you can hit the tree, throw it at

this step." The bottom step of the porch was granite, a single enormous block. "You can't miss the step."

"I'm not the sort of person—"

"Do it once."

Gilbert gingerly held the glass over the bottom step, and dropped it. It exploded in a star of splinters.

"That's not the way—" But it hadn't mattered, after all, which way Gilbert had broken the glass. He had broken the glass. He looked down at it in a kind of horrified grimness, and looked up at Reisden.

"I hated Father, Richard."

"Yes. I know."

"I'm glad he's dead and I don't want to find out who did it. But I'm going to have to because Father's dead and because someone killed Jay." Gilbert's long old mouth tightened. "I would want to forgive whoever did it, if it weren't for you and Jay, Richard."

He looked down into the star of glass as if it were the innards of some sacrificial beast. "Richard," he said, and his voice tightened with pain. "I don't want revenge, or police, or trials. But it isn't because I'm a good or forgiving man. Revenge would make me be like Father."

In the moonlight the glass glittered and reflected in his glasses, and he looked away as if he were about to be overwhelmed by what he saw. "Now you, Richard."

"I?" Reisden said.

"Break your glass," said Gilbert, as if it would be a betrayal if Reisden didn't.

Reisden drained the glass, stood up, and hefted it. It should have been easy. Army men and university men broke glasses after toasts, seeing how much broken glass they could build up in the fireplace for the servants to clear away in the morning. A stupid custom; but it was easy to break a glass. One could simply drop it, like Gilbert. But to break it, and mean it, and mean the anger behind it? He stood with the empty glass in his hand.

He was dizzy with the liquor, but not carelessly drunk. He had never got drunk that way. Because one could get out of control. Because he had to hold back something, except when he had acted in plays; and then he was someone else; but he could no longer be someone else here, if he had ever been.

Then he slammed the glass down abruptly and it shattered across the granite step. "That is acting. I don't feel angry," he said dispassionately. "I want to go back to my lab and not to be disturbed. Not to be noticed by anyone. I have nothing left inside me. Nothing to give; nothing to say. I don't want to be touched by another person again. I don't want to be hurt. I want what I can comprehend. I want nothing. I don't want to be close to anything or anyone. Not anyone here; not you."

It was not what he had expected to say either. He sat down on the steps, drained, staring at the scar of glass across the step. He looked at Gilbert. *Right; look at the audience.* Gilbert had tears in his eyes. He made as if to touch Reisden's arm; Reisden drew away.

"Richard," said Gilbert. "Do you know why I said you were Richard?"

I could not be Richard. It would be impossible to live in that much pain.

"Because you didn't want to come back here."

He thought about that for some time. It was almost funny.

"Yes," said Reisden. "That makes all the sense in the world."

·   ·   ·

ALONE in his bedroom, he thought about how it might have happened.

Who had killed Jay French? It wasn't conceivable that no one would have found him. Barns smell in summer, but the whole hayloft would have stunk as he rotted. And what had happened to Richard?

And Leo had lied. Sometime later he would think about that. Tonight it didn't matter.

Leo had lied, and Victor—had done better by Reisden than Reisden had by him.

He took out the picture of Tasy and looked again. How close could Richard Knight have been to anyone? How close had Reisden been to her? *No, surely*— He was afraid, by remembering too closely, he would lose what he had thought they had.

Tasy, did I ever tell you that I didn't remember my parents? No? Did I ever say, even then, that I wondered who I was? I told you that I loved you; but did you know it hurt me to be close to anyone? Did I tell you that sometimes I was afraid of myself, that my own emotions hurt me, so that I couldn't bear to be talked to or touched? Was I better at acting than I was with you? Was there ever a moment between us, even in bed, when part of me didn't stand aside?

Tasy's photograph said nothing, just smiled and smiled; Tasy was dead.

When he had broken with Graf Leo and gone to study chemistry under Louis, he had taken Tasy with him, knowing very well that marrying her would make the break definitive.

Did I marry you to get away from Leo?

He took out of its envelope the photograph of William Knight dead. Tasy dead on the carpet of leaves, her neck broken at that odd angle.

Did I want you dead?

William Knight dead on the carpet . . .

"All this time, darling," he asked her, "all this bad time, and not even for you?" But Tasy's photograph didn't change expression, because Tasy was dead.

And then he was angry; angry for the stupidity and for the waste of years, angry for what he had not been able to tell her, angry for everything he had failed to be. And he knew, finally, how much he had lost with his childhood.

And then, because he was Alexander Reisden who had loved her more than he had dared to know, he cried for Tasy at last; but not even that could bring her back.

CHAPTER 33

CHARLIE ADAIR and Gilbert Knight stood in the hayloft in the bright sunlight. Saturday morning had dawned hot with no breeze. Charlie nodded. "I will try to identify it for you," he said to his old friend; although he knew, Heaven knows he knew already.

When Gilbert had gone, Charlie got painfully down on his knees and picked up the horrible thing of black bone and straw and scraps of leather. By one jawbone the leather had come almost away; he got a small pair of tweezers out of his doctor's bag and picked and picked until he had cleared a section of the jaw. Then he counted teeth. Three and it would be a child, a boy of eight. Four, an adult. The body looked so small. The thin curved tweezers moved along the ridges of the teeth. One, two, three. Three. Then he found the hole where the fourth had fallen out. Four.

Jay French.

"Oh my God, I am heartily sorry that I have offended against Thee . . ." he whispered.

Jay French's murderer stood up, feeling that his legs could not support his body. He fanned his face with his old hat, as if everything were still the same.

And then he started to say the Franciscan crown once through for Jay French, as he said every day a crown for the soul of that madman, William Knight. But the words fell mocking, blasphemy and no prayers at all.

For almost nineteen years he had taken communion, and he was in mortal sin.

He sat with the beads useless in his hands. All of his prayer had been hollow and mortally sinful since the crime.

All except, Do not let me be found out.

God, dear God, Whom I have blackly offended, what shall I do?

CHARLIE ADAIR came from a Maine town. Every Sunday, young Charlie jounced over the roads with his mother and father in the grocery buckboard to the Catholic church where the loggers worshipped. He and his father and mother sat in the front, ahead of the loggers and the millworkers. Charlie thought the wooden church very grand, with its pink-and-blue paint and the saints raising their eyes to the silver stars painted on the ceiling. But his Boston-educated mother shook her head;

he was not to admire; this was a French Catholic church; and Charlie understood, even in the puzzlement of childhood, that the son of a storekeeper ranked higher than a millworker even in Heaven.

He went away to boarding school, memorized the Baltimore Catechism, and received the Body and Blood of Christ. His mother tutored him in mathematics while she baked pies. They would have given him to the priesthood (it was above them to think of anything higher—but surely His Holiness would take special notice of Father Charles). When he was admitted to medical school, his mother revised her plans only slightly. Instead of a red hat, Charlie would have a doctor's plate on a Beacon Street brownstone; he would marry a loving and submissive wife and have many good Catholic children. "Whatever you do, Charlie, you will succeed at it, and God will keep you a *good* man."

Protected by goodness, Dr. Charles Adair entered his profession in 1879, the year Richard Knight was born. To succeed in Catholic Boston, a man could take two routes: to work among the Irish, who were already developing their own strong political ties, or to become very Yankee. Charlie Adair sent his political contributions to fund-raisers for politicians named O'Brien and Fitzgerald; but he also joined the Sons of the American Revolution, and it was there that he was most often seen.

He cultivated religious discretion. He attended early Mass daily (in Cold Roast Boston, early rising is a state of grace), but was at the boathouse in time to row on the Charles River with his Episcopalian banker friends. In cases of sickness, he always suggested religious counsel, but never specifically recommended a priest. He attended deathbeds at the side of the Unitarian minister, the Quaker elders, or even the Vedantists, and learned not to think of the viaticum or of Peter, who binds and looses in Heaven. Episcopalian matrons trusted him; he was on a board with the minister of the Park Street Church. He was living proof that a good man could be Catholic and fit in.

Bless me, Father, for I have sinned . . .

But he had very little to sin about. He developed a special practice among the children of the rich, who do not die. He had never to despair about a mortal soul. Children liked him, and he them; he understood that children want to be perfect as much as they want to be loved. He liked their successes. He went to their school plays and read their letters. In this there was no calculation. He loved his patients as a priest loves God. In his early thirties, he scouted about for a suitable Catholic woman to marry. But when his suitable Catholic woman told him gently that she was called to take the veil, he found it no real deprivation to correspond with Sister Agnes rather than marry her.

He had children. He had his full share of God's holiness. He was very happy.

The boy was four years old and rich in his own right: that was all Charlie Adair knew when he agreed to be Richard Knight's doctor. The child lived in New Hampshire, four hours away by train, a most unusual and inconvenient arrangement.

"Surely you would prefer a physician who is not so far away."

"You are the best, sir, and William Knight wants the best," Jay French, William Knight's secretary, said smoothly. William Knight himself said almost nothing during the first interview in Charlie's office. His fathomless dark eyes stared past Charlie; they were almost all black, dilated, as if he had some trouble of the eye or were looking into darkness.

A local doctor would handle anything ordinary; Charlie would be called if anything serious arose. He would be paid a retainer whether his services were used or not. Charlie, uneasy, asked for far more than he thought reasonable. The little thin secretary raised his eyebrows, smiled slightly, but paid the first installment in advance, without a murmur, in gold. The two men went out together, the tall, spare, old one leaning on his cane, the younger man beside him; and Jay French's look stayed with Charlie and filled him with an almost spiritual unease.

Bless me, Father, for I have sinned . . .

It was March, when the snow is piled high on the railways. New Hampshire was cold. The Federal Hotel was closed for the season, its shutters tugging and groaning against each other in the gale. The rocks of the Little Spruce were slicked with ice, and the house rose above pines and barren fields, dark as granite, infernal. It was the time of dusk when window lights would have shone across the lake, across the fields, if anyone else had spent any part of winter in their summer houses; but all down the shore of the lake, for miles and miles, no light showed, nothing but the black-shrouded pines.

"I have come to see my patient."

They had not expected him. They brought the child out. Sturdy, solemn, his hair still in a little boy's short curls. He was dressed in deep black mourning, like his grandfather's black broadcloth and the secretary's black. There was a deep bruise on his cheek.

"The boy bruises easily."

There were welts across the backs of both small hands.

"The boy requires discipline," Jay French said.

William Knight said in a distant voice, "The boy will get his education."

The two men had chosen the best doctor for Richard they could find—four hours away.

Richard did not complain. Children his age want sticky bandages over the slightest scrape or cut, but Richard, whose hands must have hurt terribly, simply looked off into the distance with a grown man's reserve while Charlie touched them. There were other bruises on his small bony chest, some old and some newer, and old welts across the buttocks.

No more than the child did, did the old man notice how badly the boy was hurt. This was normal to them: to the man, and his secretary, and the child.

So many Saturdays, so many Sunday afternoons. Charlie came to visit his patient often. The old bruises faded and were replaced with fresh ones. The summer of 1885 came: Charlie took Richard fishing (this could happen only on Saturdays, because William Knight was strong on properly observing the Sabbath). Charlie took Richard on walks and taught him the names of trees and flowers. Charlie showed Richard the families of animals around his lake: ducks, beavers, owls, and foxes. The autumn came and the leaves fell.

"My parents are in Heaven. They don't take an interest in me if I disobey."

"Even in Heaven, those who love us look out for us. Do you pray for their souls and ask their intercession?"

The leaves fell and the snow fell. Richard's room had no fireplace. Charlie came as often as he could, knowing that while he was with Richard, the boy would be warm. They played endless games of checkers and chess in the cheerless sitting room.

"I am in mourning for my corrupt nature. I am a child of sin," the little boy said. "Grandpapa tells me so. My parents weren't married when I was conceived, and that's a sin. I must work much harder than other boys to subdue my natural temper to the discipline of Christ. Redemption is barely possible for me."

Is love a matter of taking time? Charlie Adair chose to spend more time in New Hampshire with Richard, rather than keep up the constant work in Boston that success demanded. He became less visible, taking his coloration from Richard himself, who depended on being nearly invisible. He would not have called it love. It was so much less than what he should have done.

In the spring they hunted frogs in the marshes while the iris bloomed. Richard would catch frogs, hold them for a while as if it were important to him to protect them, then let them go.

"Doctor Charlie, is Grandpapa right about religion? Christ forgives more than Grandpapa does. Christ would not whip me."

William Knight got worse.

A five-year-old will cringe from a blow; a seven-year-old will fight it. Charlie taught Richard that God was love, not discipline without relief. He would have done better to say nothing, because he taught the child to understand that what his grandfather was doing was not love. William, who thought that love disciplined the soul, caned harder. Just past Richard's seventh birthday, he caned Richard into unconsciousness for the first time; two months later, Richard ran away as far as the next town, and when he was caught, William handcuffed the boy to his iron bed and beat him with a fireplace poker.

For the first time, Charlie realized that William might kill Richard.

He spoke to the man. "You should send the boy to a good school. If he is difficult, they will reform him."

"You don't agree with my methods, Dr. Adair. But I'd send no boy of mine to school. Would they teach my boy what I'm teaching him? Deportment, eh? Business? Languages? My boy will run rings around them all. My boy's sturdy, he can hike as long as I can. Will they toughen him? Will they teach him my company? Will they do the most important thing for him, will they look after his soul?"

Richard slept curled up because the pain was too great for him to straighten out. All the skin was discolored over his stomach and liver and spleen, as if he had bled internally. His skin was grey and dusty-looking. But he sat at his little desk, by the side of his grandfather's big desk, sitting upright because if he did not he would be punished.

Bless me, Father, for I have sinned . . .

God, how could such things be? How could he hate a man so?

In dismay, Charlie Adair's well-connected confessor sent him to Father Peter O'Connell, the South End priest. In Father O'Connell's turbulent parish, the confession boxes smelled like urine, cabbage, and potatoes; and Charlie Adair sat in the dusty, malodorous dark, feeling like a failure for the first time in his life. This was the kind of Catholicism he didn't want to know about.

"The man will kill his grandson, I know it. He has

great wealth. I don't want this job. Why did the grandfather choose me?"

Father Peter's answer came through the screen between them, tired and ordinary words charged with loving.

"God chose you to prevent the child's death and save the man's soul."

Father Peter and Charlie Adair sat up in the kitchen of the parish house, drinking tea laced with whiskey, and talked about what Adair could do.

"You'll have no luck with the police. When it's a drunken Irish washerwoman, you've a chance of getting the boy away legally; but a man with money? Nothin' like this ever happens to rich children."

That was why Charlie had his practice among rich children.

"Is there anyone the boy can go to?" Father Peter asked.

"There's an uncle."

"Talk to him. Come to see me again, day or night."

Charlie traced the itinerant peddler, Gilbert Knight, to a lodging house down by Falmouth. Gilbert Knight was a reed-thin, nervous man with a droopy mustache and glasses, happy only in the company of his horse and cart. Still, he understood, though it was only with a kind of intellectual, unbelieving, guilty understanding. "Father wasn't like this when we boys were young," he kept saying over and over.

Gilbert did not know what to do. But he would do what he could. He would certainly take in Richard. "Whatever I can do," he kept repeating. "Here is a book for him. Tell him I love him."

Charlie wasn't sure that Gilbert was the right man until he read the first lines of the book, which was *The Coral Island.* "Roving has always been, and still is, my ruling passion, the joy of my heart, the very sunshine of my existence." Gilbert understood too that they needed to get the boy away. In his own way he had passed Richard a lifeline.

The summer came again. Pirate and adventure books were popular then, and Charlie passed one after another from Gilbert to Richard, who read them somehow in the no-leisure of his regimented life, as if they were promises of escape. *Treasure Island, Robinson Crusoe, Through the Looking-Glass;* books too immoral, fantastic, unsuitable for William Knight's heir. The little boy did not run much that summer; he was pale and sat too often rigid in his chair, sweating with pain. Internal injuries, healing too slowly, perhaps not healing at all.

How to get the boy away from William? And how to make sure that, once Gilbert had Richard, William wouldn't get him back? That would be the end of Richard's life.

"I will change my name," Gilbert wrote, "go with Richard to a place where no one can know us." They talked about the West, even about foreign countries. Father Peter corresponded with a bookseller in Dublin. Charlie told Richard little about this, not wanting to get the boy's hopes up or betray something.

"Talk to the grandfather," urged Father Peter, and Charlie talked to William Knight about his soul. Somewhere inside, he knew, the man wanted his grandson alive. It was faith alone that kept that knowledge clear.

"Do you deny that the Bible says that the sins of the fathers shall be visited upon the children, eh? Unto the third and fourth generation? Will indulgence root out those sins? The lazy child is beaten and becomes industrious. The stubborn child is beaten and becomes respectful. The love of the flesh is strong in this child, as it was in his father. But he shall be strong to combat it!—strong to survive!—and I'll have no weak-minded Catholic doctrine interfering in my power to make it so. You will cease to bother me or mine with your religion, Sir, or I'll make sure that you bother no others."

In some parts of Boston, Catholics were still supposed to be under the direct orders of their priests, who were in communication with the Pope, and the Pope in league with the Devil. If Charlie got the reputation of a Catholic who tried to make more Catholics, he would never work among children again.

"The boy isn't well," he ventured.

"You are his doctor, Sir! Your incompetence shall not be blamed on me."

Charlie talked privately with Jay French. His resemblance to William Knight seemed more marked, the look of a man who spent too much time in discipline.

"Surely you know what your employer is doing."

Your father is killing your nephew, he thought but would not say.

"It's my business to know everything, as a servant of the household." Jay French's pale, mocking eyes were turned up to Charlie. They were the same clear grey as Richard's, touched with the same unidentifiable color. "It is also my business, Sir, to do exactly as I am told."

Then Richard found Washington, his dog.

August sixth, 1887, was a hot Saturday, a terrible day. Both William Knight and Jay French had been away for the week, something almost unprecedented; for once

Richard was safe, alone with the servants, and unforgivably the doctor stayed down in Boston. So there was no one to tell Richard that it was wise not to play hooky and go wandering in the woods, that a little lost black-and-white puppy should not be fed or given water, should certainly not sleep in that cheerless room where Richard had spent four years. So when Charlie Adair came up to visit that Saturday afternoon, there was Richard, playing in the rose garden with a dog named Washington.

Charlie had brought a camera, training William to the idea that he had become an amateur photographer, as everyone else was doing that summer of 1887. He had hoped to get some evidence of Richard's condition on film, but Richard was unmarked that day, Richard was playing with the dog Washington; and Charlie Adair took shots of a puppy chasing a stick, a little boy throwing it, a little boy sitting in the rose garden, his arms around a black-and-white dog. And Charlie had just put the camera back in his doctor's bag, and the man and the boy were about to go inside for lemonade, when William Knight and Jay French arrived.

William Knight told Richard to hold the dog, and Richard picked up the dog and held him in his arms, the little dog squirming because Richard must have held him so tight. Richard must have thought that maybe it would all be all right, that his grandfather might let him keep the dog after all. William said something to Jay French, who nodded and went to find something. Charlie stood by Richard's side, his hand on the boy's shoulder. William Knight looked into them and through them with his staring black eyes, his long white hair wild around his collar and his hand clasped white around the knob of his lead-weighted cane. No one said anything until Jay French came back. He had in his hands a short length of thin, flexible rope.

And a gun.

There was a stake in the ground, a gardener's stake. Jay French tied one end of the rope to the stake. He took the dog. He tied the other end of the rope around the dog's neck. "Shorter," said William Knight. The dog tried to wriggle out of the rope leash. He was scrabbling frantically back along the path toward Richard. William Knight raised his cane and with one efficient blow broke the dog's back. The dog began crying, howling, the only sound in the still garden. His back legs didn't move now, but the front ones were still scrabbling, trying to drag himself along the path. His neck was pulled back by the rope. He moved in a circle leaving a trail of blood. Richard had one hand half forward, as if he were saying, "Here, boy," but so far inside himself that there was no sound and no movement of the lips, only the half-gesture of one hand. The gun Jay held was a little Civil War rat pistol, a six-shot revolver. Jay rotated the cylinder, making sure there was a bullet in each chamber. Charlie heard the click as the cylinder rotated. Jay gave the gun to William. William gave the gun to Richard.

"You didn't have permission to have a dog. Put it out of its misery."

Charlie knew what Richard was going to do; he could feel it in the way the muscles of the boy's arm tensed to rise, with the gun, toward his grandfather's face. Charlie clamped his hand on Richard's shoulder, pushing it down, holding it down, until the boy's muscles surrendered their will. "Richard, *no,*" he murmured. The boy looked up at him, once only, and Charlie only looked back, sending his whole heart along the look so that the boy would not be alone. Richard turned back toward the dog. Richard held both arms out in front of him, with the pistol held in both hands. He sighted down the barrel. He must have realized that he didn't know what he was doing, because he walked slowly forward until he was very close to Washington, and he knelt down and held the pistol close behind the dog's ear. Then Richard pulled the trigger. The little dog's front legs scrabbled once and he shuddered and died on the path; blood came out of his nostrils. Richard put down the gun. He knelt down on the path with both arms around the dog, and petted the dog's back, and the back of his head, and his ears, and lay with his cheek against the dog's body, without moving, eyes open, like a child on a monument. William raised his cane. Charlie Adair stepped between him and Richard, shielding the boy with his body.

"No," he said.

He felt the cane above him; it held for a long time. Gilbert and I have waited too long, he thought. The cane slowly descended, just clipping his shoulder; not hurting, just promising.

"Richard, go to your room. Dr. Adair, you will stay to dinner."

Charlie Adair pushed Richard down the path. Stay in your room, he thought at him. Lock the door: remembering then that Richard Knight's room locked only from the outside. He started off down the path after Richard.

"Dr. Adair, you will stay here."

William Knight and Jay French moved slowly off down the path, William leaning on his cane, saying something in a low voice to Jay, who nodded. Charlie Adair sat motionless in a garden seat with a view of the rose garden and the lake.

Eventually the flies began to buzz around the little dog's muzzle and eyes. Charlie got a spade from the garden outbuildings and buried Washington in a spot down by the barn, remembering where it was so he could tell Richard, covering it over so that William wouldn't find it. He was afraid of what the man would do. He thought of William Knight digging the body up and using it in some way against Richard. William would do that.

But William wasn't going to frighten Richard with the soil-covered body of his little dog; not now; he was going to do what he had done so often before.

He was going to beat Richard for disobedience.

Bless me, Father, for I have sinned. I have committed murder.

In his heart he had already done it.

Only Grace could save Charlie now.

And only Charlie could save Richard.

CHAPTER 34

LATE THE NEXT MORNING, viciously hung over, Reisden came down to breakfast. Harry was in the dining room, up not much earlier than he; Perdita had talked with him late last night. Reisden poured himself a cup of coffee and sat down, narrowing his eyes against the sun glaring off the tablecloth. Harry ostentatiously continued to read the paper.

It was quiet. Of course: no piano music, not from here, not over the water from the Clinic. Never again, until Harry told Perdita she could play.

I can take you, he told Harry silently. I'm Richard. Richard owns everything you thought you had. Richard has Gilbert. Give your Perdita back her music and you can have all of it. G-d knows I don't want it.

Adair had been right: One didn't want the money, but the power.

Leaving his coffee, he went outside. Gilbert had cleared away the broken glass from the porch but had missed a shard by the stair riser. Reisden picked it up, a vicious little dagger of glass. He felt as if he wanted to cut himself, to feel a placid, simple emotion like pain. He had been in this state before; he was afraid of it.

Gilbert came up from the garden. He smiled tentatively at his Richard; Reisden handed him the bit of glass. "I'm going to take the auto out for a while."

He drove a little too fast over the Knights' narrow bridge, too fast by far over the twisting unpaved roads outside town. A road he took at random came out at the top of the hills north of the lake. He was far enough away to cover with his hand the view of everything from Island Hill to the railroad station. To the south he could see across hazy green hills the view toward Boston and New York.

If I were truly sane I would drive to New York now. Everywhere but here I can be Alexander Reisden.

And what good would that do him? If being Alexander Reisden had worked, he wouldn't be here.

Did he in the least want to become Richard? If he

decided to try it there would be a long and boring fight, which he had little chance of winning. What would he do it for? Money he had enough of, he didn't need multiple millions and a full-time staff to manage it. He wouldn't have children or a wife to leave it to.

But I can.

If he was Richard, he was sane.

He sat in the car with the breath knocked out of him, looking out over the bowl of the valley. It was as if someone had left him the whole valley—which, if he was Richard, was something close to true. He couldn't see the situation all at once, not in the detail he needed.

My G-d, to be rich and sane and to have all one's chances to take again. It was a little too much to understand.

No. Most certainly no. He didn't want to be Richard.

On the other hand, he would much prefer to be sane.

He drove back slowly. Being back at the house felt awkward and tentative, like acting on a decision not really taken. He shut himself up in the telephone closet under the stairs and put through a call to New York.

"Alexandre?" Louis said through the wires.

"J'avais tort," Reisden said. "I was wrong. I didn't want to kill Tasy." He took a deep breath. Speaking French felt stiff after two months thinking and speaking in English. He massaged his temples. Thinking of Richard too much was like pushing against pain.

Long silence. "Good," Louis said.

Neither one of them knew what to say after that. The telephone line sang tensely like a cicada.

"Was that what you went off to find out?" Louis asked finally.

"Not at the time. I didn't know."

"You hurt me, up in Boston."

"Yes. Not only there."

He had never apologized to Louis; apologies for what Louis knew about him would have cost his last shred of pride. "I have been so wrong I don't know how to be right yet. This is all new. Nothing's clear."

"At least something is happening."

"Oh, my G-d, yes."

"What about Paris?"

He hadn't thought about Paris. Valleys upon valleys opening.

"Alexandre? Tu es là?"

"Yes, I'm here." Fool not to say yes, I'll go to Paris, though he knew already that someday he would. "It's all a little too early. Don't ask me yet."

"But tell Berthet not to hire anyone else? Because he hasn't."

"Don't for G-d's sake let him hire anyone else."

No sound on the other end of the line. Then finally Louis cleared his throat. *"Ouais, OK. Ça va bien."*

"Yes, everything's all right." More or less all right. Again, neither of them said anything, trying to deal with that confusion when relationships change. "Have you found anything in the lab?"

"It was good you called. O'Brien wants to send you some results. And he wants your results from last winter."

"I'll telegraph Lotmann to send them, and of course I want to see O'Brien's work. What's it about?"

Reisden could sense Louis grinning. "The package will arrive on Monday."

CHAPTER 35

"I DON'T CARE, it's too hot," Efnie complained. "Mamma, you can't possibly expect us to wear all this!"

"I expect you to look like other girls at the dance, yes. I do not expect you to shed your undergarments like a Hottentot."

"Mamma, it'll be as hot as soup at that dance. You know half the ballroom windows at the Lakeside don't open."

"These are the dresses you have, and these are the dresses you'll wear," decreed Aunt Violet. "Look at Perdita, she doesn't whine about a little heat."

The door closed definitively. "I don't have *breath* to complain," Perdita murmured.

Efnie and Perdita were laced into the corsets they would wear that evening, canvas stiffened with thin steel boning. Under their corsets they wore chemises; over them, cotton and lace corset covers, then their petticoats. Perdita was fanning herself with the fan that belonged to her dress. The dress was pale pink, edged with a deeper pink ruching, and the fan was ostrich feathers, pink and plumy. The fan-feathers moved a languid suggestion of air. She didn't feel at all like going to a party tonight. She felt a little sick; she hadn't slept at all last night, thinking about the thing in the barn. Harry had stayed very late, so that she couldn't call to Island Hill and ask

Gilbert or Richard. They might have called, but they hadn't, and she didn't know. Only the memory of that horrible smell.

"You look like a flamingo in your dress, pink doesn't suit you," Efnie said critically. "You look all pale. And my dress is ten years out of style. Nobody wears big flared skirts like this anymore. Everyone will laugh at us."

It was so hot that just standing still made the sweat come out on her. Girls weren't supposed to sweat. Perdita pushed her hair up distractedly in a coil at the top of her head. If she fainted again, the way she had in the wedding dress . . . "I don't want to go to the party."

"Of course you do. Mamma is just saving money, giving you an ostrich fan to take to a party like this. Oh, Perdita, I want to go off and buy a dress, something that'll really make the men take notice, so I can get a boyfriend like Harry. I want to dance with some man and have him know I've got a body, not a suit of armor. It's too hot not to— Oh, Perdita, don't look like that. Come with me, Mamma has an account at that New York shop on Main Street, and I saw just the dress I want."

At the shop, Perdita stood smelling the air while Efnie tried on dresses. Scents of sachet, powder, sandalwood, perfumes. One of the shop assistants let her try one of the perfumes. "Ylang-Ylang," the shop assistant said. "From Paris."

It was astringent, alcoholic, with an undertone of musk and flowers. Perdita shivered. From Paris, from all the places she had never been. She sniffed her own wrist, smelling the perfume and beneath it the odor of her skin.

"Perdita, stop smelling yourself, that's disgusting."

She hadn't thought of trying any dresses. One would be very like another to her. But if the dresses were like the perfume . . . "Please," she said, "may I try one on?"

"Why do *you* want to?" Efnie muttered. "I mean— You're engaged."

Efnie did mean it, besides the inevitable *You don't have to be fashionable, you're blind,* but it made Perdita's blood rise. "I do want to," she said, low-voiced.

"Try that one then," Efnie said carelessly, "the color suits you."

Efnie's tone made her suspicious, but the shop assistant agreed. In the changing room she unbuttoned her clothes and stepped out of them, down to her slips.

"No, the petticoat too," the shop assistant said. "You don't wear petticoats with this dress."

"None at all?" she said in a small voice.

She stood up in her chemise alone, and the shop assistant slipped the dress over her shoulders. It was lighter than anything she had ever worn. There was a little weight from the beading around her neck and shoulders; otherwise it seemed as though the dress would float away. The shop assistant pressed the snaps together around her neck.

"That *is* right." The shop assistant smiled with her voice.

"It's pretty," Efnie said almost with disappointment.

"But the one you're wearing is *your* color, it's simply you," Efnie's shop assistant gushed.

"What color is mine?" Perdita asked. "*Is* it pretty? If I get into the light, I can see it."

In the light from the front window the color was like nothing she had ever dreamed of wearing: a color like the smell of sandalwood, like that perfume from France. It was a filmy brass or gold, a color from a foreign country, not a girl's color at all. "Oh," she sighed and ran her hand down the smooth, soft fabric as gently as if it were a lion.

"The silk is Chinese. The beads are amber and iron," the shop assistant said. "And everyone at the dance will want to look like you."

"That will be good for you!" said Perdita, pleased.

"Yes, my dear; although what they want to look like, they can't buy. So we will pick you out the right shoes and fan to go with this, and— Are you dressing at the hotel? Good. Tonight Mary and I will come and dress your hair."

The two girls walked back to the hotel, their purchases under their arms, while Efnie schemed how they would dress tonight without alerting Aunt Violet. "I don't know I would wear that dress if I were you, Perdita. That color's just unearthly."

"Will Harry like it, Efnie? You know he doesn't like anything too odd." Who had she bought it for? Harry would think she was half undressed.

Richard would like it.

She thought of the two of them in the barn and for a moment shivered uncontrollably. She didn't know whether it was because of the thing in the barn, or just because he would be there.

Really, she shouldn't go.

CHAPTER 36

THE MIDSUMMER SOIRÉE was in full swing when Gilbert, Harry, and Reisden arrived at the ballroom of the Lakeside Hotel. Roar of voices, heat that made sweat stand out on the skin, and the orchestra violently sawing at the latest songs.

Reisden had not gone to a formal summer dance since Vienna. Outside, the fairy lights were strung through the tree branches as if this were a dance at Hofbrünnerstein's. The smells were the same: crushed geranium leaves, crushed flowers, perfume and punch, sex and sweat and anticipation.

A dance is sex in good clothes, in which eligible young women and men may meet, and walk, and talk, may look at each other's palms and trace each other's future with one finger, finding each other fascinating. A young man may take a young woman to see the fairy-lights strung out in the dark trees, and when the moon is full and there is a lake to reflect the moon, they may find more trees and lakes and moons than chaperones; and who knows what comes next? For a young man of good presence, the spring of a dance floor underfoot is as good as the promise of a woman. Reisden was astonished at how many women there were in the world tonight. It was a new way of forgetting when he should be thinking, but without any conscious effort he undressed them with his eyes, stripping off bugle skirts and spiky bodices to look at the astonishing curves of breasts and bellies and thighs. He was apparently going to go directly from madness to satyriasis.

"Mr. Knight," Anna Fen purred, "you called me this afternoon, my maid said."

She was a confection of tulle and lace and moon-colored charmeuse, covered with silken lilies and geraniums and glittering bugle beads. Her dress plunged on top just to the bound of discretion, so that he could see she had a beauty mark on the side of one ample breast, and rose discreetly at the hem so that her slim silk ankles showed themselves. Reisden took a long comprehensive look. Jay was dead, which he would have to tell her to learn her reaction, and he didn't like her overmuch, and the dress looked like a drunken dream. Still he looked her up and down and mentally filled in hidden details under the silk. Her eyes demurely dropped to below his waist. He mentally cursed the woman. Mrs. Fen was a public convenience, which is sometimes all that's required; but he didn't want to feel like one too. "I am so sorry she put you off. Do call again," Mrs. Fen said. "Come for tea. I shall always be at home to you." She turned and swayed away, presenting them with a magnificent rear end. Even Gilbert stared.

"Richard, you seem distracted," Gilbert said. "Are you enjoying yourself?"

"Oh, much more than I expected." He smiled.

"Have you seen Perdita?"

"No." She was expected to be in pink. He was still standing on his vantage point on the stairs and he looked over the pink dresses in the crowd, but didn't see her.

"You must dance with her when you find her," he told Gilbert.

"Harry says he's taken all her dances, but I hope he will give me one. He must give you one."

"You shall have mine, Gilbert." He thought about their dance lesson—yesterday, in the music room, when she had told him that she had given up music for Harry's sake. Then in the barn; only yesterday, in the barn? She would not want the reminder. And tonight he felt dangerous. No, not Harry's Perdita.

Charlie Adair came by, in a dark suit, not formal dress, looking tired and discouraged. Gilbert took his arm and the two men went off, moving out toward the chairs on the terrace. Reisden was besieged with requests to sign dance cards. Here, as in Vienna, the dance card was the legal tender of dances; it was a small booklet with a pencil attached on a silk cord, showing the types of dances, the music, and the order in which they would be played. "Waltz, *Fair Rose*. Two-step, *Can't You Eat a Bull-Dog?*" What?—a song about Yale. "Waltz medley, from *The Merry Widow*." Men asked for dances by asking women for permission to sign their dance cards, then writing their names for the dances they wanted. The system was cumbersome and required no little diplomacy, since once a man had permission to sign a girl's dance card, he could sign for more than one dance. Men were given no aide-mémoire, but were expected to commit to memory the combinations of women and dances with which they had been favored.

The women's system ran smoothly on a roadbed of forgeries, prevarication, and erasures—dance card pencils deliberately had no erasers, but most women learned to make do with the inside of a roll from the buffet. The stag line, on the other hand, was as full of confusion here as it was in Vienna: "Which one's Whitwell's sister? I think I've got the next dance with her, and I don't know her from a puppy." Reisden pleaded honestly that he didn't know any of them, thus could dance only with women who were not already taken for that dance. This offended all the right people. Every mamma's girl wanted to dance with the eligible bachelor Richard Knight, but none wanted to confess herself deserted for that very dance.

He danced several times with a clever girl who knew exactly what she was doing—plain face, splendid body—and once each with a series of delightful American virgins, whom he chose for their variety of body shapes like a pasha going through a harem. A little blonde so shy she almost melted in his arms; a brunette who talked about tennis while her small, round breasts jiggled; a big, warm, comfortable girl whom one could have licked like ice cream.

In Vienna—or even, say, in New York, if he had spent the summer as Louis had wanted—one part of a dance would have led very naturally to another. In Vienna, virgins were off limits but wives were not; one would move through the dances making a little verbal love here, there pressing a hand for a few extra moments; men and women cooperated very naturally, female sensuality rubbing and pressing against male, as the waltzes became slower and the hour later; eyes looked into eyes, hands pressed against lips; and when Reisden, at two or three or four o'clock in the morning, took some laughing woman up the discreet backstairs in the Schwarzenbergplatz or stripped her in her own bedroom, it was the whole dance they climaxed, all the men she had danced with, all the women he had.

Here he did not know the rules, except those Anna Fen had offered him. He didn't know what was permitted, and there were far too many virgins, who did not dance as well as in Vienna; but the same slow electricity was building up, and he played the mental game of deciding who, of all these beautiful women, he would want to end the evening with.

He took a glass of wine and stood at the top of the stairs on a little balcony with a wrought iron railing in the shape of vines. He could see across the dance floor; and out of all the wealth of women, his eye was caught by one because her dress was simpler than the rest and an odd color, almost a bronze. She was a woman of medium height, slim, with beautiful shoulders and small high breasts; the rest he had to leave to imagination under the dress, which was in the Greek style, one perfect line falling from her breasts to the floor.

She stood as gracefully as if she had been barefoot. He took one almost painful breath, swept by an emotion like the moment in music when the theme declares itself. He felt a line stretching between him and the woman, something like the tug of a fishline, a simple, painful precision of desire. She was talking with Efnie Pelham, and she gestured with one of her hands, large hands for her size, with long fingers; and he was looking at her now because he had looked at her all summer.

Perdita.

Harry shouldered his way through the crowd and took Perdita by one arm, leading her toward the dance floor. He put his arms around her in a bear hug and shuffled back and forth, out of step with the music.

Perdita kept in step with him. This was her only season for dancing. At Christmas she would be married to this oaf who couldn't dance and, knowing Harry's possessiveness of her, she would never dance with anyone else again. Reisden wanted for her a night of waltzes with someone better than Harry; but not himself, not when he so simply and impossibly wanted her. Harry danced badly, grabbing Perdita by the spine and running her up and down the dance floor like a football. Reisden wanted her; he wanted to put his hands on her and feel the curve of her hips underneath her dress; he wanted to plunge into this beautiful woman, away from everything that had happened in the last two days; and, because she was Harry's Perdita, for her sake Reisden wanted anything but that complication.

The orchestra took a pause. Harry brought Perdita back to the edge of the floor and, when the music started again, took out her cousin Efnie instead, as if there were no difference between the two. Efnie leaned her head against Harry's arm and simpered. On the edge of the dance floor, not quite out of its traffic and not near any of the few paths on which even the sighted could get from one area to another in this crowded place, Perdita was standing against a pillar. She was so beautiful Reisden's heart hurt. On the other side of the room Harry and Efnie had found a group of girls, apparently school friends of Efnie's, and she was introducing him to them, leaning against his arm. Harry stood there talking to them; someone brought him a glass of punch. He was in no hurry to come back to Perdita.

Gilbert should have been there to rescue her; but he was deep in conversation with Charlie on the other side of the room. Reisden came down the stairs toward her, too unsure of himself to be glad.

"Perdita, may I have this dance?"

He swung her onto the dance floor in something like a dazed waltz. The floor was crowded, too many people on it to have dancing room for anyone; she said something to him, but over the noise of talking and the music, he couldn't hear it. They were pressed together, body to body, and he felt the imprint of every soft inch of her.

She spoke something. "What?" He couldn't hear her, just feel her breath in his ear.

"Who . . . I'm sorry, I have to ask. What was in the barn?"

She hadn't known and he hadn't thought to tell her. Someone jostled against them.

"Come out of here," he said, breaking off the dance and leading her toward an exit door close by. "We'll go on the terrace," he meant it, no farther; they would walk, and talk, and he would do no more than hold her familiar hand.

They found themselves in a service corridor behind the ballroom. Like the ballroom, the walls were mirrored, so that the dim corridor looked spacious. Sometimes, clearly, it was used for entertaining; round banquettes lit by small electric candles curved in recesses along one wall. Tonight it was deserted but for a big silver coffee urn brewing on a rolling cart, and, on another cart, piles of clean spoons and gilt-edged cups and saucers.

"Jay," he said.

She gave one long, heaving sigh. "Not you."

"Not me in any case." Now he was lying to her.

"That's terrible."

"Yes."

She walked a few steps away from him, holding her hands fisted by her sides and shaking her head. "I don't want to *think* of it. We were talking Shakespeare on the next floor down for weeks—and Harry will—I don't want to think about that."

He recognized his own reaction. "It complicates everything."

She nodded.

"Would you like to walk, or go back to the dance? Whatever you like."

"It's awful, but I want to dance. If we go back into the ballroom, I'll have to stay with Harry. Will you dance with me here?"

The music came clearly, but muted, from the ballroom next door, the rhythm a little stronger because of what the wall did to the harmonics, one-two-three, one-two-three, a heartbeat. He said nothing but took her in his arms, in the classic dance position, and began to dance with her. Plain box step first, what he had done with a little girl in Gilbert Knight's music room yesterday, a thousand years ago; and then as they got the rhythm of each other he began to do turns with her, singly at first, then in a series, so that the corridor dizzied a little around them. He told her always to look at one thing, not to get giddy; but the place must have been too dark for her, so that she only smiled and as the music slowed she leaned her head against his arm, her breast brushing his arm. His heart beat and he held her a little more closely. The music went on with hardly a pause: a single violin, playing a slow and simple waltz, and then the whole orchestra coming in behind. He recognized it, new that year, and so popular that even scientists in Switzerland had heard it: the waltz from Lehár's *Die lustige Witwe, The Merry Widow,* bittersweet, irresistible, and Viennese.

O komme doch, O kommt ihr Ballsirenen—

They began to do turns again, the simple ones and then the Viennese turns that are a whole new category of motion, spiraling outward, circling inward to stillness. They danced, danced until they were dizzy, and the dizziness spread out of them and the world whirled, but they were as quiet in the center as two candles burning together. Their bodies were warm against each other. He put both hands on her waist, at the curve of her hips. She gave a great sigh, and their bodies fitted against each other as naturally as the rhythm of their dancing. He could not tell his body from her own. The music must have stopped at some time, because they moved more slowly; but he could not let her go, and she shuddered, and put her arms around him.

He led her over to one of the banquettes. They sat with their arms around each other. He tilted her head up. She was pale, her eyes were closed; she was panting as if she had run a race. "No?" he asked her gently, "or yes?" She nodded her head, silently, yes, as if she were taking a dare; his lips touched hers, and they were kissing desperately, the two of them enlaced in each other's arms. He stroked down the length of her side with the tips of his fingers, and felt her generous hips and thighs beneath the silk of her dress. She kissed him as if he were a wonder; kissed almost like a little girl still, half taught, half awakened. He touched the hollow at the base of her neck, ran his hand down the softness of her inner arm, touched the crook of her elbow and her shoulder blade, made her tremble. She touched his arms and his chest; moved down as far as his waist, blushed, and stopped. Every inch of his body was as sensitive to her touch as fingertips or tongue. She moved her hands to his face again, touching his face all over; she trembled and pressed her whole body against his. His need for her ached like his heart. He moved his fingertips over the round tenseness of her breasts. He wanted to go inside her as innocently as a bee inside a flower; he wanted to force her, hurt her, love her, explode inside her like a bomb; and he took her by the shoulders and gently moved her away from him.

"We had better stop now," he said, "or we'll go wrong."

Harry's Perdita. She drew one hand away and held it over her face as if she were ashamed. He wanted her to be older so that she would understand or younger so that he could simply comfort her; but he could not say the banalities that one says to women who have gone further than they intended and are ashamed. He had gone too far himself and he was no comfort to her.

In the old days in Vienna he had finished with such moments by helping the woman to rearrange her flowers and dress. One of the snaps of Perdita's beaded collar had opened and he pressed it shut. The knot of her hair had come half down. He used his own clean comb and between them they twisted it into a good approximation of the knot it had had. He looked for hairpins on the banquette, remembering a woman whose husband counted her hairpins at the beginnings and the ends of dances. He smoothed her silk dress back into its folds, trying the impossible job of touching the dress without brushing the skin beneath it. She retied his tie and had to do it twice because her hands trembled. He combed his disordered hair. They held hands. In the mirrored walls they looked the same as before and impossibly different; whatever they did, they could do nothing to change the bruised look about their mouths or the luminescence of her skin. In the mirror, as Reisden watched her standing beside him, knowing they made too obvious a couple, he saw the door from the ballroom open and Charlie Adair come through.

Reisden shook his head; no, go away. The two men's eyes met in the mirror. Charlie Adair turned away, pale, sickened, and silent. The door closed silently to Reisden's ears, but Perdita turned. "There's no one here," Reisden told her, not knowing how to protect her for this evening except by making her believe she had not been seen. He would have to talk with Charlie.

When they stepped back through the door into the ballroom, Harry had stopped dancing with Efnie, but the two were still laughing together.

CHAPTER 37

THAT NIGHT, Reisden told Anna Fen that Jay was dead. She sat in her private sitting room, on one of her deep, pillowy couches beside him, still in the gauzy deep-cut dress that she had worn to the dance, with the butterflies still in her hair. She snatched up one of the chintz pillows and screamed into it silently, and the butterflies trembled on their wires while she sobbed.

When she let the pillow drop, her makeup had run, black runnels down her cheeks like theatrical tears; but her face was square and lined with real grief. She turned to him. "Please, hold me, just hold me."

He held her in the dark perfumed silence of her house. Outside in the heat the frogs sang.

"I had red silk knickers," she said, "and he used to have me get dressed up like a housemaid and wear those underneath. Usually we met in your barn. That night he had me come over to your house."

"You were there," Reisden said.

"I was upstairs and so was he when we heard the first shot. He got up—I mean—you know what I mean. He said he'd go find out what it was. I heard his voice from downstairs, he was shouting to someone, and there were more shots. And he kept shouting. He sounded surprised and then mad. He didn't come back." She shook her head. "I knew, didn't I? I waited for him, then I went straight down the backstairs and out the kitchen door. No one noticed me because I was wearing a housemaid's uniform. I just walked home. If—if everything had been all right, I thought he'd come to my house." She gave one more shuddering sob and then another, and cried in his arms for Jay French.

She cried in his arms, and the room was dark and perfumed, and the couch was as deep and soft as a featherbed, and eventually she turned and sobbed, rather more pointedly, as if for an audience, against his chest. Reisden knew what was expected of him; Mrs. Fen wanted comforting. It was a long time since he had been shocked at what happened after funerals. He should have done it. Every muscle in his body was tight for a woman; why not, why not? The easy and pleasant and generous thing would have been to give her what she wanted, what his body wanted too. But it didn't happen; he gave her confusing signals and watched himself doing it and wondered why; he was charming and tender and just a little obtuse, and inwardly furious at himself. When he had left her, he walked back down Island Hill Road, past the Clinic, where Perdita's window was dark, and stood by the edge of the water on the Knights' shore, watching the last lights go out, one by one, on the other side of the lake. He picked up some of the flinty stones on the edge of the shore and cast them savagely out over the water.

And while he stood there, a light went on in the ground floor of the Clinic, someone no more able to sleep than he; and he heard a piano, and the music was the waltz they had danced to. He did not know whether to be afraid or exultant. He felt everything, fear and joy, want of her, need of her, need to protect her against himself, delight, estrangement from himself, as if they were data points charting a reaction, distinguishable but not separate. He could not say what he was but only *I am*. In his confusion it took him a full minute to realize that Perdita had broken her promise to Harry.

CHAPTER 38

THE NEXT DAY, Sunday, August fifth, was Perdita's birthday. Gilbert and Harry got ready for church; and Reisden, who didn't go to church, walked with them as far as the Clinic, where they would pick up Perdita. Reisden wanted to talk with Adair about last night, but when Perdita came down the stairs, blushing, dressed like a woman in a long dress and with her hair up, Adair announced that he had taken a fancy to go to church with them today. So Reisden came too.

Charlie Adair had decided on attending the Episcopal church as an act of desperation. Only the Catholic Church was a proper place for Catholics; but in mortal sin, with Jay French's murder unconfessed on him, Charlie could not take communion. Attending another church's services meant as little as a shadow in the nighttime, and it helped him to have Perdita under his eye.

She could not have done anything that she could not take to church, Charlie thought, watching her as she sat, eyes downcast, in the pew between Gilbert and Harry. But how could she have done as much as he had seen?

She wanted what Reisden told her she could have, her music. Heaven knew they were all shaken by finding Jay—Bert had said that he had got drunk with Reisden Friday night—and she had been in the barn and helped to find that dreadful thing that had been Jay. Under the brim of her straw hat her eyes looked sad and bruised. Child, dear niece, I want no nightmares for you. You shall marry Harry and be happy, you shall be a good girl. Everything that happened once shall not touch you.

The sermon was from Acts, St. Paul saying that the apostles had been called to be witnesses of the truth. The minister preached that it is holy and good and pleasant to be called to witness the truth, and that the apostles had great joy doing it. Lord, Charlie prayed, would it help if I confessed? To You I can: I killed Jay French.

I thought I only shot at him, to get him away from us.

I confess that I have taken communion many times in a state of mortal sin. I regret coming into Your Presence in a state offensive to You. Tell me what I should do to come into Your Presence again.

He stared at the stained-glass windows. Jesus among the children. What would the Clinic do for money if Charlie told Gilbert he had killed Jay? The Clinic had no endowment, it lived from year to year. Gilbert might stick by him, but the police would want to know, and then all the good ladies who sent the hundred-dollar bills at Christmas would know; and they'd ask next what happened to William Knight, and finally what happened to Richard. And would they believe Charlie when he said he didn't know where Richard was?

Stand up anyway, the Lord tempted him, and tell them you killed Jay French, and then you'll have it over with, my boy.

Ah, and wouldn't that feel fine. Confess to the priest, who would say, "Go to the police." Peter O'Connell would understand, but Peter O'Connell was dead these many years.

And what about the next girl in South Boston who didn't bring her baby to the Clinic because the doctor was a murderer in jail? And the next, and the next? You gave me Richard to save, for my redemption, over and over again, in all my Clinic children; and are You going to take him back from me and leave the children nothing?

If You will damn me for a murderer, I will die and be damned rather than hurt the children.

Behind the altar the stained-glass window showed Christ in the Garden of Gethsemane. This was Charlie's

Gethsemane, and how could he deal with it? How can I choose between my soul and the children? Is this Your work, Lord? I won't drink this cup; it's bitter; You can't make me.

The congregation stood for a hymn. Next to Charlie, Reisden was so sunk in thought he didn't notice; Charlie touched him on the arm and he jumped. He stood but didn't sing, looking over Charlie's head toward Perdita at the other end of the pew.

Confess to Richard, Charlie thought. Who doesn't remember anything and wants to know.

Ah, if Reisden were Richard.

In the churchyard after the service, Reisden took Charlie's arm and walked aside with him. "What happened between Perdita and myself last night was my fault," Reisden said. "It won't happen again."

But at the very moment Reisden said it, Charlie saw that the man was looking across the churchyard to where Perdita stood talking.

CHAPTER 39

CHARLIE HAD NO CHANCE to talk with Harry until they were back at the Clinic. He took Harry into the small parlor and looked out the window. Gilbert was out on the lawn with Reisden and Perdita; for the moment she was safe.

"You must take special care of Perdita just now," he said hesitantly to Harry. "She is young and may have her head turned."

Harry looked out the window, his hands clenched. "You mean him."

Charlie said nothing.

"He's—" Harry pounded his fists against each other. "I tell you, Charlie, I don't trust him as far as I could throw him. The thing is, we have to know that Richard's dead. We have to get Gilbert to declare him dead, or find his body, or even find Jay French and get him to tell that Richard's dead."

Charlie's skin crawled cold. Jay French was found.

"Which is more important, Richard's death or your life with my niece?"

"She isn't *realistic* about getting married," Harry said, "she isn't the way she used to be. He tells her she's going to be a famous musician and she laps it up. She's distracted from me."

He doesn't answer me, Charlie thought, and looked out the window too. Reisden and Perdita were standing together, talking. "You must be very kind to her," Charlie said urgently, "but stay close to her, close. Look after her, Harry. She is only a girl."

"She's got to stop listening to him," Harry said, "or she'll be no girl of mine."

REISDEN AND PERDITA sat with Gilbert Knight on the Clinic verandah. Gilbert fanned himself with a paper fan with the name of an ice supplier on it; and then, because it was a hot day, he fell asleep. The two of them sat together without speaking. They were sitting on the same glider, on opposite ends of it, and whenever Perdita moved, Reisden felt the motion. He watched her. Before yesterday he would have taken her hand, or she his.

"Come," said Reisden, "I want to talk with you. No, not here on this thing; come walking."

They walked down through the fields. The path of the fire was still clear in the swath of leafless trees by Mrs. Fen's fence and in the ruins of her barn. But the burnt fields had grassed themselves again; now they were sunburnt green, and burning in the fields instead, in among the green, were tall candles of purple flowers. They stood among the loosestrife. Perdita was a woman in a white dress, her long hair up. She knelt among the purple loosestrife and her dress was dappled with the reflections of its indescribable hot color.

She is in love with Harry Boulding, Reisden told himself, and engaged to Harry. I am in love with Tasy, who's dead. No. I was in love with Tasy, who died. He could not define what he felt for Perdita, only admit it. It was as though feeling was an island he had come to after a long voyage. He was too new to it, unused to the ground and the air and a little bit in love with every inhabitant, as one is in a new country. So not in love at all; no, simply astonished with her in all his senses; it was as though he could feel her skin at a distance, smell and taste her from across the room, as if she were surrounded with light.

When this enchantment moderated, she would still be kind and loving, a creative and intelligent musician; but she belonged here, which was part of her charm, and he did not; and she loved Harry.

He picked one of the flowers and looked into its heart, full of colors for which there were no words, and didn't look at her.

"My dear, thank you for last night. It was a wonderful experience, which should happen once only." The

words were the right ones, exactly what he should say;
but they sounded wrong and weak to him, as if he were
an old roué making morning-after excuses to some for-
mer virgin. "I mean——" He didn't know what he meant,
or couldn't explain it to her. "I feel stupid. I was trained
as a diplomat, but it seems not to have stuck. Last night
commits us to nothing: we do not have to go on, or to
avoid each other, or even to feel inordinately guilty. I
would like to like you and to have your friendship and
trust, as I think I have had, and to feel the same friendship for you. I don't want us ever to be awkward
together," he ended, and the whole speech felt like a
badly written formal letter. It was the truth but it didn't
feel even close enough to be an effective lie.

She was still kneeling among the flowers. He sat
down near her, not too near.

"How could I prefer . . . anyone else to Harry, how
could I prefer you, and still love Harry as I should?"
Her voice was so quiet he could hardly hear it.

"You didn't prefer me, you kissed me. You love
Harry."

"Yes. But——" She looked him full in the face. "There
shouldn't be any buts."

"You love him, but he wants you to give up your
music. I'm simple in comparison. I want you to go on.
You don't love me as you love him, and I don't love you
as he loves you, but I know where music stands with
you and he doesn't. So I'm easier. And we were shocked,
we had found Jay." He watched her face as she considered and rejected that excuse.

"It had started before then," she said in a low voice.
He didn't want to take her through any of this.

"No, no. You love him, my dear, and you want to

keep your promise to him. But you couldn't. So last night you decided you were in love with someone else, and then you could go home and play the piano. My dear, it is a cheat; you don't need a grand love for that. You simply need to win one from Harry, and you will."

Her cheeks were red. "That sounds as if I've been selfish and I've used you for Harry's sake."

"The someone else you decided you were in love with was me. That was a compliment to me, no hurt. And I needed to know I could fall in love with someone else, so I chose you; I couldn't have chosen anyone but you. I needed you." Impossible to say this to anyone without taking hands; Reisden did not take hers, and that was the only lie in what he was saying, that if he as little as held her hand it would not be true anymore.

"You needed me?"

He lay back in the grass and the flowers; they rose around him and he did not have to see her. "I want you to have your life; you're simple for me, you see; I think I can help you make that come out right, and in doing that I shall be able to feel I have—" he hesitated over the word, then used it "—loved someone without hurting her. You see that is important to me." He heard a rustle in the grass beside him; she sat beside him. Her knee brushed his shoulder; there should be no sensuality in those places of the body, but he moved away. She reached out her hand toward him, then drew it back.

Neither of them spoke. High up in the blue sky, the wind moved the clouds. The cicadas sang like their blood in their ears.

"When I am married to Harry," she said quietly, "I will live in the house with Gilbert and you. It will be strange never to touch you, not for the rest of our lives."

"I won't be there," he said quickly.

"No, you have to be there. Harry and I would go away."

"Child, you don't understand. I'm not Richard Knight. I have always told you so."

She looked out into the air. He could read her disbelief in her drawn-down brows. Ask me how much I'm lying, child, and I won't be able to tell you. So don't ask me; believe me. She passed one hand back of her neck, as though she would toss long hair back; but it was all smoothed up and pinned.

"I will go away," he repeated.

"I wish that you were Richard!" she said suddenly.

"Not worth thinking about, Perdita." She would have been eleven when he married. Twelve. And if she had been a few years older, a woman in Paris, the woman he had seen last night? Not worth thinking about. He would have Paris, but not here and not her. He wanted somebody. He had to be careful of her.

"I don't want to become Richard," he said, "but to find out what happened to him. Will you help me? Would that be too difficult?"

"I would do anything for you," she said, and he thought she was very young.

"I want to look at where he disappeared, in the Clinic, if it still exists."

They got up from the ground. He didn't help her up, which was another awkwardness. She led the way across the fields of burning purple flowers up the rise of the hill to the Clinic, through the side door, up some shadowy narrow stairs, and down a corridor. In the rooms on either side the children were taking their afternoon naps. The doors were open to let the breeze pass through, though there was no breeze. Only one of the doors was closed, and she opened it and stood aside to let him pass through.

"You won't stay?" he asked.

"No, I want to go think, I guess."

He nodded, wanting not to show disappointment, not wanting to be disappointed; then said "Yes" because she wouldn't see the nod.

She stood a moment at the door. "What we did last night . . . ? I meant to do it. I'm not sorry. I don't know what to think of myself. But I'm not."

She left him alone in the room from which Richard Knight had disappeared.

Yes, he thought, *I meant it too.*

HARRY BOULDING, when Charlie had gone, indeed looked after Perdita, and with horrible results. He saw his foolish uncle fall asleep, leaving Reisden and Harry's Perdita together. The two of them walked off together across the fields, as if by prearrangement. From upstairs he spied on them. Staring out a window on the south side of the Clinic, he saw them together in the purple-stained field, not so much as touching, but that man lying in the grass casually, stretched out while she sat next to him and talked with him, as intimate as kissing. Harry's heart sank into itself and became small and hard.

NAPPING on the sunny verandah, Gilbert had a dream. It was a pleasant dream. He dreamed he was at a funeral. He didn't know who the funeral was for, so he didn't feel mournful, rather very happy because Richard was with him. Because it was at night they were wearing evening dress; the top of the closed coffin was covered with candles, big and white, in shining candlesticks. Many people Gilbert knew were there and he pointed them out to Richard. Miss Emma Blackstone from next door was eating eclairs. Her sister Lucy was talking with Gilbert's sister Isabella and his brother Clement, who were as real and alive as she was, dressed in evening dress too, Clement talking nineteen to the dozen the way he always had and Isabella in her favorite checkered dress wearing Mother's diamond earrings, nodding her head and eating a piece of white cake.

"Whose funeral is this?" he asked Richard. "It seems just like a party."

Richard only smiled.

When Gilbert went up to the coffin and read the silver shield on the lid, it said Richard Knight; but when he turned around to protest to Richard, Richard was still there and shook his head, laughing. "You know I'm not Richard Knight."

Some people trundled the coffin away, but they somehow left the candles, and then waiters opened champagne and gave everyone at the party slices of white cake. Gilbert's was a wonderfully flavored wedding cake, thick and light, rich and sweet, with white icing roses on top. It tasted a little bit like the apple cake his mother used to make. Eating it, Gilbert was struck by a splendid idea. He tapped his glass and everyone listened to him. "I know how to give everyone what they want!" he shouted happily, but at that moment the bubbles of the champagne made him sneeze and he woke up.

CHAPTER 40

RICHARD KNIGHT had disappeared from the grandest suite in the Federal Hotel. In all the years since then the suite had not been repapered or painted. Bits of the brown figured paper had slumped away from the walls and a corner of the ceiling had fallen. Oak filing cabinets in rows filled the sitting room. Reisden pulled a drawer open: old files and the smell of decaying paper. The slatted shades were down and the rooms were shadowy and hot; Reisden pushed a window up. He opened the doors to the two bedrooms and, standing in the center of the sitting room, tried to imagine how a child could have been kidnapped from here.

Richard had been left alone for less than five minutes, in a room that was guarded on the outside. The five minutes had not been at any foreseeable time. Someone had got in, made Richard disappear, and got out, all without a sound.

Each bedroom had one window. Reisden opened Richard's: a sheer drop two stories to the gravel of the old carriage drive. A man might conceivably get up and down the side, but not unnoticed at one o'clock in the afternoon, and not carrying an eight-year-old boy.

Each bedroom had a fireplace. Reisden knelt and looked up into the chimney: narrow-throat fireplaces with dampers. A bird or cat might have got in that way. Not a human being.

Could the closets connect with another suite? The closet in Richard's bedroom was the larger, a tiny, narrow room that took up the whole width of the chimney. Its ceiling was stepped downward toward the back. Reisden lit matches and got down on his stomach to look all the way back in the bottom of the closet. Some lumps of plaster had fallen or been left there ever since the plastering. Reisden's imagination made a child there, stuffed into the narrow space under the stairs. He inched forward with matches and touched everything to make sure it was building material. Then he stood in the closet and ran his hands over the walls and knocked with his knuckles on them, to make sure there were no secret doors or hidden passages, or anything else that one does not expect to find in the closets of good hotels.

Then he brushed off his clothes, which were dusty, and lit a cigaret. His hands shook so much that he had to steady one with the other. There was a pattern of linoleum on the floor of the closet, faded squares on a dark ground. He thought he remembered it from Graz or Vienna. It was a common enough pattern. In the middle of a day hot enough to bring sweat out on a standing man, he was ice cold and shaking. He didn't want to know anything at all.

Suppose that Richard is here. Think of it like a scene in a play; he is a character. Jay is dead. Does Richard know it? He's afraid. He hides in the closet or thinks of hiding in the closet, but that's a dead end. Does he know who's going to come after him?

Who, d--n it, who?

Think about the kidnapper. If the kidnapper didn't come in while the room was being watched, he must have done it earlier. Did *he* hide in the closet? Richard is alone. The kidnapper rushes out of the closet and says, Aha, I have you. At this point imagination fails. Richard screams bloody murder, the guard outside the door rushes in with revolver drawn.

No. The kidnapper gets to Richard before Richard has a chance to cry out, and—does what? Hits Richard over the head, drags him into the closet.

What happens when Richard comes to?

Why hadn't the kidnapper simply killed Richard? Reisden's imagination furnished the room with a bed and a pillow and Richard on the bed. The kidnapper rushes out of the closet, whips the pillow out from under the boy's head, and holds it there until the boy stops struggling. Easy. Richard would fit nicely in the end of the closet and wouldn't make a sound.

Later on, the kidnapper would retrieve the body and bring it down the backstairs. Disguised as laundry, perhaps, or in a cleaning cart?

Except, Reisden thought, I'm Richard.

He followed the thought out of the suite door, which he closed again, and down the stairs to the first floor and to the basement. The kitchens and the laundry room were down here. The laundry room was in the near half of the basement: two rows of soapstone sinks, tin clothes plungers looking like big funnels with handles, shelves of irons, endless heated drying racks, ironing tables, and an auxiliary stove where the irons were heated. A double door led out into the courtyard at the rear of the Clinic, and Reisden, looking out the window, saw clotheslines of white sheets barely stirred by the air. Through that door, Reisden decided, the kidnapper took the body. He looked around the concrete, damp-smelling walls. The steam in the laundry was hard on finish plaster; the walls had been patched and repatched. Took the body out, or left it here.

He knew exactly how it could have been done. Suppose that the linen cart came around in the evening; the whole night was left to dispose of Richard. Down the hall was the kitchen, with sinks, drains, two huge commercial stoves, choppers, knives, kettles, lye, sponges, mops. Fifty or sixty pounds of meat to bone, boil, burn, grind, dissolve to jelly; there were more than enough ways to dispose of a body here. The kitchen had a door to the outside, and beyond the door were the woods, the train, the whole world to bury a child in.

If Richard were dead, it was easy.

But how could it have been done with him still alive?

Down at the kitchen end of the corridor someone was coming down the stairs. His heart beat hard once when he saw her. "Hello, Perdita," he said.

"Hello," she said shyly. "I came down here to get Uncle Gilbert a sandwich for lunch."

"I came down to find out what happened to Richard"—as if they both needed to explain why they were near each other again.

"Did you find out?"

"No," he said, "I don't think so; I don't know."

"Would you like a sandwich? If you'll fry the ham I can make ham, lettuce, and tomato."

She got fresh tomatoes and lettuce from the kitchen

garden. They took refuge in the game of how-the-blind-do-it, which had been all their conversation in their earliest days. She showed him how to slice by touch and how to work the big commercial toasting rack, and told him that blind people shouldn't fry because of the danger of grease fires, but that baking was OK and she was a good baker. She made mayonnaise while he watched because he had no idea of how to do it. They were careful not to touch each other; but they stood in the kitchen making sandwiches together, and it was intimate, even their fear of familiarity; they should have done nothing together at all.

When she was finished, she took a plate of sandwiches upstairs and stood, halfway up the stairs, turned around as if she were going to say something to him, but said nothing. He had taken one of the sandwiches and stood at the back door, not feeling hungry. It was a well-made sandwich, the toast a perfect brown, the lettuce crisp and the tomatoes sliced to the right thickness, the kind of sandwich a woman makes in her own kitchen. Was he going to keep it for a souvenir? he wondered, and took a bite. It tasted good, but he had only the one bite; then he sat thinking about Perdita and Harry.

She belongs here, he thought. That was the reason why nothing would happen.

Some of Charlie's children were playing in the high fieldgrass, some game where most of them hid and one had to find. His eye was caught by how easily they melted into the grass, into the shadows. A game small animals play to avoid predators.

He heard a sound behind him. Charlie Adair had come down to get a glass of ice water.

Reisden was still watching the children. One of them

had wriggled half into the bole of a dead tree. No adult could have persuaded him into a space so small. Reisden looked from the children to Charlie. "I'd like to speak with you, Charlie."

Charlie Adair, Perdita's uncle. He belonged here too, and Reisden did not. But Richard had.

Charlie padded over in his carpet slippers, the glass of water in his hand.

"Look out there."

Charlie peered. "Ah, that's that Billy McCrea, he'll get himself stuck—" He started out the door to rescue the boy, but Reisden held his arm.

"Charlie, what happened to Richard?"

"I don't know."

"Did you ever teach him to hide from William?"

"Yes, of course. I told him to stay away from his grandfather whenever he could."

No guilt on Charlie's face, any more than there had been on Gilbert's.

"And after everything, he hid too, and you helped him to get away, didn't you? Why?"

Charlie's face blazed white and then red. He gasped and held up the glass of water as if it were a missile, then actually threw the water from the glass at Reisden. Reisden stepped aside from the water and caught Charlie's fist.

"You d--ned, unholy man," Charlie said. "That is not true."

"Why did you do it? What was he running from?"

"You—" Charlie's face was splotched dusky red from anger and he was blinking tears from his eyes. He twisted his hand out of Reisden's grip and pointed, trembling with anger, at the spilled water on the ground.

"If someone were to say to me, all it takes to find Richard is for you to gather up every drop of that spilled water, I would start now. I did not tell that boy to go away, or help him."

"I'm sorry." But if Richard hadn't been kidnapped by force, he had cooperated. He must have left with someone he trusted. "You were the only one he would have gone with."

"You are *wrong*." Charlie's voice was thick.

How else would it have happened?

Charlie was shaking. "You—*you*—want what's Richard's, and you want more than that: I saw you with my niece, you want to take from her the peace and happiness of all the rest of her life. You have taken from Harry what is rightfully his, and made Gilbert a laughingstock and a fool. You want to rob me of my friends and my comfort and I am an old, sick man. But I will see you in H--l burning, Dr. Reisden, before I think you are Richard or support you in any of your schemes."

CHAPTER 41

"I saw you out in the grass this morning. I *saw* what you were doing, both of you."

Harry found Perdita in the music room, sitting in front of the piano with her hands clasped on the closed cover. "What we were doing this morning?" It was last night that she should have been accused of; later last night, when she had played the piano in spite of having promised Harry. "We *talked*, Harry."

"About cheating on me?"

"What? Harry!" she protested.

"I saw how he looked at you. What have you two done together? Pretended he was me?"

"Harry!"

"Get away from that piano." He took her by the shoulders and shook her, half lifted her away from the piano bench. "What happened to your promise? You're supposed to stay away from the piano. Did *he* let you off it? What did he do to you? Has he got everything he wanted?"

She could not misunderstand him. She backed away, blushing fiercely. This was not kissing at a dance. "Harry, you have got to say what you mean."

"Why don't *you* say what *you* mean?" She heard the sound of the piano cover being thrown back. Harry began to hit the piano notes one at a time, thudding his finger down on the low notes. "You always liked *me*. I thought it was *me*. Now he's got the money. And all of a sudden—" He hit a whole fistful of notes at once. "You're all around him. He says you can do every-thing—" Another fistful of notes, he was banging against the keyboard now. "Be my wife and go off to New York too. And he can say that, can't he, because he's Richard Knight and he's everything. He's *nothing*. I can send him away. Does he take you with him to New York? He won't, I can tell you that. What did he get from you, you fool?"

"Harry," she said, half crying, "I love you." But she wanted him to stop banging against the keyboard.

"You love your *music*! You're selfish, that's all you

care about. It would serve you right if I didn't care about you. You could keep on with your career, just like you want. Just stop thinking about getting married to me. Would that make you happy? You could give music lessons, and everyone would come to take music lessons from you because you're such a good pianist. And you wouldn't ever have to get married, or have children, they wouldn't get in your way."

"No, it wouldn't make me happy," she said in a low voice. But stop hurting my piano, Harry. Stop hurting me.

"Isn't that what he's been saying? Forget your marriage and get on with your career, isn't that what he says?"

He took her by the shoulders. His voice deepened and lost its sarcastic tone. "Pet, you can't go on like this. I don't think you've gone too far—look at you! blushing like a dear!—I didn't mean to talk to you like that, it's just that he's playing with you and that hurts me. Anyone can see he doesn't care anything about you. I care. I want you for my own, forever, all my own. You're the sweetest girl in the world. I want to marry you. Don't cry like that, Pet." He put his arms around her and kissed her cheek. She wasn't crying. She wanted to cry but she could not.

"I don't have to choose between you and music," she said, rigid in his arms. "Harry, it's you who say I do."

"I do say so." Harry took her left hand and tugged at the engagement ring as if he were going to pull it off. "This means something, Pet. You can't get married and expect to be who you were. I won't have any wife of mine pay more attention to some sticks and wire than to me, and I'll say it plain, I won't have any other man as much as think he can look at you. We're engaged and you're mine. Stop thinking like you could do anything and be anybody. Just love me. That's all I want you to do. I don't want you to love anybody but me."

He left her. She sat down on the piano bench again. These were his terms for loving her. I don't have any terms, she thought. I'm not allowed any, I'm only supposed to love him. Under her fingers the piano keys were quiet and familiar. She wondered if Harry had done the piano any harm by slamming his fist on it. She could check it, just by running a set of scales up it, but that would break her promise too.

Didn't she have terms for loving Harry?

If she loved Harry enough, she would close the piano cover now and wouldn't even check if there had been harm to it. She wouldn't need it anymore.

She had already gone beyond that.

After a moment she touched the lowest notes and then, one by one, each of the eighty-eight keys, and every note sounded familiar and true.

She could not marry Harry.

CHAPTER 42

OUT ON THE VERANDAH, Harry saw Gilbert still asleep and Reisden coming around the side of the hotel. "Wake up," Harry said, shaking Gilbert's shoulder.

"What? Oh, hello, my boy."

"I'm not your boy and neither is he. Come here,

Reisden." Harry knocked on the window. "Come out here, Perdita."

Reisden came as far as the verandah stairs. Perdita stood at the door, and Gilbert, still blinking, went to stand by her.

"He's not Richard," Harry said to Gilbert and Perdita. "Tell them, Reisden."

Gilbert drew a little closer to Perdita and took her hand. Reisden and he exchanged a complex look. "Harry," Reisden said, "would you walk around the corner with me a moment?"

"Tell them."

"There are things you don't know. Excuse us." Reisden gauged Harry, standing at the bottom of the stairs, and didn't try to make him follow, just stepped down from the edge of the verandah onto the grass below and walked down the gravel carriageway toward the lake. After a moment he heard Harry following. Just as he calculated Harry was about to grab his shoulder, he turned around and said, quietly enough for only the two of them to hear, "We have found Jay French."

Harry's hand closed in midair and fell.

"Where?"

"Come, I'll show you." Reisden led the way down the carriageway and across Island Hill Road. They stood underneath the pine trees. Across the flinty shore and the water they could see the Knights' barn. "There."

Harry laughed like a man who didn't understand.

"Harry, he's dead. He didn't disappear and he didn't kidnap Richard Knight; he died. The scheme has backfired and we don't have Richard's murderer."

Harry stood with his jaw open, then licked his lips.

"You're lying. I'm not stupid. That's got to be Richard's body. It's Richard we need."

Reisden thought of the blackened mass under the hay.

"We don't have him."

"I see you caring a lot about whether Richard's dead! As long as I can't prove he is, you can hang around here, can't you, playing around with my girl—"

"Very soon," Reisden said gently, "you'll say something you'll regret."

"Don't you threaten me!"

"Not a threat, Harry. A presumption on your decency."

"You bastard!"

"Harry!" Gilbert said.

He had come along behind them. He looked from one man to the other, eyes almost tearing behind his glasses.

"This is an impostor," Harry said. "Roy Daugherty found him. Ask him anything about Richard! He doesn't know."

"Harry, this is very wrong of you," Gilbert said. "I'm disappointed. This isn't polite."

Harry laughed.

"You are Richard," Gilbert said to Reisden a little breathlessly, as though the effort of making a positive statement was like climbing up a long hill. "It does you credit to say you aren't. But after all this time, Richard, there will never be certain proof, will there? And what if we should wait and wait, and I were to die? Then everything would be in turmoil. Bucky Pelham has told me so for years. Richard, I'm not entirely certain that I can do this, but—I should like to declare you dead."

Reisden's throat closed up, absurdly. He swallowed. "Do, by all means."

Harry grinned. "That's the right thing. Finally."

Gilbert nodded solemnly. "Harry, I'm glad you approve. You're a decent boy." He patted Harry's arm.

Harry snatched his arm away. "What are you talking about?"

"Perhaps I'm not being clear. Richard is Richard," Gilbert explained patiently, "and everything is his. Bucky Pelham has told me we can't give him what is his without positive proof he is Richard, which we won't have because it was so very long ago. So what I believe I must do is to declare Richard dead. Then I will have the money, and I can give it where it belongs, to you, Richard, under your own legal name, whatever name will satisfy the courts and Bucky, as if you were not Richard at all."

"You can't do that!" Harry said.

"No, you can't. Gilbert, you have gone utterly amok," Reisden said.

"Don't you tell him what he can do!" Harry said, and hit Reisden.

He plowed into Reisden with his shoulder, football-style, and sent him crashing back into the bole of one of the old pines. Gilbert shouted out. Reisden lost his footing on the gravel and was caught between the trunk and Harry, who moved in with both fists pummeling. Reisden dodged and Harry barked his knuckles on the tree. Harry twisted around and Reisden chopped at him with a right uppercut that made the breath wheeze out of Harry, but Harry came back in, shorter than Reisden but a good fifty pounds heavier, and slammed his fists into Reisden's chest and stomach again and again. Reisden fell onto the gravel. Harry drew back his foot as if to kick him; Reisden rolled and tripped Harry, bringing him down. The gravel was edged with granite paving stones, blocks the size of bricks, and under Reisden's hand one was loose. Reisden staggered to his feet still holding it, hefted the weight of it over his head. Gilbert saw Reisden standing over Harry, lips drawn back from his teeth and his eyes completely crazy, like a horse, raising the big stone over his head. Gilbert ran between them, shouting "Richard! Richard!" and shaking him. Reisden stood dead still, with the stone still in his hand; and then slowly brought it down, stared at it, and threw it away forcefully into the grass, away from any of them.

"That's not fair!" Harry shouted, jumping up.

"Fair, boy?" Reisden gasped. "I would have killed you. You've won. Go. Get away. Go."

CHAPTER 43

CHARLIE'S DOCTOR'S BAG was old, the handle mended with black cloth tape, but it was the bigger kind that doctors in his early years had used to carry. He had always packed his bag too full: lollipops, a cloth doll, candy pills. He moved everything from the bag neatly into his laundry basket and tucked the basket under the bed, in case a maid should wonder why Doctor Charlie had left his stethoscope in with his dirty shirts. From the linen-supply closet on the second floor he took the oldest and shabbiest blanket, rolled it up, and stuffed it

in the bag. Now the bag looked full. He took it downstairs, left it in the hallway by the sofa, and went outside
to speak with Gilbert.

"I'm going over to your barn, to look again at—you
know. Don't have anyone come over there." Gilbert
said he wouldn't. "And stay with Perdita." Gilbert
looked puzzled at that.

The top of the Knights' barn was full of sunlight and
heat. From downstairs in the barn, Charlie brought a flat
heavy shovel and a dustpan and brush. He put them all
down, opened the doctor's bag, and took out the blanket. The body lay like a black scrawl in the hay. The
doctor picked up the shovel from the floor, hefted it, and
held it first by its handle, then like a pick, with his hands
on the shaft. It felt awkward, but he lifted it over his
head. He thought of Jay French, long ago, with his
clear, grey, mocking eyes. *It is your business, doctor, to
look after the heir.* Charlie sighed, lowered the shovel to
the floor, and spread the shabby blanket all over the
body, from head to foot. It was a grey blanket with a red
edge. Then he lifted the shovel over his head and
brought it down onto the blanket, over and over again.
He paid special attention to the skull, which could show
that this was a man's body and not a boy's.

When he lifted the corner of the blanket to look, there
was nothing left but powder, fragments the size of a
fingertip, more like old wood than bone. Charlie's shirt
was stuck to his skin with sweat and both his arms
ached. He put the heavy shovel down and sat on the
floor for a few minutes, feeling his heart pound and the
ache twist in his arms. But he was not done. He got up
from the floor again, using the shovel as a cane to help
himself up. He took the dustpan and brush, folded back

the blanket carefully, and on his hands and knees brushed up every fragment of cloth, every bit of bone, the powder and splinters caught in the cracks of the floorboards, and dumped everything into his doctor's bag. It took surprisingly little room; there was still space for the blanket. The stain still darkened the floor, yes, there had been a body there, but impossible to tell how tall or how old.

As he got to his feet, he half stumbled across the shovel, which clanked on something in the hay, shifting it so that Charlie could see its shape: it was a revolver.

The gun was terribly heavy, a big machined piece of metal more than a foot long. It was not rusty: Charlie remembered, with terrible clarity, William Knight's age-spotted hands oiling the metal. He saw the copper-green of a percussion cap still in the cylinder. One of those bullets had been heavy and strong enough to crack a chair in half. What'll I do with this? he thought. The percussion cap would have lost its strength, the powder would not work; and what did he mean to shoot? He should throw it in the water.

Charlie put the gun in his bag with the rest, put the spade and the dustpan and brush in their places, and walked toward home. On his side of the bridge over the Little Spruce, he turned away from the path and walked up the rocky bank to the river's edge. Even in this hot August, the Spruce waters were racing. He knelt on the bank, which was covered with soft star moss, and, opening his bag, he took out the gun and the blanket and laid them down. Then, standing up and leaning out over the river, he held his doctor's bag by the two ends, turned it upside down, and shook it, the way he had done dozens of times before when some mischievous child had loaded it with treasures of sand or pebbles. Sand and pebbles and powder rained down and were caught in the foam and whirled away. Some fell on the rocks, a white powder that the next rain would mix with the earth. He shook the blanket over the water, and in a moment it was clean too. A fragment of black cloth hung for a few seconds in an eddy, and then a branch came tumbling down the river, a good-sized branch still with its green leaves, and swept everything downstream.

Now the gun. It lay bright on the moss. So big, so heavy. The Spruce waters were strong and high, but it was August; this was not the spring run when the water would sweep away a man. Charlie saw how it might be, the gun tumbling over and over until it came to the rocks in the shallow water above the Knights' bridge, then lying there, bright and gleaming, for everyone to see.

It could go into the lake, but Charlie never went rowing. If he threw it in from the shore the metal would shine in the water; someone would see it.

He sat on the moss with the gun in front of him until the water mist made him chill; the gun seemed like a weight on him and his arms ached all across his chest. The ache spread until his eyes dazzled and it was hard to breathe. He was afraid because he was not done. He leaned back on the moss and held the blanket to him, to warm him against the chill of the mist and his own sweaty body. Not yet, he prayed; he still had a letter to write and a gun to hide.

Somehow he got back to the Clinic, inside, and up the stairs with no one seeing him. In his room he wrapped the gun in the shabby blanket and thrust both deep into the bottom of the closet, behind the shelf that the hot-air pipe made. He sat at his desk. He had to hold his left arm against his chest; it felt as though the pain were something trying to crawl out of him. The fingers of his right hand felt the size of arms, uncontrollable. He wrote.

Today, Sunday, August fifth, 1906, I have examined a corpse in Gilbert Knight's barn. From the number of teeth and the growth of the bones, I have determined that the body is a male child of about eight years. I think this must be Richard Knight.

Charles Francis Adair, M.D.

He fell across his bed and closed his eyes, having told the lie that might make Gilbert end the search at last, and fell into a half-dream. Sometimes he thought he had not written the letter and he tried to get up and then fell back again. Once St. Peter, an old man with a white beard, came to him and told him all his sins had been forgiven him; and then St. Peter showed him the shabby blanket with the red edge, and laughed at him with Jay French's quiet, mocking laugh. All your sins except one, Charlie. *I have not confessed,* Charlie thought in his dream, *I will die in mortal sin.* He prayed to see Father O'Connell in his dreams, Peter O'Connell who would have known God's will in this. But he dreamed instead that he was in a confessional and asked the blessing, *Bless me, Father, for I have sinned,* and no one answered, no one ever answered.

When the shadows grew long he woke up again, sweaty, breathless, not in pain, but feeling as if he had been wrung dry, as if he had no more pain left to offer. The ceiling was covered with a network of cracks. Jay French was dead; Reisden was after Perdita, and would stay until Richard's body was found. Charlie was help-less; he had nothing to offer but lies.

And he had not got rid of the gun.

CHAPTER 44

AUNT VIOLET had set up Perdita's birthday party for four o'clock in the afternoon. It was perhaps the fate of persons like Violet Pelham always to set up events for the wrong time, Reisden speculated, as it was to say the wrong things and have the wrong ideas. Violet had no control of the heat and nothing to do with the events of about an hour before; but she might have left Harry to his excuses instead of insisting he come to the party, and might have served something other than champagne.

The party was meant to be held in the small parlor of the Clinic, but because of the heat they had all the doors open. There were not many guests, only Gilbert and Harry, Reisden, Charlie Adair, Violet and Efnie, and some of the people from the Shakespeare Club. So few of them wandering over such a large space gave a dis-agreeable effect, like a vast vase only half full of flowers. Harry drank two tulip glasses of champagne straight off, filled a third, and took Violet and Efnie off to the terrace, from which his voice rose. He was going to be very drunk.

"Richard, I'm sorry," Gilbert said.

"You're sorry?" Reisden said quietly. "I was going to hit him with a rock."

"He hit you first."

"Don't be ingenuous. And, just by the way, if you do what you threatened I'll turn around and give everything to Harry, signed and notarized. And he will throw you out and you will spend the rest of your life homeless on the streets, which will serve you right for a fool."

"Yes, Richard."

"Go out there and be polite to Violet and Efnie before he tells them everything." Most people cannot be completely appalling while eating or with more than six people in the room. Reisden sent out onto the verandah two of the caterer's helpers with trays of food, and followed them with some of the more reliable people from the Shakespeare Club. "Harry wants to rave, I'm afraid. Would you be charming and listen to him for a while?" Reisden surrounded Harry with sympathetic listeners, so many that Harry could hardly say as much as he would have said to Violet and Efnie alone, but merely muttered that he was a wronged man and drank more champagne. Eventually he staggered off around the verandah with Efnie Pelham.

"He's saying some wild things," one of the Shakespeareans said to Reisden. "He says you're not Richard Knight."

"Ah, well, we all know that, don't we?" said Reisden, smiling and sipping champagne.

"Oh," said the Shakespearean.

Charlie didn't look well. Violet Pelham said critically that she had had to get him up from a nap for Perdita's party, but he looked as if he had not slept at all, grey and fragile and old. Gilbert Knight, coming in from the terrace, took a look at him and sucked in his breath. "Richard, we shouldn't have made him look at Jay."

"No."

Perdita was drifting about inside, in the small parlor, like a ghost at her own party. There was no one else in the room at all. Reisden wondered if he should speak to her—he was likely to be the last person she wanted. But he had forgot her ability to recognize steps like voices.

"Would you come in?" she asked.

He went in, and stood over by the small central table, near the chintz-covered sofa. She stood by the French doors.

"Harry cannot possibly be such an idiot for long," Reisden said. "He has gone off to tell his troubles to your cousin, who will doubtless blame you for them. This is what relatives are for. By natural reaction he will come to his senses, and by this evening he will realize that he is very much to blame."

"I want to love him," she said in a miserable whisper. "I get *so angry* with him, but I do so want to love him."

He got her out of the room, at least, and onto the terrace, where everyone was waiting to wish her a happy birthday. She cut the first piece of cake. Gilbert joined Reisden, quietly telling him that Charlie was really not well: He had been overcome by the heat in the barn.

"Roy Daugherty will get someone in to deal with Jay," Reisden said.

"Do you suppose," Gilbert said nervously, "we shall have to give Jay a public funeral?"

Reisden and Gilbert were served pieces of cake. "I had a dream about cake," Gilbert said.

Perdita began opening her presents. She had got a package from her father and mother in the Southwest, and Violet Pelham insisted that she open it publicly. There were two presents. The first was the rattle of a rattlesnake; Perdita shook it and was delighted, and everyone passed it from hand to hand as a real curiosity. Reisden, who was rather good at presents, would never have thought of it, and he felt rather intrigued by this pair of missionaries. The other was a set of Indian jewelry, rough silver stuff with stones the color of Mediterranean water. Perdita held the earrings up to her ears. Reisden's breath caught again.

"Perdita is very pretty," Gilbert said.

"Perdita is different from pretty," Reisden said almost savagely, so that Gilbert turned and looked at him.

Gilbert had given her a case to hold her music; he had made it himself, decorating it with a spill of wonderfully, barbarically bright wildflowers in inlaid and blind-stamped leather: tiger-lilies, goldenrod, sedge grass, spiky blue-purple flowers that Reisden didn't recognize. Gilbert went pale with anxiety as she opened it and ran her hands over the blind-stamping, bringing the case out into the light to see it. "Oh, the *colors*!" because the lilies flashed gold over their dark orange and the purple flowers glittered like garnets in the sunlight. "Oh, Uncle Gilbert! It's the best you've ever done."

Reisden narrowed his eyes to see it as her shadowed sight would and it was very satisfying, a kaleidoscope of warm colors. Gilbert had made them bright so she would see them. "Good," Reisden murmured, "very good," as he would have said about fine work in the lab.

Harry had given her a vanity set, but wasn't there to see her open it; he was still out on the terrace with Efnie. Perdita opened a blouse, some handkerchiefs from Charlie, a bottle of perfume. Reisden's present for her was toward the bottom of the pile, a flat heavy box the size of an unfolded newspaper but thicker. He had meant it to be the sort of birthday present that could be given by anyone; the equivalent of, say, stationery; since Harry was what Harry was, something noninflammatory and not possibly romantic, something that she might not even need or like, and if she did, would have bought for herself sooner or later. He had found it awhile ago in Boston, at the Howe Press, after he had seen her struggling with regular-sized music.

But in the meantime Harry had associated him even with music, and it hadn't helped that he had written the card for it yesterday, Saturday, when he'd been full of indignation for the promise Harry had got from her. Twenty-four hours ago, before he had seen her at the dance.

She opened the card. He had printed it an inch and a quarter high.

PLAY
BEETHOVEN
ANYWAY
—R.

The Howe Press piano music for the partially sighted was twice regular size, half a page per broad page. She began turning over the pages one by one. Her face was so still that Reisden thought she didn't know what it was. Even this could be too small for her, or she might be used to some other way of studying music; he didn't know. And then she reached out and touched the notes.

"I can see it," she said.

She brushed a chord of notes with her fingers as if she were touching them on the piano. "Where did it come from?"

"Boston."

"Where?" she said urgently.

"The Howe Press."

"At the Perkins School?"

He thought of her with a magnifying glass, learning music one blurry circle at a time. *I could have gone so much faster,* her tone said. "I should have *known*. There are other blind piano players too, aren't there?" she said. "I still wonder how to find the piano when I play onstage; somebody must know how to do that. There are other people out there like me." She said this almost to herself, and Reisden was reminded of the long-haired girl whom he had taught to eat in a restaurant, long ago. The girl had said, *I could go out by myself.* But that was not what he had succeeded in giving her; "I don't have to do anything alone," she said to him.

"No, child, never alone."

"Thank you," she said, and he smiled.

She had kissed Gilbert and Charlie, but she didn't kiss him; they only touched hands, as formally as if they were two strangers wishing each other well. Play Beethoven, Reisden told her silently, and love Harry, who is simply foolish and will get more than he dreamed. And make him understand what it is to love you.

Gilbert and Charlie watched them. Charlie leaned over the arm of his chair and spoke to Gilbert. His voice was anxious and sharp.

But Gilbert didn't hear him, because he was thinking about another party, long ago, and Tom and Sophie.

CHAPTER 45

ROY DAUGHERTY arrived back at the Lakeside Hotel around five-thirty Sunday. At the desk he found two messages to call Reisden, and in the lobby he found Harry Boulding in person, sullenly drunk on champagne.

"I wannim out, Daugherty. Wannim out now. Reisden. He's taking my girl away from me."

Roy Daugherty had spent a relaxing Saturday and Sunday visiting with his two boys and fishing from a bridge. He sighed and took Harry up to his room. Harry sank into a chair, muttering that he wanted to throw the bastard out. Daugherty took off his glasses and polished them.

"Ought to have a little coffee first," he remarked.

"Don' want coffee. And another thing," Harry said, rousing up in his chair. "Reisden found the wrong body."

"Body?" said Daugherty, remembering that he'd got two messages to call Reisden.

He reached Reisden at the Clinic, where Perdita's birthday party was just breaking up. "Evenin', Reisden.

Harry's over here. Says you found something."

"Yes. Come over to the Knight house, will you? Leave Harry there if you can. We've had him already."

But Harry, staggering, wanted to come. Daugherty pushed him into a cab. He leaned against the back cushions, mouth open, eyes glazed, breathing with a sound like a handsaw. The cab left them by the summer kitchen where Daugherty had his office. Harry slithered out of the cab and fell onto Daugherty, and the cabman turned his horse and clattered away.

Reisden took a look at the two of them and came out to help. "Don't you touch me, you slimy crook," Harry said, drawing away from Reisden; he overbalanced and collapsed onto the gravel. Reisden stood over him.

"Foiled!" he murmured, "but I'll have you yet, my man."

"Had a nice weekend, I guess?" Daugherty asked.

"Nice implies some discrimination. Let's get him inside."

They hauled Harry, protesting, inside and sat him down in a chair.

"Perdita— He—"

Daugherty wished he could go out for a beer.

"Look, you drunk little boy," Reisden said. "Perdita loves you and you mistreat her badly. She wants exactly what she says she wants, which is to play the piano. That's the problem between you two, not me."

"Piano music," Harry said disgustedly.

"Daugherty, you can see the kind of discussion we've been having, I'm afraid." Reisden leaned down and looked Harry in the eyes. "Harry, what exactly do you think *Perdita* has done?"

Harry stammered and looked away.

"Hold that in mind," Reisden said dryly.

"Screw you." Harry pointed a looping finger at Reisden. "He's found Richard's body."

"We've found a body," said Reisden to Daugherty. "Possibly Jay's."

Daugherty looked at Reisden warily. He remembered the last idea Reisden had come up with, that Gilbert Knight had been involved in the murder. "Tell me what it looks like."

"Size of a small adult, partially mummified, extensive black stains around the body—it may have bled to death. It's been there for a long time."

"Sure about the size?"

"Sure about the impression." Reisden shook his head. "No. I'm not qualified to say. Charlie Adair took a look at it, but someone professional should do an examination."

Daugherty lumbered to his feet. "I can get someone. Mind if I try first?" He had seen a few bodies. Two of them had been supposed to be Richard Knight's. The first had been found in a drainage ditch the end of autumn after Richard had disappeared. Under the dirt and the wet dead leaves, there had still been plenty of maggots. After that, Daugherty didn't guess he was squeamish at all. "I pretty much can tell whether it's a kid or an adult."

Harry had slumped in his chair, his head back at an alarming angle. He raised it. "I wanna come," he said, and his head tipped forward and to the side. Reisden caught him and eased him down to the floor, and they rolled him onto his side. "I wanna see Richard Knight," Harry protested, and scrabbled with his feet.

"Shall I stay with him?"

"He ain't goin' nowhere. You come show me."

The two men walked down the gravel path toward the barn. The rose garden was at their right, no more than a tangle of dusty bushes now. They turned down the path toward the barn.

"What's he been drinking?"

"Champagne, and he didn't know when to stop."

"Yeah. Reisden," Daugherty muttered, "what you been doing with Perdita?"

Reisden gave him a look, sideways, sharply. "Is there never smoke without fire?"

"Just that you seem to think so high of her, you think he don't treat her right."

Reisden didn't say anything.

"Just so you know."

Reisden sighed. "Stop here a moment." They were under the elm trees; Reisden took out a cigaret and lit it. He offered them to Daugherty. Daugherty took one out of curiosity. The tobacco was strange-flavored, raw and resinous. Foreign. "She and I kissed last night at the dance. For some time. Yes, I know, that's unfortunate. She doesn't want me. She wants a husband and babies, and she wants them here; she wants to marry Harry. And Harry's so close to the right thing; if he only stops trying to make her over! She doesn't know how to tell him that and he's not picking it up for himself."

Daugherty grunted. "Think you'll be lucky if he don't hit you. Kissin' is kissin'."

"He's already hit me. It was stupid."

"Let's see that body."

They started into the barn. "Wait a moment," Reisden said. "There's another thing. Gilbert has decided that he can solve everything." He explained that Gilbert wanted to declare Richard dead and give the money to him, Reisden. "I told him he couldn't do that."

"You do anything to start this?"

"No," Reisden said, not bothering to fuss about Daugherty's having to ask the question. "Gilbert says the idea came to him in a dream. I ask you."

Daugherty took off his glasses and cleaned them: lenses inside, lenses outside, and the nosepieces, which were inclined to get greasy.

"He could do it, couldn't he," Reisden said.

"You asked me that question, I couldn't say yes," Daugherty said.

"Of course not."

"If you was trying, you couldn't a caused us more trouble. Bucky'll have cats." Daugherty reached into his jacket and looked for paper and a pencil. The only thing he had was his train ticket, blank on the back except for the logo of the Short Line, a train steaming out of a tunnel. "Lookit," Daugherty said. "You don't mind, Reisden, I want you to do something. Write down here for me that your name is Alexander Reisden, that you aren't Richard Knight, and that you don't have any claim on that money. Sign it and date it today and I'll keep it."

Using Daugherty's billfold for support, Reisden wrote on the back of the ticket, quick and sharp, and signed his name: *A. J. v Reisden.* "Honest and simple, Daugherty?"

"Yeah."

Daugherty folded up the ticket and put it away in his billfold. Can't blame me for needing to make sure, he thought. Here's a man who just said he don't have a claim on more money than most people can count. And all it is, his pride is hurt. Ain't natural. Then he thought badly of that thought and followed Reisden upstairs.

The air in the barn attic was hot, dusty, and still. Daugherty sniffed; his mind was still running on that body under the October leaves, which had smelled so. But there was no smell of rot here, only old hay and the dirty ammonia smell of mice. Daugherty grimaced and thought he heard squeaks running away from them. He saw the outline of the body on the floor, black, and he gritted his teeth.

And then he realized that it was only a shadow.

"Reisden, this ain't no body." Daugherty hunkered down on his heels and touched the stain. The floor felt different from the wood, not splintery, as if the stain were a very thin tar.

He looked up and saw Reisden, pale as plaster, kneeling beside him.

"Don't be a fool, it's gone."

They heard the door open downstairs. "Daugherty!" Harry shouted. "Reisden!"

They had left the door to the attic open. Harry's steps stumbled up the stairs. "I wanna——"

"Yes, we know, you want to see the body. Harry, it's not here."

"Want to see *Richard*." Harry swayed and waved his hand in front of his face like a man beset by flies. "I waited for this—Daugherty, have'n' I waited?"

"Someone has taken the body." Reisden didn't shout, but he clipped his words off so, he might just as well have been shouting. He still had that white look, like somebody had set off a photographer's flash in his face.

Harry stared at him fuzzily, staggered forward, and

gaped down at the shadow on the floor, then turned around so fast he almost fell. "Where's the *body?*" He launched himself at Reisden, put a hand on Reisden's shoulder, and waved the other in his face. "Where's *Richard?*"

Reisden just stared at him. "Where's Richard?" Harry howled. "What have you done with Richard?"

"What's going on, Reisden?"

"You *bastard*—" Harry swayed on his feet.

Reisden smiled; he looked like somebody had burned his eyes into his face. "What's happened? We've made—somebody—take the body away. Do you think Charlie, Roy? Or who?"

"Not Charlie," Daugherty said. "Don't think it, either."

"You're right, something is happening," Harry slurred. "You're going. Daugherty, get rid of him." Harry sat down abruptly. Daugherty moved aside with Reisden.

"He ain't going to want you here for long. Bucky neither."

"I want someone professional here. There'll be fragments left in the cracks of the floor, you'll at least be able to establish your body."

"That ain't their point—"

"I know. They want Richard. I want to know what happened to Richard. And I swear, Daugherty, that if you try to stop me now, I will make for you every bit of the trouble you think I can."

Daugherty faced him. "You better mean it, Reisden," he said, "because I can't be on your side."

CHAPTER 46

REISDEN FACED MRS. FEN in her private sitting room, with the low soft sofas and the ruffled chintz. She had answered the door herself; it was Sunday afternoon and there were no servants. Anything can happen on Sunday afternoon, her expression said. She was wearing a soft grey dress, low-cut but simple. Anything can happen on a Sunday afternoon: A man can change his mind.

"You will have a great deal of courage to do this," he said.

She looked at him over the edge of her wineglass. "What does it mean, Mr. Knight, when a man asks a woman to be brave?"

"Jay's body is gone," he said, cutting her short. "Charlie Adair saw it this morning; this afternoon it is gone. This morning I had evidence that Jay was dead. This afternoon," he said, changing tones, "the only evidence I have is yours."

It was a plea. She put her glass down. "You want me to say I was with him, don't you? But I won't."

"I don't want you to unless you are very brave." This was nonsense, clichés that Reisden's mentor in diplomacy, Graf Leo, had saved for women and other deficients. "You can see that justice is done. You can do it quite privately, through a letter; your name won't be used."

"My name——" She picked up her wine and took a long drink. "Annie Fen sleeps with a lot of men. I get talked about, but I still get invited to the parties. I like parties. I like babysitting Charlie's little Shakespeare Club. *Jay was a servant.* How many times have you slept with housemaids? When you were in prep school? For practice?" She put the glass down on the table by the window and stood looking down at it with her back to him. "Have you ever slept with a woman who slept with her butler or her chauffeur?"

"That doesn't matter."

"Have you?"

He had not.

He knew she would turn around eventually. When she did she had unbuttoned the low neck of her dress. She lifted one of her breasts out of the V of the dress, holding it in the cup of her hand with her thumb over the nipple.

"This is what I have." She moved across the room toward him and pressed herself against him, moving her hand from her breast across and around his chest. With her other hand she was unhooking, unbuttoning, easing herself out of her bodice. "He wasn't special, Jay wasn't, just another lover." She brushed her lips against his. "Sit down with me here on the sofa. Wouldn't it be a shame if Annie Fen couldn't sleep with all the men she wanted? Let me show you what they'd miss."

When he was eighteen he would have simply thrown her over the nearest sofa and made her happy. *Making love to a woman,* Graf Leo had said, *is the only way to make them stop talking.* And allowing oneself to be manipulated disarms the opposition. Now he was twenty-seven and listened, and had his doubts, and was not so sure that he was wiser; he was certainly more frustrated, because she had aroused him effortlessly and instantly. But all he did was hold the woman and tell himself, You might as well turn homosexual or cut it off for all the good it does you. He held her, responding to her gently, until she stiffened in his arms with anger instead of desire and began to cry.

"He never gave a d--n about me. Why should I do anything for him?"

SHE WALKED AROUND the room, the bodice of her dress held up, not fastened, but covering her breasts. Her hair was half down, and when she brushed it away from her face the bodice fell away from her left breast and she pushed it up again quickly, a gesture half resentful and half shy.

"I'll write a letter to the police." She added quickly, "I'll sign it. They don't have to tell everyone in the world, do they?"

"Write to Daugherty. He's private; he won't use it unless he needs to. Have it witnessed."

She sat down at a little table. "G—d, no witnesses, I won't have the nerve unless I do it now." There were pen and paper in the drawer. "I'll do one with witnesses later." She scribbled something, looked at it, balled it up, and tried again. He looked over her shoulder.

I came to visit at the Knights' house the evening William Knight was murdered. I was in the same room with Jay French. He was still there when the first shot was fired. He went downstairs to see what was going on. There were a lot of shots. I think he got shot. I never saw him again.

Anna Fen

PS—Jay and I were playing cards.

She rummaged through the drawer. Her dress fell off her shoulder again; she hitched it up, but a little more slowly than before. "I never have stamps. And my maid reads all my mail before she takes it to the post office."

"I'll take it to Daugherty if you like."

"Would you?" she asked as if she had just thought of it. "If I keep it in the house I—I'll tear it up or something."

He put it in his billfold. She turned around on her chair. She was sitting and he standing, and her eyes were just about on the level of his groin. She looked up at him deliberately and then leveled her gaze again.

"Did I do all right?" she asked.

He took her hand and drew her up out of her chair, standing next to him; the bodice slipped down again, and this time she didn't bother to pull it up. He knew exactly what was going to happen, and it did. They made love standing up, quick and rough, face to face, breath to breath. He knew how to give women pleasure, but that was out of his reach today: He had never performed more quickly, or worse, or more regretted the act during the act itself. When it was done she held her dress around her like a bathtowel and shook her hair out of her face, looking out the window where the last of the sunset was fading.

"I'm sorry," he said. He had thought of Perdita during it and all it had got him was that Mrs. Fen was

not she. It was simply dangerous to Perdita to think that
way.

"You don't care about me any more than I do," she
said quietly.

He didn't know what to say to her. It was true.

She sighed. "Maybe I'll go back to San Francisco. I
don't know. Things might be different there."

He was sorry for her, which he did not want to be.
"Sometimes they are," he said.

CHAPTER 47

IT WAS EVENING. Perdita sat with her head in her
hands, thinking, in the room from which Richard
Knight had disappeared. She had closed the door, and
the hot air smelled flat, like old paper from the files in
the next room. It was almost dark; the square of window
light by which she had oriented herself was deepening
past grey, and the rest was blind no color.

"Pet?"

Harry didn't like her sitting in the dark but she
couldn't find the light switch; she opened the door for
him. Click, and a dim orange filled with distracting
shadows. He had switched on the light. He closed the
door on the corridor outside.

"Sit down," he said. "I'm going to tell you who that
man is."

She sat down on the floor the way she had been
before. "Sit down on a *chair*," he said, "like a *real*

person, can't you?" He scraped a chair out of the shadows and pushed her down into it.

Then he told her all the story, from Charlie's seeing Reisden on the platform.

"He's an atheist, Pet, you know that kind of person. He was supposed to find out what happened to Richard. Instead he's stolen Richard's body. He was supposed to make my uncle hate Richard. You don't see that happening too well, do you? And," Harry's voice softened, "he was supposed to leave you alone. Because I love you. Instead he's making a play for you. It's like he thinks he could take over Richard's money, but we know who he is, he's not even an American, he's signed a paper saying he's not Richard. I don't know what he wants to get away with, and that scares me."

Harry's voice went on and on like a buzzing in her ears and she sat with her hands in her lap and heard only phrases. "Maybe he thought it would be fun to ruin you for me. Maybe he thought Gilbert wouldn't like that." Gilbert wanted her here. "Dazzled you, but it was easy to dazzle you, wasn't it? You heard what you wanted to hear, *piano music,* and—"

No. She crossed her arms over her breasts. She didn't know whether she was being stubborn or scared.

"If you want to be my woman, act like it," Harry said, and the door opened and closed.

HARRY found Reisden on the shore of the lake. "I told her everything you are," Harry said. "See how she likes you now."

PERDITA had turned out the lights again. She sat in the chair because Harry would dislike her if she sat on the floor. She would have cried if she had been with somebody who could give her comfort, but she was all alone and so sat in a blankness beyond tears.

She heard steps outside the door; *his,* not Harry's. She did and didn't want to see him. He did not knock or ask whether he could come in but only stood outside, as if not knowing that she could hear him and unsure of what to do. She got up and took a step closer to the door. Stillness and silence. She was afraid that he would go away without speaking to her; she put her hand on the knob and felt him do the same from the other side. He took his hand away again, and she twisted the knob, opening the door wide just as he began to knock. They were so awkward with each other, she was afraid.

"Come in."

She closed the door to the corridor. He didn't ask for the lights to be turned on; she stood, and he didn't ask her to sit down.

"What you have heard is probably true," he said finally. "I agreed to impersonate Richard Knight. I am not Richard. I know I told you I wasn't, but you didn't believe it and I didn't make you believe it. Gilbert Knight was intended not to believe I was Richard; but he did. It will be part of my job to tell him he's wrong. I didn't take Jay's body." He gave a small explosive sigh. "That's all," he said after a while.

"It was what he said about me," she said. "I had no brains and no wants. Everything that I thought had come from you."

"Is that true?" he asked.

"Neither one of you has anything to do with my wanting to play the piano!"

He didn't say anything. After a moment he asked her

if he could smoke; she said yes and he opened the window and, she thought, sat on the windowsill. She came over and stood by him.

"Who are you?" she asked.

He said, "When it comes to you and Harry, I don't know what's driving me."

She waited for him to go on. In the evening air, in the hot room, she could smell soap on him, as if he had just showered, but she could also smell the distinctive scent of his body and an undertone of muskiness that made her skin feel sensitive.

"I was twenty when I married," he said, "Harry's age; and my wife was eighteen, your age. I don't know how to tell you this, or even if I should. At your age, Tasy wouldn't have understood."

Perdita moved closer to him, so that their hands were touching, only lightly. "Don't," he said. She moved away.

"I was, and am, very lonely," he said, "and I do things that I ought not. I wondered, sometimes, after her, if I had married her because I had been about to quarrel with my guardian, and had wanted someone to convince me I wasn't merely selfish. So be careful of me." He lit a cigaret, and while he was doing it he moved away from her. "She was a very good musician, a singer; she had a career and so did I. And we decided that we weren't going to have children. No," he said after a hesitation. "I decided. I knew she wanted children eventually. I took precautions, thinking, Perhaps someday. I really didn't mean us ever to have children. But when she died . . ." he said, ". . . when she died . . . It wouldn't have been in any sense easier for me if there had been a child. But there was nothing left of her. So you see, you had better have the music and Harry too, and Harry's children. And quickly, because there's not always time."

Perdita said nothing for a minute. She felt his closeness in the dark. "How did your wife die?" she asked.

"She was in an automobile," he said, and after a long time, "I drove it. She died."

She felt for his hand. He shook hers away, then took it and held on hard.

"When she died," he said, "they did an autopsy and she was about a month along with child. I hope she never knew. I hope that she didn't know, because if she did, she didn't tell me." He didn't speak for a long time. "I was driving the car she died in. I thought I had killed her and the child. I thought I knew she was pregnant." He took his hand away. "So now, Perdita, I think you know the very worst about me."

She said into the darkness, "Richard?"

And the darkness did not answer her.

"No," he said. "Not at all. I've told you."

"I know what happened to Richard," she said.

He didn't say anything.

"He was scared," she said, "and he hid."

"He went away with—someone, I think."

"No," she said, surprised, and realized, then, exactly what she would be saying, and to whom.

"Richard," she said, "he ran away. He'd done it before. That time he did it."

"No," he said after a very long while. "That cannot be."

If she had not known him she would have thought his

voice calm, but she heard something in him like violin strings stretched too tight. She touched his face. He brushed her hand away.

"He didn't mean to do anything wrong, or run far away," she said. "Kids do run. He just wanted the adults to fix it, then he'd come back. But he must have gone too far, or forgot how to get back——"

He interrupted her.

"You and Harry are going to make it up, you see," he said. "You are a musician, you're going to be married, you'll be all right. Everything will be all right. Except you can see that I wanted you to keep your music. I made you up. It wasn't even personal, d--n it."

"You can't make me up," she said. "And I'm not her. If I play the piano in every concert hall in the universe, it won't matter to her; your wife will still be dead and she'll never be able to sing anymore. And Harry's children won't be yours, and Harry isn't you. You made *him* up but he doesn't fit. He——" Her voice wavered and she went on. "I think he really isn't going to let me play the piano."

"He will have to."

"He won't let me go to New York."

"No," he said finally. "He won't. I have wronged you. I should have left you alone."

"You wronged Harry and me," she said, "and yourself too. You can't make yourself up or stop being who you are."

He said, "I'm not Richard. Charlie is right, you're wrong. Richard couldn't have done this to himself. Richard died, he was in the barn, I was wrong when I thought it was Jay."

"If you lie now," she said, "you'll have to lie the rest of your life."

He laughed bleakly.

"Take my hand," she said.

"Why?"

"I'm going to make you a promise."

He took her hand in both of his. His hands were cold.

"I won't tell," she said. "I love Gilbert but I won't tell him, because I know you're going to ask me not to."

She reached out with her other hand, and he held it hard, hard enough to hurt, but she didn't say anything. After a long while something like a shudder went through his body. "Not to tell?" he asked, with a wry, tired trace of amusement in his voice. "That was what Richard said," he seemed to think aloud, and there was another long time when he didn't say anything.

"Then don't tell," he said.

THEY SAT on the floor together, their backs leaning against the wall, their arms around each other. They told each other things about themselves, whispering, like children telling stories in the dark. He talked for a long time, as if he needed to share with her everything he had been and done; he told her stories about places and trifles, giving them to her, as if it had been so long since he had talked. "I saw an elephant once in Africa." He talked about finding the first half of *Hamlet* in a torn book, and not knowing for a couple of years how it ended. He moved his hand up and down her arm. "This is my hand. Why does it move?" he said.

"I like your voice," she said.

He laughed, and kept talking; and eventually his

voice became lower and more tired, and he said that he had to go back to the house, but he fell asleep with his head against her arm. The birds began to sing, one by one, in the darkness, and she heard the lark's climbing call.

It was Monday, August sixth, 1906, the nineteenth anniversary of William Knight's murder.

CHAPTER 48

REISDEN WOKE UP with the dawn in his eyes, disoriented for a moment, confused by the happiness he felt. It was quiet, he was quiet, as if he had had a noise in his ears for so long that silence had wakened him. This was natural, to be quiet and unafraid like this, to wake up early in the morning next to someone, happy. Sometime during the short night, Perdita had fallen asleep, snuggled up against him with her head pillowed on his arm. Oh, we're in trouble, Reisden thought, wondering whether anyone had checked her whereabouts or his; but with an illogical sense that it would be all right, rested next to her, enjoying the warmth of her body and her weight against him.

"Child," he said finally. "Perdita."

She opened her eyes with a start, looked at his face next to hers, and blushed.

"Fair beauty," he murmured, "you are in my power."

She looked at him dubiously. "We didn't—?"

"No, believe me, you will notice when you do. But if you're not in your room, the difference won't be distinguishable to the untrained eye. Come on."

They slipped through still-dark halls, past the rooms that smelled like sleeping children, and up to her room in the dark and deserted north wing. They kissed shyly outside the door like two good teenagers, but kept kissing with the heat rising between them until she took fright and he said, "Go inside, close the door, goodnight," and when the door was closed, he leaned against it on the outside, frustrated, with his palm against the door, thinking censorable thoughts about how to make her bed look slept in. They had not solved that between them; they had not solved anything.

The stairs to the basement were deserted. He slipped out the door and walked quickly across the fields toward the Island Hill bridge—it was no distance, perhaps two hundred feet, but when he looked back he had made a dark trail in the dewy grass. So, by the bridge, he looked back through the fence to see whether anyone was noticing the path he'd made, until two dogs from the Clinic ran barking through the misty field, zigzagging through the grass until it was a palimpsest of dark lines. The dogs shook condensation off their coats and trotted away. He sat on the bridge, looking down the river to the lake, light-filled and fogged at this hour, and up the streambed. The heat and dryness had lowered the water level until the current was murmuring at the bottom of the cut, but scoured and darkened rocks made a high-water mark man-high.

Tranquil stream, tranquil morning. He wanted Perdita. He wanted her to sleep in his bed, wanted to wake next to her in the morning, every morning, with her head on his shoulder. He also wanted her to have what she wanted for herself. She was eighteen and ready to make commitments he could not make. He scooped up pieces of gravel from the mossy floorboards of the bridge and threw them one by one, in a kind of meditative frustration, down at the rocky bed of the stream: *tak, tak, tak.* Then he walked through the woods toward Island Hill and wandered awhile over the lawn and through the rose garden, sitting on the edge of the shore, staring out over the bright, calm, empty lake.

He went back to the house and showered and shaved and changed, still the first one awake except the servants, and read through half the paper, drinking coffee in the dining room. Still he did not know what to think, sleepy in this odd, deep relaxation, in a thought-less funk about her. From time to time thoughts would break through—not even thoughts; words that spoke themselves silently in his brain, that invited him to think about them: She knows. And: I don't know how to be alone anymore. He had been open with her, had needed to be, and afterward he had been comforted. But she was eighteen, and he wanted her with a force that scared him. He wanted to make love to her, to sit next to her and feel her body against his; he wanted to taste her, touch her, fill his senses with her; and in the end, he supposed, he wanted from her exactly what Harry wanted—by loving her to control her, to make her not so unbearably close to him as she had been last night.

Because I won't tell. He shivered, then controlled himself as Gilbert walked into the room.

"Richard, did you sleep well last night?" Gilbert looked haggard. Reisden poured him a cup of coffee, wondering if the question were a polite inquiry after his whereabouts, and decided to treat it as though it were.

"I was at the Clinic, trying to find out what had happened; and when Perdita left, I went back to the summer kitchen to think. Did you look for me there? No? I'm afraid I fell asleep there and woke up only an hour or so ago." Perhaps too circumstantial, but a good gentleman's lie. "Were you looking for me?"

"I just didn't know where you were." Gilbert sat down, looking paper-thin. He stared at his coffee without drinking it, then at the newspaper. "Richard, I wonder if you could let me know where you are, when I don't see you, this time of year?"

This time of year? G-d. August sixth. "Don't tell yourself ghost stories," Reisden said sharply.

"It's very silly."

"It is." He added, "But I'm sorry you worried. I didn't remember what day it is."

Gilbert looked at him, surprised and as offended as Gilbert could possibly be. "I suppose that is a mercy," Gilbert said after a minute.

Gilbert went over to the sideboard, where Mrs. Stelling had set out eggs and bacon, but, as if reluctantly, he looked out into the hall and was drawn out there. After a moment Reisden followed with his cup of coffee. Gilbert was staring at the open door of William's parlor: still unfurnished, still plain white plaster walls and holystoned oak floor.

"I always see you when I come by here," Gilbert said. "Father dead there, and you halfway up the stairs."

"Was I halfway up the stairs? Do you know that?"

"I suppose I think that if you saw it, you would have been there."

"Where was William when he died?"

Gilbert stood in the hall, with his cup cradled in his hand, looking up the stairs, then back into the room as if the place were full of people, and all of them frightened him.

"He was there." Gilbert moved a few steps inside the room, knelt down and touched the floor. "That was where he died, lying in front of his rocking chair. I saw—a day or so later, you know, when I came up here. Everything was still—much the way it had been—they'd taken Father away, of course. But it was like a battlefield. The smell, and everything broken. Worse because it was at home." Gilbert looked down for a moment at something invisible, then got to his feet.

"Often I see the headlines about Father's death in the paper," Gilbert said. "When I've only half unfolded it, you know. Or dream that someone calls me up and tells me Father is dead. There's a spot in Charlie's hall, right by the door. I can never go by it without feeling odd all over, and hearing that guard coming down the stairs and asking, 'Do you know where your nephew Richard is? Because we can't find him.' "

"Come out of here," Reisden said.

He took Gilbert by the arm and led him out onto the porch.

"It never really finishes," Reisden said, "does it?"

"Oh, someday—I hope, Richard. Someday."

"Perhaps when we know."

Gilbert stirred his coffee but didn't drink it. "Perhaps. I wonder if, in a way, it won't be one of those things that we won't really *know*. Like the war. Just . . ." he hesitated, "finish with. And yet that would seem very sad."

"Tell me how it was at Charlie's the day I disappeared."

"Oh—" Gilbert looked out over the water. "I don't remember much that happened during the morning, I suppose it was a quiet day. It was the day before the inquest. Charlie was in and out because people were asking if you could testify. I didn't think you could. You seemed babyish to me and frightened of putting your hand on the Bible. You asked me to read to you, though you could read quite well, and I read some of *The Coral Island*, the soothing parts, you know, Richard. You had understood some of what Charlie and I meant to do for you, and you asked me if we would still go away to a foreign country. I said no." Gilbert's voice trembled. "I said we didn't need to now. There was nothing to be frightened of at all."

Yes. Reisden knew what had happened to Richard.

"Charlie came to get me for some business about the inquest. We went downstairs together and into the little parlor, where Perdita keeps her piano now, you know, and he and I had just come out when the guard told us . . ." Gilbert's voice wavered and stopped.

But, Reisden thought, I don't know what made Richard run, off to that coral island where he thought he'd be safe. Safe from what?

"I thought we could be happy now that you are back," Gilbert said. "That we could simply—forget it, you know. That, I don't really know how to say this!—that we deserved to forget it because you and I are . . ." He drifted for a moment, looking for the right word. "We are not bad people. What do we have to do with murders? I wanted to shut my eyes tight and have it go away."

We have everything to do with murders, everything, our whole lives. "I don't want to know about the murders but I have to. And I don't know how." Reisden stood up and looked through the door into the hallway: a natural square proscenium. He shivered. "I can't remember it. If I try, it's as though I—" He couldn't think of a metaphor. "F. J. Child once wrote an article about reconstructing an Elizabethan play of which he had only the stage directions and a very corrupt text. Unreadable actions around conjectures and blanks. This feels like acting in that play."

"You may remember someday."

Someday, Reisden thought, five or twenty years from now, when it is long unbelievable that I am Richard Knight and I've no way to verify what I think I remember. How much more time would Harry leave him here? As little as possible. And memory wasn't evidence, not the kind of memory he would have.

Something was chasing around in his head. What was he thinking of? Francis Child using stage directions as scaffolding to reconstruct the true order of text.

Reisden said, "I directed a few plays when I was at university." Gilbert blinked. "No, there really is some relevance here. A director has some data points, stage directions, places where the characters must be and actions they must do. And between those points the director makes a structure of the play. Movements, gestures. The right action creates the play."

"Richard, do you mean you would make a play about it? Like a scene from Shakespeare?"

The play's the thing, wherein I'll catch the conscience—of someone. Perhaps my own. "No, I simply meant to block it out on paper, as an experiment."

"But perhaps you should use real people. I would help if you wanted me to. And if it were a play," Gilbert said, "it might be easier to deal with somehow."

Reisden looked through the door into the hall. He could see part of William's parlor. An empty space full of imaginings: a stage. "I don't want to do it." Gilbert was about to agree with him that of course he didn't have to; but, of course, that wasn't what either of them meant.

"Charlie would do it too if we asked him."

Not Shakespeare but Sophocles. I do not want to know but I must know.

Reisden stood in the middle of the empty hall. "We would need four people. William, Jay, Charlie, Richard." It was as if he were calling them from the walls. "We would start when Charlie talked to William. While he walked down to Mrs. Fen's point, from which he saw Jay run out of the house, William would be murdered here . . ." They would need a fifth person: the shadow, the stand-in for whoever murdered William and Jay. He found he had begun to block the movements of all of them in his head. It was not easier to think of them as a play, but it was not thought at all, it was the sense of their closeness.

"When would you have the play, Richard?"

The two men exchanged glances. Not tonight, Gilbert's pale face said. Not tonight, Reisden thought. It would be tasteless on the anniversary.

"Tonight."

CHAPTER 49

CHARLIE ADAIR brought in the mail, five minutes after Perdita arrived to speak with Harry.

Charlie had his own play to put on. He intended to find the body gone this morning and to tell Gilbert that the body had been Richard. But what he saw instead, through the hall doors into the dining room, was delicate, edgy intimacy: Gilbert was gone from the breakfast room for the moment, Harry was not yet up, and Perdita and Reisden were having breakfast together. Perdita was bringing food for both of them. When she gave Reisden his plate she sat next to him, as if it were natural, as though there were no other chairs anyplace around that whole large table. "Do you want coffee?" Reisden asked her quietly. "It will help with being sleepy." Charlie's heart contracted with a pain that was not all physical. They both looked tired, both relaxed, but Reisden was wary of her, and Charlie knew what he was seeing.

"Child, you must learn to drink coffee." Reisden looked across at her with the wry look that a grownup gives a child. He had debauched her all the same, Charlie thought, and was debauching her now with those eyes that could not leave her, those tired and hungry and wary eyes, looking at her as if he wanted to eat her, slowly, with the salt of her new experiences. The two of them had done something; the question was only how much. More than Charlie had seen at the dance? He thought so. Was it over completely for her? Reisden had a look of holding himself back from her; ah, it didn't mean he had held back *then*. So many didn't, and then left the girls to pay.

Heaven save her and let her have her goodness still.

Charlie turned away. Inside his jacket pocket, over his strained and burning heart, he felt the sharp pricking of the letter that said *This body is Richard*. Charlie had to sit on a hall chair. His chest was bursting; his muscles pained him all up and down his arms. It was like when he had been backing away from Jay French, trying to focus the gun on something that would stop Jay, not wanting to hurt Jay but simply to stop him, the gun going *pop, pop, pop,* but he knew that he could not stop anything at all. He could not stop Reisden now.

But he had stopped Jay.

The pain passed and left Charlie limp in the chair. He could not stop Reisden, because he knew only one way to do it. The gun was still in his closet, wrapped in the blanket behind the shelf that the hot-air pipe made. Not me. Not me.

He sat in the hall for minutes with his head in his hands, trying not to understand what he might do. He wanted salvation, love and friendship, a quiet old age. Lord, let this cup pass from me, Charlie prayed humbly, a murderer quoting God's words.

And who needed them more, who needed mercy more?

CHAPTER 50

CHARLIE ADAIR watched while Daugherty opened his letter. The big lawyer read it, reread it, and then scrubbed the palm of his hand over his short hair.

"You sure?"

"I counted the teeth," Charlie said.

"Sure you got all of 'em?"

"Yes. Only three molars had come in. It is Richard."

"How sure?— I ain't doubting you, Charlie, it's just I'm asking what other folks are going to." Daugherty sighed. "You know the body's gone."

"Yes."

"Reisden took a look at it, said it was an adult. Gilbert thought the same thing. You got measurements of the bones and stuff?"

Charlie Adair hesitated. "Yes."

"Let's see 'em."

Charlie took a deep breath and let it out again. "No. No, I don't."

"Charlie, don't you lie to me, I ain't the right one to lie to. You ain't an expert on identifying bodies, and I got to have good evidence for this one."

"I know about children's teeth," Charlie said as quietly as he could. If he was going to lie he must be believed.

"Yes, and that goes some ways, don't think it don't."

Daugherty scrubbed at his head with his palm again. Through his thick glasses his eyes squinted at the paper. "I got to get me some new glasses, these ain't worth much. How's your sight, Charlie? You wear glasses too?"

"My sight is fine with glasses."

"How was the light in that barn? Morning or afternoon?"

"Midday. The light was very good."

"Hot, was it? Have any trouble with the heat? Your handwriting's kinda scriggly here."

Charlie remembered the barn at noon, full of sun and heat, and in the center that black horror. "No," he said, "I didn't have trouble."

Daugherty looked at the paper in his hand, crossed his legs, uncrossed them again. "Charlie, this is as good as you got, I know, and I appreciate your writing it down and showing it to me. It's going to be real useful if things ever come to court."

"Don't you see that *it is Richard?*" Because only Richard stood between them and Reisden. For a moment, dizzyingly, he thought of confessing to killing Richard. Or to sending Richard away, as Reisden had said. But he hadn't and he wouldn't and no one would believe him, not even himself. He was nice Uncle Charlie, who didn't commit murders. Why should they think he was anything else? Uncle Charlie was all he wanted to be.

"I don't want Reisden to stay," Charlie said with a little gasp. "He's an immoral man."

Daugherty coughed behind his hand; Charlie heard the chuckle underneath. "Been messing around with Annie Fen or something, has he?"

"I don't know." Charlie did know. "I think he has been, 'messing around,' as you call it. But there's another woman. A girl."

Daugherty looked across at him, one swift frightened stare.

"You know whom I mean," Charlie said.

"He ain't done nothing." Daugherty shook his head. "He said he didn't. That was only just yesterday afternoon."

But what might have happened since then? Charlie saw Perdita's tired softness this morning. He couldn't bear to remember it. "I've seen more than 'nothing,' Mr. Daugherty, and earlier than yesterday afternoon, and later, too! She behaves around him so, with such confidence, so familiar, and he looks—he *looks* at her—how can a man of decency even encourage such a thing? She is engaged to another man."

"It ain't so. Reisden's decent enough by his lights; he wouldn't do her harm."

"Mr. Daugherty—" Charlie felt he was being driven to say more than anyone should ever have to. "He wants her. Perhaps he even believes he'd do her no harm. Mr. Daugherty, tell her what kind of a man he is—what he is doing here!"

"No," Daugherty said. "It's too late for that."

"What?"

"Harry told me this morning. She already knows he's Reisden."

Charlie sat down in his chair, and his heart banged and scrabbled like a trapped animal. Reisden could stop pretending to be Richard. But he had taught her to go out to restaurants by herself, to take cabs. He had told her to go to New York, and this morning there had been a big packet of mail for Reisden from New York; Charlie had seen it on Gilbert's hall table. Reisden's Swiss address was in the big book Daugherty had shown him, the European nobility book. They could guard Perdita from him forever, but could they guard her against herself if she thought she cared for the man?

"Get him away," Charlie gasped. "Where she can never find him."

"He ain't going to be here for too much longer, Charlie."

"Every moment is too much."

Daugherty got up and stood by the window. He turned around. "I hate to say this to a man like you, Charlie, and I hope you don't mistake me. I got to have more than counting teeth. I got to have measurements. I got to have drawings of how the teeth looked."

He could save her yet, if she could be saved. Charlie's heart banged in his chest, but regular, steady. "You will have measurements," Charlie said. Lies like that were honorable in comparison. "You'll have drawings of the teeth and of how far the skull sutures had closed."

The two men looked at each other for a moment, Daugherty sizing Charlie up. "You had 'em today, you just forgot to bring 'em."

"You will have them," Charlie said a little stiffly. "Today, if you'll come to the Clinic the end of this afternoon."

"They're dated yesterday. Just like that note."

"You will see they are dated," Charlie said.

"OK. I'll get Reisden out of here."

CHAPTER 51

THE LAB NOTES from Maurice O'Brien and Louis arrived in the morning mail, a big envelope a half-inch thick. Reisden took the envelope outside onto the porch and dragged two of the porch chairs next to each other, spreading out the notes on one. And for an hour he was only who he had been, in the lab again among Louis' scribbles—sketches of the Statue of Liberty as a pig, of O'Brien as a pig—and O'Brien's neat, lucid, beautifully reported lab work.

About eleven-thirty Gilbert came out on the porch, whispered that Harry was up, and added, did Richard want to go for a walk with him? "Harry's rather sad," Gilbert said in a low voice, "and I believe Perdita has been waiting around to see him. Perhaps we would be—more than was quite needed, for a while."

Gilbert had brought a book. Reisden put his papers back into the envelope and took it with him. The two men cut through the woods until they came to the end of the iron bridge that William Knight had built. The cut of the Little Spruce lay before them, a long streambed of tumbled rocks cut deep into the green star moss of its banks. Gilbert peered down into the confusion of rocks, at the glitter of water ten or twelve feet below, and stepped back quickly. The water was so low that they could barely feel the mist rising from it, but it still raced over the bottom of the cut. The air was cool. Gilbert gave one of the sandwiches he had brought to Richard then sat down underneath the trees, but Richard sat by the edge of the cut, dangerously close, with one foot over the edge. Not eating, throwing rocks down into the water and reading his papers.

Gilbert bit his tongue and didn't tell Richard to get back. Gilbert chewed his sandwich, twenty times each bite, and thought: I have made Harry my heir and been faithful to Richard. And Harry has been so unhappy that he cannot trust Perdita as he ought. And even Richard says that I should choose Harry over him. But Gilbert had no choice, he had never had one; and so he had to wait here, while Harry and Perdita made up their quarrel, or not, between them: between the boy Gilbert had never been able to make his son, and the girl who was effortlessly his daughter. And Richard, who would not marry her, sat on the edge of the cut and threw flints over the edge and looked white and tired.

Gilbert got out his book, opened it, and closed it again.

Richard, Gilbert thought, don't end up like me. If it doesn't work out between Harry and Perdita, speak to her.

But he only asked what Richard was reading.

"Notes from chemical experiments." Richard came over and sat down beside him: away from the edge, thank Heaven. He showed them to Gilbert. Formulae and foreign languages, and a sketch of a pear with a mustache.

"Gilbert, I want you to do something for Perdita."

"Anything, Richard; what shall I do?"

"When she and Harry get married, insist she take her

lessons in New York. If she wants to."

"What, go down once a week, go away from Harry?"

"Harry can breathe unassisted for a day. Supposing that she is a musician, I want someone to give her the train fare and the lesson money."

"I can't come between a man and his wife."

"You can," Reisden said dryly, "better than she can herself." There was no use thinking of her, but she was there, mixed up with Louis' notes and the lab. "What are you reading, Gilbert? Read to me."

Gilbert began slowly:

> Like he who sees in dreams, and in the light
> Feels yet the passion of the glory seen,
> But keeps no memory of all his sight,
> My vision is departed—

Reisden smiled. "Dante? Not the right thing."

"Richard," Gilbert said in a rush, "you love Perdita as much as I do, I think. What is best for her?"

Reisden shook his head. "The music. That's all I know."

"But Harry—?"

"I can't speak about Harry."

And so Gilbert returned to his book, and read silently the last cantos of Dante's Paradise, read about the Light that one can never turn one's eyes from, because the Good that is the object of the will is all collected in it; read about that Light Eternal which is alone Itself, not to be seen with light alone or with thinking, but in a lightning flash, in the granting of a wish; and all the time he mourned, because Perdita might not marry Harry, and if she did it might not be the best thing for her. The sun moved through the sky, drawn in its wheel by the

Love that moves the sun and other stars; and the shadows of the pine trees moved over the star moss, and over the white dust and fragments that were all that was left of Jay French.

Reisden sat with Louis' and O'Brien's lab notes across his knee, reading and comparing. Perdita would make up her quarrel with Harry. Reisden had created a woman he wanted to save, a musician; but he was trying to save himself. She had helped him as much as she should. Because I won't tell, her voice said; she was bright fragments, impressions and memories, a girl with apple blossoms falling on her hair, a girl at a piano. Now, from here on, he was on his own.

He read. O'Brien had got what they considered to be anomalous results in measuring the energy produced at one stage of the recovery reaction. And, since anomalous results shouldn't be replicable, he had done the same thing again, and got them again. Did Reisden have any idea why he should have got this amount of free energy? Reisden studied the data, then went back and reread all the summer's lab notes slowly. And then two pieces of the lab notes came together in his head with something Peter Miller had said about coenzymes, and then more, and five years of his own experiments with them, so that he sat back and said aloud, "No, it goes *this* way," and grabbed for a pencil and began to work out the empirical equations on the margins and the backs of O'Brien's typewritten sheets, having for one moment the whole wheel of life together in his head; and it moved, and it changed, and he knew, not all, but a little more, why his hands moved.

When he finished, the shadows had changed and grown longer, and under the trees it was hot, golden, and very quiet. He read over his notes once and then again, made two corrections in them, and stretched, leaning back against the rough bark of one of the pines, more exhausted than he had ever been but complete, whole. One moment of such completion makes a life. Gilbert Knight was still sitting on the ground, with his closed book in his lap, looking at him as uncomprehendingly as a squirrel. Reisden smiled at him. "Did you know that—" But the chemistry of muscle motion is a difficult music, and not everyone hears it or needs to. "I've got to call New York," he said.

So at three o'clock Reisden and Gilbert were in the summer kitchen, out where they would make no difference to Harry and Perdita, and Reisden was dictating formulae over the phone to O'Brien.

"Question mark question mark question mark," he finished the last one. "I think that's what's happening. If it's right, the process has at least two steps. I found something along similar lines last winter and didn't know what I was looking at; my lab assistant in Lausanne should be telegraphing the results to you. *Louis, Lotmann t'a déjà envoyé les résultats? Merde.* No, of course he won't have, it's the middle of the night over there. All right, let me see what I can remember."

He was bringing up the results in his head and reading them off—he could do it, but it took concentration—when Perdita walked in, alone.

Reisden turned around to look at her.

Gilbert had taken her hands; now he held her left hand only, pressed it with both of his, as if he were feeling the difference with blinded and untrained fingers. "Oh, my dear," he said desolately.

She leaned her forehead against Gilbert's shoulder, only a tired little girl. "I wish I could have!" she said only. "I wanted it so. . . ."

Reisden lost his place. "Excuse me," he said to O'Brien on the phone, then laid it down and came around the edge of the table and put his arm around her. And then he could not let her go.

"Perdita," he said, not knowing what he meant, only being there.

Eventually he reached across the table and got the telephone, mouthpiece and earpiece, and juggled them somehow into position so that he could keep on talking with O'Brien.

When he hung up the phone, Gilbert had gone and they were alone in the room. He wanted to let her go; he wanted to tell her sensible things, harsh things. When she got wholly away from Harry, she would not need him. They were too dissimilar. But she was the one who spoke first. "Is that your piano music?" she said, and he laughed. So he kept his arms around her and gave her comfort, so quiet and shy they were with each other that they barely kissed, but held each other, more tentative and more tender, more complicated, and no less close than lovers.

CHAPTER 52

AT SEVEN O'CLOCK the play was ready. Harry hadn't been back to the house since Perdita and he had talked. The servants had been sent home early. Gilbert had pushed and pulled furniture around in the hall, so that the table and chair and umbrella stand were where they had been in 1887, the chair by the bottom of the stairs instead of over by the table, the umbrella stand back next to the big mirror.

In William's parlor Gilbert watched while Richard drew the shadows of furniture in charcoal, a rectangle by the wall for the side table Gilbert remembered, a half-circle for a big leather-padded rocking chair, a tambour table next to it. And on the wall more shadows, outlines of pictures and of the old banjo clock painted with the fight of the *Guerrière* and the *Bonhomme Richard*. Gilbert remembered the pictures of a ship sailing across a stormy sea and a ship at harbor; the little chairs with their hooped backs carved with grapes; the bronze statue of the Stag at Bay and the black marble clock ticking slowly on the black mantel.

Richard opened the door of the fuse box at the top of the basement stairs and unscrewed fuses one by one, until all through that part of the house the rose-yellow electric lamps died and only the gaslight flared through the Welsbach burners, sharp and green-white, all glares and shadows, like something photographed by the police.

It was not dark outside but the light was shadowed, strange, gaslight competing with the last of the sun. Clouds were building up over the hills and there was rain chill in the air. Reisden sat outside on the porch, suddenly feeling his exhaustion. Perdita came by with sandwiches and he took one but just looked at it, too tired or too nervous to eat.

There would be four of them tonight, Reisden himself, Gilbert, Perdita, and Charlie Adair.

William. Richard. Charlie. Jay.

Perdita sat down by him. "Odd request, my dear," he asked; "will you play the piano?" It was hardly for his ears, since the music room was on the other side of the house; he heard only fragments and the little roughnesses that meant she had not practiced since she gave her word to Harry.

Now she was free.

And what about him? Would he learn enough tonight to free himself?

Gilbert sat down at the other side of the steps. "Gilbert, if she has trouble getting the money for New York, will you help her?"

"Of course, but, Richard, you'll have the money."

Reisden smiled and shook his head. "We have enough to discuss tonight without that."

Charlie Adair was standing at the bottom of the steps. He had brought his doctor's bag, as if there would be use for his services. He looked around at the arrangement of the furniture, recognizing it.

"Charlie, good evening," Gilbert said. Still looking at the furniture, Charlie didn't answer. His face was waxy, and Gilbert moved to help him to a seat. Despite Charlie's health, he couldn't be left out of this; how much did he know?

"Didn't Roy Daugherty talk to you?" Charlie asked sharply. "Is Harry here?"

"Uncle Charlie, hello." Perdita appeared at the door as if she had been waiting for him. "I don't think Harry will be here tonight. Uncle Charlie, you should know that Harry and I have decided—not to be married."

The doctor sat down as if unable to stand. He leaned his elbows on his knees and put his face in his hands.

No one said anything for a minute. Charlie Adair looked up at her. "Do you know what a bad girl is, Perdita?"

"Yes, I do, Uncle Charlie."

"You are deceiving yourself if you think this is only about music."

She said nothing for a long, long time. "No," she said, not looking at Reisden, "it's not all about piano music, Uncle Charlie." And then, very quietly, she added, "But I am going to New York."

Yes, thought Reisden. And someday, so am I.

SINCE CHARLIE was not too well, Gilbert was given the job of taking Charlie's walk, down to the point of land by Mrs. Fen's house where Charlie had seen Jay French run away from Island Hill.

"You will walk down there at a steady pace. You hear the shots, you go out to the point to see what's happening, you pretend to see Jay running away from the house. You then run back to see what's wrong, come into the hall, and look for Richard."

Richard sounded very much like a director, very

professional. He showed Gilbert how to use his stopwatch. (Richard's pocket watch *would* have a stopwatch built in, Gilbert thought, enjoying his nephew's quirks.)

Rain was coming. The trees outside seemed black-green and black-brown, every leaf, every fissure on each trunk visible; the sky was fading to a colorless charged light. Grey clouds edged with brightness massed in the west above the fields. Gilbert thought of umbrellas, then thought of lightning striking umbrellas.

"Wait, Uncle Gilbert."

Perdita caught up with him, bringing an umbrella. Gilbert took it; if lightning struck, only he would be burnt to a crisp. They walked down the gravel drive, trying to keep to whatever Charlie's pace had been on that hot August night.

"I only wanted you to know," she said, "Harry's a good man. I didn't want you to think it has anything to do with Harry."

"My dear, I know that."

They came to the bridge over the Little Spruce River and stopped on the bridge while Gilbert looked at the water. It must have been raining in the mountains; the grey water was rushing thinly over stones that had been bare that morning. In a few hours it would be deep. The trees hung black over the river.

"Harry won't stay with me without you. Richard has his chemistry."

She nodded.

"Richard will have to go away, Uncle Gilbert. He belongs someplace else."

"I hope not, my dear, but I am so afraid. We will all scatter." The oaks were black shadows in the stream, and one dark leaf was blown off by the wind, plastering

against a rock. In one crack of granite a bunch of leaves
had caught, huddled there by the water and the wind.
"Oh, child, Perdita, stay close with me," Gilbert said.
"I have no one else but you."

They got as far as the point of Mrs. Fen's land when
the rain began to rattle the leaves above them. They
punched the stopwatch, started it again, and ran back in
earnest, holding hands while they stumbled on the road.
Through Mrs. Fen's screen of trees they saw her house
all dark. At the Clinic a few children were still trying to
play in the rain and the nurses were shooing them inside.
They ran through the woods and up onto the porch, and
the rain came down on the roof like stage thunder.
Puffing, Gilbert punched the stopwatch button again:
seven minutes, thirty-four seconds to walk to Mrs. Fen's
point; three minutes, twelve seconds to get home.

"Now?" Reisden said to Daugherty.

"Bucky wants you out now. This hour."

"No."

Daugherty wiped his neck with his handkerchief. He
had been on the telephone with Bucky Pelham, not
wanting to tell Bucky what the real issues were and not
knowing how to tell him anything else.

"You ain't real surprised, Reisden. We got a body
now."

"The body is not Richard's," Reisden said forcefully
to Charlie. He took a quick look at the sketches, spread
on the hall table. "Lovely, Charlie, but you've cooked
them. I remember at least one of the front teeth was out;
you've put them all in. And look at the shading. I don't
put shading in my lab sketches and I don't know a

person who does. There may be sketches you made at the time and I'd like to see them. But you drew these later and you drew what you wanted to see."

"Reisden, that's evidence," Daugherty said.

"I have evidence too. Hello, Gilbert, Perdita; you're wet. Go and make yourselves dry. Then we'll begin."

"Let's see your evidence," said Daugherty. Reisden followed Gilbert with his eyes as he went upstairs for towels. He took the letter from his billfold and handed it to Daugherty.

"This is private unless it needs to be used; you can see why."

Daugherty opened the envelope and read the single sheet. It looked small in his hands.

"Where'd you get this? It ain't true."

"Check it."

"Telephone?" Daugherty asked. Reisden gestured toward the new telephone closet under the stairs. As Daugherty clicked for the operator, Gilbert Knight came down the stairs again and peered over the banister at him.

"Oh, Mr. Daugherty, you should be very careful of using a telephone in a thunderstorm. Quite often the lightning comes right down the wires and directly into your brain."

"I got rubber-soled shoes," Daugherty muttered. "Operator? Could you put me on with Anna Fen's house. . . ." Reisden waited for what he would say, but the conversation was only "Uh huh" and "Yup." The phone clicked off and Daugherty came out from under the stairway.

"She's gone."

"Gone where?"

"Gone for a visit, her maid says. Don't know when she'll be back."

Long enough to let the letter do its work. "I rather imagine she's traceable, Daugherty."

Daugherty took a long look at the letter and abruptly crushed it. "It ain't so, Reisden. You can see why it ain't so." Daugherty stuffed the crushed ball in his pocket.

"That doesn't make it go away," Reisden said quietly.

"She didn't have it witnessed. I don't want to see nothing."

"Richard is putting on a play for us," Gilbert's voice floated down from upstairs; "Mr. Daugherty, I hope you will help."

"Don't," Reisden said quietly.

"What kind of play?" Looking around the hall, Daugherty sucked in his breath as he answered his own questions.

"I don't know what I'm going to find."

Daugherty looked balefully up at Gilbert. "I'll watch," he muttered.

CHAPTER 53

"PERDITA IS RICHARD." Reisden assigned Perdita to her role first, because protecting her was important for Gilbert and Charlie. "Gilbert, I'm going to cast you against type; you will be your father. Charlie, you're yourself. We need a Jay. Daugherty, can you take him?"

Daugherty shook his head. "I'm going to watch. You?"

"No, I'm going to direct traffic. Gilbert, you'll still be William. Charlie, your role is over early; are you well enough to take Jay?"

Charlie Adair looked grim, devastated, shrunken. He just nodded.

"If you're not, say so; we'll stop."

He pitched his voice to carry. "This is a walkthrough. No one knows exactly what happened here to the Knights and to Jay French. I will walk us through what we think they did. Any of you can stop at any time, ask questions at any time.

"We have several constraints. First, there was furniture here. It is represented by black squares. As you move around, you can't walk through the furniture.

"The second constraint is time. Charlie Adair was at Anna Fen's point of land when he heard the first shot. Gilbert and Perdita did that walk again just before the rain started. It took them seven minutes, and whatever happens here can take no more.

"The third constraint is that we know where the shots landed and that the last one came in from outside. It broke this window—" Reisden tapped the middle of the three long windows in the parlor.

"I have some photographs of how this room looked afterward, which I won't show around, but will use for checking what we get. Daugherty, you haven't seen these. Would you like to do the checking?"

Victor's police photographs were on the hall table in a manila envelope. Daugherty took them under the gaslight to examine them. "Whew. Reisden, where'd you get these?"

"A friend."

"You got strange friends." Daugherty slid the photographs back into their envelope and mashed down the little metal tab with his thumb, holding the envelope close to his side. He sat down on the stairs in the hall and rubbed his free hand over his skull, looking from one to the other of them.

"Right, let's start," said Reisden.

He brought two chairs from the dining room to William Knight's front room. "We are in the front parlor. William Knight is sitting in a leather-upholstered rocking chair. There's a small tambour table next to him, and on it is a board about eighteen inches long, on which are mounted four guns. He is cleaning the guns and talking to Charlie Adair. Charlie, were you standing or sitting when you talked with him?"

"Standing."

"Good. Where? Close to that chair? Good. Stand there." Reisden placed one of the dining-room chairs there, the other where William's rocker had been. "William, sit down."

Gilbert sat down in the other chair. "How does William look, Charlie? Is he smiling?"

"No."

"Not smiling. Is he indifferent, sad, stern, or angry?"

"Angry." The doctor cleared his throat. "Very angry."

"At you? Why is he angry? What is he saying to you?"

Charlie cleared his throat.

"He was angry about a dog. Richard had got a puppy—"

"Oh, surely not," Gilbert interrupted in a low voice. "Father didn't believe in pets."

"He'd been away, Bert, and Richard found a puppy in the woods. That black-and-white dog, the one I took photographs of. The one in the painting. I knew Richard would have to give it up, but William came back unexpectedly and he was very angry."

"Oh." From his tone, Gilbert knew what Father would have done when he was angry at an animal. "And he was angry at you, too, Charlie, because you had let Richard have the dog."

"Was that the only reason?" Reisden asked. "Is that why he's angry at you?"

Charlie Adair looked down at the floor. "Yes."

"And any other reason?" Reisden asked.

"No," said Adair.

"And the dog. Is it out in the barn? Is it down in the cellar, howling?"

Out of the corner of his eye Reisden saw Gilbert shake his head, no. Reisden held up his hand to stop Gilbert. Charlie looked from side to side and then back to Reisden.

"The dog is dead. I buried the dog."

"Oh," Perdita said in a low voice from upstairs.

Reisden saw for a moment the picture of Richard Knight he had first seen in Gilbert's library. Little boy in a rose garden, petting a black-and-white puppy, smiling.

"If I had known, I wouldn't have had that dog put in the picture," Gilbert said, distressed. "Richard didn't know that his dog was dead, did he, Charlie?"

"No, of course he didn't know. Richard was very

happy that afternoon, Bert." Reisden had moved between the two of them, so Gilbert didn't see Charlie's white and miserable face. Reisden did. "Richard loved his dog, though he didn't have it long. He would have liked to be painted with it."

"Who killed the dog?"

"It had just died," Charlie said.

There was a little silence.

"Did Father kill the dog, Charlie?" Gilbert asked.

Charlie nodded.

"Oh, dear." Gilbert raised his hand to his mouth. "Oh, dear."

Reisden continued. "So the dog is dead and Richard doesn't know. William is angry with you. Where is Jay and where is Richard?"

"Richard is upstairs in his room." Upstairs, Perdita felt her way silently along the wall to stand at the door of Richard's old room. "Jay is in the upstairs office."

Gilbert asked a question. "Was Richard—was he well, Charlie?"

"William hadn't touched him," Charlie said.

Gilbert looked desolately surprised. "Was that unusual?" Reisden asked.

After a long time Charlie said, "Yes."

HAVE I TOLD TOO MUCH? Charlie thought. Should I have told him about William making Richard shoot the dog? Should I have talked about the flies on Washington's muzzle?

"He was angry at you," Reisden said for perhaps the fifth time. "Tell me what you said."

"What I said? Nothing."

"Were you angry?"

"I couldn't afford to be angry. I was afraid he would fire me. He threatened to." William Knight had never threatened anything unless threats were worse than doing. "I told him I had to go. To see another patient." Charlie knew with a twitch of anguish just what would have happened if he had done that. "I left him alone with Richard."

I could never have done that.

"And you actually did what?"

"I left the room and left the house." He improvised, almost sure of himself. "I walked toward town but I was afraid. I didn't know what I could do. I was ready to turn back when I heard the shots."

"You were afraid he would hurt Richard."

He would kill Richard. Charlie Adair tasted again the choking panic he had felt on that hot night. *Dispense with your services as easily as I do now . . . When I am done with Richard, Sir, his soul shall be scoured clean of you.* That night it would have happened. Charlie reached out and touched the chair arm. "I was very afraid of it."

"But as it turned out," Reisden said, "Jay French killed William, or someone killed William and Jay."

Charlie felt the hunt veer away from him, and gasped. It was almost a disappointment. He was like a fox, hunted in plain sight with the hounds behind him, and suddenly the hounds were swerving to follow a new scent. The fox had become invisible, as if dead, as if unimportant. Don't you see me?

"What about Richard?" Daugherty said. "Who killed him?"

"Not our business tonight," said Reisden. "Charlie, do you know why Jay and William might have quarreled?"

"I never knew that," Charlie Adair said.

"Or why anyone else would have quarreled with them?"

He shook his head, no. His heart was beating too hard. "Am I done? May I sit down?"

"Of course, Charlie."

He sat down in the chair, took one of his little pills and let it dissolve under his tongue while he winced through the momentary sharp headache the pill induced. It began to slow his heart. He was sitting where he could look right at the place where he had stood, and he imagined he saw himself there, thinner, with all his hair still red, with his greatest miseries and joys still unthought of. Poor young man.

"Gilbert, set the stage for us. You're playing William. If William quarreled with Charlie, what would he say?"

Gilbert half got up from his chair, as if he were making room for his father, then sat down again. "Why, Richard, I don't know."

"But if you did know, what would it be?"

"He would say that . . . that dogs are verminous—are vermin, Sir!—that's what he'd say. Charlie is Richard's doctor, he should not expose him to such filth. Any doctor who would do such a thing is no doctor at all. He would say—he would bring in the Bible. Is the laborer worthy of his hire, Sir? Does the shepherd nurture his flock? Did God see you when you did this, Sir? Did you think of God?" Every word heavy, separate, sharp, like hammer blows. For a moment, the man who rose from his chair and raised his right fist was William himself, with his wild funeral eyes and his long hair. Charlie stared, but it was Bert who sat down, tame, dithery

Gilbert who had never even wanted to know what his father had been.

"Oh, Richard, if you don't mind, I'd rather just be killed for Father," Gilbert said.

Reisden said something that Charlie heard but didn't understand. "Go ahead, smash the glass. We already know it's not your style."

"I don't want that, Richard."

"Does it surprise you?" Reisden murmured. "You're more afraid of his anger than of him." All this so quiet that Charlie hardly heard it. There were only the three of them in the parlor, but now there were five. Bert, cowardly Gilbert, carried William Knight around in his skin even to the very gestures; and Reisden had seen that. And here also was red-haired Charlie as he had been nineteen years ago, just about to do the most important thing of his life, and Reisden was ignoring him. Charlie's life was slipping and changing, as if he were nothing, only a witness. It frightened Charlie: He ought to know all the answers, but he didn't understand.

"Don't hear you," Daugherty called from the front hall.

"It doesn't matter," Reisden raised his voice. "We were just saying that William was angry with Charlie. Charlie goes out—don't move, Charlie." Reisden followed an invisible Charlie with his eyes and Charlie saw him too, a young man walking out the front door into insignificance. "Now William is left alone.

"He has seven minutes to live."

Reisden stood at the door, leaned against the doorway. Reisden's dark eyes moved to Gilbert—to William—and lingered speculatively, and Charlie watched him, as Gilbert was watching, as Daugherty was;

Daugherty got up and stood at the bottom of the steps as if he were waiting for somebody. Reisden looked up the steps too, then back to Gilbert. "Presumably he is still cleaning his guns—here, William, here's a gun to clean." Reisden tossed something black at Gilbert and Charlie started before he saw that it was Reisden's own black pen. Gilbert held it in his hands, mesmerized.

"Does William like to be alone, Charlie, or always together with someone?" Reisden asked.

"Together."

"Does he go to seek out people or call them to him?"

"He calls them."

"Then he will call for someone now. He did not call for an upstairs servant. Three possibilities remain."

"Three?" Charlie asked.

"He called Jay, or Richard, or he called no one because someone came from outside the house."

Charlie felt odd, half protesting, half laughing. It hadn't been that way; some part of him was enjoying how far Reisden was getting from the truth. "Richard," he said. "Try Richard."

Reisden looked at him inquiringly. "All right. William calls, 'Richard, come down!' "

"Richard, come down!" Gilbert said.

"If he's going to hit me, I don't want to come down," Perdita said from the door of Richard's room.

"Charlie, does Richard come down or stay upstairs?"

Charlie got up from his chair and went out into the hall to look. Perdita was standing by Richard's door, a pale shadow in her white dress, her back against the wall. What would that little boy have done, who had had to shoot his own dog that afternoon? "Stay upstairs," Charlie pleaded. "Don't come down."

"And what does William do when the boy doesn't come down? Does he give up, go upstairs, or keep calling?"

"He stands there. Where you are. He keeps calling."

Reisden stood at the bottom of the stairs; and Daugherty moved back as though people were going up and down the stairs, but there was no one, just the wavering, glaring green light. The light fell on Perdita at the top of the stairs, outlining her against the dark wallpaper. She moved a little and then stood still, eyes wide, listening. Reisden didn't say anything, nor did Gilbert, nor Daugherty, nor Perdita, and the silence built precariously like a house of cards, and Charlie's heartbeat banged in his ears. Finally Reisden said, as quietly and precisely as if he were laying a card on top of the house of cards,

"Come down, Richard, or it will be much worse for you."

Perdita groped her way forward until she found the banister at the top of the stairs. "Uncle Charlie, I'd go down," she called. "He's right, it would be worse—" She felt her way down the steps, one by one, until she was standing in the hall, looking up at Reisden and he down at her. Reisden very slowly raised his fist, brought it down, not touching her. "Body falls," he murmured, "curtain." Charlie could see them, the old man with his wild white hair and the little boy, his face pale, too proud to act afraid of his grandfather, and the old man raising his cane— That was how it would have happened. William would not have waited to say a word.

"But William didn't call him," Charlie said aloud. I didn't leave.

"No," said Reisden, "probably not. Ruining a splendid dramatic situation. Richard refuses to come down, Jay drags him down, which gets both of them in the hall or the parlor. Or Richard comes downstairs, then gets away and," he glanced around the hall, "runs into the closet, shutting himself in to protect himself. But there's no lock on the inside of the closet door"—he opened it to look—"why would there be? And the door opens outward, and a boy cannot hold a door without a handle against a man." He closed the closet door again. "Richard was not in the closet and was not beaten, so he was probably upstairs. You're still waiting to be called down, Perdita, love. William has decided to do something else first."

Perdita moved a few steps up the stairs.

"He calls for Jay," Daugherty said.

"Good. The classic explanation. They quarreled, Jay shot William. For the moment we'll leave aside what I showed you earlier, unless you'd like to do it as the letter suggested?" Reisden looked at Daugherty. Daugherty shook his head violently. "All right. The time is sometime before the first shot. William calls Jay, Jay comes downstairs."

Charlie moved forward. "Do you want me to go upstairs and come down again?"

"What? No, sit down, Charlie. I'll use you soon. There's a bit of going up and down stairs in this part; I'll play Jay for the moment, if you don't mind."

This was safe, Charlie thought. It hadn't happened this way.

"How did William call Jay?" Reisden asked.

"If William were in the parlor and Jay were upstairs in the office, he would ask a servant to do it," Charlie said.

"And if the servants were upstairs?"

Charlie walked over and touched the speaking tube by the door to the downstairs office. "He would use this."

"Which would whistle upstairs. In the office?"

"In the office and in Jay French's room."

"And Jay would come down. Which stairs would he use?"

Charlie thought back. "Sometimes the front stairs, sometimes the back."

"It didn't matter?"

"No," Charlie said.

"We'll try both, then. Jay comes down the back stairs and through the door from the downstairs office, into the parlor here." Daugherty heaved himself up and stood at the door of William's parlor. Charlie looked into the parlor under Daugherty's arm. Gilbert was still sitting in the chair with the pen in his hands. Reisden opened and closed the door, then walked over close to Gilbert, facing him, with a hand on the back of his chair. "William quarrels with Jay."

"Why does he, Richard?" Gilbert asked.

"I don't know. Why?"

Because of Richard? Because of something Jay had done. What would Jay have done? He was always accurate and reliable, he was William's. The silence stretched on. Reisden shrugged. "No one knows, of course. Let's leave it for the moment and concentrate on the action. Jay reaches out—" Reisden stretched out his hand "—and picks out a little pistol, it looks like a .22-caliber, from this board of guns. Daugherty, do you have the photographs? Yes. There is the gun on the board. Look how easy it would be to get it out of the fasteners; one would only give it a tug.

"Now the other gun is much larger. It was a Civil War revolver, which disappeared during the murder so we've no pictures of it. It was a Colt .36-caliber six-shot Navy revolver, a much larger-barreled gun, about a foot long, with much larger bullets. The difference in caliber is important because there were bullet holes all over this room. Big bullets make big holes, small bullets usually make smaller. It's possible to tell which bullet holes came from which gun."

Reisden looked through the material in the envelope and came out with a piece of paper.

"This is a drawing of where those bullet holes were. Daugherty, would you draw them on the wall with this red chalk? You'll be able to feel where the wall has been patched. There should be eight: five on this north wall, two on the south, one on the east by the door. Mark each big or small."

Daugherty took the drawing. "Where'd you get this?"

"I made it from the police report."

Daugherty turned it around suspiciously. "The big ones are all on the north wall and the little ones are on the south and east."

"As you'd expect if William had the big gun and Jay were standing by the office door with the little one. But there's something interesting about those bullet holes. Draw them in."

They were in entirely different places from the ones Charlie remembered. He thought he had pointed at Jay all the time, but one of the little bullet holes was way over to the right of the doors (had Jay ever been there?) and one was almost in the ceiling; Daugherty had to stand on a chair to draw it. The big bullet holes were spaced very close together around the north wall and the mantelpiece. One was over the mantelpiece, where one of the pictures had hung. The bullet had ripped through the canvas—what had it been, a picture of a ship? Sunset in a harbor, or perhaps sunrise. The walls had smoked with plaster dust.

"So you see," said Reisden, "they're shooting at each other. Little Gun's first three shots go wide. Big Gun gets off four or five shots; the one that hit the picture may be a ricochet from the mantelpiece, here." He pointed at the scar. Charlie remembered its whine. No, there had been five shots; that one had come earlier. "There are six shots in that revolver, which William Knight keeps loaded, so there is at least one bullet left."

Charlie remembered the copper-green percussion cap in the chamber when he had dug the gun out from under the hay. The gun was in his doctor's bag now; what would Reisden say if he knew that?

"Little Gun's fourth shot hits William and kills him. It hits him here." Reisden touched the inner edge of his left eye. "I'm sorry, but I've got to talk details. The bullet goes through the eye, does extensive damage to the brain, and goes out the top left of the skull. The entrance hole is small and very neat and around it is a kind of tattooing. I have—had—a friend who studied murder, and he knew what that mark was because he'd seen it before. It was powder from the muzzle of the small, not very powerful pistol. William Knight was killed with the muzzle of the gun not more than a few inches away.

"Gilbert, would you help me with this?" Gilbert,

startled, nodded yes. "I am Jay, you are William. Shoot at me as I walk toward you." They were about ten feet away from one another.

"Shoot at you?"

"With the fountain pen. You should get off four or five shots."

"Do I have to, Richard? All right," Gilbert quavered.

Reisden walked forward shooting an invisible gun. Gilbert pointed the fountain pen at him and whispered, "Bang, bang, bang, bang, bang!" Reisden's shots looked real somehow—oh, Charlie thought: His hand jerked up a little with the recoil every time he shot. Not as much as the real guns had.

"Wait a second," Daugherty said. Gilbert had fired five shots; Reisden was still about four feet away. Daugherty came back and stood by Charlie, arms folded. "That don't make sense," he said. "Try it faster, Reisden."

"Shall I shoot more slowly, Richard?" Gilbert murmured.

Daugherty shook his head. Reisden moved faster this time, low, dodging; he almost reached Gilbert by the time Gilbert had fired his five shots, didn't stop himself in time and stumbled into Gilbert's chair. He reached out the hand with the invisible gun to shoot Gilbert in the eye, but instead turned to look at the big lawyer.

"Daugherty?" Reisden said.

"Well, you got him, you probably got him, but you're dead, you *been* dead about two seconds now. And he's going to get you once more before you get him."

"Yes, that's what I think."

"Can you try it with Jay coming in this way?— Get outa the door a minute, Charlie." Reisden moved to stand in the door and Gilbert turned to face him. "S'pose they had the same fight, but he's here, try that, it's closer. Now you go at him from here."

"Should I shoot at Richard," Gilbert asked, "or at the wall?" He turned a full quarter circle toward the wall where the large bullet holes were. Daugherty squinted at the wall, then back at the door.

"Well, I will be," he said. "That don't make much sense either. Reisden, you got any ideas?"

"Yes. Try it the other way. As the letter said."

Daugherty glared at him.

"Try it," Reisden said quietly.

"Reisden, we know who done it, we just don't know how yet. I don't want no complications."

"Do it. Here, Charlie, stand there." Reisden pushed Charlie toward the chair where he had been sitting. "Where you were before."

"Who am I?"

"We don't know. You're the third hypothesis, the man who came in, the one who kept William from calling for either Jay or Richard."

"Someone we don't know about?" Charlie said.

"Yes, someone new. William, sit down. You have the big gun. The little gun is on the board."

"Where's Jay?"

"Jay is still upstairs. Charlie, walk forward. You've come to see William about something. Something quite desperate perhaps. You're talking to William. Stand right in front of him, that's it. Reach forward." Reisden was kneeling by Gilbert's chair with the black pen in his hand. He held it by one end for Charlie to take. "Pick up the small gun from the board, tug it out of its fasteners, it comes easily. Now shoot William."

Charlie reached forward, moved Gilbert's glasses aside, and touched the inner cantus of William's eye with the end of the pen. The gun exploded all the air in the room. His heart was full of blood, too full to pump; it labored, and the aching fullness drained, and it went painfully on. He dropped the pen.

"What shall I do?" Charlie asked Reisden.

"Sit in the chair."

He sat, the gun between his hands. He saw the blurred whiteness of Perdita's dress at the door. Daugherty was there, arms crossed, watching him, as they were all watching, Gilbert looking at him solemnly, Reisden gazing with black unreadable eyes; and William was dead on the floor. Don't you know who I am? he said to all of them. Gilbert, without anyone telling him, lay down on the floor, a dead body. "Jay comes downstairs; he's at the door to the hall. He comes inside. He sees William dead on the floor and the murderer there with a gun. He takes the big gun and begins shooting at the murderer. The murderer has the little gun and shoots back." Charlie raised his arm, hypnotized; he stood up, he pointed the gun at Reisden, he began shooting, and Reisden was firing back, accurate, the gun kicking in his hand. *They all see, they see who I am,* but Charlie could not stop firing. "He fires at Jay, and Jay runs away from him, outside, then fires at him again through the glass," said Reisden. "There is a third man." He pointed at Charlie. "And he is there—just there."

Charlie sat down in the chair, not able to stand. Reisden was looking directly at Charlie, and Charlie saw the cold intelligence in his eyes fade away and be replaced by a look of very human confusion. "Charlie?" asked Reisden, so very quietly that no one knew except the two of them. Charlie gasped and put his hand to his chest, though for once it didn't hurt at all. Daugherty took his arm.

"Whoa, Charlie, sit down! He don't mean *you*. Reisden, what do you think you're doing?"

Reisden looked from one to the other of them. He closed his eyes for a moment, then walked over to the wall and leaned his back against it as if he needed its support, suddenly pale all the way to the lips. "I don't know," he said. He looked as if he had been shot himself. He sat down rather abruptly on the floor. "No critical sense. Also no sleep last night, and all at once that's catching up with me."

Charlie leaned forward on his chair. "Who was the third man?"

"There wa'n't no third man. Reisden is makin' all this up. Reisden, what you want to do that for?"

Perdita knelt beside Reisden with a mug of coffee. He tasted it and said something to her, something like a thanks under his breath. "Do you think I know who the third man was?" he asked Daugherty.

"Jay come down before the first shot. He shot William. Then he made it look like there was some kind of fight. He shot one gun first and the other one after. That was it."

"And the letter?"

Daugherty looked at Reisden. He took a piece of paper out of his pocket and ripped it in half, then again, then again, until it was unreadably small. He put the pieces back in his pocket.

"There ain't no letter." He looked at Gilbert, then back at Reisden and Charlie. "We got evidence, we got drawings, we got measurements. We don't need more.

It's finished, Reisden. You got anything more to say?"

"No," said Reisden. "I don't think so."

"You don't mind, me and Gilbert are going to start talking. Come on into the library, Mr. Knight."

"Are you all right, Richard?" Gilbert leaned over him. "Don't you think you had better have a sandwich? Mrs. Stelling has left some—"

"I'm all right, Gilbert." Reisden smiled up at him. "Go with Daugherty."

Perdita was still kneeling by him. He watched as Gilbert left the room with Daugherty, then turned to her. "Help Gilbert. This is the end of Richard; he'll need you." She put her arms around him, and he drew her to him and held her tightly. "As soon as I can, I'll see you, love; as soon as ever I can."

And then there were only the two of them, Charlie and Reisden, alone in William's parlor. Charlie was still sitting on the chair. Reisden blew on his coffee to cool it and looked up at Charlie.

"I am not your 'third man,' " Charlie said.

"There was no third man. You didn't go away."

Charlie's heart squeezed.

Reisden spoke very quietly, almost pedantically. "Blocking is useful, Charlie. When one starts blocking a scene, one has the actors moving here and there, and so often they come back where they started and one realizes one simply shouldn't have moved them. You went off as Charlie and came back as the third man. And I didn't have to move you. You were talking with William, then you were the third man picking up the gun. . . . I don't have a chance of proving it. But I'd like to know that it's true."

"No," Charlie said. "It isn't true."

How you would like to control me, Dr. Reisden. You would say I killed Richard. Or that you are Richard. That I destroyed Jay's body to protect myself. And you would have Richard's place, Richard's money; Gilbert and Perdita would give it to you and would be glad of it.

Nineteen years ago a young man had walked out the front door into insignificance: Then he had turned and come back. Charlie got up and followed his young self with his eyes. "I went out the door, but I didn't go far. William called Richard to come down. And Richard came. William brought him back here into the parlor." Charlie felt, through nineteen years, the little boy's arm tense and try to rise under his hand, to point the rat pistol at his grandfather.

Richard, forgive me.

"Afterward it happened the way you said. Jay came downstairs after the first shot. I was in the parlor with Richard. He shot at us both and I pushed Richard down to the floor and I shot at Jay. I must have hurt him. But he ran, he didn't seem hurt. I must have killed him, and God save me, because I took communion all these years.

"But it was Richard who killed William Knight."

CHAPTER 54

THE RAIN RATTLED the windows. Inside the house there was no sound. Then, faintly from across the hall, Reisden heard Gilbert's voice raised in short, sharp protest. Daugherty had told him; Richard is dead, Reisden thought.

"You never told Gilbert?" Reisden asked.

"No, no, certainly not."

"You needn't worry. I won't tell." Richard's words. Of course Richard wouldn't tell. They had protected each other, Charlie and Richard.

"What happened to Richard?" Charlie asked, very pat, as if he were quite innocent of what had happened to Richard, or at least wanted to reassure Reisden that he knew nothing.

"Jay killed him."

Charlie looked up at him, questioning.

"Stick to your story, Charlie. I'm not so omniscient as you think me, and not so cruel either. If you could get your little boy back I wouldn't hide him."

"And Perdita?"

"I didn't hurt her."

No? Not until now. Reisden would not think about her now, her or anyone.

Charlie picked up his bag. "I feel—" He hesitated at the door. "I hope I have misjudged you, Dr. Reisden. I feel I've hurt you."

"No, Charlie, you were right. I only wanted something I couldn't have."

Charlie closed the door behind him, leaving Reisden alone in the white room. He sat there, a shadow in the light, quite numb. Staying numb was a job, like carrying a large beaker of some corrosive liquid. Something might break.

"Reisden?" Daugherty knocked quietly at the door. *Leave me alone.* But Daugherty opened the door.

"You all right?"

"Fine," he said dispassionately.

"I'd like your help for a minute. Gilbert don't believe me, about it bein' Richard in the barn."

Why should he? I was supposed to be convincing. "Let me get what I need; then I'll talk to him."

Upstairs, he had some idea of packing. He opened drawers, then stood overcome, keeping very still as though he were being hunted by something. He closed one drawer after another. In the top drawer was his box of collar studs, and behind that the gun he had used five years ago and the bullets he had bought at the Scollay Square shooting gallery the night he had met Harry. He stared at them. He could not look one moment beyond the instant he was in. He knew what he could do with the bullets in the red cardboard box and the grip of the gun and the trigger, and he didn't know what else he could do.

The chemistry notes were on top of the bureau. They seemed still warm from this afternoon's sun. (He put the gun in one jacket pocket and the box of bullets in the other. This is my hand. Put the gun down, fool. Leave it. Let it go.) He took the chemistry notes, as though he could assert that he had some future in which he could use them.

Gilbert was in the library, sitting pale and hunched by the fire. Perdita was by him. He looked up when he saw Reisden come in. "Richard?"

"No," Reisden said. "Not Richard."

He said what was required. He could not listen to himself other than to know he was saying something that Gilbert would believe. "I'm sorry. In the beginning I didn't expect you to believe it. I told you not to. Then eventually, to be human, to be Richard, I lied to you and said I was he." He saw how, as he spoke, Gilbert's face went white and old. He did not look at Perdita at all.

He kept going until Daugherty touched him on the arm. "That's enough, Reisden."

Out on the porch the rain sluiced across the granite step where Gilbert had dropped the glass. "Reisden, I got your coat and a couple umbrellas. You want to go and wait for the train together?"

"No. I'm going to drive the automobile."

"You better not, it's pretty wet."

"It's all right."

Daugherty held out his hand. Reisden didn't take it.

"Well," Daugherty said finally, "I guess that finishes up then. I'll clean up in the office." He opened his umbrella. It made a sound like a bat's wings, and whatever else he might have said was drowned in the roar of the rain. He trudged off down the drive, toward the summer kitchen.

Reisden lit the acetylene headlights of the car and then cranked the engine, and it started with a coughing roar. He adjusted the spark and the fuel mixture. Autos were not built for weather like this. Water was coming in through the leather roof. The rubber blade scraped back and forth on the windshield, clearing it for a moment before the rain opaqued it again.

Tasy's blood smeared across the windshield, turning the light from the headlamps red. I am a murderer. Not hers. Killing William was easy to live with by comparison; it ought to be easy.

He drove the black auto down the long sweep of the drive and into the road that snaked through the woods, and then, once in the woods, he accelerated, the stiff steering bucking against his arms. Leaves whipped at the windshield and bloody water runneled across the glass like snakes. In the acetylene light, when the wiper swept away the rain, he saw the road in jerks and flashes. A tree trunk brushed close enough to scrape paint; he saw the pattern on the bark. Suddenly he was through the woods and close to the bridge and the gates and the chasm.

He knew exactly how the wheels would slip on the clay by the gates, how the auto would slew and roll and fall into the narrow cut of the Spruce. He had no sense of being able to stop it. The gate pillar was stone and about four feet across; the auto went into a long skid, down the grade, its headlights full of granite, and hit the gate. It slewed, spun a quarter turn around, and slipped toward the ditch, passenger side crumpling, rearing like a horse about to roll over and crush him underneath it. At the height of the roll there was a moment of intense, quiet balance, without weight or motion, as complete as being at work in the lab. He had time to think of everything. Louis in New York, Maurice O'Brien . . . An elephant trumpeting in sunlight. He had time to smile at that. He thought of Perdita last night; "I won't tell." No, never, but she would know. He couldn't let that happen to her; except that he had not much choice now. He threw his weight away from the direction of the roll.

The car lost balance and crashed down the way it had come, landing upright.

He closed his eyes as the windshield exploded. Stone sliced through the right side of the car, shearing metal, and the impact knocked the breath out of him. The car jounced and swung back and forth and screamed metallically, settling onto a broken spring.

He leaned against the steering wheel, gasping. My G-d, my G-d.

One of the headlamps was half smashed and guttering, throwing a haze of light into the air; the other still worked. He unclipped that one and looked at the auto. It was broken. All four wheels were smashed, the thick hubs splintered. Most of the passenger side was bits of metal on the ground. It would take wrecking equipment to move it. He was still overwhelmed by that calm like death or a prayer, and the absolute terror of knowing what he knew and being still alive.

Outside the car the gravel rolled under his feet and the path blurred into the water-soaked grass, whipping in the wind. He turned and the rain beat into his eyes, stinging like tears. He had cut open the back of his hand, a deep cut runneling blood, and it stung. The rain hit his face like a fistful of needles. But in the middle of the storm there was the quiet, which he had no name for. The wind howled and pounded at him. By the wrecked car and the paint-scored gate was a tree, a pine; he turned away from the car and ducked under its branches for shelter, but when he touched the hard bole of the trunk, pine sap smelling in the dark, he began pounding his fist against it and could not stop.

I will not remember, I will not even imagine, what happened to Richard Knight to bring him to murder. I will not let myself know what it would be to kill someone, even someone you hated; to be full of that terrible desolation, and to be eight years old—

But that was what the quiet was, it was the same thing as the pain and the desolation; it was Richard.

The wind and rain thrashed the branches against him, he was wet through, and he scooped up a handful of the pine-needles and stones under the tree, hurling them into the wind. Nothing more ridiculous, nothing more futile; he should have laughed at himself but he threw grass and stones at the darkness, where the wind blew them back again in his face, but he picked them up again and threw them at the wind as if he were still Richard Knight and William Knight this storm.

He remembered nothing, nothing at all; but he screamed and swore at the storm, and damned William Knight, and finally cried for Richard, until he was exhausted.

He leaned against the pine bole. Can't I stop now? He wanted to be out of the storm, out of everything he was feeling, wanted to be warm and dry and someone else. He wanted to make rational, considered judgments, to drink hot tea with rum, to be grown up, and to agree with someone that the poor child was not in the least to blame.

The only thing the poor child had not known was how he would feel for the rest of his life.

Through the screen of trees he saw the shape of the auto, the smashup six years ago. There is a body right there, he thought, on the ground beside the car. He saw it in the rainy darkness, knowing this was the last time he would really see it; from now on it would be memories. This time the body was recognizable as William, an old man with long white hair, flung facedown. I've killed him, Reisden thought confusedly. He was glad, so glad he was shaking and frightened, but horrified, and wrenched by loneliness, as if he were lost in an unimaginably far place with no landmarks and no way to get back, and he was afraid to kneel down and turn the body over for fear he would see someone he loved. He stood in the rain with the water streaming down his face, and it only slowly came to him that he was crying still, and that the person he was crying for was his grandfather; it was ludicrous, appalling, but he cried.

Twenty feet back was the near gate of the bridge. He held up the lantern and looked through the bridge rail and the grating at the river he had not driven into, and he let the rest of the numbness go, feeling Richard in anger and terror, in vengefulness and pain and sorrow, and in the quiet too.

Underneath him the water raged, grey and twisting, and the rain cried down in sheets through the open cage of the bridge. The storm soaked him, whipped him with the force of the wind. He held the lantern over the water, barely three feet below the bridge, and the river was terrible, full of grimaces and twists like mad faces. He set the lantern on the decking and with cold, stiff fingers took the gun out of one wet jacket pocket, took the bullets out of the other, and loaded the gun.

The lantern at his feet fell over and went out, and he stared into the blind dark. Did God see you, Sir, when you did this? Did you think of God? Every victim has one hold on his tormentor; Richard's had been that he could get sick. Richard could die.

No, William. Now we make peace.

He stretched out his hand with the loaded gun in it, held the gun over what he hoped was the river, and let it go. It fell down, away from him, into the dark and the water's roar, and he threw the rest of the bullets after it.

CHARLIE ADAIR sat in the hall chair while Dr. Reisden talked to Gilbert Knight. Charlie hardly listened. He hugged the pain in his chest and arm as if it were a secret. It spread slowly like a viscous liquid.

The door slammed behind Dr. Reisden. He's gone, Charlie thought with incredulous relief.

Perdita was standing in the hall, looking after Reisden with pain and disbelief written on her face. Charlie looked up at her, standing by the door, poor child, listening sightless to the storm.

Dr. Reisden was lying all summer, my dear. Not tonight.

He leaned back for a moment, breathing shallowly to make the pain go away, then bent painfully over and rummaged in his doctor's bag. His fingers felt the barrel of the revolver, wrapped in its scrap of blanket, and flinched away from it. He brought out his prayer book and turned to the sacrament of Penance, marked with a well-worn purple ribbon.

"Examination before the Confession. Fifth Commandment. Thou shalt not kill."

Have I done evil to my neighbor? Through scorn or vengeance? In wishing him death? . . . In speaking injuriously of him? . . . Have I done harm to children?

Bless me, Father, for I have sinned. But I did the best I could.

Lord, let it all go back the way it was.

Lord, he prayed uselessly, why did I have to know what I have done?

I won't ever tell, Perdita repeated to herself.

Then don't tell.

He hadn't been lying when he said he was Richard. He couldn't have. So he was lying now.

She stood in front of the doctor, her long woman's skirts whispering. "Uncle Charlie?"

"My dear?"

"Uncle Charlie, what did you say to—to Dr. Reisden?"

A long silence. "Only that I knew he was not Richard. The body was a child's. I think he would have wanted to believe he could be Richard."

Her eyes stung. She opened the door and listened for the automobile motor. At night its sound carried far; she had heard it sometimes, lying awake in her bed. But tonight the rain clapped too hard on the porch roof.

"What did you say to him then?" she asked. "What did he say?"

"Dr. Reisden is gone," Uncle Charlie said. "He's gone, my dear; no use looking after him." He came over to her, patted her arm. She drew back. "You're unhappy. Wait here for Harry, if you'll take my advice."

"No," she said under her breath. When she left this house tonight she would not have a place in the Knight family anymore. She was afraid to put that moment off too long. Harry would come back and she wouldn't know what to do; he would plead with her again, the way he had this afternoon when he realized she meant to go away. He is Richard, she said under her breath.

"Uncle Charlie, please stay here with Uncle Gilbert. Don't make him be alone tonight and don't make me stay."

"Child, you won't wait for *that man* to call you?"

That was exactly what she was doing. No matter how long it took. "Please."

Charlie Adair gathered up his missal and his doctor's bag. She heard his breath wheezing and laboring. "Uncle Charlie, don't go. You're not well. Please, let the three of us stay here together."

"Perdita," Charlie said. "He won't come back."

Outside on the porch he closed his missal on the Confession and dropped it into his bag. His old coat had capacious pockets and there was a hole in the bottom of the right-hand one; the foot-long Civil War pistol fit into it like into a holster, rucking the flap up a little. It was the same coat he had worn at a train station in Switzerland when he had seen Richard Knight.

He left his doctor's bag on the glider, taking only his flashlight, and as he turned it on he saw a coat on the porch next to an envelope full of papers. The address read, "M. le Baron Alexandre von Reisden."

Reisden had left his papers and his coat, and he would come back. He'd had to, he'd say. And Perdita would be there. Would he go back into the house, or take Perdita away with him?

I can't stop him, Charlie thought. He took the papers and the coat. How can I stop him?

Outside, the rain drummed on his umbrella. He stumped down the drive, the pain spreading again, burning every vein and artery like corrosive blood. Lord, use me as You will, take my death into Your service. Let me confess to you.

Bless me, Father, for I have sinned.

The Lord be on your lips and in your heart that you may properly confess all your sins. . . .

Seven minutes, they had said, for Charlie to get through the woods and to Anna Fen's house. Young slim Charlie had been faster; it took old Charlie longer than that to get to the gate, breathing around the rod of pain in his chest, listening for Reisden. He thought he would find him before reaching the woods, or somewhere in the tangle of trees, perhaps where the cherry tree had fallen.

But when he left the trees he saw the black car skewed to the road.

It had claw-marked the driveway. Its big wheels had gouged the gravel and one of its headlights was gone. The other pointed up at a skewed angle, making a pool of light in the rain. Charlie stood in the light from the single headlamp, peering at the front seat, looking for a slumped body, blood.

I have wished my neighbor harm. . . .

"Charlie."

I have contemplated violence.

Reisden stood at the edge of the light by the bridge.

I have been driven toward violence.

"Dr. Reisden, where are you going?" Charlie asked. "The train station is the other way. Here, I have your coat."

"I left the notes," Reisden said as if it surprised him. "Put them in the car. I'm not going to the train station, Charlie; I'm going back. Will you come with me?"

Charlie dropped the coat. He switched the handle of the umbrella from his right hand to his left and tucked the flashlight under his arm. There was enough light. Reisden had unclipped the other headlamp from the car. It was a halo of white light around him. Charlie stepped back.

"Don't play games with me, Dr. Reisden, not now."

"No, Charlie." His eyes looked dark and exhausted, but he focused on Charlie and suddenly he was almost smiling. "I don't want to do any of what I am going to do now. Except get out of this rain."

The devils in Hell face the worst there is, and have all the feelings burnt out of them, and then get that light in their eyes, the deathly amused light of survival: Is this all there is to Hell? I am still here.

"I am going to tell Gilbert and Perdita what happened."

"What will you do?" Charlie asked. "The Clinic—"

"Come back to the house, Charlie, and we will brew a strong pot of coffee and start a fire. Then Gilbert and Perdita and you and I are going to sit around the kitchen table, like four grownups, and you and I are going to tell him and her how Richard killed his grandfather." He took a long breath. "I took this on alone most of my life. I can't do it anymore."

Will you speak like Richard? You are not Richard, you damned man. "The Clinic—"

"I don't know what he'll think, Charlie. Of either of us."

"Go away," Charlie said to him. "Get away from me."

At the same time he fumbled the flap back from his coat pocket. It was awkward because of the wet, and the gun being so far down in the pocket and sticking. Dr. Reisden saw what Charlie was doing. His head went back and he shouted, "Charlie, *no*!" like a warning. The children are the kingdom of Heaven. Lord, take this cup from me. I'm afraid. Charlie tensed his hand. The sound was just as he remembered, a thick flat clap like a dictionary being slammed closed. The bullet seemed to crawl away from the gun so that Charlie could have grabbed it in his fist and crushed it like a fly. "You'll never—" Dr. Reisden said and shook his head violently, and the impact slammed him against the rail. The whole iron bridge rang.

· · ·

GILBERT HAD COME OUT of the library into the front hall and was looking up the stairs. "If I had run away with Richard," Gilbert was saying. "If I had *done something* about Father. We would have Richard——" His breath caught in his throat. "Ah, my dear——but we have *him*—— No one else is Richard. That's how it hurts me."

He is Richard.

She had promised not to tell. It is stupid, Richard had said about something else, like locking yourself in a closet. What would he want her to do? He had lied to Gilbert and had never wanted to be Richard Knight.

If you lie, she'd said, you'll have to lie all your life. And so will Gilbert, and so will I.

But he had never wanted it known——

They heard the shot.

I CONFESS to Almighty God, to Blessed Mary ever Virgin, to Blessed Michael the Archangel . . .

Charlie knelt in the rain by Reisden, who had fallen against the bridge rail, both hands pressed against his chest, his eyes wide open. He was breathing in great heaving gasps like a runner fallen in a race. "Charlie," he said.

. . . that I have sinned exceedingly in thought, word, and deed . . .

"Confess yourself," Charlie said to Reisden.

"Tell them," Reisden said urgently, looking up at Charlie. "Or you'll never be able to talk to anyone."

. . . my fault, my most grievous . . . "Why didn't you go?" he asked the man.

The man only laughed, a breathy grimace. "I couldn't go. I'm Richard."

"Don't lie, man, you're dying."

You are not Richard, Charlie thought. You have no right. I didn't want to shoot you. I wish a man's death. I have shot a man. Please die. Charlie's imagined priest was gone and nobody here but this man. He is no one. Reisden moved his head back and forth and drew his lips back a little from his teeth as if the pain distracted him.

"Charlie," he said slowly, "I never told. Do you want them never to tell?"

REISDEN FELT A BLOW, himself falling; then he was lying on the gridded floor of the bridge. He was confused for a moment. Tasy? There's been an accident. She's dead. When he tried to breathe, Reisden heard water rushing; he could get no air at all. He tried to keep talking to Charlie. Tasy, he had asked her once, why those endless death scenes in opera? She had laughed. *But when they stop singing,* she said, *they are gone.*

I must stay conscious. Charlie—

If Charlie is at all clever he'll put me in the car and throw the headlamp at the wreck. The gas tanks must have ruptured. And then there will be an explosion and they'll think I died being stupid. That would be the way to do it. And the notes gone too. Did I tell O'Brien everything? Charlie, how did you keep them from finding Jay? Did you know about Jay?

He tried to raise his head. Blind dizziness washed over him.

Charlie! Tell Gilbert and Perdita that what I told them was nonsense. They know who I am. Tell her to go to New York. When she is there she is to see a man named Louis Dalloz. Maurice O'Brien in the chemistry department will reach him. Tell her to tell him, he is to

take her out to dinner and talk about pigs. . . . I loved
her. . . . The water was falling silent. Perhaps it was not
raining any more. Nothing is worth being alone forever.

"Charlie," Reisden managed. Please. Stop it now.
Tell them everything. Please. "Tell."

"I will tell," Perdita said.

Perdita had got ahead of Gilbert, familiar with the
road in the dark. In the circle of light, under the wet-
ground smells of the rain, she smelled gunpowder,
smoke, and a diluted, sheared-copper smell that for a
moment she did not know as blood. "Uncle Charlie."
He rose to his feet, wheezing and gasping, and she saw
the glitter of the gun in his hand. He left his shadow on
the ground behind him, a darkness crumpled on the
bridge, and she was back in the barn again, seeing the
shadow on the floor. She knew what had happened
before she could give it names or words.

"Uncle Charlie? Richard?"

"Lord God," her uncle said thickly.

She was terrified of Uncle Charlie but she held out her
hands to him. She had loved Uncle Charlie all of her life.
She laid both her hands across the gun, loosening it from
him while keeping hold of his hand. She laid the gun on
the bridge. "Uncle Charlie," she said.

He did not shrink back from her. He held her hand
for a moment, and then knelt down by the man he had
shot. "He is not Richard," he started to say to her, but
the words died on his lips. He felt for Reisden's pulse;
in the white light from the lantern she saw his hands
blurred and red.

"What did he tell you?" Charlie cried out to her.

"How did he make you believe him?"

"I told *him*——" It didn't make much sense, but Uncle Charlie understood.

"Richard?" he said, and repeated in a terrible gasping voice, "Richard?" He tried to gather Richard up, take him in his arms, but Richard seemed too heavy for him, and suddenly Uncle Charlie slipped and fell down on the ground. He didn't get up. He said a few words indistinctly and she thought she heard Richard say something, but she didn't know what.

She knelt down beside Charlie and touched him to help him get up, and he half rose, but at that moment she felt him die under her hand. He grunted something, his hand jerked once as if she had given him a shock, and then he fell toward her, but what she caught was butcher meat, old bones sliding under loose skin. She eased him to the ground, feeling no pulse under his old frayed collar, no Uncle Charlie there at all.

CHARLIE is saying an act of contrition, Reisden thought, recognizing the pattern without the words. My God, I am heartily sorry to have offended against Thee. . . .

The rain was drowning him. He coughed and tried to move his head, but it was filling his lungs. Now? And Gilbert and Perdita were not here.

No one will save you, Charlie. No one will listen to your penance or absolve you. We are alone. No one will know what happened here, and Gilbert and Perdita will never be sure enough to tell.

He freed the only person he could.

I absolve you, Charlie, from every bond of excommunication and interdict, to the extent of my power and your need. And finally, I absolve you from your sins. . . .

He couldn't remember any more.

PERDITA held her hand next to Richard's mouth and felt his desperate shallow breathing. Under his arm she felt the littler bullet wound and in his back the bigger one, where the blood ran out between her fingers. Uncle Gilbert dropped to his knees beside her. She was tearing material from her underskirt for the pressure bandage Uncle Gilbert was making. Charlie had taught her and Gilbert to do what they could. That was all she could understand for now. Richard's hand stirred and she turned from her work for a moment, holding him. "You're safe," she said as she would have said to a child, and then amended it, "you're with us." And she crouched in the rain while Uncle Gilbert ran for help, holding on to Richard in the darkness, breathing with him, breath for breath.

"Are you *here?*" he whispered once.

"Yes," she said. Yes.

CHARLIE felt a terrible clawing pain up his arm. It was as if he had touched a live wire. He cried out but the pain kept on, up and down his arm and spreading across his chest.

Bless me, Father, for I have sinned—

I am no murderer, he shouted at Perdita, I would never hurt you. He heard no sound.

The pain eased suddenly and Charlie sat up. All the lights went on at once. He was surprised to see he was back at Island Hill. Reisden was leaning against the wall, arms crossed, eyes dilated to black in a chalk-white face.

In one of Reisden's chalked mirrors Charlie caught a glimpse of his own reflection, a young man with red hair. Reisden sat in William's chair. "Here," he said, and tossed Charlie the Navy revolver. "Now shoot." Charlie raised the gun and sighted, but in the clear moment before the shot, he saw that it was Richard in the chair, Richard eight years old. He's only something I'm dreaming, Charlie thought, but with surprise and relief he put the gun down.

"Come on!" Richard said. "We can still get away!"

Richard and Charlie ran hand in hand through the dark down Island Hill's long gravel drive, across the iron bridge that echoed with the clang of their boots. Oh, Charlie thought, it is a dream, but it seemed so much as if it were real, as though they were really escaping at last. They ran through the fields by the old Federal Hotel, deserted and boarded up, the eagle tilted on its cupola. Trying to keep up with Richard's quick legs, Charlie was panting like an old man.

They ran into the hotel and up the wide empty staircase. The rooms were dimly lit but Charlie found the right one, the place where he had lost Richard, by its moldy smell and its closed shutters. They wedged between a chest of drawers and the window and Richard tilted a shutter slat to look outside. He was holding a lantern and the light profiled his face. He was half laughing with excitement, doing a little dance. It was as though he were playing cowboys and Indians. Charlie was astonished to see him so happy.

"Richard, let me see you."

Richard held up the lamp obligingly. Clear eyes in a thin face. The run had given him color and his eyes were laughing.

"Do you know me?" Richard said.

You never laughed, Charlie thought. I would have known you if I hadn't been so— Charlie blinked back tears. Child, I was foolish. You had to come back. But when you did I had to be afraid.

He had made up a man chasing him and it was only the child.

"No one's after us," Richard said, squinting through the shutters. "Look."

It was only the empty dawn road beside the Clinic, just as Charlie had seen it so many times before. Nothing there except night and trees. The grey road stretched out empty all the way back to William Knight's house.

"No, no one," Charlie said. "We should never have run away. Forgive me."

"I forgive you," Richard said soberly.

"I thought—" Charlie tried to explain. "The police would have put me in jail or killed me. I don't know what I thought."

"They might have," Richard said.

"And then the Clinic—it's a strange thing. There wasn't a blessed soul but me with a real motive . . . but the more I showed them that I loved children, the more they said, 'Ah, go on, you couldn't have done it.' I must have begun to think I was the saint they said I was. You haven't a notion what that does to you, being told who you are; you get to be an actor, Richard."

Richard laughed a little. "I know."

Richard played with the catch on the shutters, jiggling it up and down, beginning to be impatient. He was more grown up than Charlie remembered him, but still a child.

"What is it, Richard?"

"Can we open the shutters now? It's almost morning."

"No, it can't be yet." Children always want the light. Adults need the dimness sometimes. What'll we do today, Richard, in this day dawning? Play chess if it's raining. Go fishing, but you'll throw the fish back. Today we will see God. And here I've left my rosary somewhere, no one confessed me, my soul's in a muddle. What will God think of me?

Charlie only thought that, but Richard heard.

Richard drawled in a perfect imitation of Alexander Reisden. "Ah, Charlie, when you think of all the other things you and I don't know, how can we possibly know that?"

Charlie laughed and Richard laughed with him.

"Now," said Charlie.

Richard opened the shutters and let in the day.

Epilogue

ANY BOOK is a light shone into a darkness, and we are reaching the limits of the light. Outside it, in the darkness of the century, anything may happen. Harry and Perdita may make the best of things after all, or Reisden and Perdita, or none of them; Perdita may do something with her music, or dwindle down to memories, to piano scores in an old cupboard and a pretty leather case for sheet music. Outside of books there are no guarantees. This beautiful Commonwealth Avenue, with its wide double street, will be narrowed with parked cars, and college dormitories and condominiums will fill the rooms where families lived. Old newspapers will crumble to dust and carry away the last memories of the Knight case, without even Lizzie Borden's four lines of doggerel to immortalize Jay French and Richard Knight; and August sixth will no longer be the day Gilbert trembled at, but the terrible morning of Hiroshima.

But that is another book, and this one ends now, in this year of 1906, on the tenth of September, a Monday, at four in the afternoon. The servants are on holiday today and Harry has gone out to see Efnie, in whose company he finds himself more and more often nowadays. Gilbert is at home alone and answers the door himself, and Reisden comes inside.

They have had more than enough chance to talk while Reisden was in the hospital; it is not talking that Reisden came for. They have learned as much as they will know. Gilbert knows what Charlie said he did and Richard did. There are great ragged holes in the story. How was it that no one found Jay's body? Could Richard have run away himself, or did Charlie help him? This side of death no one will know what is true. What matters, Reisden has said, is what one is willing to be responsible for.

So Gilbert has spoken at Charlie's funeral, and said what a good man he was; that much he knew, and knows still.

Charlie's children will not suffer. Gilbert has renewed his commitment to sponsor the Clinic. The money is all his now because Richard has been declared dead; Charlie's drawings convinced the judge.

Roy Daugherty has come in to see Reisden often in the hospital and, one day, has happened to mention he knows about a ship, the three-masted *Wanderer,* that sailed from Boston Harbor going to Port Elizabeth, South Africa, twenty-first of August 1887. He could make some inquiries as to whether a boy, or some such, stowed away on her. But Reisden has said, "No, don't," and Gilbert has said nothing, has only remembered the name of the ship.

No, Gilbert and Richard are only going to say good-bye to each other, because tonight, on the late train, Richard is going to New York, and from there to Paris.

They sit in chairs in the garden, which is beginning to look like fall; in the late sunshine the lilac leaves are olive dusted with white and the chrysanthemums are spreading their curled petals, fall colors, golden and bronze. In the center of the garden the apple tree is bowed under its fruit, and a few apples have fallen, red rayed with gold on the ground. Reisden stands looking at it, oddly surprised. "My G-d, you forget that apple blossoms turn to apples." He picks one up from the ground and looks at it. Gilbert picks two from the tree and gives one to him. Father planted this tree, he tells Reisden; the fruit is always very good. "I have tasted of the tree of the knowledge of good and evil," Reisden murmurs, looking at the apple, and polishes it on the sleeve of his jacket—gingerly, his left side is still giving him trouble—and eats it, bite by bite, tasting sweetness and a crispness like winter snow, and all the summer; and Gilbert loyally eats his too. "I remember Perdita standing under that tree," Reisden says.

"Often," Gilbert says.

"What will you do?" Reisden asks Gilbert.

What will Gilbert do? He will be alone. Gilbert has met Richard's working partners, the people in his lab, the big old Frenchman and the man from New York; he understands that Richard is going to work with them again. Gilbert has seen how the men from Richard's laboratory talk to him, and how they need him; he has a place there. Richard is not Gilbert's now, whatever share Gilbert might have had in him; and Gilbert will never keep a bookstore in Falmouth and no little boy will ever keep it with him, because Gilbert has no more children.

"I have got a job," Gilbert says. Actually he does not have it, because he has only just now thought of the idea, but he sees no reason why he might not. "With the Harvard Library. I am collecting bookbindings for them, a little collection, you know. I am acquainted with the bookbinders a bit, you see, Miss Sears and Miss Creese Green, some of the others as well, and actually, I wonder if I could ask you a favor."

"Yes, Gilbert. Of course."

"I suppose that most of what I do will be American, but I *do* do early North Italian bindings from time to time, and . . . I wonder if perhaps you could—I know you will be there from time to time—the Italian libraries are so extremely desultory, I wonder if you could look up some references for me."

"It would keep us in touch," Richard says.

"It would." Richard has seen through him, of course; but Richard is sitting on the chaise lounge, with his hand over his eyes so that Gilbert won't see, because Richard was always private and proud. Gilbert sits down on the edge of the chaise, gingerly, and hesitates, and after a moment he hugs his nephew in both arms and thumps him on the back, the way that men do. And Richard hugs him back.

"Oh, Gilbert, the arm," Reisden says eventually and leans back in the chair. He half smiles at Gilbert. "Sorry. The thought of dealing with the staff at the Marciana, I imagine." And then he closes his eyes, and says very carefully after a moment, "I wasn't sure you would want to keep in touch. And I would have missed you."

"Richard," Gilbert says, "are you sure you are doing what you want, and going where you ought to?"

"The h--l of it is," Reisden says, "I know exactly who I am."

Not long afterward the doorbell rings again, and this time it is Perdita. She has taken a cab, for practice she says, because in a few days she is going to New York. She looks very grown up in a grey skirt and jacket. Looking at her with her hair up, for a moment Gilbert finds it hard to remember how she looked as a girl with her long hair down her back. Gilbert takes them both into the kitchen. He has soaked codfish for codfish cakes, and Perdita and Reisden sit and talk with him while he flours the cakes with corn meal and fries them in his old black frying pan. They eat fishcakes and baked beans, and Reisden makes coffee on the stove, and for dessert they eat more of the apples from the garden; and they sit talking while the twilight changes to darkness. To-night there is no reading, no music, just three people talking, as if they must find in this night all of the little inconsequential pleasures of a lifetime; and at the end of the evening, Gilbert brings out one of the old bottles of sherry and three old glasses and they toast each other. None of them say anything. Gilbert thinks, To Perdita in New York, and thinks of the dead and missing. To

Jay French, whose name is still uncleared. To Charlie, my dear friend. Richard, he thinks. And, surprisingly, Father.

They have taken a cab to South Station; they are on the platform and the train is about to leave. The lights are scattered all down the platform; they stand in a pool of light in the darkness. They shake hands. "Alexander Reisden," Gilbert says, not goodbye. Perdita only looks after Richard as he climbs the train steps.

And then he is gone, in the train somewhere. Not gone far, only to New York where she will be in a few days; but by the time she is there, he will be somewhere on the seas to Europe. Not far either, not gone, but not within the reach of hands; and Perdita stretches out her hands—

"My dear," says Gilbert, "he doesn't know everything! Go to him."

And she is gone, seeing nothing in this darkness, but feeling her way along the side of the train. The conductor has helped her up. She is standing, a young woman at a lighted door. The wheels scream; the train pulls from the station. Gilbert thinks he sees the two of them together, but in a second the train is gone.

So Perdita Halley and Alexander Reisden left Boston, in an evening at the end of summer, 1906, and Gilbert Knight looked after their train until the platform was empty and everyone had gone. *Charlie, it all happened the way you thought it would; Perdita ran away with him.* What would happen next? She was still very young, and Richard—and Alexander—had far to go before he had finished with all his shadows; they were neither of them ready for each other. He would put her out at the next station, Gilbert thought; it was the sensible thing to do, and Richard had always done the sensible thing, more or less. Gilbert walked through South Station and saw porters and baggage handlers, rumpled men who had worked late and were waiting for the train to Quincy, an old woman with a dreaming look, a man with a grin, a mother hugging her little boy; and with all of these lives he seemed for a moment entangled. He hesitated at the crossing in front of South Station and crossed the street, walking through Boston and looking into every face that he saw, every man and woman and child. We are together, he thought. For no reason, he was very happy. He walked on, across all Boston, through the streets full of people, through the dark streets, in the gentle night, toward home.

ACKNOWLEDGMENTS

ANY CREATED THING is many people's work. This book owes special thanks to the following people who have contributed criticism, knowledge, and advice. The richness they have given it is theirs; the inaccuracies are wholly mine.

This book has been shaped by outstanding criticism from William Alfred and from members of the Cambridge Speculative Fiction Workshop: Alexander Jablokov, Steven Popkes, and D. Alexander Smith, who wields a fine editorial machete, as well as Jon Burrowes, Steve Caine, Geoffrey Landis, Dee Morrison Meancy, and Resa Nelson. It wouldn't have been the same without you, friends—it wouldn't have been.

Jane Otte, my knowledgeable and supportive agent, together with her husband and partner David Otte, have been a continuing delight to work with. Thank you both.

At Ballantine, Bob Wyatt has provided editorial help and friendship far beyond the call of duty. There are real editors; Bob Wyatt proves it. Julie Garriott line-edited the book beautifully, and her knowledge of music provided delightful details. Thanks also, Iris Bass and Jim Freed!

Special thanks to a network of readers, advisors, and friends: to Eric and Martha; Alice Wiser; Pat Rabby, for empowerment and dragons; Darcy and Brian Drayton; Margie Ploch; Lisa Raphals; Elaine Sternberg, for midnight pies; Sacha and Christine Jordis; Vincent Brome; Thomas, for bones; Terri Windling, who said the right thing at the right time; James Turner; Denise Lee; Steve Marcus; Mary Gilbert; Meridel Holland; Nancy Paisner; Betty Woodbury; "Sarah's circle"; Aroo; and Jim Morrow.

- Jerry Rosen, violinist, composer, programmer, and raconteur extraordinaire, gave valuable help on Perdita's music and the Boston musical scene around 1900.
- The late Carroll Williams, whose lectures long ago started *me* wondering "Why does it move?", pointed me toward the best people to look at in early twentieth-century biochemistry. James Novick and Steve Popkes also gave extremely valuable suggestions.
- Dr. Kenneth P. Stuckey, director of the S. P. Hayes Reference Library at the Perkins School for the Blind, and Diane Morreo, volunteer at the Hayes Library, introduced me to "doing things blindly," from the social history of blindness to how to organize a plate and a closet.
- Christopher Schwabacher, Marion Fremont-Smith, and David Alexander Smith (thank you again, David!) consulted on the legal aspects of Bucky's dilemma. The way Bucky solved them is all his.
- Peter G. Dowd explained the workings of Colt per-

cussion revolvers and shared with me some lovely anecdotes about black powder.

• Harley Holden, Director of the Harvard University Archives, and the Archives staff gave help on the calendar of 1906 Harvard. For the sake of the story I bent the chronology, for which they are not to blame.

• William Alfred, whose own writing and wise humanity are a continuing inspiration, helped me fill in the background of nineteenth-century Catholicism. Thanks also to F.P. for priestly advice on how a confessor might approach murder.

• Mary Jackson and the late Robert Lee Wolff helped point me toward the right Victorian children's reading—I wish Robert Wolff had been here to take pleasure in this work, as I did in his. Thanks as well to Mary Wolff and Raymond and Mary Harriet Jackson, for civilized teatimes in Cambridge and New York.

• The scholarly work of James Reed, Dorothy Needham, Norah Waugh, John Rowe Townsend, Keith Lucas, and Bela Siki has been particularly useful to me; Siki's *Piano Repertoire* is paraphrased in Perdita's piano-playing scenes. To understand what the ATP reaction is really about, I used Isaac Asimov's very clear introduction, *Life and Energy*.

• Thanks also to the staff of Widener Library, Harvard University, the Boston Public Library, the New York Public Library, and the Brookline, Mass., Public Library, as well as to the staff of the Victorian Society.

• Richard Knight's story owes something to that of Charley Ross, with its extraordinary epilogue over fifty years later. Five other victims of Victorian tragedies contributed their deaths: W.E.B.; W.E.B., Jr., disappeared; C.E.B. and C.E.B., Jr.; and James Cutler Doane Lawrence. S.M.B., beloved storyteller, told their histories and let the Knights be murdered in her house.

· F.S.P. III, July 15–17, 1982, taught me all I need to know of grief and of a child's death. Little boy, you are remembered.

Dear Fred, my beloved husband and partner, noodged me and got the kids to school for six months; Mariah was proud of me (as I am of her); and Justus kindly helped with occasional typing and sticky kisses.

About the Author

SARAH SMITH has lived in Japan, London, and Paris, and received her Ph.D. from Harvard. She has taught film and eighteenth-century literature and now writes and designs documentation for advanced computer products. She has written the hypertext science-fiction novel, *King of Space*, as well as several nonfiction books. A Quaker, she lives near Boston with her husband and children and her 22-pound cat, Vicious.